PENGUIN BOOKS
Rush

Emilee is a self-proclaimed Somerset cowgirl, born and raised in a seaside town in Somerset, England, where she's one of few people wearing cowboy boots to the pub.

With her dad, who spent years working in Formula 1 while Emilee was growing up, she began attending World Endurance Championship races. Her love for motorsport grew rapidly, and Spa-Francorchamps started to feel like home.

When she isn't writing, she is holed up in local seaside restaurants (Greek food is her fave), hanging out with her dog, Fudge, or rewatching *Grey's Anatomy* for the millionth time.

Rush

EMILEE CARTER

PENGUIN BOOKS

PENGUIN BOOKS

UK | USA | Canada | Ireland | Australia
India | New Zealand | South Africa

Penguin Books is part of the Penguin Random House group of companies
whose addresses can be found at global.penguinrandomhouse.com

Penguin Random House UK,
One Embassy Gardens, 8 Viaduct Gardens, London SW11 7BW

penguin.co.uk

First published 2025

001

Copyright © Emilee Carter, 2025

The moral right of the author has been asserted

Penguin Random House values and supports copyright.
Copyright fuels creativity, encourages diverse voices, promotes freedom
of expression and supports a vibrant culture. Thank you for purchasing
an authorized edition of this book and for respecting intellectual property
laws by not reproducing, scanning or distributing any part of it by any
means without permission. You are supporting authors and enabling
Penguin Random House to continue to publish books for everyone.
No part of this book may be used or reproduced in any manner for the
purpose of training artificial intelligence technologies or systems. In accordance
with Article 4(3) of the DSM Directive 2019/790, Penguin Random House
expressly reserves this work from the text and data mining exception.

Set in 12.5/14.75 pt Garamond MT
Typeset by Falcon Oast Graphic Art Ltd
Printed and bound in Great Britain by Clays Ltd, Elcograf S.p.A.

The authorized representative in the EEA is Penguin Random House Ireland,
Morrison Chambers, 32 Nassau Street, Dublin D02 YH68

A CIP catalogue record for this book is available from the British Library

ISBN: 978–1–405–97903–0

Penguin Random House is committed to a sustainable future
for our business, our readers and our planet. This book is made from
Forest Stewardship Council® certified paper

For the girls who spent so long being a toned-down version of themselves so they didn't cause a stir, who just need to be reminded they are enough exactly as they are.

I

The morning sun streamed through the lace curtains of Savi's childhood bedroom, painting the sage green walls in soft, golden hues. Her safe Wyoming haven was a cosy, comforting mix of past and present: posters still adorned the walls, a stack of second-hand romance books she had thrifted last week sat on the bedside table, her cherry red claw clip on top, and an open suitcase lay on the floor by her closet, half-filled with clothes from her recent trip.

Savi stood in front of the antique gold mirror, toying with the pendant her birth mother had passed down to her, reminding her that her family downstairs were not the only people who loved her enough to make promises that had the power to change her life.

Her fingers trembled slightly as she fastened the clasp, the weight of the day ahead pressing on her. Today wasn't just another day on the ranch – it was the day she'd step out into the world she'd dreamed of for so long, one which had been just within reach for years and was finally hers for the taking.

Her mum's voice drifted up the stairs, snapping her out of her daydream. 'Sav! Breakfast is ready and our guest is starving!'

'Coming!' she called back, smoothing the front of her dress. She caught her reflection again, tilting her head.

The confident young woman staring back at her looked polished, grown-up, but there was still a glimmer of the girl who used to sneak out to parties in farmers' fields two towns over and climb trees in the backyard, showing up to dinner with muddy knees.

Savi turned and scanned the room one last time. She spotted the photo on her dresser, the black and white chequered frame resembling a racing flag. She picked it up, her smile matching that of her eighteen-year-old self. It was from her very first race, her teammates flanking her on either side, their faces glowing with pride. She set it down carefully, grateful for the reminder of how far she'd come and how much further she had to go.

The kitchen was bustling with activity; her dad was flipping pancakes while her mum fussed over a basket of fresh fruit, her brother moved around the kitchen pretending like he was helping while all he was doing was helping himself to the food that had already been put out on the table. Then there was their guest, sat reading the local newspaper, like the CEO of a racing organisation needed to know what was happening in a tiny town in the midwestern United States, thousands of miles away from his home.

'There she is,' her dad said with a grin, flipping a pancake onto the growing stack. 'All dressed up and ready to conquer the world of motorsport.'

Savi blushed. 'I have been doing that for a few years now, Dad . . . The IEC is just on a way bigger scale. And millions more people will know my name. But anyway, it's just another contract,' she sighed. That was how she had to look at it if she wanted to keep her nerves at bay.

'Just another contract?' her mum echoed, setting the fruit bowl on the table. 'Honey, this is the opportunity you've been working for. Don't downplay it. The money, the reputation, the power that all comes with it. This is monumental for your career.'

'Don't be nervous, Hart.' Gabriel, her *big* boss and sponsor who had become part of the family, looked up from his paper and grinned. 'I moulded you into the perfect woman for the job.'

Savi took a seat at the table, her nerves easing slightly. Her dad slid a plate in front of her, and she took a bite of the maple syrup-coated pancake, savouring the familiar taste. She had grown up eating these on a Sunday morning, and today might be Monday, but special occasions called for special measures.

'You're going to be amazing, kiddo,' her brother said, moving to sit beside her and placing a hand over hers, squeezing it tight. 'Just be yourself, only way less annoying.'

'Thanks Weston.' She frowned at him, 'I think.'

After breakfast, Savi grabbed her favourite pen and headed towards her dad's home office with Gabriel following closely behind. Her parents trailed after them, her mum adjusting the collar of her denim jacket and her dad giving her a quick squeeze on the shoulder.

'Come and get us as soon as it's over,' her dad said. 'We want to hear everything.'

'You guys know I'm just signing a piece of paper and taking some photos for social media, right? It's not even an official meeting, just Gabriel and I going into a room . . .'

'Well, you'll be on a video call with your new team principal! That'll be exciting.'

'I guess,' Savi raised an eyebrow.

She had met Jasper a few times, most recently when he had been trying to get her into the International Endurance Championship and onto team Revolution Racing, visiting her in the Jaehn Racing garage over the last Formula Voltz season.

'Let's do this, Hart,' Gabriel ushered her in excitedly, 'Jasper should be waiting on the other side of the screen.'

Her heart was beating rapidly, but she felt ready. On the old oak dining table, handed down through generations of the Hart family, lay a single document that was set to transform every aspect of her life for the better. Driving for the first all-female team in the IEC, opposite three of the biggest names in motorsport. This was what little Savi Hart had waited half her life for. Joining Savi in the all-female car, there was Kodie Gray and Miko Kajima. Two fellow IEC rookies, who were equally as sought after for appearances and interviews thanks to their fast progress in junior championships.

Savi adjusted the cuffs of her jacket, finding comfort in the familiar rough denim under her fingertips. Her fun, Western-inspired outfits would soon be replaced once again by a racing suit, this time in Revolution Racing red. Her heart raced – not from nerves, but from the thrill of the opportunity before her. Across the table sat Gabriel's laptop, and Jasper Kotosovski, a sharp-eyed man whose grey hair did nothing to soften his commanding presence. If she didn't know of his kind nature and his love for his drivers, she would be petrified.

'Morning, Savi. So, this is it. The big day,' Jasper said, smiling warmly at her. 'Today you sign your two-year deal with one of the most prestigious teams in the International Endurance Championship and help us make history with our brand new all-female team. When we decided to add our second car, we knew we wanted you. We've been watching you since you started out in the smaller support races, but you have outdone yourself in Formula Voltz the last couple of years, Savi. Your performance last season speaks for itself, and we cannot wait to have you be part of our racing family.'

Savi's lips twitched into a small smile as she glanced down at the paper. The words swam before her for a moment, the reality of it sinking in. Her name – Savannah Hart – boldly typed at the top, alongside the team's logo. She reached for her lucky pen, its weight solid and cool in her hand. She used it to sign anything important, and it was the same one her brother had used to sign his own contracts for the rodeo.

'I wouldn't have got the start I did if it weren't for you, Gabriel. Your belief in me as a little girl, your investment in my future and your trust in my talent,' she said, her voice steady but tinged with emotion. 'Every karting championship, every late night in the simulator, every race where I had to prove I deserved to be on that grid . . . it's all led to this. I get to make history in part because of you.'

Gabriel nodded. 'But you're not just here because of me, and you're not here by luck. You're here because you earned it. And if you sign, you'll have the resources, the car, and the team to fight for the championship of your dreams.'

She took a deep breath, her fingers tightening around the pen. The team's logo stared back at her, a silent promise of the future she'd always dreamed of. Memories of her journey flashed through her mind: the gruelling training sessions, the moments of doubt, the podium finishes, and the roar of the crowd chanting her name.

This contract would kick things up a notch, more than she could even fathom as she sat at a table at her family's ranch in Sheridan, Wyoming. The world was wide, and she was about to walk into it with an open heart, an open mind, and an overwhelming desire to shape the industry for women in motorsport.

Savi's signature flowed onto the paper in a smooth, deliberate motion. As she set the pen down, a wave of triumph washed over her.

'Welcome to Revolution Racing,' Jasper said, looking equally as proud as Gabriel.

'Thank you,' she replied. 'I won't let you down.'

The door to the office creaked open, and her family peered in. 'Smile for the camera!' her mum said brightly. Savi turned to the lens, holding the signed contract in one hand and letting Gabriel envelop her in a one-armed hug. The camera clicked, capturing a moment that would soon be plastered across the media. A candid shot, captured with love.

As Savi said her goodbyes to her principal and stepped out into the hallway, her mind was already all over the place, envisioning the roar of engines and the thrill of the track. She'd been at IEC races before, provided entertainment for the very same crowds of fans. But she'd never truly been part of it, not like this.

With a fire ignited in her chest, Savi walked down the porch steps and out into the fresh air, inhaling deeply. She was ready to take her place among racing legends, and forever be known as one.

2

Babysitting a heartbroken racing driver, and her new teammate, on the bathroom floor of his team's motorhome at Spa, had not been on Savi Hart's bingo card this race season.

They had just spent a weekend at Julien's, one of the other drivers for her new team, and she had somehow found herself glued to Marco De Luca's side. She had known him since she was a junior racing driver and he was already making a name for himself in the International Endurance Championship, with their paths crossing numerous times on the weekends she drove in the support races that were meant to provide entertainment to the fans while they waited for the big guns to come out on track.

As a result of their familiarity, she had wound up spending most of the pre-race week shenanigans playing beer pong with him as an out for her anxiety.

It was safe to assume Savi and Marco were bonded for life after this weekend, only she hadn't intended on being a shoulder to cry on *after* the alcohol had left his system and they were supposed to be back in work mode. He could have timed this better.

'I miss her so much,' Marco sighed, getting a mouthful of fluffy towel as a result of being sat right next to the rail. His hazel eyes glistened with tears and while she tried to pity him, it was kind of hard given how unlike himself he was behaving. She knew he was a sensitive soul at times, and he was polite and respectful and the kind of guy you would want to take home to your parents, but this was different.

'Marco, I don't know who you mean.'

'Esme!' he growled, but Savi didn't take the minor aggression personally.

She wasn't sure how he could miss his rival's social media manager when she was here at the track with them. They had seen her mere minutes ago, her bright yellow Converse dazzling them as she ran down the pit lane with her camera in her hand, chasing after one of her drivers. Mind you, it was right then that Marco had bolted in here and yanked Savi by the arm, forcing her to follow him. She should've clocked it immediately.

'Wait, you and . . .' she trailed off, confused as hell.

'Yes, me and dot dot dot.' He threw his arms up like she was supposed to just know.

She'd had no idea anything had gone on between them. As far as Savi knew, Esme had been on and off, or in her words, in a 'casual entanglement' with Thalia for the last few months. Yes, Esme was friends with Marco, but had they crossed a line?

'Ugh,' Marco groaned again, this time following it up with a sniffle. He'd got himself worked up enough that his olive complexion had a hint of red to it.

'Why don't you come and sit out on the sofas so you can quit eating the towels? It can't be hygienic.' She felt bad for laughing at his sad and sorrowful state, but how could she not? He was one of the world's most famous racing drivers, usually so laid back and calm in every situation, and here he was, having a heartbreak-induced meltdown whilst stone-cold sober.

'I'm comfortable down here. It makes me feel grounded.'

'Oh, honey. A bathroom floor ain't gonna cut it. You need to be in the mountains. Get some good old country air in you.'

'I'm no cowboy.' Marco scowled but slowly clambered to his feet and followed her.

'No, you're quite clearly a city boy through and through.'

'Hey!' He looked genuinely offended.

'No need to get all defensive, Mr Monaco,' she smirked. From the few times she'd hung out with the team, she had already established that his teammates Brett Anderson and Julien Moretz loved getting their hands dirty on their Malmedy farms, whereas Marco would rather sit on the balcony of his Monegasque apartment and watch the world go by with a sparkling water.

'We can't all rock cowboy boots.' He gestured down at Savi's choice in footwear. Cherry-red cowboy boots with white detailing, her pride and joy. Lucie Carolan had expressed her admiration for them the second she'd laid eyes on them at Julien's. She'd got them at a vintage store back home when she was seventeen and they were still going strong six years later.

Savi may be about to embark on another tour of Europe and beyond in her new role as a racing driver for one of the most reputable International Endurance Championship teams, but you couldn't take the Wyoming cowgirl out of her. It was kind of becoming her brand.

Anderson's thing was being the sober positive mental health rep, Moretz was the family man, she was the USA native being thrown in at the deep end and Marco . . . well, Marco De Luca was currently the emotional mess of the team.

'Right, are you done getting all emotional on me? No offence, but I came here to work and bond with the team. Not to babysit your ass.' Savi took a swig of water.

'I'm done, promise. Think that was the residual weekend hangover doing the talking there. Sorry for the snapping and the dramatic as fuck sighs, not my finest moment.'

'You don't say.'

'Oh, shit. You're friends with Ez aren't you?' Marco looked like a deer in headlights, running a hand through his chocolatey curls and causing them to become even more dishevelled.

'Yeah, but I didn't know about you two. Not even an inkling,' Savi shrugged, trying to act like she wasn't bothered.

'That's because there was never really an *us*, Savannah. I really liked her, but she's too caught up in her shenanigans with that girl.'

'Okay, first of all, you don't get to use my government name. It's Savi, to you. We have been over this so many times, De Luca, please. You may not know me well, but you have known me long enough and still haven't learnt. Second, you are a millionaire racing driver with multiple world championship titles under your belt. Thalia doesn't even have a podium win. She's still considered a rookie after four seasons.'

'But she has Esme's heart. And I don't.'

'What I'm saying, Marco, is if you want her, go get her. It's not like Thalia Kotas is here to stop you, is she?' Savi raised an eyebrow then thought about it further, and frowned, 'At least, I don't think her team is here yet . . .'

'You're right, damn it Savannah, you've always had a bit of a way with words.' Marco stood up and put his hands on his hips in somewhat of a superhero pose. 'I'm gonna get her back. I'm gonna get my Esmerelda back.' Despite the conviction with which he said it, he stayed put, silence filling the motorhome.

'Esmerelda?' Savi frowned.

'I was not supposed to tell you that. Fuck it, you got a pen and paper? I'll write up an NDA.'

'No need, I can keep a secret.'

'I'll take your word for it.'

She sipped her bottle of water, waiting for the supposedly bold and courageous driver to get his ass into gear. Except Marco was still in the same pose, gazing longingly at the door as though Esme were going to materialise. She was going to have to give him a hard shove in her friend's direction.

'Marco, if you're going to make a grand gesture you can't stay in this overpriced metal box forever. Come on, let's go down the pit lane together.' She held her hand out, coaxing him out into the unknown. 'You've got this.'

'I one hundred per cent have not got this, but I appreciate the encouragement.' He grabbed her water out of her hand and took a big swig, gulping it down.

'You're fine, this is no big deal.' She laughed and tugged him down the trailer steps, back towards the Revolution

Racing garage. Savi watched as Marco did his best to snap out of his sad and sorrowful energy and feign confidence as he walked past his team.

'Were you guys getting down and dirty in the team motorhome?' Brett gave them a once-over, earning himself a slap on the arm from Lucie, his wife and one of Revolution's two social media managers.

'No, Anderson, because my heart is elsewhere.'

'Uh, so is mine!' Savi defended herself, not letting Marco make it sound like she had been rejected by him back there. If they had seen the state of him, on the brink of tears over a woman, he'd be mortified.

'Savannah actually gave me a pep talk, and it was quite effective. Gave me a kick up the ass. I'm going after Ez.' He continued walking out of the garage and down the pit lane, gathering a crowd as the team trailed behind him.

'Whatever he's about to do, this is going to go so wrong . . .' Miko grimaced, as she and Kodie rushed to follow their teammate, watching in horror as Marco marched himself into another team's garage in the middle of their workday, uninvited, on the hunt for Esme.

'Can I have everyone's attention please!'

'Oh no . . .' Savi cast nervous glances back at her new teammates, her eyes silently screaming for help. Esme put her camera down and looked at Marco like he'd lost his damn mind.

'I think you might have helped get him into this mess,' Brett grinned in response, leaning against the entrance to Eden Racing's garage and enjoying the show. 'I vote you don't get him out of it. It's been years since Mars made a fool of himself like this. About time someone took the title from me.'

Esme ran towards them in a state of panic, bypassing Marco who still looked to be preparing his grand speech, 'Savi, what have you done? What did he tell you?' she whisper-yelled.

'I don't know, *Esmerelda*, what have *you* done?! You broke him! The man is about to declare his love to you in front of all these people. A usually very sane, very rational man.'

'We never even slept together! Might've kissed once, just once, but that's all.' Poor Esme looked genuinely concerned for him, as she should be.

'Well apparently that one kiss has ruined his life. You sure there wasn't more to it?'

They waited for Marco to complete his deep breathing exercises, the same ones he did before a race. Could they just get his therapist on a video call right now? This was *so* far from what Savi had meant when she told him to go get his girl. There were so many more discreet ways he could have gone about this. Like a text message, which was her speciality. Type your feelings, hit send and launch your phone across the room. Job done.

'There was. I liked him, and there was something between us. But then Thalia got in touch again, said she was ready, and I couldn't say no to her.'

'Then I think it should be you dragging him out of here, not me.'

'I'm ready!' They were cut off by Marco's yell and Faith, Julien's wife and the second social media manager for Revolution Racing, paused the music playing over the garage speakers, making the whole situation ten times more dramatic. Marco was so going to regret this when the adrenaline wore off and rumours started circling the paddock.

'Marco, maybe now isn't the time,' Savi called out to him.

'With Esme and I, there will never be a right time. I've got to say this now or else I won't say it at all. Esme, we had something special. And I know I don't have lady parts, but I know that doesn't bother you. So yeah, maybe Thalia Kotas can give you everything you want, but I could give you everything you need. I'm stable, dependable, a hopeless romantic which is super obvious based on the fact I'm doing this right now, and I would go to the ends of the earth for the people I care about. Don't throw that away over someone who can't commit.'

'Mars, can we have this conversation elsewhere?' Esme pleaded. 'This isn't how I want to do this, let's go to your trailer.'

'Whatever you have to say to me, you can say in front of our friends. Doesn't bother me.'

Savi thought he should be thanking his lucky stars that there was no press around; the fans would never let this go. Then again, neither would the guys.

'I'm going straight to hell for this,' Esme muttered under her breath. 'Mars, I'm sorry. Thalia and I are good. We're exclusive, and we're happy, and I love her. That's not to say we didn't have something, because we did and I think you're a really great guy, but I have to let Thalia in.'

Marco stood motionless in the middle of the garage, a few of Eden Racing's engineers looking extremely uncomfortable while others looked downright disappointed that their rival's grand declaration had gone unrequited.

He blinked, hard, like he was trying to place himself back into reality. 'Well, shit. Good luck to you, Ez. Jules, we're going back to the hotel in twenty, right? Choose me the best whisky they've got behind the bar. I'm taking it to my room.' Marco walked straight back out of the garage through the back door, likely to go and hide in the trailer for the foreseeable.

'I'll pay you back for it, Julien,' Esme looked uncomfortable.

'No need. He deserves it after that shit show.'

'You crushed Mars. I didn't think it was possible,' Brett chuckled. 'He'll get over it quick, don't worry. A few therapy sessions, a race win and a holiday and he'll be right as rain.'

'I can't believe you didn't tell me about him,' Savi turned to her friend with a scathing glare.

'Do you tell me about every guy you kiss?' Esme challenged.

Savi thought about it for a second and determined that actually, yes, she did. Esme was the only person who knew about Jesse. She was also the only person in the racing world who knew a lot of things about her, like the fact half the reason Savi was pursuing her racing career so hard was so her parents could keep their ranch in Wyoming.

Or that Savi's brother, Weston Hart, was a famous bull rider in the United States who was now paralysed from the waist down after being thrown off a bull six years ago. Another reason Savi needed this career; medical bills were expensive, and Weston's money had run out.

'Yes. You owe me, I had to go full therapist mode in that trailer and now I'm going to have to do it all over again with a *very* different approach.'

'When I found him on Saturday night hiding away in the guest bedroom, he was weeping.' Julien interjected. 'Not crying exactly, but actually weeping like he'd sprung a leak. It was right after you mentioned Thalia in passing, in fact. I should've clocked it sooner.'

'I am a terrible person.' Esme looked genuinely upset with herself.

'You can't help who you love, Esme. Don't stress. But Savi, you're on damage control,' Faith instructed. 'Cheer him up. I don't care how you do it but maybe consider vegan chocolate chip pancakes from room service. He loves them.'

Savi inwardly sighed as she headed after Marco. She was supposed to be video calling Jesse tonight to catch him up on how her trip was going, but if she was still on babysitting duties, it wasn't going to happen.

Back at the hotel an hour later, Savi successfully intercepted room service with a stack of pancakes and, with some convincing through the door from Julien, was begrudgingly granted access into Marco's room while he sat on the sofa and sulked. Despite his initial disgruntlement at the sight of two of his teammates, guilt plastered all over their faces, he seemed to mostly be over his embarrassment when he caught the scent of pancake batter.

'You did this for me?' he mumbled through a mouthful.

'Got to make it up to you somehow.' Savi sat down next

to him, relaxing back into the tan leather couch and a sea of textured cushions. It would appear that when you've been with a well-established racing team from the start, you got some room upgrades.

'You've got a whole season for that, Savannah.'

'Savi,' she scowled.

'I like Savannah better.'

'I hate it.' She grabbed the can of non-dairy whipped cream, which she had all but physically fought for at the front desk, insisting Marco would need extra, and sprayed it directly into her mouth, as though her manners had been left back home on the ranch. It was almost enough to distract her teammate from his train of thought, his eyes dancing over her in what some might call adoration. She wondered if it was more disgust than anything else.

'Yeah, well I like hanging out with people who *stop* me doing stupid shit in the name of love, but we can't always get what we want.'

'Marco –' There it was again, that feeling that she was out of her league here.

'Nope. I was feeling pretty vulnerable, Savannah, which you knew, and you stood back and watched as I poured my heart out to your best friend, who you know is in a stable, happy relationship. Pretty shitty move if you ask me.'

She could have defended herself. She could've told him that he was already worked up when she reached him, or that she *did* make a weak attempt to stop him. But truthfully, Savi liked this side of her new teammate. The media always got the soft, gentle Marco De Luca, but turns out he had some bite. That, she could get on board with.

3

'Red is your colour.' Marco's hushed voice in Savi's ear caused her to jump, her heart racing more than it had when she'd *almost* spun out on the track during testing. That had been Marco's fault, too. He'd got in her way and had the cheek to laugh over the radio.

'Why are you in my trailer?' she snapped.

He leaned against her closet door while she pulled her socks on. 'I'm your buddy for race week. So you can treat me like your own personal fountain of knowledge, take all your stress out on me . . .' Marco smirked like he wanted to add more to that last part. Perhaps she was imagining it, or maybe he really was attempting to flirt. Regardless, she was going to ignore it. They didn't have that kind of dynamic in their relationship.

Savi slammed the door to her shoe cupboard. 'I don't need a buddy.'

'Has the big boss not spoken to you?'

'About . . . ?' She looked at him quizzically, because of course Jasper had spoken to her. Countless times over the last few days. But clearly, somewhere along the line their team principal had failed to fill her in on something.

'He's matched you, Miko and Kodie up with Julien, Brett and I to guide you through your first season with the team.' He grinned. A genuine, enthusiastic smile that threatened to piss her off even further.

'Great, my team principal is playing cupid.' She rolled her eyes, more so at his obvious enthusiasm, and shooed him out of the way so she could finish putting the last of her things in the closet. 'I don't need a buddy, Marco. I may be a rookie in this championship, but I have been a racing driver for a number of years. You've seen me in the support races, might I add. Watched my name rise to the top of the leaderboard. I know the drill by now.'

Marco smirked again, eyeing her up and down. 'You haven't driven for Revolution Racing before. We do things a certain way round here.'

His fixated gaze on her was making her feel very hot and bothered but she put it down to anxiety, something she had struggled with for years. 'I've had a lot of in-depth talks with the socials team. I know what Faith and Lucie are expecting of me. The PR team, too.'

'Savannah, let me do my job.'

He looked irritated now too, and it gave her a thrill. Savi had always been up for a challenge, and she performed better when she had a point to prove. 'Let me do mine.'

With a blasé glance over her shoulder, she hopped down the steps of the trailer and left him standing there with his hands on his hips. Less of a superhero pose this time, and more of a pissed off co-worker vibe.

Savi played the role of sweet, wholesome country girl in front of the cameras, fans and her bosses but her friends and family knew she had some fire in her. She never would've picked an equally sweet and wholesome Marco De Luca as her equal, but the way he had looked at her in her race suit had made it quite clear she hadn't given him enough credit.

She was happy with Jesse, and she definitely didn't see Marco in that way, regardless of his European charm and effortlessly good looks, but if she could get him riled up and frustrated with her, it would create one hell of a race out there.

'Ready, girls?' She joined Miko and Kodie outside the conference room, where they were standing with Julien and Brett. Matching red and zebra stripe racing suits on, other teams milling around nearby and talking animatedly.

The outside of the conference room could be compared to a zoo; everyone talking at once, yelling across the crowd and exuding chaos, and the atmosphere inside would be the same. The drivers may switch into professional mode, but it was the media who would start acting like animals to get the stories they wanted out of them.

Despite this, everyone looked raring to go. Hadn't anyone warned them there would be an onslaught of invasive questions and borderline harassment from the media? Savi had done this before. She knew what to expect. But her rookie teammates were inexperienced and had only just started racing a couple of years ago. Daddy's money and a private school education couldn't buy them a backbone.

'Oh! Is Marco your buddy?' Miko looked excited, her long dark hair swishing around her shoulders. You wouldn't catch that girl with her hair up unless she was putting her race helmet on. She'd got lucky with Brett as her glorified tour guide slash babysitter, and Savi couldn't help but think that Brett was more suited to her own personality. Sarcastic, always cracking jokes. Jasper's foresight hadn't been the best here.

'Something like that,' Savi shrugged, catching the way Brett tried to hide his grin behind his hand. 'Can I help you, Anderson?'

'No, no. Just . . . Lucie warned us about you.'

'What?' Savi frowned. She thought she'd been getting on well with the socials team.

'She didn't say anything bad about you, at all. Sang your praises, in fact. She just said you were fiery. So, God only knows why the boss paired you up with baby Mars.'

'Oh, someone agrees!' She high-fived him, although from the sudden one-sided flirting and lust-filled gazes she had been on the receiving end of just now, she could safely say there was nothing *baby* about Marco De Luca.

'Agrees with what?' Marco appeared behind her, almost managing to murmur into her ear for a second time today. Only this time, it didn't send shivers down her spine, it just wound her up. She wasn't in the mood, given the hell they were about to walk into.

Savi crossed her arms, 'You and me, we don't work.'

'Just as well we're not getting married then, ain't it Savannah?' His Italian accent, which she had grown rather fond of, had a weird twang to it all of a sudden.

'I'm sorry, was that meant to be my accent?' she shot back.

'It's time to go in.' Kodie shoved Savi through the door before they could cause a scene.

The girls headed straight for the stage while the guys lined the back wall, alongside Jasper and the socials team. As the only all-female team in the entire IEC, the Revolution Racing girls had a spotlight on them this season and it made Savi nervous. She had to make a name for herself all over again in a new championship, and it meant answering questions and avoiding conversations she had managed to steer clear of over the course of her career so far.

Privacy was a privilege most drivers weren't entitled to, especially when they were put in rooms like this where all the attention was on them and it was their job to provide stories and headlines. Savi kept her brother's identity under wraps for a multitude of reasons, but there had been a couple of reporters who had been paid to keep quiet over the years. Journalists who were desperate to get a reputation for the dirt they could dig up, but valued the money her team's lawyers could offer more.

If people really wanted to know every detail of her life, they could probably figure it out with a deep dive on the internet but for the most part, thanks to cheques and the good graces of people in her hometown and in the rodeo circuit, she had been able to maintain that privacy when it came to her family.

As the first reporter stood up from her seat, clutching her microphone and recording device, Jasper shot them a supportive thumbs up.

'Savi, this first one is for you. It is widely known you had offers from multiple teams this season. What made you choose Revolution Racing over and above the others?'

Savi had to fight to keep the sarcasm at bay as she whipped up an Oscar-winning answer in record time. Obviously it was the money primarily, but she wasn't going to say that. 'Not only are they consistently at the top of the leader board with very few mistakes and strategic misjudgements,' she nodded at her boss, 'but thanks to their incredibly fast growth on social media in recent years, I could see that this team puts their relationships first.'

'Could you expand?' The reporter smiled, encouraging her to keep going.

'Well, their bond is next level, and I wanted in on that. When you're on the road for so long and your whole life revolves around your job, you need to be in a team where everyone has your back. I'm also very easy going, and as much as I am a professional, I want to be able to have fun with it. Nobody does that better than Revolution Racing.'

The reporter nodded politely and moved on to Miko, while the rest of the team gave Savi a silent cheer from the back of the room. She sat back and let the others have their time answering questions, chiming in when necessary, and waiting patiently for the more personal ones.

Then she spotted him, his tortoiseshell frames perched on the end of his nose in that same precocious way they always did. The reporter who had been at her first-ever press conference years ago and seemed to have a personal vendetta against her. Hugo Schmitt, ego the size of Jupiter, zero manners and a serious problem with boundaries. He had made it his mission to find out every single detail of her personal life, although she did have to laugh at his lack of knowledge regarding her dating history.

Her team back then had paid him off so he didn't reveal too much about her family, but since her new team didn't know, they couldn't protect her from him. She knew she should've listened to her agent when he'd told her to come clean to Jasper.

Mr Schmitt all but yanked the microphone from the moderator, itching to fuck up Savi's day and attempt to humiliate her again. For the first time in a while, she worried he might succeed.

'Savannah, what do your family think about you abandoning them to chase your dreams?'

There it was. A personal attack thinly veiled as an innocent question, meant to get a reaction out of her. Family was a sore spot for Savi, because her parents and her brother didn't choose this life. They wanted no part of the media attention that came with her career, the invasive nature of journalists and the lack of respect for what they had been through.

It was bad enough when Weston had hit the big time, and they'd had camera crews trying to sneak onto the ranch to capture behind-the-scenes footage of the rodeo's newest star. Savi was much younger then, but she had seen the stress it had caused and how much worse it all got after his accident. Constant headlines, rumours on social media and letters from crazed fans. She was determined to keep them very far away from all of this, and she wasn't going to let this one man and his cheap, tacky suit get in the way of that.

'I don't think I've abandoned my family at all. I had a childhood dream and did exactly what you said, chased it. They're very supportive of my career. I'm sure the families of every driver on the grid feel the same way.' She resisted the urge to shrug, which was code for *I win*. That was the thing; whatever negative things he had to say about her choices in life were simply untrue. He could have an opinion, but it wasn't fact.

'What about your brother? Is he not jealous?' He stared her dead in the eye, refusing to waver. Savi glanced around at her teammates who looked confused, just like every other journalist in the room, as if they hadn't got the memo.

She would tell her team one day, but today was not that day. It was too soon, and she didn't know if she could trust them just yet. While Savi clenched her jaw and tried to re-centre herself, for a split second she debated letting it all out in the open and then holding everyone hostage in the conference room until they'd signed NDAs. Except they didn't have time for that, and there were at least six other teams who were yet to give their own interviews.

Schmitt would come off far worse if he exposed Weston's identity. Savi and Wes had decided between them very early on to keep their familial connection a secret. At first, because she didn't want to ride his coat-tails and have opportunities handed to her as a result of his own sporting success, and then later, after his accident, because he didn't want pity. He had enough people feeling sorry for him, he didn't need anyone comparing him to his kid sister who was still able to do the job she loved while he was stuck back home in Wyoming with hordes of medical bills.

'My brother understands what it means to want something so badly that you would give up everything. He encourages me every day to live my life the way I want to while I can.'

There was more confusion radiating from her team, but when she looked over at Jasper there was an underlying sense of understanding. Recognition for the fact she was making an active choice to hold things back from him.

'You didn't come from money, did you? Not like your teammates here.'

'No, I didn't,' she frowned. 'But money doesn't buy talent, and you can't get into an industry like this, a championship as big as the IEC, without it.' She wanted to say more in defence of Kodie and Miko, but she didn't want to be labelled as difficult. She was already treading in dangerous territory and Savi was not a difficult person.

Schmitt narrowed his eyes at her, getting frustrated that his victim of the day had an answer for everything. Not only did she have years of media training, but so did her entire family. She knew all the right things to say. 'Do you ever feel guilty?'

'I'm sorry, for what exactly?' she pushed, almost wishing she hadn't. This could be it. The follow-up question that tore it all apart.

'Your parents would have spent a lot of money on your karting lessons and travel expenses over the years. If they weren't very well off, wouldn't they have struggled?'

'I got lucky. I was sponsored by someone in the industry and my lessons were free. That's no secret, the world knows that the CEO of this championship gave me the opportunity so many kids dream of. But my parents gave me the most important thing of all, their time and their love.' Savi looked over at Gabriel Lopez, her knight in shining armour and the man who got her here. He was practically bursting with pride.

'Hmm. No more questions,' Schmitt huffed, sitting back down. It took a lot to shut that guy up once he got going, but despite his slight dig at her teammates, he didn't have any more to say to them. Probably didn't want to contend with the potential legal issues that came with going after such a big racing team.

There were a couple of questions about Miko's father's investment in the team, and Kodie's education, but they handled them well. On the outside, at least. Most drivers were good at coming across as balanced and level-headed on the outside, in front of the cameras and the media and in situations where it mattered, while their emotions worked overtime and they were fighting constant battles on the inside.

She could see it in her teammates; there was only so much they could take from the tortoise-emblazoned moron, listening to their friends and colleagues take hit after hit and try to defend themselves and the mistakes or choices they had made. Kodie looked particularly miffed as they got up from their seats, shuffling out of the room like the life had been sucked out of them.

'I hate that guy,' she muttered. 'Just because my family has money, it doesn't mean I can't drive a fucking car. And I'm fast, too. Bet he drives a Fiat.'

Brett joined them as they reached the door, 'He's definitely a Smart Car kind of bloke. The kind who drives way below the speed limit and cries when he goes over a speed bump.'

She tried to engage, to laugh at their jokes and pretend what happened in there hadn't bothered her at all. But the anxiety had well and truly set in, and Savi couldn't get away from them fast enough. 'I'll catch you guys later, I've got some things I need to take care of.'

She said her goodbyes, barely giving anyone a chance to respond, and darted across the paddock, slamming the trailer door shut behind her. Her heart was beating rapidly, heat rising up through her body while she tried to stop her hands trembling.

She couldn't stand this; the way she became detached from her body and had to claw her way back to reality. Her chest ached and she knew she'd lost total control over herself. This happened a lot, and it didn't matter if she dealt with it alone or in a room full of people, it was never any less embarrassing. To know there was nothing she could do about it made her feel weak. Anxiety attacks, she could handle. The warning signs were there, and she had time to put a stop to them, focus on her coping mechanisms and ground herself before they took over. But the panic attacks? She didn't know they were coming until it was too late.

She was mid-panic attack when Kodie and Miko flung the door open, worry etched across their faces as they studied her battling her own body.

'Savi?' Miko knelt in front of the sofa she was perched on and placed a hand on her knee, while Kodie put an arm around her, squeezing her tight.

'What's up, Sav?' Miko smoothed her hair down for her, tucking it behind her ears so it didn't get stuck to her wet cheeks.

'I just hate talking about my family. It's nobody's business.' And yes, that did unfortunately include her teammates no matter how lovely they were. 'I don't know why they can't stick to questions about the job.'

'He was a dick,' Miko agreed. 'But what's this all about?' She gestured to the mess Savi had made of herself in the few moments that she'd managed to escape an audience.

'I get anxiety around interviews, because of questions like that.' She was even uncomfortable now, talking about it. Her whole face was burning red, and the nausea was rising in her throat. Savi didn't do this, ever. She didn't break down in front of near strangers but here she was, crying to her teammates before the first race had begun.

'Have you . . . seen the team therapist yet? Talked about this? Maybe bring it up to Jasper, too? He can have the moderator ban questions about your family, if that's something you aren't willing to talk about publicly,' Kodie suggested.

'You can talk to us, too,' Miko added. 'Don't feel obligated, but we're your teammates. Built-in best friends, sisters. Whatever this is, you haven't got to bottle it all up. We're sworn to secrecy, Savi. Promise.'

'Thanks, girls.' She swallowed roughly and reached forward for her water bottle. 'I just honestly don't know that I'm ready to disclose my family issues with anyone. It's not just my story to tell.'

'Oh . . . okay.' Kodie squeezed her shoulder, sounding somewhat disappointed. 'Makes sense. Do you need a second, or do you just want to get up and crack on?'

'How's my face?' Savi sniffed and wiped her tears away, calming her breathing down. She didn't want this to be her reputation in the team, she wanted to be reliable and strong and let Kodie and Miko know they could depend on her to take them to victory, that she wasn't going to crumble. This wasn't a good look so early on.

'Flawless, as always,' Miko smiled.

'Well then, I'll crack on. Thanks, ladies.'

Shaking herself out, she let Kodie lead the way out of the trailer, her hand not even on the door handle before it rattled, and she jumped backwards. 'Who the f—'

'Savannah?' Marco's head poked through the gap. 'Can I have a moment alone with Savi please, girls? I fear I might have pissed her off earlier.'

Her teammates looked between his guilt-ridden face and her rosy, blotchy one and waited for her to give the go-ahead. She nodded, with an eye roll for dramatic effect. They hurried out and let Marco in, giving Savi about three seconds to pull herself together enough that he wouldn't know anything had been wrong in the first place.

'What's up, De Luca?' She crossed her arms, wishing she could just get a few minutes alone around here. She'd been at the track for three days and the only time she'd had to herself was when she'd been asleep. Even then, she'd be lying if she said Marco ignoring her for that short time after the Esme ordeal hadn't kept her up at night. Her own emotions were proving too much today, she wasn't sure she could handle his, too.

'About the buddy thing . . .' He was coming across as incredibly shy and much more like the Marco she had been witness to before that night at Julien's. 'I get it. You don't want to be babysat. So, with that being said, if you want me to go to Jasper and tell him this isn't going to work, that I have an issue with it, I will.'

She felt awful. Yes, it would be fun to have a bit of rivalry out on track, but that was possible without making

Marco feel like his help and guidance weren't valued. Savi still had a lot to learn, and there was a lot she didn't know about this championship and its inner workings. While she wasn't the type to admit that, it wouldn't hurt to let Marco in. A smidge.

'One demeaning comment or mild insult and I'm kicking off. That includes about my cowboy boots.' She was even wearing them now. Jasper hadn't given them a uniform as such, just asked that they keep it work-appropriate and wear their race suits in the garage. So of course, for press day she had paired a red Revolution Racing shirt with a white, tiered miniskirt, her red boots, and a red bow in her hair.

'As long as you don't start walking around in a cowboy hat too, I will keep my mouth shut and try to remember that you do sort of know what you're doing and have been behind the wheel of a race car hundreds of times before you signed with us, and won championship titles before, even if they weren't quite as impressive as winning the International Endurance Championship.'

Savi bit her lip and eyed the coffee table where her trusty black hat sat waiting. She had only left it in the trailer because she'd been in a rush after Marco had irritated her earlier, otherwise it would have been firmly planted on her head for the first day of media duties.

'I should've known.' He feigned genuine disappointment, picking it up and placing it on his head. 'Do you actually wear this, like . . . in public?'

'Please take that off your head immediately.' She snatched it back from him and blushed, memories of four summers ago coming back to haunt her.

'Okay, sensitive about the hat. Noted.' He smirked at her again, but in her head, Marco's smirk was replaced with Jesse's. The owner of said hat.

He had been wearing it the summer they met at the Sheridan County Fair and less than six hours later, she'd been wearing it on her own head while they . . . she . . . never mind. That saying, wear the hat, ride the cowboy? Well, that had been the start of her and Jesse's journey. A journey which she feared may be about to end during the most important summer of her life.

Marco De Luca was no cowboy, and he was definitely no Jesse Montalvo. That cowboy hat wasn't his to wear.

4

Savi was all dressed up in her Revolution Racing race suit and she felt like a million bucks, even if she'd had to abandon the cowboy boots for the day to meet health and safety standards. The adrenaline that had been coursing through her veins since she woke up that morning only heightened when Jesse's name appeared on her phone screen for the first time all week in bold, white letters, her favourite photo of him staring back at her.

'Hi, baby.' His deep, gravelly tone sent shivers down her spine. 'How's my superstar?'

'I'm good, better now I finally get to hear your voice.'

'You can hear my voice any time you turn on a country music station on the radio, darlin'.'

'You know that's not my Jesse, that's the Jesse Montalvo the rest of the world gets access to. The shiny, polished version.'

'Ah, yeah, I forget you like it rough.' She could practically hear the smirk in his tone, and she went weak at the knees.

Jesse Montalvo, her secret boyfriend of four years, was a global country music sensation. Born and raised in Story, Wyoming, just twenty minutes away from Sheridan, he was one of few people who had ever made it out of the state and been launched into stardom before he could legally drink. Savi was close behind him.

He was touring North America, so he'd been singing love songs to everyone but her and she had been wrapped up in pre-race season preparation. They hadn't seen each other for four months, and there was only so much they could do over video calls and texts. It had been four years of hiding in the shadows and pursuing their dreams, the trials and tribulations of a long-distance relationship still not quite destroying that spark they'd had when they first met.

Even now when there was so much pressure on her shoulders, he was there as her safety net, reminding her where she came from and how hard she had worked to get there. If anyone could make her believe she deserved this, it was him.

'How's the tour going?' She never liked the answer to that question. He always told her how incredible it was to do something he was so passionate about, and she knew what that was like. That wasn't the problem. The problem was she had never been part of his world, and he had never been part of hers. Not when it came to work. It always left a bitter taste in her mouth.

'Well, I get a whole two weeks off come Sunday morning...' His voice trailed off like he was more annoyed than happy about that.

'Since when?!'

'Since the arena in South Carolina got flooded and we had to reschedule. My stupid ass donated thirty grand to help fix it and now they're not sure they can fit me into their schedule, so I'm gonna have to find a new venue and do a show later this month. Sucks for the fans.'

'It was out of your hands, Jess.' She imagined they would feel how motorsport fans felt when a race got red-flagged. She'd driven in a few of those, and it was never a nice feeling.

'Mm. Anyway, I mentioned it because I want to fly you out during your break. It's such a long one. You, me, two weeks in the mountains. Potentially a quick trip to Nashville if I can get security sorted out in time. I want to celebrate your first race with you since I can't be there.'

'I would love that.'

'How about I send a jet to pick you up from Brussels tomorrow evening? You can fly overnight, and I'll have someone meet you at the airport and bring you right to me.'

'Can't you come and get me yourself?' she pouted, thankful that he couldn't see her. She didn't like to seem ungrateful, but she was tired of being ferried around by his security team. She just wanted to sit in the passenger seat of his truck, and she could only do that at home in Wyoming. Except they rarely went back there together these days, because locals liked to talk.

'You know it's not that simple, baby. Tell you what, I'll wait on the side of the road a few miles away from the airport, security can drop you to me and you can switch cars. Then we can road trip into the mountains together.'

'To your cabin, right?'

'Exactly.'

She couldn't help but smile at that. The journey to Jesse's cabin was stunning, if not a bit treacherous as you got closer. They had spent many days holed up in there, away from prying eyes and soaking up their time together before one of them inevitably had to leave.

Sometimes she liked being a secret, but on days like today, she wanted him here. She wanted to run into his arms when she crossed the finish line, but as the years went on, she started to doubt if he would ever be willing to expose their relationship to the public.

He'd always told her that when he got down on one knee, the whole world would know about it. But the idea of marriage hadn't been mentioned for over a year now, and she wasn't sure it was on the cards with the direction their lives were heading in.

'I can't wait to see you, Jess.'

'Me too, Sav. It feels like forever. And so much has changed for us both, this trip is definitely needed. I just want to hold you in my arms and enjoy you.' She sat there grinning like a lovesick idiot as he spoke. 'Text me when you get out of the car safely, okay?' That was their rule. He texted her after his shows and she texted him after every race. Not a day on this tour had gone by where she hadn't woken up to a message from him, even if it was a whiskey-influenced outpouring of love in the form of a voice message.

'I will. And I will see you in less than forty-eight hours.'

'See you soon. Good luck, Superstar.'

'Back at you.'

She would never tire of him calling her that. In her eyes, he was the superstar. His fame was on a totally different level to hers. But she had her own fans, and he was up there as one of the biggest along with her family. Her brother especially. Speaking of, he was still waiting for his own phone call, and she didn't have much time to spare.

'Nice of you to show up!' Weston huffed before his face came into view.

'Sorry, I was talking to Jesse. What's up?' She flipped him off as he fake-gagged at the mention of the country singer he hated most of all.

'What's up?! My baby sister is about to do her first race as a rookie for one of the biggest racing teams in motorsport history, that's what's up!' He cheered like a rowdy frat boy, threatening to deafen her and making her phone's speaker crackle.

'Wes! My ears!' she laughed. 'Damn, you're louder than my race car.'

'Hi, honey!' Her mum appeared behind him, leaning down to Weston's level and beaming into the camera, albeit way too close. Their parents weren't the best with technology which was a real pain when Savi was thousands of miles away most of the year.

'Hi, Ma. How's it going?' She shook her head as Wes had to physically wheel away from her, so her head was no longer blocking him from Savi's view.

'Weston has set the television up with his computer plugged in so we can watch your race!'

'Think I finally convinced them to get a bigger TV, you can thank me later.' Wes winked.

'Send me a link to the one you want, and I'll order it.'

'Shut up.' Wes rolled his eyes and changed the topic, listing all the snacks they had got to watch the race with. Better hope the livestream didn't cut out. Any time Savi tried to buy things for Weston's benefit, he got cagey. He hated it. Hated that he couldn't afford small luxuries like he used to and that his little sister had to help him out, but Savi wouldn't see him go without the things he needed or wanted.

'Where's Dad?' Savi frowned, realising he hadn't joined them.

'Oh, he's sorry he couldn't join in on the call! He's just out with the horses, Mocha got out again so he's securing the fence.'

'Does the fence need replacing, Ma?'

'Not yet!' She said it with enthusiasm, but Savi knew she was sugar-coating it. Their horses were their babies, they couldn't be escaping on the daily. She mentally added it to her list of tasks. It was better to just send someone to the ranch to fix it without warning than for Savi to send money that her family wouldn't want to accept.

'You'd better get moving, Sav. We just wanted to wish you luck with your race.' Weston wheeled back towards their mum.

'Yes, good luck! You'll smash it.' She blew a kiss. 'Oh! Wait, not literally!'

'Thanks guys, I'll call you after!'

'Ma, you can't say that when she's about to careen a race car –'

Savi cut them off and sat back on the sofa, absorbing the few moments of silence she always allowed herself before she got in the car. This was her pre-race ritual. Some drivers meditated, some worked out, some gathered in their teams, but Savi spoke to her loved ones, gave herself two minutes of me-time and then got back out there.

She left the trailer and headed into the garage, trying

not to get upset over the fact Miko and Kodie had their families here today and her own family couldn't be with her. Weston couldn't travel all that way easily, and her parents stayed behind to care for him, and Jesse, well he just couldn't show his face in a place like this.

'Savannah.' Marco rushed up to her before she'd even got over the threshold. 'Got something to show you.'

'Okay . . .' She reluctantly let him lead her to his side of the double garage with his hands covering her eyes. She didn't like this.

'Ta da!' He moved his hands, and Savi opened her eyes to none other than her dad standing there with his arms open wide. *Out with the horses.* Of course she'd fallen for that.

'Dad!' she squealed, jumping into his arms. Just as well he still had the whole lumberjack thing going on at the age of fifty-six and could support her weight. 'How did you get here?'

'On a plane.' He spun her round, her hair flying out behind her.

'No shit.' She breathed out a laugh, in disbelief that he was actually in front of her.

'We weren't going to let you do this solo, Savi. I had to come and support our little girl. Marco suggested it after realising you'd be the only driver on the team without someone from home here with you for your first race, we planned it days ago.' He set her down.

'You . . .' She looked at Marco, who couldn't wipe the soppy grin off his face. 'Thanks, De Luca.' Savi gave him a quick hug of appreciation. She had spent all this time thinking he was genuinely mad at her for the whole Esme thing, while he'd been in cahoots with her dad to fly him halfway across the world for her.

'It was my pleasure. But you,' he pointed at her, 'need to get your ass in that car. And you, sir, need to go get your headphones so you can listen to every swear word your daughter fires out when I overtake her.'

'Oh, I can't wait for this.' Her dad chuckled and wandered off to find Jasper.

'You mean to tell me we're starting the race together?'

'Side by side, Cowgirl.' He pulled his helmet on before handing Savi her own, a custom pink leopard print design. The whole animal print theme Revolution Racing had going on really spoke to her soul, even if leopard and zebra clashed.

'That's not really how the grid works.'

'No, you're right. In that case, I'll be slightly in front of you. Then I'll get farther and farther away until I'm a speck of dust.'

'Make sure you wave goodbye when I speed off ahead, yeah?' He knocked on her helmet and walked off, leaving her the perfect level of fired up.

'Good luck, Sav!' Kodie called out from her spot by the side of the grid.

'Take care of our car!' Miko chimed in, both of them hurrying back to the garage as the drivers all got in position.

Savi loved this car. Her seat was just right, and she much preferred it to some of the cars she'd driven in the past. This one was in a league of its own, and she'd spent the last few months really getting to grips with it in preparation for today. This one, singular day which had the potential to make or break her career with the IEC. No pressure.

'Good luck, sweetheart.' Her dad's voice came over the headset, and she knew how special he must have felt when Jasper gave him permission to do that.

'Thanks, dad. See you on the other side.'

As the lights counted down, one by one, Savi psyched herself up for the next two hours. Driving a race car round a circuit at high speed for that long took a physical toll on drivers' bodies and minds. From the g-force impacting their necks and spines to the sheer concentration that was required; there was a reason this sport was so hard to succeed in.

But despite the battle against gravity, speed, weather and most importantly her competition, this was what Savi loved to do. It was just her and the car. That was what she told herself. She had to ignore the presence of the other cars on the track and just drive, letting the fear of failing slip away.

Go. The car instantly felt like it belonged to her. It responded to every movement flawlessly and before she knew it, that sacred two-hour stint was coming to an end, and she was climbing Eau Rouge less than a second behind Marco. She knew she could get past him; it was just a matter of timing it right.

As they sped down the Mulsanne straight multiple laps later with only a few minutes before they both had to return to the pits and swap with their teammates, she knew it was now or never. It was as though she was one with the car as she sailed past him, cackling with laughter at the thought of what must be going through his mind watching the back of her car move into view.

This was what racing was all about. The innocent rivalry, pushing yourself and proving yourself. She had overtaken a multi-championship winning driver during her first race, and she knew Julien would probably claim the spot back from Miko within the next ten laps but still, she would get people talking. Her name would be in the mouths of the presenters and commentators and plastered across social media for all the right reasons. She couldn't wait to watch the footage back and re-live the satisfaction.

Savi pitted the car and helped Miko clamber in, connecting her drinking tube for her, then headed into the garage with pure euphoria written all over her features. Lucie had a camera on her in seconds, allowing her the space to come back to reality but making sure the team had essential content for their platforms.

'Nice going, Cowgirl.' Marco high-fived her.

'Not so bad yourself, De Luca. Shame you couldn't keep up.'

'I might start wearing cowboy boots if it makes me as cocky as you.' He winked at her and then in the next moment, she was enveloped in a smothering group hug from Kodie and her dad, her teammate's brunette ponytail whipping her in the face amidst all the excitement.

'I am so damn proud of you, Sav. *So* proud. And your ma and brother are too.'

And that was the part that set off the waterworks. Weston. Because even though this career was her dream, he was the driving force behind it.

5

'I can't go up there, Savi!' Her dad pulled on her arm, begging for her to let him stay down and watch her go up. 'The podium is *sacred*.'

'Dad, we are telling you that you can come with us. It's not a big deal; you can stand off to one side with Miko's and Kodie's parents. You're not going to be front and centre.'

He faltered again, looking very unsure of himself and a million miles out of his comfort zone, and Savi was starting to feel bad. 'Sav, are you sure you want me invading your moment?'

'Oh, Dad . . .' She smiled softly and wrapped him up in her arms, 'You've been an integral part of my journey so far, of course I want you on the podium with me.'

'Come on, Mr Hart!' Marco breezed past, clapping her dad on the shoulder as he went. 'You can hold Savi's helmet for her while I spray her with champers.'

'Is it really champagne . . .' he whispered to Savi, 'or is it rosewater?'

'We're in Belgium, so it's real champagne. We only have rosewater in countries where alcohol is prohibited, and it doesn't fizz up the same so it's nowhere near as fun.'

'Cool . . .' He nodded away, getting lost in the chaos of all the podium-winners gathering at the foot of the steps, talking animatedly and getting rowdier by the minute. The podium trackside celebrations weren't a patch on the party Faith and Julien threw after this very race every year, but they were cherished among the drivers. A valued tradition. 'You go with your team, I'll see you up there.'

Savi left him hovering near Marco's cousin, only turning her back when she saw him get pulled into a conversation. She made her way over to her teammates and finally let out a breath, her anxiety at bay so far. The race was done and dusted, but after these celebrations they had a couple of interviews with journalists and television presenters, followed by a debrief in the team's temporary paddock headquarters. There was plenty of time to stress but this wasn't it.

'You okay?' Kodie mouthed, as if Savi now had a flashing neon sign above her head that read '*Anxious. Handle with care.*' It was the primary reason she hadn't wanted anyone knowing.

Nodding and smiling appreciatively, she found herself glued to Marco's side again. That was twice this week she'd relied on him for support, unbeknownst to him. Before signing with this team, she had never once considered him as someone she could trust. He was just Marco De Luca, fellow racing driver who didn't mind holding a conversation when they crossed paths. Now, he was a teammate, potential friend and a safety net. 'That was a great drive, De Luca.'

He threw an arm around her and pulled her into his side, casual intimacy feeling very normal and appropriate for their new dynamic. She hadn't experienced this with a male teammate before, and it made her feel strange. What would Jesse think? 'Thanks, Savannah. It was nice having you to challenge me out there.'

'She didn't just challenge you, mate,' Brett laughed, 'she destroyed you on that track. Never seen a rookie drive like that in their first race. Outstanding I have to say.'

Marco shrugged, 'I was mildly distracted. You know, what with the recent heartbreak and everything. Didn't have time to squeeze in a therapy session beforehand. But yeah, she is outstanding. If anyone was going to show me up like that, I'm glad it was her.'

He didn't seem bothered at all, despite his teammate's dig, but she also didn't buy the fact he had been distracted by thoughts of Esme. That just wasn't the done thing. You leave your personal issues in the garage, every driver knew that. And regardless of the unprofessional location of Marco's meltdown at the start of the week, he didn't strike her as the type to let his feelings control his driving. Even so, she caught him gazing after Esme in her team uniform, capturing video content of Eden's drivers who had earned third position.

'Hey,' she elbowed his side, 'enjoy this. I know you've done it hundreds of times before, but you and the guys won. Our *whole* team won. Take your focus off Esme until you're home safe in Monaco, or wherever it is you're heading next. That's when you let yourself feel it all.'

'Same goes for you.' He removed his arm and stretched out, gearing up to walk up the steps.

She frowned at him, tuning out the rest of the team, 'What?'

'I don't know what's up, but you look like you're fighting

one hell of an inner battle. Your cheeks are burning up, and no matter how much you try to hide it, your breathing is off. I can hear it, feel it, see it. The way your chest rises and falls with hesitation, how you're gasping for breath. Save it for later, Cowgirl. Push it all down until you're free to let it all out.'

Savi was still processing the way he had been able to see right through her when they got the signal to make their way to the podium, a crowd of their biggest supporters traipsing along behind them and Marco's hand on the small of her back. It was a small gesture which could so easily have gone unnoticed, but it grounded her. And then when she got to the top of the steps and Marco had to leave her to go to his place on first, Kodie took over.

She, Kodie and Miko joined hands and helped each other up, pausing to smile at one another and soak it all in privately, before they turned to face their audience. Hundreds of people, from team principals, drivers, engineers, mechanics, VIP guests, and the fans beyond the pit wall who had rushed from the grandstands to the track just to get close enough to celebrate with them. She had experienced this before, but it was different now. Revolution Racing were in a league of their own, and the International Endurance Championship was home to some of the best drivers in the world. Now she was considered one of them. Podium position in her very first race. How many people on the planet could say that?

Medals were hung around their necks, trophies handed over and hands shaken by people so high up in the motorsport industry that Savi did all she could not to hug them and thank them for letting this championship exist. It took a village, and this team was just a very small part of it, but it was hers.

Glancing to the side, she spotted her dad bursting with pride out of view of the cameras, all but crying on the shoulder of Julien's mum who had also come alone, and looked like she'd been weeping for days. She was proof that this feeling would never get old, for drivers or their loved ones. And then she looked over to the podium next to theirs, watching the guys get into position for photos while her own team did the same. Arms around shoulders, all beaming and revelling in the magic of the moment.

'Savannah,' Marco approached the three of them, clutching his champagne bottle with Julien and Brett in tow. 'How do you feel?' he shouted above the applause and excessively loud cheers from down below.

'Like I'm in heaven!' she laughed.

'Probably the closest we'll ever get,' Miko added.

Then the spray hit. Sticky, sweet champagne that coated their racing suits, dousing them in a reminder of everything they had achieved today. This week. In their careers thus far. Savi wanted this forever, which she knew wasn't possible, but she'd be behind the wheel of a race car until she was old and grey and couldn't see to drive anymore or she didn't have the reactions necessary for a sport so elite. Revolution Racing was her world.

'Come in!' Jasper beckoned them into the conference room. 'Take a seat, everyone.'

The team, engineers included, made themselves

comfortable around the long, rectangular table in the middle of the room. Her first official race debrief for the IEC. Savi was excited even if some of the engineers looked nervous. She supposed there was, in a sense, a lot more pressure on them. They were the ones deploying the race strategy to the drivers in the car and taking the brunt of it when the drivers went against team orders. Not that any of them had done that this time, but Savi had taken a risk when she'd chosen to overtake Marco in the first two hours.

'No food this time, Jasper?' Brett sulked.

'Faith and Julien will have a buffet at their place later, consider me depriving you now as a favour.' He rolled his eyes playfully. 'How were post-race interviews?'

'Same as always,' Julien stated. 'But I guess the girls might have had a different experience. Less mundane, more exciting.'

'They just made us talk about our feelings.' Savi scrunched her nose up. 'Get all sentimental on camera. Would've been better off showing our parents crying and calling it a day.'

'They do like to try and tug on the heartstrings,' Jasper grimaced. 'You'll probably get that kind of approach to interviews all through this first season.'

'It's worth it,' Kodie shrugged.

'Let's crack on with the debrief, then . . .' Their boss sat down at the head of the table with his notes, before tossing them to one side. 'Who am I kidding? You guys all did a stellar job. Truly. I don't know if I've ever been so relaxed during a race, but you had everything under control from the moment those lights turned green. Your engineers were on the ball, each of you made strategic risks that paid off. I couldn't be prouder. To have a brand-new team of drivers in a car we've never raced before do so well, it's almost unheard of. And frankly, it's a big screw you to anyone who thinks women don't have a place here.'

Savi swallowed the lump in her throat, all signs of anxiety replaced by an overwhelming sense of gratitude for her younger self, her family, Gabriel Lopez for sponsoring her, her teammates and her boss and everyone who had worked to give women opportunities like this. Especially women from backgrounds such as hers, where you had to rely on being in the right place at the right time and the possibility that someone with the power to make dreams come true might see something in you.

'He's right, we're all about making statements in this team,' Marco added. 'This is the biggest one of all, and it's already paying off. Because of you.'

Jasper nodded along. 'You each deserve all the success you have created for yourselves, and I am so glad the rest of this team made the active decision to dedicate our second car to the three of you, and the future of women in motorsport.'

'So . . .' Julien said. 'Anything you want to tell anyone off for?'

His attention shot to Savi and Marco, who were sitting side by side. Sort of. Marco was leaning back in his chair, his foot hooked around the metal leg of her own. 'Us?!' he scowled.

'Well, you two were playing a bit of a dangerous game at

the start of the race but I trusted that you knew what you were doing. Trust is a big thing, and I could see you pulling back when needed, Savi. You made the move when you knew it was safe to do so, and it worked out well for you.'

'Until I got the position back from Miko!' Julien grinned, high-fiving a startled Miko who had been keeping to herself, mid-daydream.

Miko frowned. 'I'm not sure that warrants a high-five on my part, but sure.'

'Now, before we all head into Malmedy for the after party, I will issue my annual reminder that there will be a lot of people there tonight. They may be drivers like you, but that doesn't mean they have the same standards for privacy. Your behaviour offtrack is a reflection on the team, and if you take things too far . . . Well, please don't make the PR team have to do any damage control tomorrow morning. That's all I ask.'

Brett let out a snort. 'Jasper, need we remind you of your actions last year?'

'I am well aware of what I got up to, Anderson. I could have created the biggest scandal this team has ever faced with my naked rendition of "Bohemian Rhapsody" on the balcony, but thankfully we avoided the video getting out. I have since joined you in your journey of sobriety.'

'Speaking of,' Brett stood up, 'if we're all done here, I'd like to go and wash off the champers before we head to Julien's. I think I'm going to have to peel my racing suit off like a second skin.' He shuddered. He had decided when he first made his comeback to the sport that he could handle alcohol being sprayed on the podium, but he never liked to sit covered in it longer than a few minutes if he could help it.

'And I,' Marco rose from his chair, 'am calling dibs on being second in the shower.'

The two of them left, closely followed by Julien, leaving Savi and her female teammates sitting in a room with Jasper and a few engineers. 'Jasper, can we look into getting brand deals and sponsorship from some female-led brands and businesses next season?' Savi asked, knowing each of them had signed a two-year contract so they would be here to see it out.

Miko sat up straight, 'Oh, please! That's genius!'

'Yeah, we've already got a partnership with Faith and Lucie's motorsport academy, what's a few more?' Kodie added.

Jasper smiled knowingly at them, shuffling his stack of notes. 'Did you really think I'd introduce this second car to the team without having such plans up my sleeve already? I'm in talks with a few, but I'd love to get you in some meetings. Send me a list of your own recommendations, too. We'll discuss it.'

That was why she was here, with this team. It wasn't just about status and relationships and everything Revolution Racing could give her. She wanted to give back. To all the little girls who dreamed of growing up to be just like her, and to the women who were already in this industry and tired of the sexism from the people who didn't understand what it took to get here. It was about progress. Making history. And while she had a long way to go, she knew her future was bright.

6

The flight from Brussels to Nashville seemed to last a lifetime. It was like the Le Mans twenty-four-hour race of flights; it dragged on so long it felt like she'd been ten thousand feet in the air for a whole day. In reality, it was only around eleven hours with a stop for fuel. But still, she'd had eleven hours to sit and mull over the chaotic weekend she'd just experienced.

The post-race parties at Faith and Julien's farmhouse were not for the faint hearted, and this one had been even wilder than the Revolution team bonding party. She was certain every driver on the grid had been in attendance, and the mechanical bull, a longtime Revolution Racing tradition, had been violated to the point where they had managed to break it before she even got a chance to show them how it was done.

Even her dad had been invited and had a go on it before waking up still drunk at three a.m. and hitching a ride back to the hotel in someone else's cab, so he didn't miss his flight home. Whether they let him on the plane whilst intoxicated was a different story.

She was sitting in the back of a blacked-out SUV now, racing on the back burner for at least a few days, en route to some random road amongst the trees where Jesse was waiting for her. She was nervous – not to see him, but because pulling over in a car like this and getting into a beefed-up pick-up truck was going to look like a drug deal or kidnapping or something, not like the reunion of two loved-up celebrities trying to hide away from the world.

Her car had barely stopped before she was jumping out of it, closing the gap and wrapping her cowboy-boot-clad calves around Jesse's waist, nearly knocking his hat from his head.

'Hi, baby.' He held her tight with one arm, pushing her hair back with the other and planting a kiss on her. It was a sweet, innocent kiss but it was filled with months' worth of affection they hadn't been able to give, and it left her wanting more.

'Hi.' She kissed him again. 'I missed you.'

'I missed you more. Trust me.' He gazed into her eyes and she admired the ocean-blue hues of his own. There was nothing like this. Sometimes the weeks and months apart were worth it just for the feeling she got when they saw each other again. But if she told him that, he might not do crazy things like fly her halfway across the world in the middle of his insanely busy tour just to lie tangled up in bedsheets for two weeks.

'Ahem.' Her driver coughed, subtly gesturing to Savi's suitcases which he was waiting to put in the trunk of Jesse's truck for them.

'Sorry, man. Here, I'll do it.' Jesse grabbed them and did it himself, tipping the driver generously. So generously, in fact, that Savi's eyes nearly fell out of her head.

'Thank you, sir. Let me know if you need me at all over the next two weeks.'

Just like that, they were alone at last. He held the passenger door open for her, ever the gentleman, and snuck in an extra kiss as he buckled her in. 'Will never get tired of doing that.'

'Well, then I'm in for a treat.'

Jesse's truck was one of Savi's favourite things about him. It wasn't flashy or over-the-top, it was a beat-up old Chevy that he'd had since high school and it belonged to the same guy she'd fallen for, before fame got in the way. Not that there was anything wrong with him being famous, she just sometimes missed that tiny snippet of a summer when it was them against the world. Now it felt like it was the world against them.

'So, tell me about the race.' He removed one hand from the steering wheel and placed it on her knee, causing goosebumps to rise. 'What was your personal highlight?'

'Overtaking Marco,' she laughed.

'No shit, I bet that felt good.'

'I'm no stranger to the fact that he's a better driver than me, all the guys on the team are. For now, at least. Us girls are new to this level of endurance racing, with a car as fast and as high spec as this. But knowing I'm capable of that so early on in my career with the IEC? Makes me wonder where this will take me.'

'Formula One, baby.'

'I don't want to race in that championship,' she laughed. 'Endurance racing has my heart, you know that. I like the unpredictability, the challenge. The longer a race is, the more chance that things can go wrong or they can change. It feels like more of a fight.'

'Wouldn't you give it a try?' Jesse eyed her and squeezed her upper thigh. 'Would be a hell of a legacy to leave behind one day.'

'I'd consider a season. Or a spot as a reserve driver, maybe. But if it meant sacrificing my place on the team or dropping out of the IEC and risking not getting back into it, absolutely not. Besides, F1 is a whole different ball game. What if I failed?' Savi had never really suffered from a fear of failure, but endurance racing was what she was good at.

So many drivers switched between the two and were great at one and not so great at the other. She knew of F1 drivers who had come across to the IEC, stolen the spotlight and had all the fanfare, and then flopped so badly that they'd either gone back to what they knew or retired from racing entirely. It was just different. And as much as Jesse always encouraged her to shoot for the stars, *this* was her dream. She was right where she wanted to be.

'Enough said,' he smiled. 'There are snacks in the glove box, by the way. I stocked up on your favourites.'

She dived straight in, her eyes lighting up at the sight of Reese's Peanut Butter Cups. She was lucky that they were easy to find in Europe. 'Tell me about the tour, then. What's the latest?'

'Uhm, well, my manager is pregnant. So that's a real pain in the ass.'

'Sapphire's having a baby?!' Savi gasped. Sapphire was one of very few people who knew about Jesse's relationship status, and that was only because she along with his PR team were responsible for helping to keep it under wraps. Savi had met her a few times.

'Yep,' he replied, popping the 'p'. He didn't seem happy about it at all.

'Let me guess, you're sulking because she'll have to go on maternity leave?' She ripped open the packet and bit into chocolatey, nutty heaven.

'Yeah! She's been my manager since day dot. So I'm gonna have to find someone else while she's raising a kid, and then what if she doesn't come back?' He seemed genuinely stressed out, but Savi couldn't help but find it amusing.

'That's just life, Jess. People move on. But I'm sure Sapph will come back to you, she's the one who got you to where you are.'

'Exactly! I can't do it without her.' He put his other hand back on the wheel and Savi missed the warmth of his touch.

'You can. But anyway, you're stressing over something that might not even happen.' She held out the rest of her peanut butter cup for him to take. More to shut him up and get him back into cheerful-boyfriend mode. The boyfriend who was focused on living in the moment.

'Sorry, this trip is supposed to be about us and I'm already complaining,' he sighed, stopping at a red light. Savi silently leaned over the centre console, forcing him to look at her.

'Hey, I love you.' She traced his jaw with her fingertips and was met with a kiss. It started out slow, and then it became a race against the traffic light system. How long did they have before he had to hit the accelerator?

Approximately thirty seconds, apparently, as a car pulled

up behind them and hit the horn. It was typical that on such a quiet road, they would still be interrupted. 'Shit. Quit distracting me, Sav, you know I can't resist you when you get all cute on me.'

Savi felt her heart sink a little. That had happened a few times lately when she was with him or talking to him. He hadn't told her he loved her back for a while, and although he wasn't a words of affirmation kind of guy and showed her how he felt with physical touch instead, it still played on her mind every time she said it and he didn't.

The cabin came into sight three hours later, after a very bumpy ride on a dirt road that was sure to have damaged Jesse's truck. He spent a fortune keeping the thing running but he refused to cave and buy himself a shiny new one, even with the millions he earned.

The cabin, however, was very shiny and very new. It screamed dollar signs. A-frame cabins like this one were popular in California and Jesse loved the architecture, but he wasn't a California type of man. It sat amongst hundreds of trees, and you really wouldn't know it was here unless you were looking for it. That was what made it the perfect hideout for the two of them. They had spent winters holed up here, some visits extended because they were snowed in.

When the sun set and moonlight descended on the mountains, the cosy, ambient lighting from inside and out turned the dark and moody black structure into a luxurious sanctuary.

Inside, Jesse had decorated with white, black and soft grey with faux fur rugs, cushions and blankets everywhere, making nights in front of the log fire a dream. Savi loved spending time here, with him, away from everyone and everything. Even if he had got Wi-Fi installed last summer so he could work from home when needed.

'Home sweet home.' Savi dropped onto the sofa and put her feet up on the oak coffee table, admiring the landscape from the floor-to-ceiling window. They never shut the blinds here, choosing to soak in the views and wake with the sun.

Jesse dumped the bags by the front door and closed it behind him, sealing them into their perfect, private bubble. Until they ran out of groceries and had to make a trip into town, that was. He peeled his jacket off, placed his cowboy hat on the sideboard and made a beeline for her. 'You keeping the boots on while I devour you?'

Oh. Savi sat up straight and looked him dead in the eye. She didn't realise he was planning on getting down to business within seconds of getting through the door, but really, she should have. He'd been pretty tense the last stretch of the journey, post-kiss. She'd thought he was still frustrated about his manager but maybe the frustration was all sexual.

'Boots and lingerie is a look, right?' She raised an eyebrow.

'One hundred per cent, but I know you. You won't have taken lingerie to Europe, because I'm the only person you need to wear it for. So I suggest you get your cute little ass in that bedroom and find my favourite set from the drawer.' He sat on a kitchen bar stool and leaned on the counter, waiting.

Savi launched into action and pulled out a classic black, lacy set from the dresser. Suspender belt and all. She wasn't going to deny that she felt incredibly sexy in it, but she was weirdly nervous. It had just been so long since he'd had his hands on her, she always worried she wasn't what he wanted anymore. But then she opened the bedroom door, cowboy boots still on, and found him right where she'd left him. Staring her down. And she knew he hadn't taken his eyes off the door the whole time she'd been in there.

'I'm ready.' She kicked one leg out in front of her, faking confidence.

'You're missing something.' Jesse got up, his black T-shirt stretched to the max over his biceps, and headed back towards the entryway. 'This,' he said, coming closer until he was directly in front of her, 'belongs to you.'

'Wear the hat . . .' she grinned.

'Ride the cowboy.'

His lips crashed against hers and his hands were in her hair in an instant, walking her backwards until they reached the bed. He gestured for her to sit down, and she did as she was told, resting her hands on the mattress and leaning back on them. The only time Savi liked to be dominated was in the bedroom.

'I've been waiting for this,' she breathed out as he lifted his shirt over his head.

'You have no idea how bad I've missed this, baby.' He unbuckled his belt, not letting her do it for him. Jesse was the opposite to her; he wasn't in control of his personal life because his management team were so overbearing, so he took control in situations like this. She, on the other hand, had a lot more say in her job and a lot more freedom, so she didn't mind handing the reins to him sometimes.

Savi's mouth practically watered at the sight of it. He was already hard, and she imagined he had been since she'd wrapped her legs around his waist three hours ago. She spat on her hand while gazing up at him through long, dark lashes, taking hold of him and stroking his length at an agonisingly slow pace. For both of them. Because she had been dripping wet since they'd stopped at that red light, and she was ready now.

'Fuck, do we need to bother with the foreplay? I don't think I can wait any longer to be inside you, Sav.' He gripped her wrist and watched in awe as she took her other hand and slipped her fingers inside her lace thong. Holding her hand up to him, his eyes went dark as he took her fingers into his mouth.

'I think that's a firm no.' She stood up and turned around, so her back was to him. This was his favourite position, and he was stressed. It was the least she could do.

'Bend over for me, darlin'.' His voice had got even huskier and it was killing her. How could time move so slowly? They'd only been in here about two minutes, if that. She leaned over, already gripping the bed sheets in preparation. His cowboy hat fell off her head and bounced onto the floor.

Jesse pulled her underwear to one side, slowly inserting two fingers into her like he didn't fully believe she was ready for him. He really did underestimate the effect he had on her.

'Jess. Hurry the fuck up,' Savi whined, earning a laugh.

'Ready?' He slapped her on the ass, hard. She jumped, but it didn't deter her at all. She cried out in a mix of pleasure and pain.

'I've *been* ready.' And with her verbal consent, he entered her with a soft moan from the pair of them. 'Oh my God.'

'Savannah, holy fuck.' This was one of few times he would get away with calling her by her full name, and the only other person who got away with it all the time was her pain in the ass teammate. How could she argue with Jesse when he was buried inside her? 'I know you're gonna kill me for calling you that but god, it's like you were made for me.'

'I'm starting to think I was,' she mumbled as he began thrusting his hips, filling her completely. 'Faster.'

'This is about to be the best forty-five seconds of my life.' Jesse gripped her hips and slammed into her, laughing in disbelief.

'We've got two weeks to . . .' And then she gave up speaking. Because her face was buried in the mattress, and she was totally breathless. Her whole body felt like it was on fire in the best way.

They were usually all about the foreplay and taking their time with each other, but today Jesse seemed to be on a mission. Like he had some sort of point to prove. To whom? She wasn't sure, but she wasn't about to complain. This was quite possibly the best sex they'd had, and they'd had a lot over the last four years. It was often all they did, because they couldn't go anywhere. That meant they'd also experimented a lot, but today was proving that simplicity was key. Simple was good.

'Savannah.' Jesse's voice was strained, but Savi didn't even have the energy to answer him. She was about to explode, and she knew he was too. If she spoke and ruined her focus, she might be delayed, and there was no doubt that reaching a climax in unison was the best way to do it.

Mere seconds later, he came inside her with a groan so loud, she wouldn't be surprised if they heard it all the way down the mountain. Her entire body shook, and he held onto her tightly, letting her have her moment. He wasn't lying when he said forty-five seconds.

He waited for her to get it all out of her system, stroking her back, before he collapsed on top of her. Still buried inside her, he kissed her neck. 'Sav?'

'Yeah?' she murmured, enjoying the warmth of his bare chest against her shoulders.

'I love you.'

7

Savi woke up to an arm thrown across her torso, crushing her and holding her hostage in bed. A very big, very comfortable bed that was moulded to her body. Jesse lay next to her, gently snoring away. She studied his face in awe. It was no wonder the rest of the world adored him so much, had calendars of him on their walls and social media accounts dedicated to him.

She remembered seeing a viral photo of a girl at one of his concerts a couple of years ago who held up a sign that read 'Jesse Montalvo will you be my baby daddy?' and she laughed.

Would her fans ever do something like that for her? Actually, yes, they probably would. Some of them were pretty creepy. She had been rising in popularity the last few years, which was part of the reason she was constantly waiting for her brother's identity to be made public, and she liked to hole up at the family ranch to get away from it all when she could.

First day at the cabin tradition was Danish pastries and fruit juice, which were always stocked by someone from Jesse's team. It was usually his personal assistant, but knowing Jess, he would have given her a few days off and got one of his security team to do it before they arrived.

She always liked to surprise him with breakfast in bed,

but this morning it was proving impossible. It was like his arm was made of concrete. Savi spent a lot of time in the gym, but even she couldn't shift it without his input.

'What are you doing?' he mumbled, his face squashed into the pillows. Her pillow, not just his. Jesse never stayed on his side of the bed, and he never slept with his back to her. He was always on her.

'Trying to be the world's best girlfriend and bring you breakfast.'

'You're my breakfast.' One eye opened and he had a devilish grin on his face. He looked more adorable than sexy, which Savi was certain wasn't what he was going for. Nonetheless, her body reacted accordingly.

'Pastries after. Can you pull the blinds across? The sun is not my friend this morning.' She squinted, holding her arm over her face. Jesse got up and plunged the room into darkness, ambling back toward her.

A whole hour and two rounds of mind-blowing sex later, Savi was satisfied with a croissant, OJ and multiple orgasms. It had turned from her spoiling Jesse to him spoiling her, but she was enjoying every second.

She had to kick him out of the shower just so she could deep condition her hair without him distracting her, but even then he had gone down on her before he left. He'd ended up with the conditioner from her hands in his own hair, too.

'Baby, I've got to make a work call. I'll be in my office,' he called out as she was doing her hair. She'd thrown on one of his oversized tour t-shirts with a pair of boxer shorts, her uniform for a lazy day at the cabin.

'Okay! I'm going to call Ez.' She hunted down Jesse's spare laptop and went to sit out on the deck. The internet connection worked surprisingly well out here. Well enough that she could have a catch up with her best friend, anyway.

'He hasn't kidnapped you, then?' Esme's face appeared on the screen.

'Of course not. We're at the cabin.'

'Ah, yes. The love shack.'

'Ez!' Savi rolled her eyes. Her friend didn't exactly approve of the way Savi and Jesse spent their time together. She couldn't understand why they didn't just go public and then sue the hell out of anyone who published degrading articles about them.

'Sorry, would you rather I refer to it as a sex dungeon?'

'You're cutting out!' Savi yelled, shaking the laptop slightly so the picture wobbled.

Esme tutted. 'Fine, I'll shut up. Nice shirt, by the way. Better not post any photos on social media in it. Fans will go wild for that.'

'Plenty of young women have t-shirts with Jesse Montalvo's name and face on them, thank you very much. It's not a big deal.'

'But you've posted that you're in the mountains, Jesse has posted that he's in the mountains, so . . . if you post a photo in that shirt, someone somewhere is gonna put two and two together.' Esme shrugged like it was obvious, and it should have been. But Savi was so caught up in La La Land that she probably wouldn't have noticed until it was too late.

'What the hell am I meant to post for two weeks? I post *every* day. I've got a brand to keep alive.' Savi ran a hand over her face. Why did this have to be so complicated? 'I usually plan in advance to avoid situations like this. We can't show us being in the same house.'

'Better dig up some good old throwback photos.'

'Some days I just want to post a photo of him and call it a day on this whole secrecy thing. It's tiring. You know, we haven't had a real date in years? The last one was two years ago, he flew us out to Bali where nobody knew us. And then he visited there again last year, solo, and got swarmed by fans. There's no escape.'

'Stop escaping, then. Just get it all out there and go on with your lives.' Esme suggested.

Savi had thought about it endlessly. But she had brought it up with Jesse before, and he wasn't game. He was right, though. Their life together as they knew it would be over. Jesse's world was an intimidating one, and he was just trying to keep Savi out of it.

'What's new with you?' she sighed.

'Sav, I saw you three days ago. I know you're trying to change the subject. But anyway, there is nothing new with me, my life is very mundane and boring, and my relationship is perfect.'

'Great, thank you for rubbing salt in the wound.' Savi wished she had a beer.

'You're very welcome,' Esme teased. 'Oh, have you seen any of the articles about Marco?'

'Articles?' Savi questioned. She had been steering clear of her phone, trying to fully unwind and enjoy her time with Jesse before being dragged back to reality. She was only chatting to Esme because he was on a call.

'He's gone off the rails!' Esme said it like it was exciting, something fun to gossip about.

'In what sense?!'

'Oh, not in a Brett-Anderson-Drinking-Problem sense,' she waved her off, referring to Brett's battle a couple of seasons ago. 'But he was seen leaving a club in Paris with *two* leggy blondes last night and yesterday lunchtime he was photographed kissing a completely different woman slap bang in the middle of the viewing platform on the Eiffel Tower. Then, today –'

'Wait, wait, wait. Slow down, Ez,' Savi hushed her right as Jesse appeared, shirtless. He gestured for her to continue her call and sat down opposite her, taking a bite into his Danish. 'Marco isn't that kind of guy, is he?'

'No, which is why this is such a huge thing! So today, he was snapped on his yacht in Monaco, stark naked with a *fourth* woman!' Esme's eyes were wide.

'He's just living his life, let the poor man be!' Savi knew this wasn't like him, but why shouldn't he have a little fun? Everyone was entitled to; it was just unfortunate that his adventures were being documented in the press.

'But do you think this is because of me?' Esme grimaced.

'Umm . . . honestly? Probably. But it might not be! Maybe you rejecting him has made him shift his perspective and he figured life's too short.'

'I reckon this is the new Marco, you know. I hope it is. Anything to stop him crying at parties over me. God, that was horrendous.'

'Maybe he's mad at you now. And me, for letting him pour his heart out. He's channelling his rage into a string of meaningless sex.'

'Can you blame the bloke?' Jesse chimed in from across the table. 'He's heartbroken, gotta let him get it out of his system. Sex is a good release.'

'Hey, Jesse!' Esme shouted.

'Howdy, Esmerelda,' he replied, to which Savi offered her a sheepish smile.

'How did you kn—' But before she could finish, Jesse had leaned over, shut the computer lid on her and taken Savi's face in his hands, leaning in close to capture her lips with his own.

'We were talking,' Savi smiled up at him, not in the least bit offended. It was his and Esme's thing, fighting over having Savi to themselves.

'I know. But I also know she'll call you when this Marco guy hits the press with his fifth sexual conquest of the week.'

'Want to hike to the waterfall?' Savi asked, desperate to get her nature fix. Despite growing up on a ranch, surrounded by dust and dirt, she was a water baby at heart. Lakes, rivers, pools. It was where she was happiest.

'Sure. Let me go and pack the essentials.' By that, he meant beer, water, snacks and sunscreen. None of which he would let her carry, despite the fact she was an athlete and was more than capable of lugging a backpack over some rocky terrain.

It wasn't until they reached their favourite waterfall an hour later that Jesse finally relaxed. He may have done this same hike every time they came here, but he was pretty pathetic at it. He complained that everything hurt, that his walking shoes were rubbing, the bag was heavy, he could feel the sunburn coming on and that the hike was far longer than he remembered. The view, aka Savi stripping off and standing on a rock with zero clothing on, shut him up.

'You always do this,' he smirked.

'Why wouldn't I? Nobody's around. Just you, me, and nature.'

'Guess I'll join you, then.' He set the bag down and copied her.

'I didn't come here to stand on this rock all day, let's swim.'

She trod carefully into the water, cautious of slipping like she had two years prior. Her old phone was still down there, somewhere. Surrendered to the fish.

'Do you ever regret leaving Wyoming?' Jesse caught up to her and ducked under the waterfall, reaching for her as he shook his soaking wet, dark hair out.

'Never,' she responded firmly, and she meant it.

'Even with Wes?' Jesse frowned.

'What's that supposed to mean?'

'Don't you ever wish you could be there to help him?'

'I'm his sister. I'm not his caregiver. Us keeping our distance and me travelling has made our relationship stronger. He doesn't need to be a witness to my sympathy. Besides, how else is he gonna afford the level of care he gets if I'm not earning the big bucks?'

'That's a fair point.'

'Do *you* regret leaving Wyoming?' She studied his

features for a moment, noting the frown lines that had formed. Jesse never used to be so serious, but now it was hard to get him to have any real fun. To let loose. He just seemed to use sex as an outlet.

'Every damn day.' He breathed out a sarcastic laugh.

'Really? You have it all, Jess. Isn't this exactly what you wanted?'

'Do I? How can I have it all when I can't go anywhere without a security team unless I want the whole world knowing about it? How can I have it all when I can't show off the woman I love without people tearing her apart?'

'I'm in the spotlight myself, Jess. If that was a change you wanted to make, I could handle it.'

'They'll dig, Sav. They'll dig and dig, and they won't stop until your secrets are spread like wildfire. Weston's identity will be uncovered, his accident will be a hot topic again, you'll be scrutinised. We've been through this. We are on totally different levels of fame, in two vastly different industries. You don't understand what it's like for me.' He looked ready to cry, and she looped her arms around his neck, making him look at her instead of past her.

'Okay, you're right. I'm sorry. If this is too hard . . .'

'No. That's not what I mean. I'm just fucking tired, Savi.'

'That's why we're here, right?' She offered him a small smile, unsure of what she could possibly do to make this situation any better. The only thing she could do was not have the career she had or the family she had or the life she had. She had to not be *her*.

'Yeah. I'm just sorry being with me feels like a secret military operation, sometimes.'

'You're worth it, Jesse.'

He planted a gentle kiss on her forehead and pulled her further into the water, where they proceeded to lose themselves in each other until hunger hit and they realised they were still an hour from food. That was something that sucked about being here; they couldn't just drive to a restaurant and have a proper date. It was a home-cooked meal or nothing.

They were in the process of making quesadillas for lunch when there was a knock on the door. Savi opened it to reveal Jesse's head of security.

'Hi, ma'am.' He was stone-faced as usual but even Savi could tell something was wrong.

'Hi, Sloan. Need to come in?' She opened the door wider, and he stepped past her, squeezing his arms in against himself like he was scared to touch her. He always tried so hard to be respectful that it just made her laugh.

'Sir.' He nodded at Jesse, and one look at his employee's face was enough to make him drop the spatula on the counter. 'We need to talk.'

'Then talk.' Jesse's jaw tensed.

'We just found a photographer hiding in the shed out back. Not sure how long he's been there, but we chased him off. Well, we tried to catch him, and he ran. We haven't seen any vehicles, so we have no idea where he came from.'

'How the hell did he get past you?' Jesse spat.

'Jess . . .' Savi tried to calm him down.

'No, this isn't good enough. You're not just meant to be

protecting me, Sloan. You're protecting my girl, too. I need to know that we're safe.'

'The guys are out scanning the perimeter now, and we've got a second team in.' There was nothing Sloan could say to defend himself and Jesse was getting more anxious by the minute, pacing back and forth.

'Did he have a camera, or was he just being a creep?' Savi questioned him with a far gentler, less snappy approach. Maybe he should come and work for her instead.

'We didn't get a chance to see.'

'Great. I need to go and call my PR team so they can be prepared.' Jesse all but shooed Sloan back out of the cabin and reached for his phone. 'Sav, I suggest you speak to your team.'

Offering her apologies to Jesse's no doubt soon-to-be-fired security guard as his boss stormed off into his office, Savi sat on the sofa and debated whether to make the call.

It seemed silly, telling her bosses that she was dating someone high profile and it might hit the headlines. It almost felt like she was bragging, making herself sound like she was as big a deal as him. Would Jasper understand? Would he reassure her or would he scold her for not being upfront when she signed her contract? Maybe it was better to keep quiet for now, let Jesse's team take care of damage control.

'Baby . . .' Jesse stood in the doorway, white as a ghost.

'What's wrong?' She shot up.

He held his phone out to her, and she felt sick to her stomach. There on his screen was an article. *Jesse Montalvo and Mystery Woman Snapped During a Wild Night of Passion.*

There were multiple shots of the two of them in a compromising position from the night before, lights on, curtains open. That man must have caught them through the window, and they were so wrapped up in the moment that they hadn't noticed. The only saving grace? Her face was buried in the covers.

8

Savi had never been so glad to be back at the racetrack. After two weeks cooped up at the cabin, avoiding being seen in public and walking around with the curtains closed like she was a hostage, Monza felt like her safe haven.

'Savannah.' Marco appeared next to her at the coffee cart, his curls dishevelled. Savi knew he had a girl here with him this weekend, but could he not control his new-found urges?

'De Luca.' Savi grabbed three cubes of sugar and dropped them in her deliciously strong pool of liquid. The caffeine hit was needed after the long flight from Tennessee.

'Good couple of weeks off?' He nudged her arm in an overly friendly manner. It was just as well the IEC race season was spread out with longish breaks between races, because he was all up in her personal space and she could only handle him in small doses.

'Yep. You?' She started walking and he trailed behind her.

'Wonderful.'

'Which port was your favourite? Saint Lucia, Dubrovnik?'

'Hmm, Saint Lucia. Great company. So, which position was yours and Jesse Montalvo's favourite?' he challenged.

Savi stopped in her tracks, almost spilling her coffee

when he bumped into her. 'How the hell do you know about that?' she whispered.

'You told me the morning of your flight that you were going to Tennessee . . . Then all of a sudden, photos have gone viral of Jesse Montalvo with a girl with hair just like yours,' he twirled a strand round his fingers, 'in the Tennessee mountains.'

'Shit . . .' Her face got hot.

'But also, I know you have a tattoo of a horseshoe on your ankle. I saw it at Julien's party when you jumped in the pool. It was visible in the photos . . . after I zoomed in which yes, is weird, sorry. Curiosity got the better of me, but it confirmed my theory. You've been sleeping with him!'

She kept that tattoo hidden because she'd got it done underage and it was awful and faded. She should've known someone would notice it at some point. She was surprised people weren't roasting her for it on social media, commenting on how bad it was.

'You can't tell anyone it was me, Marco. Please. I will do anything.'

'Anything? Like being my own personal assistant for the season?' He gave her a cheeky grin and if she didn't know better, she'd think he was being serious. 'I'm kidding, I've got one of those already. Your secret is safe with me. But seriously, you're dating a country music superstar? How did that come about?'

'It's not a new thing, we've been dating four years. Ever since we met at a county fair back home.'

'That is the most hillbilly thing I've ever heard.'

'Shut up.' Savi kept walking, desperate to get away from him.

'That's no way to talk to someone who knows what you did in the mountains.'

Marco wandered off to his side of the garage while Savi pretended to be engaged in a conversation with Kodie and Faith, not taking in a word they said about social media schedules or content ideas. That was the last thing on her mind, and it shouldn't be that way. Work needed to be her number one focus. Was Jesse a distraction?

She was entitled to be happy and to have a personal life, but *was* she happy? She was Jesse Montalvo's dirty little secret, emphasis on the dirty. If the public managed to link her to the photos, the team could drop her, and they would have every right to do so.

The cabin was supposed to be a sanctuary, somewhere she and Jesse could live as normal a life as possible, and that had been taken from them. Where else were they supposed to go? How were they going to be together now? Was all this worth losing everything?

'Savi?' Faith waved a hand in front of her face.

'Huh?' She blinked, snapping out of her daze.

'You on the same planet as us?' Faith laughed. 'I said what about a video of you, Kodie and Miko doing a tour of all the different food trucks here at the circuit?'

'All of them?' Savi winced. That was a lot of food they probably shouldn't be consuming during race week, when they were supposed to be eating nutritional, whole foods only. She hadn't even picked up an energy drink this week.

'Yeah, you could share. I heard the stone-baked pizza

truck does a mango and ricotta one. Lucie and I will finish your leftovers.'

'Mango on pizza?' Savi fake gagged.

'Don't knock it until you try it!'

'Can't believe they're allowed to sell something like that at a racetrack in Italy. Does Marco know about this? He's anti-pineapple, can't imagine how he'd feel about mango.'

'Marco is keen to try it, Lucie on the other hand? Acted like someone had died when she saw the menu.' They laughed. Lucie was born and raised in Los Angeles with Italian heritage and was the perfect combination of a classic California girl and a stereotypical fiery Italian.

This one conversation was enough to drag Savi away from conjuring up every worst-case scenario and she did the one thing she knew how to: threw herself into work. She was underneath the car with a mechanic, looking at the chassis, when Marco called down to her.

She scooted out to find him crouched over her. 'When did you last speak to him?'

'Who?' she scowled, quickly shutting her mouth when he side-eyed her mechanic in a silent signal that he couldn't say the name out loud with people around. 'Oh. Yesterday.'

'How did he sound?' Marco asked.

'Stressed . . .' How else would he sound at a time like this?

'Stressed enough to send someone out here?'

'He what . . . ?'

'There's a guy here. Says he knows you. Blake something.'

She shot to her feet and pulled Marco out of the garage with her. 'Where is he?'

'Team HQ. More importantly, *who* is he? Because he's not just here for you, Savi.' Marco looked nervous. 'He wants to speak to me, too.'

'What?' She was more confused than ever. 'He's Jesse's PR rep.'

'Well, he knew my name and who I was and told me to come and get you. Said he'd wait all day if he had to, and that Jesse sent him here to talk to us both. He seemed serious enough that I abandoned what I was doing, so this had better be worth it.'

'What the hell?' She peered through the tinted windows of the team headquarters and saw Blake sitting there with a cup of coffee and a slice of cake, looking very relaxed. He usually did, because it was his job to be calm in a crisis.

'You can keep standing out here if you want but I'm going in there to find out why I'm being dragged into your shenanigans.'

Marco scanned himself in and held the door for her.

'Savi, good to see you.' Blake stood up and reached out to shake her hand, shaking the crumbs from his suit jacket.

'Hi, Blake,' she smiled. 'This is Marco De Luca, but I hear you've already met.'

Marco shook his hand and had barely sat down before Blake stopped him. 'Is there somewhere more private we could go? A conference room or something?' He glanced around at various team members occupying the tables, all within earshot.

'My trailer?' Marco suggested.

They led the way and while Blake made himself comfortable on the sofa, Savi and Marco stayed standing up, waiting for what he had to say. Whatever it was, Savi knew it couldn't be good if he had to fly halfway across the world to say it.

'I'll cut to the chase, Jesse and I have been talking about damage control. Now, Savi, I know your identity hasn't been exposed but we need to throw people off the scent. Jesse mentioned that Mr De Luca, you, uh . . . have been dating around, shall we say.'

'We get it, I'm a man whore. What's my sex life got to do with Savannah and Jesse?'

'We think you two should pretend you're dating.'

The two of them stood there in utter silence, dumbfounded by his announcement. Was her boyfriend out of his damn mind? It made zero sense. 'Why, exactly?' She cast a hesitant glance at Marco, who was still quiet but smirking to himself.

'Think about it, Savi!' Blake said with genuine excitement in his tone. 'People are going to be hunting for the girl in the photos, so if you're already seen to be with someone, it's unlikely anyone will clock it was you.'

'But Jesse and I have no links to each other according to the outside world, so how is anyone going to link us? Why would they suspect me?'

'He follows you on social media, for a start. You know what people are like, that alone can sometimes be enough for the fans and media to run wild with theories. And you grew up not far away from each other. I wouldn't put it past people, Savi. Please consider this, just as a precaution. Jesse doesn't want to risk it, and we feel that this is a good solution. Plus, it's good publicity for your team.'

'For the team, maybe. Not for me. An IEC rookie dating

her teammate mere weeks into the start of the race season? I'm fighting for my spot at the top of the leaderboard, trying to be taken seriously as an athlete. I don't want to be known for my dating history.' She could already imagine the derogatory comments, as if women in motorsport didn't get enough of those.

'I mean, it worked for Faith and Julien when they got together. The fans love a bit of romance,' Marco shrugged, totally unbothered by the idea.

'What, you're down for this? What about your yacht groupies?' She narrowed her eyes.

'I can boot them to one side for a season, Savannah. If it throws people off the scent and helps you out, I'd be more than willing to do it.'

She was suspicious, not just that he was offering to stop sleeping with other women for an entire race season but also that he was acting so nonchalant about it. This was a huge PR stunt, and there would be rules. Enforced by Jesse, who she was equally suspicious of because what man wanted another guy's hands all over his girl?

'What's in it for you?' she questioned, noting that Blake was still smiling away while they went back and forth.

'Nothing, but I'm your buddy, remember? We're teammates. I don't take that relationship lightly, Savannah. If you need me to do this, I'm all in. Plus, you know . . . if there's even a tiny chance that it might get Esme riled up then even better.'

'And there it is,' she scoffed. 'You're still not over her?'

'Nope, which is why I need to get under you. You know, in a metaphorical sense.'

'Uh...' Blake interjected. 'This isn't a physical agreement.'

'No, no. I am aware. Savannah and I are not... Wouldn't dream of it. But, how are the fans going to think we're more than friends? We have to do something to suggest that there is a romantic element, a kiss on the cheek here and there. If it's not believable, fans aren't going to get invested.'

Savi studied Marco's features, trying hard to admire him in that kind of light. But she wasn't going to lie, as attractive as he was, there was nothing there. Her body didn't react in the slightest. How was she supposed to kiss him without standing dead still, arms glued to her sides and her lips unable to move with his? She had always been awkward around guys, but the chemistry between her and Jesse had been undeniable. She wasn't so sure she could be convincing enough for this.

'Jesse will write up a contract if that's what you both want, make sure the lines are clear as day, but he trusts Savi enough not to worry about it. A contract is just another thing that could be exposed in the press, so it would be better to do it without one. However, Mr De Luca, he would like to make it very clear that he is also trusting *you*, man to man. No crossing boundaries, and Savi is to be the one who sets them.'

That hurt Savi's heart. Shouldn't Jesse at least be talking to *her* about it? Not only was he actively encouraging her to pretend to be in a relationship with someone else, but he had no interest in putting anything on paper. It was bizarre. This whole thing was out of pocket, and she still didn't know if it was a good idea. For anyone.

'I can talk to him. Tell him what's what. If he wants. Other than that, just tell us from a professional perspective how you think we should launch this relationship into the media, and we'll crack on and chat to our PR team, assuming Savannah is keen.'

'Keen might not be the right word,' she grimaced. 'But if you think this will work, then let's give it a go. Just for a couple of months until all the fuss about the photos has died down. There's no need to drag this out over a whole race season.'

'Well, actually... Jesse thinks we need to give it six months minimum. So that will take us through to November. You can announce a break-up before the festive season, then you'll have the winter break to "heal" before you see each other at work again in January.'

'He's really thought of everything, huh?' Savannah's tone dripped with sarcasm.

'You don't have to do this, Savi. But we're doing it for you. It doesn't make a difference to Jesse if you're linked to the photos, his privacy has already been violated, but you're a rookie in this championship. It's not a good look for your sponsors.'

She felt her skin getting hot under the pressure of having to make a decision that had seemingly already been made for her. He was right and everyone in this room plus Jesse knew it.

'Okay,' she breathed out, wiping her wet palms on her race suit.

'You sure, Cowgirl?' Marco looked to her for reassurance.

'No, but we can try.'

Blake started to rise from his seat, his business here done the second she'd agreed. 'You can back out of this, Savi. Just understand the consequences. And I strongly suggest you have a word with your team principal, plus Esme.'

'Esme?' Marco crossed his arms.

'She knows about Jesse and I.'

'Yes, and she needs to think you two broke up. If you have to tell anyone, the only people who can know you and Marco are faking it are you two, Jesse, your PR team, your boss, immediate family, and me. That's it.' If this was such a serious matter, why no contract? It wasn't adding up, but she trusted Jesse. She didn't tell Blake that she would absolutely be telling Esme the whole truth; no way was she lying to her best friend. She'd already kept the secret about Jesse for four years, and she trusted her with her life. She regretted having to ask her to lie to everyone, but she knew Ez would do it in a heartbeat.

'So, what's the first step?' Savi asked as Blake reached the door, ready to see himself out.

'That's up to you two to figure out.' He shrugged, and without so much as a goodbye, Blake was gone. Leaving Savi and Marco to process what the hell had just happened.

9

'Did you even consider that I might not want to do this?' Savi was pacing her hotel room with Jesse on loudspeaker, along with the buzz of whatever bar he was in on the Nashville strip. She knew this wasn't the best time for him, but she was past caring.

'Sav, come on. You know Blake and I wouldn't do this without good reason. I don't want you getting caught up in this mess, I'm just trying to take care of you.'

'I got caught up in this mess the second you signed your record deal, Jess.'

'Don't be so dramatic, Savi. Please. You don't understand what it's like in my world, it's harsh and there's a lot of pressure. You see the things they say about me in the press, I don't want that for you.'

'My world is not all that different. You think I'm not already subjected to criticism and misogyny on a daily basis? Sure, it might not be on such a wide scale, but I know how to handle myself. Don't you think if we had been public from the very beginning of your career that media attention might have died down by now? We're four years in, Jesse. Where is this going if you don't think I belong in your world? We should be able to love each other out loud, not in the shadows of secluded cabins and hotel suites.'

'Are you saying you don't want me anymore?' he shot

back, almost cutting her off with his bluntness. It was a defence mechanism, but it still stung.

'No, of course not, I'm just saying I think we need to reevaluate what it is we're doing here. I can't do another four years of sneaking around.' Her confidence wavered and her voice lowered to a whisper. She almost wished he hadn't heard over the noise of a group of men cheering in the background, because she was not the type of girl to give ultimatums. She had kept quiet for their whole relationship, not voicing her concerns out of fear of losing him altogether. She was exhausted.

'Just give it six months of this PR stunt, Sav. Okay? We'll talk about it then, look at how to launch our own relationship into the media slowly, avoid any drama.'

Jesse was romantically linked with every woman in his vicinity, all the time. It was a huge insecurity of Savi's, but she had learned to live with it, because she knew she was the one he always came home to. When work allowed.

'Fine, but I'm not happy about it. And I'm not waiting until those six months are up to discuss this again.' She was already reaching for her jacket, desperate to get some fresh air and clear her head before she'd even ended the call.

'You've made that pretty clear. Can I get back to my boys now?' She could hear him heading back into the bar he'd come from.

She hung up without another word. He'd always had a blasé attitude about a lot of things, important life things that required deep thought and honest conversations, but it was beginning to annoy Savi more than it used to. They seemed to be heading down different paths, and she wasn't quite ready to accept that their future was looking a little shaky. She wanted to believe fame hadn't changed him, like it hadn't changed her except for making her more resilient, but she was struggling to deny that he wasn't the same Jesse she'd been introduced to at a food truck all that time ago.

Suede jacket in hand, she headed down the corridor to Marco's room. At least someone was being rational in this whole debacle, even if her real boyfriend wasn't. Jesse was supposed to be her teammate, too. Maybe he should take notes from Marco, who upon opening the door looked happy to see her.

'What's up, Cowgirl?' He leaned against the doorframe, arms crossed as he took her in.

'Are you busy?' She peered past him and took note of his open laptop.

'I can make time for you.' And without questioning a thing, he shoved his feet into his trainers, grabbed his sunglasses and phone and shut the door on whatever it was he'd been doing and took her out for lunch.

'You want to what?' Marco stared at her, not quite believing his ears. He'd sat down barely fifteen minutes ago and she was already jumping in at the deep end. He studied her face which was slowly turning a pretty shade of pink, trying not to smirk as she defended her idea.

'Our first kiss can't be in front of the cameras, Marco. What if we're, like . . . clunky.'

'Clunky?' he laughed, regretting it when she looked genuinely embarrassed.

He was great at putting his foot in his mouth with the

women in his life, platonic or not. This was new territory for both of them, and they had gone from casual conversations at the track to teammates to fake lovers in very quick succession. They had known each other for years, but they didn't *know* each other.

They had gone out for food away from the track, to a place that did fresh pasta and had outdoor seating. They might as well soak up the sunshine while trying to get their heads around this journey they were about to embark on. Tomorrow was qualifying day, and their heads needed to be fully focused on the race. They had to get the awkwardness out of the way first. Except the look of sheer panic on Savannah's face told him this might be uncomfortable for a number of weeks yet, if not for the duration of their unofficial contract.

She hesitated, cheeks burning. 'We don't know each other's techniques.'

'Relax, Cowgirl. This ain't my first rodeo.' He was saying anything he could to make this easier, and that included using his nickname for her. That was their thing. If they were going to survive this, they needed a thing.

'De Luca,' she sighed.

'Fine,' he laughed, giving in to her request no matter how strange it felt. 'Come here.'

Savannah shook her head. 'Absolutely not. Not *now*. There are so many people around, Marco. We've been disturbed by fans three times already.'

'Savannah.' He put a hand on each side of her wicker chair and promptly yanked it across the paving slabs, so she was closer to him. 'You can trust me.' And then he put one hand on her waist and leaned in, closer and closer until she couldn't back up anymore. He went for gentle, but the reality was, he was a little afraid of her. His flirting had been intentional of late, but he never imagined being in a position where he might get to cross a line even if it was all a lie.

It only lasted a few seconds before he pulled back, but when he did, he rested his forehead on hers. Just for a moment, so he could soak it all in. He knew from that kiss alone, he had made a mistake. But as long as Savannah needed him in her corner, that was where he would be.

'Have you done this before?'

'What, kissed a cowgirl?'

'No,' she rolled her eyes, 'faked it.'

'Oh. No. Also never kissed a cowgirl, so there's a first time for everything.' He winked and then snuck in another quick peck before settling back in his seat, making it look so natural to the outside world and ignoring how it felt on the inside. He would have to keep the kisses to a minimum throughout this whole thing.

'Jesse has been drunk texting me since our argument. Apologising profusely, telling me he loves me, and he trusts me.' She bit into a piece of chicken and checked her phone again.

'If you were mine and I knew some other guy was gonna be all over you, I'd want to at least talk to you about the details. I get that he couldn't show his face at the track and have a meeting with us, but was he just going to rely on his messenger pigeon and not have a *real* conversation about it? You guys should be outlining every tiny little thing, what you're both okay with and what you're not. I mean, what if I grab your ass and he flips out?'

'Simple, don't grab my ass. Be civilised, respectful, and there shouldn't be an issue.'

'Okay, but hear me out . . . an ass grab will *really* sell it,' he teased, hoping she understood him well enough to know he was joking. Sort of. He was attracted to her, but he had nothing but respect for both her and her relationship. He just couldn't help but flirt, it was in his nature.

'You're going to have to stop flirting with me for this to work, De Luca.' She sipped her water, choking as she did. 'That was not still. God, I hate sparkling.'

'You're gonna have to stop stealing my drinks.' He took his glass out of her hand. 'See the lip gloss stain?' Marco pointed at the rim of her own glass. 'Yours.'

'I'm serious. Doesn't matter how harmless it is, that's how lines get blurred.'

'Yeah, yeah, and you're super happy in your relationship so this,' he gestured between them, 'is always going to be an act.'

'You're getting it. Even if you are a sarcastic little –'

'Language, Cowgirl,' he smirked.

'Don't start acting all prim and proper, Monaco. Your recent antics have proved you're anything but.'

He thought she should give him credit where it was due, he had truly shocked his friends when he'd emerged with model number two, and then three . . . With his fellow male drivers on the team now married off, it was Marco's turn to be the stereotypical rich and famous playboy. It just didn't really suit him, not when he'd been crying over Esme a short while ago. He was trying too hard to be someone he wasn't.

'And my recent antics are why I'm so willing to do this. I know what it's like to have my sex life talked about by those who have nothing better to do, and I don't want that for you. So, we need this to look like we're really in love, not just fooling around. The world needs to believe that this is different, that you're special. I won't let them put you in the same category as those other women.'

'I am special,' she argued. 'But you are never taking me on a yacht or to a club. Or a log cabin, come to think of it . . .' She trailed off and stared down at the last few bites of pasta.

'You're getting all mopey and weird now, where's the sassy Savannah I've come to know?' He gently kicked her shin under the table, bringing her out of her own head.

'Don't kick me, I bruise easily.' She scowled and kicked him back, only a little harder.

'Ow!' He cradled his leg.

'I can give as good as I get, don't forget that,' she shrugged. 'Anyway, tell me more about yourself. I know you live in Monaco, are pathetic when you're heartbroken, you own a yacht, and you drive for Revolution Racing. After all these years of running in the same circles, somehow that's all I've got . . .'

'Someone hasn't paid much attention to our social media content the last few years.'

Savannah's phone buzzed with another string of texts from her boyfriend, who had interrupted them multiple times already this afternoon. Marco sighed as she apologised yet again. It wasn't her fault, but it was damn annoying. She turned her phone over, so it was face down, and gave him her undivided attention. 'I saw enough to know I wanted to be part of it, but I was busy focusing on my own career. Plus, I'd like to hear it from you.'

'Okay . . . Uh, I was born in Italy and raised in Monaco.'

'So is your mum Monegasque?'

'Yeah. She may or may not be friends with the royals.'

Savi's jaw dropped. 'What, like the king of England?'

'Savannah . . . Fucking hell, are you even on the same planet? You know Monaco has a royal family, right? As does Denmark, Bahrain, Malaysia . . . The list goes on. The Windsors are not the only ones. God, you're so American.' He laughed so hard her cheeks flushed.

'So, your mum?'

'Is not a royal. Just grew up with one of them. But she moved to Italy for university where she met my father. We were born and raised there.'

'We?'

'My brother and I.'

'Ah,' she nodded and smiled, 'tell me more.'

'My brother, Rafael, lives in Switzerland with his wife and kids. I try to see them all a few times a year, I take a lot of diversions in between work trips. The three boys are pretty into cars, so of course I'm the coolest uncle ever.'

'You have three nephews?' Her eyes widened.

'And two nieces. Raf started young. Eighteen, actually. Caused quite the scandal.'

She grinned. 'Scandals seem to run in your family.'

'Yeah, well, I wouldn't have resorted to my shenanigans

if, you know . . .' He frowned, finishing his bowl of penne arrabiata.

'Spit it out, Monaco . . . Come on, still not over it?'

'Do you think Thalia is gonna ruin Esme's life?' He leaned back in his seat and crossed his arms, annoyed with himself. The yacht groupies were a distraction technique which evidently had not worked. He still thought about Esme more than he should, even if he knew there was no hope for them.

'Possibly. But you could say the same thing about Jesse and me, or about your brother and his wife, Faith and Julien, Lucie and Brett . . . You never know where life is going to take you. Just got to focus on yourself.'

'What is it about Jesse Montalvo?' Marco narrowed his eyes.

'What do you mean?' She signalled to the waiter that they wanted to order dessert, like she was hoping to steer the conversation towards tiramisu and away from an interrogation into the deepest, darkest parts of her relationship.

'Sell him to me. Why are you with him, how do you know he's the one?'

'I don't know if I believe in the one.'

'Oh.' He was taken aback. That was the polar opposite to his own beliefs, but he was a hopeless romantic and had been raised that way. 'Well, still . . . why him?'

'I . . . I love him.' She swallowed. 'I've never answered this out loud . . . Um, he makes me feel wanted, he's ambitious, strong. He's been through hell and come out the other side still standing, and he remembers the little things. He's romantic and he still flirts with me to this day. Still slow dances with me in the kitchen while we're cooking dinner, still behaves like he's trying to win me over.'

'But he's not the one.' Marco gazed at her intensely, seeing right through her. The way she spoke about him sounded like the words of someone who did believe in soulmates, but maybe, as much as she liked to pretend she was, she wasn't living a fairytale.

She lifted a shoulder, and the corners of her mouth turned up ever so slightly. 'I don't know.'

'It's okay to not know, Cowgirl. The spectrum of human emotion is complex.'

'Can you order dessert for us? I need to use the bathroom.' She grabbed her phone, cow-print case looking up at her, and headed inside.

Marco wasn't afraid of hard topics, and he often worried it put people off. Sometimes he started conversations others weren't ready to have, or he overstepped, and he spent the next few minutes stressing that he had just done exactly that. He wanted Savannah to trust him and feel safe with him, enough that she could tell him anything that was on her mind.

By the time she headed back to the table, her face looking a little brighter and her voice full of enthusiasm, he had her favourite dessert sitting in front of her. Jesse wasn't the only one who remembered the little things.

Savannah sat down, their chairs still close from their practice kiss, and took a deep breath. 'Jesse wants to fly us out to Los Angeles and meet the man who is fake-dating his girlfriend.'

10

Race day seemed to have taken an age to arrive, and Savi and her teammates had been wide awake since stupid o'clock, sitting in the hotel restaurant and eating what their team principal called a breakfast of champions.

'How's your buddy situation been going, Savi?' Miko asked. 'You two getting on okay?'

'Great,' she grinned. That was the truth, Marco had spent yesterday evening going over race strategies with her and teaching her everything he knew about the circuit. The best places to overtake, the areas to avoid the risk. He was taking his roles as a teammate and a buddy seriously, in addition to his one as fake boyfriend.

'It's so unfair,' Kodie whined. 'You get De Luca at your disposal whenever you want, but I keep losing Julien to babysitting duties.'

'He's not babysitting, Kodie. They're his kids.'

'Yeah but he brings them to our meetings. I had to hold Emmy through lunch the other day. I get there are two of them, because they were unfortunate enough to be cursed with *twins*, but couldn't he have put one in a highchair or something while he held the other, rather than dragging me into it? Better yet, get Faith to have them?'

'Faith was filming content with me and Brett,' Miko sheepishly admitted. Julien had let slip he was debating retiring in a couple of years, but Savi couldn't imagine him not being their teammate. The three guys were part of the furniture at this point.

'It must be hard trying to balance everything. They only use their nanny on quali and race days, they give her the rest of race week off to see all the sights.'

'Screw sightseeing, Sav! This rookie needs help!'

'You don't need help,' Miko reassured her. 'You're great out there, Kodie. We all are.'

'Morning, ladies.' Brett swanned in with Marco and Jules hot on his tail, each holding one of the Moretz twins. Faith and Lucie followed soon after with camera bags and pushchairs. It was the picture of chaos, but it put a smile on Savi's face. Revolution Racing was beginning to feel more like family for her.

'Hi.' Marco dropped down and greeted Savi with a kiss on the cheek, part of their plan to ease the team into the idea of them, and then Margot was reaching for her. She semi-reluctantly held her arms out and the almost-one year old crawled onto her lap.

'Please don't hand me the other one,' Kodie winced.

'Not a fan of kids, Kodie?' Faith patted her on the shoulder and took her daughter from Julien so he could go and get breakfast from the continental buffet.

'Absolutely not. Yours are cute, though. I'm not a witch, just . . . they're loud. The most noise I can handle is that of an engine.' She said it matter of factly, but she still sat there playing with Margot's stuffed tiger.

'Oh, I think Emmy wants Uncle Mars.' Faith let the other twin clamber across to Marco who had seated himself next to Savi, squashed up in the booth seat. He was in the process of helping himself to her untouched cup of coffee.

'Of course she does,' Brett rolled his eyes. 'Uncle Brett's love and affection is never enough.' He removed himself from the table to join Julien while Savi and Marco found themselves making a tiger and a panda interact with squeaky voices.

'You nervous about today?' Marco spoke quietly.

'A little,' she confessed. 'Although I'm not sure why. You've taught me everything you can about the track, and it's not like it's my first race.'

'Could it be because this is our debut?'

'There's that, too. I'm mostly nervous for how the rest of the team will react.'

She would be lying if she said it hadn't kept her awake last night, tossing and turning for hours and trying to quash the feeling of dread. Photos of their kiss at lunch hadn't hit the media yet, and they may not. Cameras didn't always follow them everywhere. But that meant there was more pressure on today, and their pre- or post-race kiss, whichever they opted for, would be an even bigger deal. It didn't help matters that she hadn't heard from Jesse since he'd invited her and Marco to LA.

'We've got this, Cowgirl.' He nudged her arm.

But as Margot cuddled up to her and Savi let herself get lost in baby snuggles and a drama-free breakfast, pushing all thoughts of Jesse aside in an effort to get her head back on race day, the butterflies in her stomach continued to flutter.

*

'Savi, Mars, can we have a quick chat?' A very dishevelled-looking Jasper pulled them aside on their way into the garage. There was a lot more pressure on his shoulders since bringing in a second car this season.

They followed him to team HQ and into a conference room, which was just a big table and chairs with some leafy green potted plants in the corner. It was basic, but it did the job. This was where they held drivers' briefings, and also where they argued back and forth and analysed the race result on days things didn't go quite right. To be dragged in for a private meeting was a whole different ball game, but Savi knew what this was about.

'Sir,' Marco nodded at their boss, prompting him to start talking.

'I understand that the two of you are seeing each other.' He tried to hide his smile and stay in super serious Jasper-mode. 'I don't know how serious it is, but I will say the same to you as I did to Brett, Lucie, Julien and Faith . . .' The poor man, what other team principal was put in this position three times by four of his drivers?

'Don't let it impact the team.' Marco and Savi said in unison, earning a grin from Jasper and unleashing his obvious excitement at the prospect of them being a couple.

'I needn't have bothered with this meeting. You're not kids, you know how to handle yourselves,' he stated, except Savi was still a kid compared to some members of the team. She was only twenty-four and Marco was in his early thirties. 'I got the PR team to prevent photos being leaked yesterday of you two kissing at lunch, because I was worried you weren't ready to go public . . .'

'Nah, this has been brewing for a couple of months. Pretty much since Savi first joined the team. We just kind of clicked instantly even if it only got serious in the last week or so, so we're down to go public. We don't want to go through the trouble of trying to keep it secret.' Marco was so quick with it, so smooth, it was as if he'd been rehearsing what to say. Perhaps he had been, and perhaps Savi should have, too.

'Yeah, why bother trying to cover it up? It would soon come out anyway.'

'Noted. So should I tell PR to expect lots of stories in the press after today's race that are totally unrelated to the results?' he laughed.

Savi knew he was joking but she still felt weird about it, because he was right. Two teammates dating was hot gossip for the fans, and it would be talked about on a much larger scale than their fastest lap time or what position they were in the championship. It shouldn't be like that, just like the fact she was a female racing driver for a top team shouldn't be such a big deal, but they didn't have the power to change it.

She was worried about the backlash she'd receive for dating her teammate, but it would never be as bad as the backlash that came with having her identity attached to indecent photos with a country music superstar. No matter how bad opinions of this situation with Marco got, she had to remind herself of that.

It also helped that although Marco was more famous than her, he had nowhere near the legions of dedicated fans and press attention that Jesse got, which meant there wasn't the same risk of scrutiny on his personal life, and therefore hers. It was still a risk, but it was a much safer one.

'You've done this twice before, Jasper. I don't even think fans will be shocked. It was my turn to create waves, bring some excitement.'

'*I'm* excited. Have you told Gabriel?' He directed his question at Savi.

'Not yet. I'm thinking we surprise him when he sees it on TV.'

'The man might have a heart attack at his prodigy finding happiness so close to home, but yes, I agree. I will ensure he's in the Revolution Racing garage before the end of the race so I can witness his reaction in real time. Right, you guys had better get back to work!'

Savi and Marco ambled back down the paddock, hand in hand, just to really drive it home. If it was going to be this easy the whole time, they'd have no problems. It wasn't that it felt natural, it just didn't feel wrong. And it certainly didn't feel like she was holding her brother's hand . . .

'I knew something was going on!' Lucie pounced on them as soon as they stepped over the threshold, and the entire team turned around to take notice of the new couple's arrival. 'When he kissed you on the cheek this morning we all pretended not to see it, but I knew!' she beamed.

'Let's not make a big deal out of it,' Savi mumbled, earning a squeeze of the hand from Marco before he let her go and reached for his helmet from its cubby at the back of the garage.

His helmet this season was Revolution red with white detailing and sat right next to hers, a turquoise and purple design with a lucky horseshoe design on the back. It had much better detail than her poor excuse of an ankle tattoo.

Savi always tried to incorporate a little bit of home into her helmet, to make it feel like her family were with her even though they couldn't leave the ranch. Her dad being there for the first race of the season had meant the world to her, and she wished he could be at every one. She wished Weston would stop shying away from his new reality and join her, that her ma could finally witness her daughter crossing the finish line with her own eyes and not through the lens of a camera. But she understood their predicament, and had learned to accept that Weston just wasn't ready to take that step.

'Hey, Sav?' Faith pulled her aside, away from Lucie's squealing, and beckoned Marco over to join them. 'Guys, can we make a tiny bit of a deal out of this?' she pleaded.

'You mean you want to use us as this season's guinea pigs?' Marco raised an eyebrow in suspicion. 'I know your game plan, Jensen.'

'Well . . .' Faith feigned innocence.

'I don't see anything wrong with it,' Savi agreed, albeit cautiously. 'Just don't make us the new stars of the team's social media, a few posts here and there is fine. I know it's going to be hard to avoid but I don't want to be known solely as the girl dating Marco De Luca.'

'Oh, no, of course not! We will really be pushing yours, Kodie's and Miko's presence on the team this season, especially in the first half and at Le Mans. But the fans do love our boys.' Faith ruffled Marco's curls, and he batted her hand away. 'We just won't hide the fact you're together. Brett and Lucie made us do that when they went official and it was a nightmare, the fans recognised something was off immediately. We went from posting about them every day to acting like Lucie wasn't even around half the time.'

'Savi! Come over here!' Miko called out, her and Kodie looking very excited. The reactions of her teammates made her uncomfortable. She didn't mind lying to the public, but lying to them? They were her extended family, and she wouldn't dare lie to her actual family.

Right on cue, Weston texted her. He wanted to know if today was their big debut and said he hoped Jesse cried himself to sleep tonight, knowing he caused this. He wasn't his biggest fan. Her family hadn't been impressed when they heard about the photos, but thanks to a life shielded from social media and gossip mags, they hadn't seen them. Weston, however . . . His reaction had been explosive. Almost enough to get him on a plane to kidnap his sister and bring her home where he could keep her safe.

'Stay cool,' Savi whispered, pretending to be embarrassed.

'How long has this been a thing?!' Kodie gripped her arm tightly.

'Not very long.' She focused on getting her helmet on, seeing as the race was starting soon.

'But the chemistry was just undeniable, right?' Miko might as well have hearts for irises.

'Yep,' she nodded.

'How serious is it?'

'Uh . . .' That was something they hadn't discussed, not

that they'd really discussed much at all. What were they telling people? 'Serious enough that we're going public?' It wasn't much of an answer, but it did the trick and shut them up.

Savi pulled her helmet down over her head and blocked them out, trying to shake out the nerves and stress of the day. Every race day was significant, but this one even more so. She shot a glance at Marco, who was still helmet-less and caught her eye through her open visor. Upon noticing that she looked ready to explode, he made a beeline for her and her teammates scarpered, leaving them in what they thought was their loved-up bubble.

'You okay?' he whispered.

'No.' Savi shook her head quickly.

'Do you need me to call someone for you? Jesse or your dad?'

'No. I just need you to stand with me until it's time to get in the car.'

'I can do that,' he nodded and took her hand in his. 'Come on, let's go take a seat. We're both last in the cars, so we've got time. You plan on keeping the helmet on?'

'Potentially. This all feels overwhelming,' she admitted. She hadn't told him about her panic attacks, and she didn't want to, but she could feel one brewing. Not now, not in front of everyone. Not on camera.

'Take the helmet off, Cowgirl. I can see the pressure building, and I know what panic looks like. If you keep it on, you're going to add to it. You need to take some deep breaths.'

When she gave a weak nod of agreement but made no effort to remove it, he took her helmet in his hands and lifted it off for her, revealing rosy cheeks and hair plastered to her forehead with sweat. Not a good look. 'Sorry.'

'You have nothing to apologise for. I'm sure he won't mind me saying, but Brett has panic attacks and anxiety attacks quite a lot, too. I know all the signs, and I can help you out of it.'

'I don't think it's going to come to anything. I just need to sit, relax. Try not to think too much about anything other than the task at hand.'

'You're right. You know what you're capable of, Savannah. You've really proved yourself, before you came to this championship and again since you signed your Revolution contract and got in that car for the first time. Put all thoughts of "us" aside, forget the rest of the world exists. It's you versus you.'

She had been so absorbed in his words and trying to feel normal again that she hadn't even noticed his hands gently massaging her shoulders, easing some of the physical tension in addition to the mental. Jesse had never seen her like this, because he'd never been with her in race-mode. And for some reason, her anxiety was never an issue away from the racetrack.

'Thank you, for looking out for me.' She breathed in and out, slowly. 'And for making me feel like I belong here. I wasn't quite sure what to make of you at first, but you've shown yourself to be a pretty decent guy, Monaco.'

'I take my role as a teammate and assigned buddy very seriously, you know. But the most important role I play is as a friend, and you can consider me yours.'

*

Savi's new favourite track position was the one where she was moments away from overtaking Marco towards the end of the race, the thirty-five other cars barely a speck in her mirrors. If this could be a regular thing, she'd be quite happy. She liked racing Julien in the wet, too. Pushing the boundaries. He was always up for a challenge and didn't let her off easy. But she and Marco had a stronger connection, and it brought with it a more intense rush of adrenaline.

This was the part of the circuit where Marco had told her it was near-impossible to overtake unless the stars and planets aligned and conditions were perfect, and yet here she was. Hundreds of fans on their feet as she approached the chicane, flags waving with flashes of Revolution Racing red, the sharp, tangy aroma of burnt rubber filling the car.

Her tyres were struggling but she was relentless in her approach, wanting to prove again that she could do it, prove she belonged here. Performing well was one thing, but if she could keep going above and beyond, she knew they wouldn't let her go at the end of her contract. She needed this. The exhilarating feeling that racing gave her, similar to the rides at the fairs she grew up going to. But this was like being in a different world, and she would never be able to match it.

'Savi, watch those tyres.' Her engineer's voice came over the radio, which irritated her. She liked to be left alone when she was in the car, but she knew he was just doing his job.

'Got it. I know my limits.' Her voice was confident, because that's exactly what she was. Even as she got distracted and let Marco get away from her, she knew she would catch him up again. And that was exactly what she did on the last lap, seconds from the finish. She shot past him, the chequered flag waved and her engineer all but screamed in her ear.

Marco pulled up side by side and joined her as they waved to the fans, soaking up the atmosphere. There was red smoke everywhere, the crowds were going wild and Savi felt euphoric. They drove into the pits and up to the signs for first and second position, Jasper and Gabriel and the teams already there to greet them.

But it wasn't any of them who got to Savi first to congratulate her, it was Marco. Their helmets were off, eyes full of pride, and emotions running high. She knew it was coming. It wasn't planned, but it made perfect sense. And as his lips found hers and he lifted her into his arms in full view of the entire media crew, broadcast to millions, Savi knew their entire world was about to be turned upside down.

11

Savi was sprawled across Miko's bed in her gym wear, having just gone for an hour-long run through the streets of Monza. She had decided to stay on an extra couple of days, filling time before she and Marco flew to Los Angeles for Jesse's show. She hadn't expected everyone else to stick around too, but it was a nice surprise.

They were also keeping her sane in the wake of her and Marco being the latest hot topic in the world of motorsport. She wasn't used to this kind of media attention and while most fans were being complimentary and showing genuine excitement, there were always going to be some who had nothing nice to say. There had been comments on her upbringing, her skin colour and texture, her cowboy boots. Anything they didn't like about her made her unworthy of Marco's affection, in their eyes. She had been prepared, but it still stung. They were doing a fantastic job at putting her off ever going public with Jesse, and she was finally seeing his point. She was also acutely aware that someone somewhere was probably going to do enough digging that they uncovered her brother's identity, and she felt sick to her stomach. If that ever got out, she wanted it to be on Weston's terms.

'Give me your phone,' Esme demanded, still disappointed in Jesse for his fake-dating plan but deciding to play along to keep her friend happy. Her eyes had brightened at the prospect of him having to watch the woman he loved in the arms of another man. She had never particularly liked him; she thought he had lost touch with reality when he made it big. 'You need to stop reading things, it's no good for you. Who gives a damn what anyone else thinks?'

'An IEC rookie. That's who,' Savi huffed, rolling over and burying her face in a pillow.

'Savi, people just like to cause a stir online. They want likes and views, and controversial opinions are the best way to get a reaction.'

'Okay, I'm going to take action.' She sat herself up with a sudden newfound vigour. This was the best year of her life, and she didn't want other people's negativity to take the enjoyment out of it. She had a seat on a team she'd dreamt of being part of since she started out in the sport, her family were incredibly supportive, she was forming wonderful friendships and Jesse was . . . well, he was hers. For the most part, she was happy.

'That's our girl.' Kodie took the phone from Esme and tossed it back onto the bed. 'Just don't go on the warpath.'

'No, no. I'm just doing a cleanse.' She unlocked it and proceeded to delete all her social media apps and silence her text notifications.

She'd been flooded with messages from people back home who all had questions, and she couldn't really blame them. Savi had maintained relationships with almost everyone from her tiny, close-knit graduating class and they had bi-annual reunions at a local bar. She was the only one who had left Wyoming behind for something different, everyone else choosing to embrace small-town life and settle down. Savi loved her hometown, and she was all for settling down, but she had the best of both worlds and she wasn't in a rush.

'On the plus side, you looked really hot in the footage and photos,' Kodie grinned.

'I did *not*.' Savi rolled her eyes.

'You did!' Miko agreed.

'You're just trying to make me feel better. I had helmet indentations on my cheeks, I was a sweaty mess, and my hair was flat as a three-day-old opened can of Coca Cola.'

'Marco's hands in your hair gave it some volume,' Esme teased.

Savi was convinced they were going to hell for lying to their friends about this. She was good at keeping secrets but if the truth ever came out, they were never going to understand. How could they? It was a miracle that Marco got it. They were less than twenty-four hours in, and she felt awful. Miko was ready to plan a wedding, she was so happy for them.

'I think I'm going to go back to my room for a bit,' Savi sighed and rose from the bed, itching to wallow in peace and not have everyone trying to cheer her up. It wasn't that she was miserable and regretting it, she was just processing. This was a big, sudden adjustment. One that Marco was handling much better than her.

On her way out of the door, after saying her goodbyes and promising to meet up for dinner, she shot back a response to the group chat of girls from back home and gave them very brief, very basic details. Just enough to stop them hassling her until next time she went home and saw them. She was already dreading that trip to the bar. Even the barman was all up in her business. Funny how she could be thousands of miles away and still wrapped up in that small-town environment. You could take the girl out of Sheridan but . . . well, it would always be part of her life in more ways than one.

Swerving the corridor that led to her room, she took the elevator straight down to the lobby and made a swift exit. It probably wasn't the wisest idea given that it was only one day since the race and there were still fans hanging around the area, but she needed fresh air. She had followed a running route recommended by Brett that morning and managed to avoid people, but she could already sense she wouldn't be so lucky later in the day.

She hadn't even got to the end of the street before someone recognised her and snapped a photo without acknowledging her with so much as a 'hello'. Savi hated that. She wasn't a monster, and she would much prefer being interrupted than people trying to be sneaky. Nevertheless, she shot the girl a smile and kept walking.

'Jesse?' She breathed a sigh of relief when he picked up after the first ring.

'Hi, baby. Everything okay?' His voice was warm, comforting, and she would give anything to have him here with her now. They had talked last night, he had even excused himself from a meeting for her sake, and she'd woken up to an audio message where he'd told her he loved her and the buzz around those photos was dying down on his end.

It was looking promising, and she was sure this fake-dating arrangement wouldn't have to be dragged out for as long as they initially thought.

'Yeah, I'm fine. It's just a lot.' She sighed and found a seat on a park bench.

'I know, but it'll be worth it when you come out the other side and you and I can move forward. Together.' He emphasised that last word. 'But you know the media attention is going to be far worse when we do, don't you? Think of this like training for that. You've got to learn to block it all out and just live your life.'

'I just miss you more when I'm stressed.' She was fighting back tears now. What she really wanted was to go home. To Jesse, her family, her horses. She shouldn't have chosen to stay in Monza for longer, not with all of this going on. But at least she was with Marco who was also being dragged through hell in the press.

'I miss you too, Sav. But I'll see you at the LA show at the end of the week. Kind of a shame Marco will be there too, but it will be good to meet him.'

'I think you'll like him.'

'I don't like many people.'

'No,' she laughed, 'I'm aware. But hopefully you guys can get along.'

'As long as he doesn't touch my girl in front of me,' Jesse huffed.

'Jess . . . he's not an idiot. He wouldn't have agreed to come to your show if he didn't respect you and want to get to know you. He keeps his hands to himself unless there's a camera in the vicinity, and even then, he doesn't overstep.'

She didn't mention the odd bit of flirting because as far as she was concerned, it was totally harmless.

'I guess. I just don't want to regret this decision. I know you're still not totally sold on this whole idea, and yeah, it might not work. But I think it will . . . You search up my name alongside yours online and nothing comes up. At all. I want it to stay that way.'

'Hopefully it will. I'm just thankful my hair was so messed up in the photos that nobody will recognise it when *we* go public.'

'Mm, yeah. Most of it was buried in the bed sheets while I railed you from behind.'

'Jess!' Her cheeks were tinged pink, and she felt all hot and bothered. 'But it does beg the question, is all this really necessary? Is pretending to date someone else not a bit extreme?'

'Just ask yourself what your sponsors would think if it did get out, and that's your answer. Remind yourself of that every time you start to doubt it, every time you think of ending the agreement. This is for you, Savi.'

'I know. And I appreciate you for thinking of the idea, for protecting me the best way you know how. Even if it does all feel very strange.' Strange was an understatement. It still felt like she was betraying him, even if he didn't seem fussed.

'Well, just know it's always going to be me you get to come home to.'

Except that was such a rare occurrence, it wasn't really true. When Jesse wasn't on tour, he was in the recording studio for months at a time and Savi was either travelling to different racetracks or she was at home with her family.

They got a week or two together in the cabin every now and then, or Jesse would sometimes manage to spend a few days on her family's ranch with her when he was visiting his own hometown just down the road, but they weren't likely to ever share a home together or start a family. It just seemed impossible.

Savi had accepted it a couple of years into their relationship, but it was playing on her mind more and more as time went on. It wasn't the case that she desperately wanted marriage and a family and four walls to call hers, but what if she reached a point in her life where she had to choose between that, and him?

'Hey, I need to get going. I've got to give my brother a call. I promised. He's got a doctors' appointment today and he wanted to hear my voice before he goes.'

'Okay, give him my best. I'll talk to you later. Love you.'

'Uh, yeah. Will do . . . Bye.' Now who was avoiding the L word?

She leaned her head back and gazed up at the dull grey sky, watching the clouds drift across and letting herself momentarily forget who she was and where she was before she came back to reality. She needed to call Weston. Not just for his sake, but for hers, too. He was her anchor.

'About time! I'm leaving in twenty minutes!' Weston berated her for her timing, forgetting that she had always struggled to stay on top of their time differences wherever she was in the world. 'Let me guess, you were talking to the rock star?'

'I was.' She rolled her eyes at his nickname for his sort-of brother-in-law. 'You excited about your appointment?'

'Why would I be excited to have a doctor lift me in and out of my chair and be stared at like I'm some sort of animal?' he bit out.

'Alright, misery guts. First of all, you know you're only being stared at because the ladies at the doctor's office all have a crush on you and want your autograph which you refuse to give them. Second of all, you're being lifted in and out of your chair because you're getting a brand spanking new one with loads of cool features. You're gonna be the new Lightning McQueen in no time,' she teased, knowing he was super strict about the speed people pushed his wheelchair at. She had once let him roll down a slope out by the barns and he'd screamed the whole time.

'I will be driving the thing *slowly*. And none of you can take over because I've got control of this one at all times.'

'No drunk driving.'

Savi had used some of her money from her contract signing to gift him a new wheelchair which was a lot more comfortable and convenient for him. He had complained for days about not wanting to take her money, until she'd told him it was either that or she paid for an extension on the main house, so he had his own space. That was a lot more expensive than the chair, so he'd shut up and accepted her generosity.

'When are you coming home so I can annoy you in person? It's not the same over the phone, for example, I can't crash into you or run your foot over when you piss me off.'

'Thanks, Wes. I'm so lucky to have you as my big brother.' She recalled the last time she visited when she told him he was being a baby for ignoring an invitation to go out with his old friends, and he'd literally wheeled away and faced the wall, refusing to speak to her. They still fought like kids, and they drove each other insane, but their bond was stronger than ever since his accident.

'I'm lucky to have you as my kid sister, too. I mean that. I don't thank you often and I don't want you to think I'm not appreciative, but Savi ... I couldn't do this without you. You take care of me in so many ways even when you're so far away, even down to reminding me to take my medication and arranging my appointments on my behalf. You took so much on when I had my accident, and I'm so proud of you.'

'Okay, now is not the time to be mushy. Also, it doesn't suit you. I prefer it when you bully me, it feels more natural. But thank you, seriously. You're my best friend, Weston.'

'I won't be saying anything nice for the next three hundred and sixty-five days, you have reached your quota for the year.'

'Go to your appointment. And give the doctor's office ladies their autograph! Maybe even dig out an old charity rodeo calendar for them. Bet they'd love to hang that up.'

'Never in a million years. Bye, loser.'

'Bye, idiot.'

She hung up and headed to a nearby café for her final caffeine intake of the day. The team were heading out for dinner later, the Jensen-Moretz twins in tow, and she would be switching to cocktails for the evening. Her last team hadn't been close-knit in the slightest, and she had spent many evenings alone in her hotel room with room service. She loved Revolution Racing's way of doing things. Together. Like a family. It made being away from Wyoming a little less heavy on her heart.

She was seated outside a cute little bakery when a group of fans spotted her and asked for photos and autographs, and she was halfway through her latte when said group tripled in size. It was too much. Savi never had to deal with situations like this alone, she always had a teammate or someone with her, and now with the Marco thing, she felt like a circus animal. They all had questions and opinions, and they weren't shy about getting in her face. It was the girl who took a seat at her table who sent her over the edge, and she could feel the panic starting to rise in her chest, threatening to take over.

If she left, she would be viewed as rude. Her fans would think she didn't appreciate them. If she stayed, it was only going to get more awkward and intense, and she was going to have an anxiety attack in public. This was the last thing she wanted.

They continued to swarm around her like bees and she continued to choke out responses and fake smiles for them all, praying at least one of them would get the hint, but they were all getting too carried away with themselves. She got it. They'd travelled miles for the race and here was one of the drivers, sitting here casually enjoying a coffee on her own. What could they possibly be interrupting other than her peace and quiet and her sanity?

Right when her eyes pricked with tears, two familiar faces appeared amongst the crowd of strangers. Marco and Julien. Her knights in shining armour, who caused quite a stir themselves. The crowd parted like the Red Sea to let them through, fans going from merely invasive to full-on screaming and thrusting their phones at them for photos.

'Savi, what are you still doing here? We've gotta go, urgent meeting.' Julien picked her bag up off the floor and held it out to her, and she took it gratefully.

'If we hurry, we can make it.' Marco rushed her out of there, his hand placed on the small of her back. 'Deep breaths, you've got this,' he murmured.

'Everyone step back, please!' Julien called out. 'Sorry, we don't have time to stop. Thank you all for being here this weekend and for the support.'

As her teammates walked her back to the safety of the hotel, she couldn't stop the panicky feeling from overruling all sense of reality. Her whole team was going to know this was something she had to deal with, and she was embarrassed about it. Brett may have been ready to open up about his own struggles, but he'd earned enough respect from the world over his more than a decade-long career for his voice to be heard. Savi wasn't quite there yet.

'I'm gonna come hang out in your room for a bit, just until I know you're okay.' Marco buzzed them up to the sixth floor and took her bag from her, fumbling around until he found her key card.

'Let me know if you need anything. I'm right down the hall, Savi.' Julien disappeared while Marco and Savi headed to her room in silence. Aside from her heavy breathing.

'This is so embarrassing,' she mumbled.

'Hey . . .' He placed a hand on her arm, stopping her

outside her door. 'No, it isn't. It happens to the best of us. Nobody is immune to this kind of thing, Cowgirl.'

'You?' She blinked up at him.

'From time to time, yes.' Marco gave her a reassuring smile and scanned them into her room, ushering her in. 'Take a seat, I'll get you something to drink.'

Savi clambered onto the bed and hugged one of the spare pillows to her body, still trembling slightly and struggling to steady her breathing. There wasn't enough oxygen in the room. Her life had got so out of control so fast and there was no way to stop it now. She was at a stage in her career where she had to constantly worry about being recognised everywhere she went in Europe, and it was all because of a man. Two men. One of whom, thanks to their growing connection as teammates and friends, was willing to deal with the onslaught of attention, and one who cared for her enough that he was in no rush to put her in a position where that attention was crippling, so she couldn't go anywhere or do anything across the globe without being criticised.

If she couldn't handle this with Marco, how would she handle it with Jesse? They were on two opposite ends of the spectrum when it came to fame and popularity and Savi was too weak for any of it.

'Here.' Marco handed her a bottle of water straight from the mini fridge. 'Got to hydrate, replace the liquid lost from those tears.' He sat down on the edge of the bed and dabbed at her rosy cheeks with a tissue.

'Sorry.' She gulped down some of the icy cold liquid, finally feeling more human now she was in the comfort of the four walls she'd been calling home for the last eight days.

'Don't apologise. You feeling better?'

'I think so,' she nodded, batting his hand away. 'I can wipe my own tears, Monaco.'

Marco laughed and handed her the tissue, his fingers brushing against hers so fast, if she wasn't so hyper-aware of every sensation her body was feeling right now, she might have missed it. Savi inhaled sharply. At some point, they had crossed a line from teammates to what could be a real, genuine friendship, rather than just one of circumstance.

Maybe it was because they had been thrown together in the most unlikely of circumstances, or maybe it was because Marco was warm and kind and he made Savi feel like she could let her walls down every now and then. He was someone she could feel safe with when her whole world was being flipped upside down and she was thousands of miles from everyone she loved. He had brought home to her. Plus, it helped that he kept calling her Cowgirl and liked learning about her life growing up on the ranch.

He had practically begged to visit and meet Mocha one day. He hadn't grown up around horses; the closest he'd gotten was a donkey ride in Greece, so Savi had told him regrettably that Mocha would be too much for him to handle. If, and it was a strong if, he ever did visit her home in Wyoming, he'd be lumbered with Java. He was smaller and calmer, and they used him to teach the local, more advanced kids.

'We've still got a few hours until dinner. Why don't we

watch a film? Unless . . . you want to call Jesse. Or you just want me to leave. I don't mind.' He looked at her like she was made of glass and she hated it. Right now, it felt like she was. But Marco knew the fiery side of her, that had been his first impression of her when they were introduced and until now, was the only side of her he knew. She didn't want to lose that. This was a blip.

'I'd like you to stay, only if you agree to a few alcoholic drinks from the mini fridge before we go out.' She gestured at the fridge which was tucked under a desk. Why did so many hotel rooms have desks? She was sure the likes of Faith and Lucie used them when they disappeared to work on *Girls Off Track* and continue cementing the future of women in motorsport, but she'd rather do business in the restaurants and bars of hotels.

'We're going to have to order some room service wine, all they've got in there is champagne.' He turned his nose up. 'I'm sick of that stuff, I managed to inhale it through my nose at the last podium. Surprised the cameras didn't catch me gagging.'

'I'll call down, then,' she laughed. 'Red or white? Or perhaps you're a rosé kinda guy.'

'Red it is,' he chuckled. 'But we'll wait to drink it until your heart rate is back to normal, alcohol isn't going to help your anxiety.'

'My heart rate is just fine, see?' She didn't know what possessed her to do it, but she grabbed his hand and placed it on her chest, right over her heart.

It was only when his breath hitched in his throat and he swallowed nervously that she realised her breasts were exposed in the camisole she was wearing. This wasn't what friends did, and it was certainly crossing the line that Jesse had not yet drawn, but she had just felt so at ease, so comfortable in Marco's presence, that she had momentarily forgotten he wasn't Miko or Kodie or Esme. He was her male teammate, her fake boyfriend, and her real one might well have punched him square in the face had he walked in and witnessed it.

'Yeah, mine isn't . . .' he whispered. 'Let's watch that film.'

As Marco shuffled into his spot on the bed next to her, Savi tensed up, and in that same moment, her walls shot up sky high. She needed him to meet Jesse, see the love they shared, so she was certain he wouldn't read into whatever the hell that was.

12

Marco was fucked. There was no other way to put it. Despite being publicly snapped all over his teammate, his phone had been blowing up with late-night texts from models and socialites. He'd spent the past few months wrapped up in bedsheets with anyone who'd shown interest, within reason, trying to wipe any trace of Esme Keelan from his mind. And it had worked.

He could watch Esme and her girlfriend walk down the pit lane hand in hand and not bat an eye. He could attend dinners with both of them present and be genuinely happy that they had figured it out, because he had accepted that Esme wasn't the woman for him.

Only now, he was ignoring those texts and calls and avoiding every woman on his roster, and it wasn't because he was still heartbroken. It was because Esme's friend, his teammate and his fake girlfriend, had weaselled her way into his heart without even trying, and was the only thing on his mind except racing. All the time. He woke up thinking of her, fell asleep wishing she were next to him, and spent his days watching her across the garage and thoroughly taking advantage of every second he was allowed to touch her. This wasn't just another infatuation; there was something special about his favourite Wyoming cowgirl and unfortunately for him, he was falling hard and fast.

It wasn't right. It wasn't okay. He knew that, and he knew if her boyfriend ever found out he would make Marco's life hell. It wasn't fair that he was falling for her. On Savannah or on him or on Jesse Montalvo. And Marco had seen enough of Jesse Montalvo in the press to know he wasn't keen on the bloke and thought Savannah deserved better, but it wasn't his place. Or maybe it was? He felt somewhat responsible for her wellbeing considering he was lying to the world, to his friends and family to protect her. Telling her he thought her superstar boyfriend was an asshole was looking out for her, right?

Marco knew what guys were like, he knew the red flags and Jesse had a lot of them, but it was too soon to break bro code. Not that he felt loyal to him over Savannah, but he had to witness their relationship first hand before he could really judge.

He should answer one of those texts, entertain one of his recent conquests on the yacht again. Take his mind off things. Harriet was a riot, as was her friend Gianna. He could get an NDA drawn up, save it going public. Protect his and Savannah's façade. But he wasn't willing to risk it, and he would much rather hang out with Savannah anyway, lounge around in bed with their clothes on and drink the most expensive wine on the room service menu.

Except she had drifted off to sleep on his shoulder forty-five minutes ago and he had coaxed her wine glass out of her hand and placed it on the bedside table. He had to wake her up soon so she could get ready for dinner; he thought she looked beautiful as she was, but she wouldn't be his biggest fan if he let her go out with smudged eye makeup and hair that resembled a bird's nest. All that crying must have taken it out of her, and he had been trying to drift off alongside her, but his mind kept going back to his hand on her chest.

Feeling her heartbeat had been so intimate it had made his head spin, although he knew she hadn't meant for it to be like that. She hadn't been thinking, that much had been clear, and she had done a stellar job of acting totally normal in the moments that followed. It was just him reading into it. As he always did.

He paid little attention to the film playing, some action movie that they had taken forever to agree on. His back was starting to lock up, having stayed in an awkward position so as not to disturb the sleeping cowgirl, and he used it as his opportunity to wake her up gently. Shifting his body, he heard a soft little moan escape her lips. It went straight to his groin, and he prayed she wasn't awake enough to notice, not that she ever looked at that part of him anyway. He was the only one who ever did the staring here.

'Shit, are we late?' Savi shot up, rubbing her eyes and further smudging her mascara. With full lips and rosy cheeks, she looked more like they'd gone a few rounds in bed than she did an anxious, crying wreck. Perfect look for dinner since they were showing up together and were likely to be twenty minutes late if she didn't move at the speed of light.

'Not quite. You go sort yourself out, I'll tidy up.' He started gathering the empty bottles and glasses and straightened the bed sheets, not wanting Savannah to have any visual reminders of her emotional breakdown when she came to bed tonight.

'Mars?' she called out from the bathroom and the nickname made his heart flutter in his chest. She had hardly called him that since they met, it was either his full name or Monaco. Another nickname that worked for him, and one that turned him on more than anything.

'What's up?' He poked his head round the door and was met with her naked, tanned back and shoulders. She was more muscular than he'd expected, and he could see the effort she put into her training. It was the body of an athlete.

He couldn't help but picture the rest of her, most importantly those legs wrapped around his waist when he carried her through his hotel room door. Which wasn't going to happen, because yet again he had fallen for someone who was otherwise engaged.

'I can't zip this stupid thing up.' She gestured to the white corset dress she was clutching to herself and sighed, clearly getting flustered at the delay it was causing. If there was one thing he'd noticed about her it was that she was punctual. Always on time or early to every team meeting, every press conference aside from the one after they'd been cornered by her boyfriend's PR guy.

'Allow me.' He refused to let their eyes meet in the mirror, already feeling like he was majorly overstepping and should have asked one of her female friends to look after her.

'Do I look okay?' she asked. 'Be honest, because I'm not feeling so hot right now.'

'You look perfect,' he murmured. 'What's bothering you?'

Savi sighed, and he felt his heart break just that little bit more knowing he couldn't take her pain away. 'I feel like everyone will know I've been crying even if Julien doesn't tell them, and they'll see right through me. The wine was supposed to get me tipsy in time for dinner so I'm a little less self-conscious and instead, I slept it off. I think I even drooled on your shoulder, which is not part of the deal and not at all what you signed up for.'

'What I signed up for is irrelevant, Savannah,' he murmured as he held the fabric together and zipped her into the corset. 'We're teammates over and above everything else and what are teammates for if not for drooling on one another in their sleep? Besides, Brett has done it to me numerous times.' He watched as she let go of her curls and they fell over her shoulders.

'It's still gross.' She scrunched her nose up.

'Oh, and by the way . . .' He chose that moment to look up at her reflection, catching her gaze in his and making sure he spoke with confidence so she could really feel his next words and know that they were the truth: 'You look incredible. Never seen red cowboy boots and a corset look so good.'

'Thanks, Monaco,' she smiled back at him.

'Julien won't tell anyone, you know.' He fixed his hair, running his hands through it and making sure his own curls were perfectly placed. 'It's highly unlikely he even told his wife but if he did, Faith will keep it hush hush. She's a girl's girl, and also a teammate, you haven't got to worry about it.'

'I just don't want people to see me as weak,' she said, frowning as she put her jewellery on. Without a word, he took her necklace from her and looped it around her neck, focusing on the clasp at her nape. Jewellery was so fiddly, but he often wore a chain, so he was used to it.

'Your anxiety doesn't make you weak, Savannah. It makes you strong. Because you constantly choose to fight it instead of letting it win. And look where that strength has got you . . .' He put his hands on her shoulders, gripping them tightly as if his touch would really drive it home. 'You're a badass, Savannah. I don't label many people that, but you've earned it. And I don't even know half of your story.'

He wanted to know. Savannah didn't talk about her family much, not unless it was directly related to their support of her racing career. But he didn't know the little things; what was her favourite family recipe, the best holiday she'd been on, did she go to prom or was she too cool for it? There wasn't always a reason for anxiety, some people were just born with it, but a lot of the time it came from trauma and Marco knew nobody's life was perfect. Savannah seemed like the type to keep parts of her past, and present, a secret unless someone had earned the right to know, and he hoped he would qualify one day.

'We should probably get going if we don't want them to accuse us of something we haven't been doing. No amount of liquid blush will hide *that* kind of embarrassment.' She shooed him out of the bathroom and towards the door. 'Your shirt is creased.'

'My shirt is always creased; I have developed a bit of a reputation for it. I don't even have an iron in my apartment.' He held the door for her, and she ducked under his arm.

'Don't you have a housekeeper?'

'Yes, but she doesn't do my laundry. Just cleans once a week whenever I'm not home.'

'Chef?' she quizzed.

'Chef slash nutritionist. He works for Jules, too. You should get one of those.'

'I don't need a chef; I've got my ma. Nobody on this planet can cook like her, but I come in close,' Savi beamed with pride. 'As for a nutritionist? Google exists. I don't need to pay somebody to tell me what I can research for free.'

'Shh. Don't let Ben hear you say that.' He put his hand over her mouth, chuckling when she licked his palm to force him to let go.

'You can keep him. He should consider himself lucky that his racing driver clients are too damn lazy to teach themselves.'

'Also don't tell him I'm going to stuff my face with a very expensive vegan burger with all the trimmings and side dishes.'

'You're vegan?' Savi looked genuinely surprised. 'Huh, I never noticed.'

'I wouldn't survive long in Wyoming, I take it.'

'Not a second. Although my family does a lot of barbecues so if you like corn then I guess you wouldn't starve to death.'

'Might be nice to attend one some time.' He was pushing his luck a little, especially considering he didn't think even Esme had been invited to visit Savannah's family. And they were thick as thieves.

'Maybe,' she shrugged, smiling when she must've thought he wasn't looking.

The moment they stepped through the door of the restaurant, they realised not only were they very late, but all eyes were on them. Marco hated causing a scene, not that you would know based on his public behaviour after Esme shut him down. Brett sat there grinning at them and Marco knew he was about to yell out to them and make their presence known.

'There's the happy couple!' And just like that, the entire restaurant looked up and the phones came out, cameras pointed right at them. They had found a local, family-owned place. The kind of establishment where the waiters liked to chit chat and the walls were lined with black and white photos of previous generations. It was full of fans wearing racing merchandise, a hint that perhaps the team should start taking advantage of their bank accounts and exploring higher-end places where everyone else was trying to be private, too. Marco reached for Savannah's hand in a rush to put her at ease, because while he was used to this, she still wasn't.

He ushered her into the empty seat next to Kodie and sat down next to her, only letting go of her hand so she could shakily reach for a glass of water. 'Hi, sorry we're late.'

'Don't stress.' Faith shot her a smile across the table and Marco reassuringly squeezed her thigh before finally leaving her be. He didn't want to overdo it. 'We waited to order. We've been sampling the mocktails, though. Brett's influence. Highly recommend the watermelon spritzer.'

'So, who's headed where after this little extended trip?' Lucie asked the table.

Racing drivers never stayed in one place for long, but as the years went on, the Revolution team tended to adopt home bases and go there as often as they could. Marco's was Monaco.

'Faith and I are off home to Oahu to spend as much of the summer break as we can with my biggest kid while she's home from college,' Julien said. His daughter's mum had passed when she was a baby, and that was right around when Marco met Jasmine. He had quickly fallen into the role of Uncle Mars and he loved it just as much as he loved watching Faith take on the role of stepmum, blending their family over the last few years. 'She wants to be around her friends and told us if we take the twins to Malmedy and away from her, she'll never forgive us. Claims she hates kids but is the first to offer to play with them, take care of them. Bit scary watching her take on a maternal role but it means Faith and I can go off on waterfall hikes and drive round the island to find the best acai bowls.'

'We'll be in Malmedy so if you want us to look after Ford, let us know,' Brett added. 'As long as he doesn't get muddy paw prints on our new carpets.'

'Why would you get carpets when you've got two young nieces down the road and you dog-sit our giant Husky on the regular?' Julien demanded.

'It feels soft under my feet,' Brett argued without a care in the world. Marco gave it two years before Lucie convinced him to rip it up and put hardwood down.

'I'm going home to Japan,' Miko smiled softly. 'Haven't seen my cat in a while.'

'Your cat?' Faith laughed. 'Not your family?'

'We're not super close, they're always in business mode. Mochi is a Persian, she's my pride and joy. I have one of those clear cat backpacks for her and everything.'

'Oh my god. I love it,' Savi giggled at the photos Miko showed off.

'I am going wherever the wind takes me,' Kodie shrugged. 'With Esme and Thalia and their friends, because life is short, and the world is wide. We're thinking Kenya first.'

'Then Tanzania, too. But that will be after Le Mans. We want to do some volunteering so we're looking into that,' Esme added.

'Savannah and I are off to Los Angeles. Gonna go to the Santa Monica Pier, Venice Beach, the Hollywood Walk of Fame and see some concerts.'

'I'm going to force him to listen to some country music,' Savannah grinned. 'He can't wait.'

Marco smiled back at her, not letting his distaste show. He did actually like country, he just didn't like the particular artist they were going to see or the complications for his poor, wounded heart that came with it. If he was being honest, he was dreading this week.

What if Jesse could tell that Marco was into his girlfriend? What if he was jealous and possessive and called this whole thing off? That would be beneficial in lifting the weight of responsibility from Marco's shoulders and would mean he could focus on just being friends with Savannah, but it would mean he didn't get to kiss her and touch her without consequence.

He sounded insane. He knew he did. He was repeating the Esme situation, only this was worse and a million times more complicated. He couldn't believe that his feelings for the cowgirl were already stronger than the ones he'd held for Esme. He was going to be ruined. Why couldn't he fall for someone who was open and available and wanted him back just once in his life?

This had all started in nursery when he'd chased Caterina Rossi across the playground and she'd screamed, cried and pushed him over to get away from him. His luck with women was great when it came to casual, no-strings-attached hookups, but he'd never had a real relationship. He had high standards, and he wasn't going to forge ahead with someone who he knew wasn't likely to be his soulmate. He was a romantic, and he didn't settle for anything less than perfect.

That was the problem. Savannah Hart was perfect, and it had taken him a very short time to realise it. But she was perfect for someone else, a man who refused to show her off to the world. Marco would show her off, he was already doing it. He just wished he could wake up and have it all be real.

13

Savi couldn't sit still. She and Marco been flown out on Jesse's private jet, and they were on their way to his show before they'd even checked in at the hotel. His assistant's assistant had met them at the airport and taken their bags for them so they could head straight to the venue, and Savi was yet again irritated that he hadn't got his security detail together so that he could personally welcome them on the runway.

It wasn't just about her. Marco was a guest of theirs, personally invited by Jesse so they could get to know one another, and Jesse didn't have the decency to show up.

His excuse? Well, he hadn't given one. She was used to his poor communication skills, but she was embarrassed by his lack of regard for her.

'So . . . are we going to be shoved at the back of the arena, out of view?' Marco asked, helping himself to the free champagne that had been provided in the back of the limousine. Savi was surprised by the choice of car, it seemed too flashy, but maybe Jesse was trying to make up for his absence.

'Honestly, I have no idea. I've never been to one of his shows.'

'What?!' His genuine shock made her uncomfortable and she knew she shouldn't have told him. She could no longer pretend that her boyfriend didn't have a fair few red flags, and neither he nor she was giving Marco a good first impression of him.

'The timing has never been in our favour.' She shrugged it off, but Marco wasn't shy about side-eyeing her suspiciously. The truth was, Jesse had never invited her, and she'd never asked.

'I hope we're not surrounded by screaming women, wherever we're seated. I can't deal with that kind of energy in my vicinity tonight,' he grumbled.

'You should be used to that, Monaco.' She patted his knee to emphasise that she was making fun of him. They would most likely be standing the whole show, with other celebrities who were in the same boat, wanting to be undetected. She doubted Jesse would leave them to the wolves with no security.

'Yeah but it's fine when they're screaming for me.' He rolled his eyes. 'What is it about cowboys, anyway? Racing drivers are way sexier.'

'Should've put that theory to the test and worn your race suit to the show.'

'It's in the wash. But do you think Jesse will let me borrow a cowboy hat so nobody recognises me? I don't want the humiliation of people exposing me as a Jesse Montalvo fan, because that I am not.'

'Oh,' she frowned, 'we were going to get you a tour t-shirt to wear.'

'No offence,' he shot her a look, 'I am not wearing your boyfriend's name *or* face on my body. I worked hard to look this good, I would be doing myself a disservice.'

'Fine, I'll wear one on my own.' She had a whole collection of his tour shirts which she wore to bed each night back home. Her brother hated seeing them out on the washing line.

'Sorry, but I don't think my fake girlfriend should be wearing another man's face on her shirt, either. I will happily argue with the both of you about it.'

'We're here.' She peered out the window as they drove to the back entrance of the arena. It was huge, and so unlike any music venue she'd been to before. She was used to bars and pubs with live bands, not huge events with tens of thousands of fans screaming along at the top of their lungs. She didn't know if her anxiety could handle it, to be frank, but at least Marco was now aware of her struggles and could keep an eye out for the warning signs.

'Oh, wonderful. I cannot wait.' Marco was laying it on thick with the fake enthusiasm, but it was just making Savi more amused. This must be strange for him, and for Jesse. It was certainly an interesting predicament for her.

They were let out of the limo by their chauffeur and shown into the backstage area by a member of the venue staff. It was like a maze back there. Posters of various artists lined the walls, from rock bands to pop princesses and country legends. Some were autographed, some not, and iconic tour outfits were in glass display cases. A classic bedazzled jumpsuit belonging to Dolly Parton was among them, and Savi stopped to sneak a photo. They even spotted one of Slash's guitars which Marco spent a good couple of minutes drooling over, much to the annoyance of their guide.

They finally reached Jesse's dressing room, with his name on the door on a laminated, white A4 sheet of paper. Underneath 'Jesse Montalvo' it read 'Artist'. Savi wasn't sure why she felt so nervous, why her anxiety was spiking. Was it because she was about to introduce Jesse and Marco, or was it because she was finally being let into Jesse's world? A world she'd been excluded from for four years. She didn't know if she was ready to be exposed to the reality he lived in, and one that she was going to be faced with in six months' time when this fake-dating drama was over and done with and she and Jesse moved forward together.

The security guy guarding the door looked terrifying. His jaw was set, arms crossed. He also sort of looked like the social worker from Lilo and Stitch, but she wouldn't dare tell him that. Then he opened his mouth, and his scary façade crumbled.

'Hey, y'all! You must be Mr Montalvo's VIP guests for tonight's show.'

'Hi, Savi and Marco. He should be expecting us.' Savi played with her rings as the man knocked on the door and stepped aside again. *Please be in a good mood, Jess.*

'Hi, baby!' Jesse greeted her with a huge smile adorning his features and pulled her into his arms for a kiss. He didn't shy away from showing her how much he'd missed her, sliding a hand down over her ass and clutching her tightly. It was awkward with Marco and the security personnel standing directly behind her, just watching, because what else were they supposed to do? This was the kind of PDA she couldn't quite get on board with.

'Hi. Jess, meet Marco.' She detached herself from him and turned her body, inviting Marco into the conversation. That was certainly one way for Jesse to assert dominance.

'Mr De Luca, good to meet you.' His face dropped as he stuck out his hand and shook Marco's in a firm grip, even Savi able to tell that it was already a battle of testosterone between them. Something was in the air, and she didn't like it one bit.

'Montalvo.' Marco was blunter in his response, but at least he mustered a smile.

'Come in, guys.' He held the door for them and welcomed them into the dressing room, where Savi was met with the intense scent of his aftershave. They were underground and there were no windows, but still, how did he not feel the need to sneeze non-stop? 'How was your flight? My crew took good care of you, I hope.'

'The drinks and salted peanuts were my favourite part,' Marco said. 'The Revolution jet is alcohol free for the most part, because of Brett's past issues, and it sucks.'

'But we do usually only use it to get to and from work events,' Savi pointed out.

'Yeah, there is that,' he agreed. 'So, is this all yours, Jesse? Or do you share with your band?' Marco wasted no time in wandering around the room, taking it all in.

The dressing table was lined with basic makeup and hair products and sat underneath huge light-up mirrors, Jesse's collection of one-of-a-kind guitars had a home next to the leather sofas, and the dressing table held a selection of whiskey, bourbon and the same champers the limo had been stocked with. His cowboy boots were all lined up in a row of red, black, dark brown and beige and the closet was stocked with an array of plaid and denim shirts, suede jackets and plain V-neck t-shirts. The whole room screamed Jesse, right down to the bags of Swedish Fish jelly sweets on the coffee table. He never went anywhere without them.

It was strange seeing his home away from home, but she concluded it wasn't much different to her own lifestyle. Her hotel rooms were all personalised by her boots and hats and race suits wherever she went, and both of them moved those things from place to place, city to city. But as for personal belongings? Photos and keepsakes, memories. Those things all stayed in their childhood bedrooms in Wyoming. They were valuable, too valuable to take on the road.

'The band has their own dressing room down the corridor. It's a hell of a lot louder in there than it is in here, I need my own space. I can't deal with their bickering or constant strumming, not in the lead-up to a show. Once we make it to sound check, different story. That's when we morph into one.'

'Knock knock!' a female voice called out and Savi immediately felt the hairs on the back of her neck stand up. It was the one thing that made her nervous with Jesse's job: the female attention that typically came along with the fame. She wanted to trust that Jesse wouldn't stray, but could you ever *fully* trust anyone? But then Jesse's manager appeared and her worries washed away.

'Sapphire!' She rushed towards her and wrapped her up in a warm hug.

'Hi, Sav.' The petite brunette returned the embrace, rubbing Savi's back like no time had passed. They'd mostly interacted via video calls over the last four years, when Jesse had been beckoned into work meetings while they were hiding out in the cabin, but they'd managed to hang out at Jesse's place in Wyoming a few times, too. 'It's so good to see you again.'

'Congratulations on the baby.' Savi stepped back and smiled affectionately at the tiny bump she had. Well, it wasn't that tiny really, not compared to Sapphire's dinky little frame.

'Congratulations on the fake boyfriend,' she replied, then lowering her voice to a whisper, she glanced at Marco who was checking out Jesse's vintage Fender without daring to touch it. 'He's quite the catch.'

Jesse cleared his throat from his position next to the sofa. 'I'm right here.'

'You should've picked someone ugly for her if you didn't want us to gossip.'

'It's alright, Jesse.' Marco dragged his attention away from the guitar. 'We both have women falling at our feet, but your cowgirl has only got eyes for you.'

'He's a possessive guy. Comes with the whole brooding cowboy thing he's got going on,' Sapphire teased, earning a deadly look from her client.

'I get it, Savannah is a great girl. But anyway, Sapphire, you looking for a stepdad for that little one?' He pointed at her bump, laughing wickedly when Savi smacked him on the arm. Sapphire's jaw dropped before she broke out into a fit of giggles, and Jesse's jaw got tighter and tighter. If he wasn't careful, he'd break his molars.

So, Marco was breaking out his flirtatious side, was he? As long as he didn't use it on Savi in front of Jesse, they should all be safe. Although it seemed even flirting with a member of his staff was a step too far, judging by the way he turned his back on them all and poured himself a whiskey. Neat. All Marco could offer Savi was an apologetic shrug which was followed by a smirk. He wasn't sorry at all; he was having a field day with this.

'Hello?' another voice called out, joining the chaos. Blake stepped into the room, dressed in a full suit. The same uniform he had worn when he'd cornered them at the track to kick this whole fake relationship scenario off. Slight overkill considering the star of the show was currently wearing jeans and a vintage Dallas Cowboys sweatshirt, but Blake was ever the professional.

'Blake.' Marco shook his hand, and Blake was much less intense than Jesse had been.

'How are things going with you two?' he asked, looking pleased to see them both there together. 'I've seen a large number of headlines, and photos and videos. You guys are naturals.'

'Ahem.' Jesse cleared his throat, shifting uncomfortably.

'I don't mean it like that, Jess,' Blake tutted. 'Jealousy doesn't suit you.'

The tension in the room shifted even further into uncomfortable territory, and Savi was about ready to leave and abandon the whole idea. She should have introduced them at dinner or something, not hours before Jesse performed. He was stressed and this was only adding to it. Marco, meanwhile, was still peering around and clearly being nosy, which seemed to be irritating Jesse even more. Savi couldn't blame her teammate, not many people had the opportunity to be in the dressing room of one of the world's biggest country music stars.

'So, Sapphire, when's your last day with Jess?' Savi asked the one thing she'd been dying to know. How long did she have before Jesse's work life imploded, and he started claiming he didn't want to be a musician anymore? As if there was nobody else capable of doing Sapphire's job in the entire music industry.

'I've got three more months,' she smiled nervously. 'The label has got a replacement lined up. She's great, he's in good hands.'

'She's an intern,' Jesse scoffed and took a swig of his whiskey.

'An intern who I have personally been training, Jess. You need to chill.'

'You'll be fine, you knew Sapph wasn't gonna stay with you forever.'

'I wanted to believe she would,' he shrugged. 'Anyway, we're ignoring Marco. Sorry, man.' Jesse clapped him on the shoulder, his large frame overpowering Marco's slimmer, athletic build. They couldn't be more different.

'Oh, don't worry about me. I'm just happy to be here.'

'So, you're Italian, right? Early thirties, been racing since you were sixteen. Still living in Monaco when you're not travelling the world with the team, although that's slowed down since Julien and his wife had kids.' Jesse reeled off the basics of Marco's life story, his attitude thankfully shifting for the better.

Marco nodded. 'Half Italian, half Monegasque, but you're spot on with the rest. You've done your research.'

'Well, yeah. I wanted to know who has their tongue shoved down my girlfriend's throat.'

And he was back. Insecure, jealous Jesse who ideally needed to kick everyone out of his dressing room, have a strong drink and focus on tonight's show. But it seemed he wanted to make poor Marco squirm, and all Marco was doing was smirking, his eyes sparkling with amusement.

'Definitely not crossed that line,' Marco assured.

'Yeah, it's all been totally PG, Jess.' Savi put her hands in her back pockets, unable to reach for Jesse because he was stood too far away. She never knew if she should lay on the PDA when they were around Sapphire and Blake, because they were never actually *in* public together.

'Better not cross it, either,' he sulked.

A lot of women liked a man who behaved like this, who warned other men off their girl, but it was getting under Savi's skin. Pretending to date Marco and kiss and hold hands and behave like a couple had been Jesse's idea, he'd pushed for it, and now she and Marco had travelled halfway across the world for Mars to be treated like an outsider, someone who was doing something wrong by simply doing as he had been asked. Doing a favour. A favour which was getting in the way of his own dating life for the next six months.

'How about we all give Jess some space and take a little trip to catering,' Sapphire suggested, hurrying them out of the room before Jesse got carried away with himself and knocked Marco out. It had happened before and was another reason Savi's brother hated him. He had anger issues, especially in bars. 'I bet you guys are starving.'

Before they could shut the door behind them, Jesse pulled Savi back into the room with a sad and sorrowful look on his face. 'I'm sorry. Apologise to him for me, this is just new, and I don't know how to feel about it. He's a handsome guy, and I've seen the reactions of your fans. Everyone's obsessed with the idea of the two of you, and it makes me want to just steal you away from your world and take you back to the cabin.'

'You don't need to worry about him, Jess. You know I've only got eyes for you.'

'I know.' He gave a gruff nod.

'I love you.' She leaned up and gave him a quick kiss.

'Enjoy the show, Superstar.' He walked away, her excitement for the show somewhat dulled down by the fact that once again he hadn't said 'I love you' back.

14

Savi had forgotten how much she loved live music, even more so when it was her boyfriend performing. She really should take advantage of the free concerts provided at certain races, plus go to more shows back home in the US. She and Marco were in their element in their security-heavy VIP section, soaking up every moment.

The atmosphere was electric, thousands of people were screaming every lyric out of Jesse's mouth, the bass was making Savi's heart leap out of her chest with every beat, the lights almost blinding them but simultaneously transporting them to another world. She got it. She finally, truly understood why Jesse had chosen this career.

He was loving it; she could see it written all over his face. He was interacting with his fans in between songs, cracking jokes with his band and moving around the stage like he owned it. He was good, he deserved to be where he was. Savi had never doubted that. She'd seen him in the studio both at the label's headquarters and at home in the cabin, watched him work into the night on melodies and verses, letting his creativity flow until he was confident he had a hit.

And this is what it got him; an arena full of people who were there just for him. To feel something. She had never held it against him when he had to leave Wyoming for months at a time because she had been doing the same thing in her last championship, and being part of Revolution Racing came with more opportunities and more responsibilities. It took her away from home far more often. Except now when she was lying in bed at night, feeling the distance between them, she could remember this. Remember *his* reasons for not being by her side.

And she could also remember Marco yelling phrases like 'I wanna be a cowboy, baby!' at the top of his lungs without a care in the world, proudly showing off his Jesse Montalvo tour t-shirt despite previously claiming over a mouthful of vegan cauliflower wings that Savi's boyfriend was an 'arrogant son of a bitch'.

She had a t-shirt too, a freebie to add to her collection, but she'd let Marco have the one that *didn't* have Jesse's face on it. It simply said his name on the front above a rodeo graphic, and had the US tour dates on the back. It looked like something he'd picked up at a thrift shop, not something thousands of teenage girls were also wearing tonight. Savi already had that one in her dresser at the cabin.

'Is LA a good place for cowboy boots?' Marco asked while Jesse was between sets.

'Absolutely not. If you're going to invest in a pair, they've gotta come from Wyoming, Texas or Tennessee. A state where cowboys originate from.'

'Cool, we'll go to Wyoming after one of our upcoming races. I've got nowhere to be.'

'Oh, I'm taking you back home, am I?' She raised an eyebrow.

'Fuck yeah, I want to ride horses and be a proper cowboy.

I've been converted.' He grinned, his curls plastered to his forehead. He'd exerted so much energy tonight, and they still had at least six songs left before the end. She dreaded to think how he'd behave during the encore, when everyone let out every last bit of emotion and the confetti rained down on them. She'd seen endless videos, and few artists did an encore quite like her boyfriend.

Their conversation ended abruptly as Jesse started singing again, silencing Savi as she took in the lyrics. This was her song. Nobody else knew that, but it was called 'Wyoming Cowgirl' and mentioned their first date-slash-meeting at the country fair. Jesse had written it for his debut album and it had been a hit single, but she had heard it months before the record label had. That was before he'd built the cabin, when they spent days at her family's ranch and rode horses at sunset. It was during one of those sunset rides that he'd pulled out his guitar and sung it for her, and she'd fallen in love right there and then. No going back.

She was tearing up by the second verse and soon found Marco's arm wrapped around her shoulders. 'It's about you, isn't it?' he asked.

'Yeah. Gets me every time.'

'I knew as soon as he mentioned red cowboy boots.'

'Sorry, I don't mean to get all emotional on you.'

'No, it's sweet.' He squeezed her arm and pulled her in closer.

It had become very clear even this early on that this sort-of contract she and Marco were involved in was going to result in a lifelong companionship. People just didn't do this for each other, it wasn't your run-of-the-mill friendship, and he had already seen some of the deepest, most hidden parts of her over the last few weeks. It was special. He was special, and he made her feel a little less alone amidst all the chaos. Marco De Luca was the very definition of a teammate.

'How do you feel?' Savi looked up at him as the lights came up and Jesse departed the stage for the final time, leaving everyone in a post-concert daze as they began to trail out of the arena like zombies.

'You know, I am not a fan of your boyfriend as a man but my god, he can put on a show. Don't tell him I enjoyed it as much as I did though, I don't want to feed his ego. I'll tell him it was just alright.'

'You're literally wearing his merchandise, Monaco.'

'Shit.'

Savi laughed and tugged him back to where they needed to be to get backstage, VIP passes around their necks. They'd been standing amongst other VIP guests, mostly other musicians she recognised and a few influencer types, none of them in the same circles as her and Marco, so there hadn't been much attention on them. A few fans around them had recognised them, and they'd been tagged in videos from people zooming in on them through the crowd, but for the most part they had been left alone to enjoy their evening.

'Guys! Follow me.' Sapphire met them at the door and led them back through the tunnels, towards Jesse's dressing room. 'How did you like it?'

'It was amazing!' Savi exclaimed. 'I can't believe it's taken me four years to see him live.'

'You'll have to come to more shows on the tour when you can, don't forget the European leg starts next spring. That'll probably work better for your schedule since you race out there most of the time,' she said. 'Marco, what did you think? You a country fan now?'

'Yeah, it was alright,' he mumbled, earning a quick glance from Savi. 'Oh, who am I kidding? The man's unreal. Don't you dare tell him I said that.' He pointed at Sapphire.

'Your secret is safe with me,' she laughed. 'Right, don't freak out when you see the amount of people surrounding him. He has to cater to the VIP fans after the show, we always select some to come backstage and hang out for half an hour or so. He'll be all yours soon, no doubt he'll kick them out early tonight.'

They rounded the corner where Jesse was being swarmed by more than ten young women, all of whom looked to be in their early to mid-twenties and all in mini dresses, long legs on display. Swarmed might to be too much of an understatement. Mauled was more like it. They were practically hanging off him, two women in particular all but fighting over him, hands on his chest as he pretended they didn't exist and spoke to the others. Savi felt sick. She hadn't been warned about this, and she'd stupidly thought she would get a few minutes by herself with him. Instead, she was watching him provide random fans with access to him like his girlfriend wasn't stood metres away.

And then, in a move that almost made her keel over with shock, Jesse took his cowboy hat off his head and placed it on the blonde woman clinging to his left bicep. *Wear the hat, ride the cowboy.* That was his and Savi's thing. She was the only woman who had ever worn one of his cowboy hats, or so he had told her.

'Hey, this happens every night,' Sapphire tried to reassure her. 'It's part of his brand. He entertains them backstage for a bit, plays a couple of songs for them in his dressing room, and then they leave. That's all it is. Oh, look, he's spotted us!'

Jesse waved at them and subtly detached the girls from his body before signing a few autographs, snapping some selfies and sending them on their way. He beckoned Savi and Marco over, and Savi hoped her face showed how disgusted she felt.

'Hey, guys. What did you think?'

'It was great, man. I'm impressed. Told Savi I might have to get some boots.'

'You definitely should,' Jesse chuckled. 'You mind if I have a second with my girl?'

'Oh, sure. I'll wait out here,' Marco agreed, and Sapphire herded him down the corridor to a spare room where the crew hung out.

'Hi, baby.' He kissed her on the cheek and led her into the dressing room, shutting the door behind them to give them some privacy. He poured himself another whiskey and got her a beer from the mini fridge. It was her favourite brand, and it was hard to find. Evidently he had given her *some* thought. 'You okay?'

'Feel a bit weird about whatever that was I just witnessed.'

'Oh, those girls? That's just part of the contract. No

different to how you have to kiss Marco in public, it's all fake. A necessary evil.' Jesse crossed the room to her. 'It doesn't mean anything, baby; *they* don't mean anything. You're the only girl I want and the only one who gets to wear my cowboy hats. That one I just gave away was a prop, purchased specifically for that reason.'

'Hmm,' she frowned, refusing to meet his gaze.

'Hey . . .' He tipped her chin up and forced her to look at him. 'I love you, Sav.'

'I love you, too.'

'What did you think of the show?'

'Hated it.' She broke out into a smile, annoyed with herself over how easy it was for him to win her over when she was supposed to be mad at him.

'Oh, yeah?' he smirked back at her.

'Yeah. Should've taken your shirt off.'

She squealed as he lifted her into his arms and spun her round, her back against the door. He locked it behind them, pushing his hips into her and biting at her neck. 'Don't ever let Marco do *this*. There are some parts of you he'll never have access to.'

'Stop giving cowboy hats to random women,' she counteracted, not that she would let Marco kiss her neck for the sake of the cameras anyway. There was no need, ever.

'It's a done deal, Superstar.'

'There's only one superstar in this room right now, and that's you.' She gripped his jaw with her hand, his lips inches away from hers. 'You were breathtaking, Jess. I've never seen you so . . . you. It was like watching you in your truest form, like you were on a different planet except you took me with you.'

'I just wish I could have you front row every night. My girl, waiting for me in my dressing room at the end of every show,' he murmured against her lips. 'The VIPs wouldn't even make it past security before I sent them home so I could devour you.'

'You're doing way too much talking right now,' she whispered, and that was all she needed to say for him to finally shut up and kiss her. His tongue battled hers in a fight for dominance, and Savi couldn't help but grind her hips against him while he held her up. The door was old, and every movement she made caused it to shift. People on the other side would know what they were up to, but she didn't care.

'I really want to take you right here in this dressing room, but I have to get my shit and get out of here by a certain time and I know you'll keep me busy for way too long.'

'Fuck you, getting me all excited,' she scowled. 'Thought you were the kind of man who always finishes what he's started? That's the Jesse Montalvo I know.'

'Who said I won't? Go back to the hotel, have a couple of drinks, and then meet me in the room. *Our* room.' He placed one singular kiss on her neck and handed her a hotel key card. 'I've booked a suite for us. I go to Texas tomorrow night, but you and Marco have an extra night on me.'

'You're my favourite, you know that?' she sighed with contentment.

'Right back at you, Superstar.'

She missed his touch as soon as he set her down on

the ground, and she watched his expression with adoration as he fixed her hair for her. Her dark curls always got mussed up thanks to him, but he knew how to make her look put-together again. It was part of the Jesse Montalvo package. He straightened out her dress, too, before opening the door and sending her back out to find Marco.

'See you later?' She turned back and smiled at him, almost like she didn't believe he was coming home to her tonight.

'I'll be back at the hotel before one a.m. I've got some press shit to do.'

She located Marco three doors down, one beer deep with a mountain of food in front of him. Pizza, cauliflower wings, vegan nachos and fries. Someone on Jesse's team had gone above and beyond to cater for Marco's diet, and she hoped it was Jesse himself. He was happily chatting away to Blake and some members of the band while someone played guitar in the background, and Savi almost felt bad for keeping Jesse away from this.

'Hey, wanna head back?' Savi laughed as Marco dropped a fry in the barbecue sauce.

'Let's go, Cowgirl.'

'Fancy a drink?' Marco held the door to the hotel lobby open for her, taking on the role of doorman while the actual doorman observed them with an expression of fondness.

'Or five,' Savi laughed. 'We're not exactly dressed for a trip to the bar, though.' She gestured down at the merchandise they still had on.

'Oh, who cares? We're not going to be seen in here, it'll be all rich businessmen who are too worried about themselves to pay us any mind.'

'We fit right in if you take bank accounts into consideration,' Savi laughed, taking a seat on one of the velvet-cushioned bar stools.

'Not that we should be discussing contracts, but did any other teams offer you more money than Revolution?' Marco waved down the barman, ordering them a strawberry daiquiri each. He'd remembered her order from the last bar they were at with the team.

'One, actually. Talos Sport. But I wasn't in this for the money. Sure, it helps, but whatever sum I was offered was going to be life altering so it didn't matter to me. I wanted this.'

'A fake boyfriend?' Marco frowned.

'No, you idiot. A team that feels like family. You know, I text or video call Kodie and Miko every single day that we're not together? And Lucie sends me updates on the goats, Faith on the twins. Brett sends me memes and Julien asks me for advice on his horses. Then obviously there's Esme, who may be our rival but still fits right in, and she knows almost everything there is to know about me. And here I am now, sitting in a bar with you after just introducing you to my world-famous boyfriend who less than ten people know about. I've never had this.'

'Really? Never?' he asked. 'I imagined Sheridan, Wyoming, to be close-knit where everyone knows everything about each other.'

'I mean, you're right. It is like that, and I love everyone

back home, but this team is in a different league, Monaco. Think about it. We travel the world together, risk our lives together every time we go out on that track. Nobody else is under the kind of pressure we are, it's unique to our sport. And we get to support each other through every loss, every win and everything in between. I spent years in my last championship watching you guys, waiting to be part of something big. Something magical.' She couldn't help but tear up. She had never cried happy tears as much as she had since the day she signed her contract.

'And here you are.' Marco nudged her arm and raised his glass to her.

'Here I am,' Savi smiled, clinking her pink drink against his.

'We're lucky to have you with us, Cowgirl.'

15

The bed was empty. Savi was lying amongst the white cotton sheets, staring past the spot where Jesse should have been and out the window at a view of the Hollywood sign. Jesse hadn't come home last night. Her boyfriend, who had begged her to wait in their room for him, was a no-show. No texts, and all eight calls of hers had gone to voicemail. She was used to him doing this when she was away for work, but not when she was right here. For him. She would have spent the whole break with her family in Wyoming, but instead she had jumped on a jet to Los Angeles the minute Jesse clicked his fingers.

Now she was pissed. Never in a million years would she have done this to him, but then again, Jesse never got on a plane for her. Ever. She would understand if it weren't for the fact he had his own property in Story, near his parents. They could be alone there, away from prying eyes. But Jesse rarely came home if it wasn't someone's birthday, and it didn't seem to matter to him that Savi spent a lot of time at home when she wasn't working. It was always Tennessee or nothing. His terms.

She and Jess were meant to be taking Marco for lunch at some celebrity hotspot. A place where people like them went because they didn't want to be photographed. It was so secret, the paparazzi didn't even know about it.

But apparently they served incredible vegan dishes to suit Marco's diet, and garlic and rosemary focaccia to die for, and you had to be of a certain reputation to get in. Even if Savi and Marco didn't meet requirements out here in the United States where motorsports weren't as popular as in Europe, Jesse did.

Savi reluctantly dragged herself out of bed, not sure whether anger or disappointment was the strongest emotion clouding her brain this morning. A mixture of both, with a little fear sprinkled in for the part of her that wondered if Jesse was physically okay and who he had been with last night. She couldn't escape the image of the girl wearing his cowboy hat.

She shot her teammate a text to ensure he was awake, before filling in the girls on how last night had gone. Their phones had been firmly put away most of the evening, and Kodie was furious that the group chat wasn't flooded with videos of *the* Jesse Montalvo performing.

Confirming Marco was up and alive but treating himself to a room service breakfast before they headed out for the day, Savi took her sweet time getting ready, trying to put on a brave face. If Jesse could go about his day without giving her a second thought, she could do the same. She wasn't big into makeup, just the basics. But her hair took time, and she had mistakenly scheduled hair wash day for this morning and was regretting it. Her curls took a lot of work, and her arms ached. Throwing on her red cowboy boots, she wished the restaurant they were going to later was the kind of place where it was appropriate to wear a cowboy hat. It would've saved her from the hassle of doing her hair, and then tomorrow she would be on a private plane without a care in the world what she looked like anyway.

She was halfway out the door when Jesse appeared at the end of the corridor, stepping out of the elevator. He looked like shit. Like he hadn't slept a wink. Was he hungover? Still drunk? He didn't look right, but that could be the guilt she hoped to god he was feeling for abandoning her like that. 'Sav?'

'Nice of you to show up.' Her tone dripped with bitterness once she had processed that he was safe.

'I'm sorry, Sav.' His face dropped and he took three big strides towards her.

'Are you, Jess?' She held her arms out so he couldn't get close enough to touch her. 'You didn't even attempt to get in contact.'

'I was recording.'

'How many times have I heard that one?' She laughed sarcastically. 'It's your code for drinking in bars and acting like I don't exist. You've done it from day one.'

'I'm telling you the truth, Sav. The lyrics just came to me after you'd gone, and then we came up with the melody. Time got away with me. I didn't mean to stay out all night.' He rubbed the back of his neck, doing a really good job of looking uncomfortable. 'We stopped for breakfast on the way back here which made us even later. I was hoping you'd still be asleep.'

'What, so you could just crawl into bed next to me and act like you'd been there all night, thinking I wouldn't notice?' she demanded.

He didn't say anything. Just stood there, unable to defend himself any further. He couldn't. There was no excuse for it, he could have found ten seconds to let her know where he was. Then she would try to understand his side, even if it still hurt that he had chosen work over the limited amount of time they had together. But lately Jesse's actions and lack of respect or care had started to pile up and Savi was beginning to realise just how many red flags there were. Asking another man to pretend to date her and not bothering to state his boundaries wasn't even half the issue. This was so much bigger than Marco.

'I don't know what to say, Sav.' He cast his eyes down, his scuffed boots much more interesting than coming up with an apology that sounded genuine.

'I'm going out. Meet us at that restaurant at two, so you can be a man and show my teammate the respect you owe him.' She slammed the door behind her so he would have to find his own key card to get in, and walked towards him. 'Don't you dare be late.'

'Morning, Cowgirl. How ya feeling, this morning?' Marco was bright-eyed and bushy-tailed, the total opposite of Savi. She had a mild hangover, but it was overpowered by the anger bubbling inside her. She needed Marco to work his magic and make her forget about reality.

'Jesse never came back to the room.' She clenched her jaw and shoved the lobby door open, startling the doorman. Veering left, she and Marco made their way to the Hollywood Walk of Fame. She was most excited to see Dolly Parton's star. Savi and her brother had grown up serenading their parents with 'Dumb Blonde', Weston donning a blonde wig and balloons stuffed under his shirt.

'He what?!' Marco rushed to keep up with her as she stormed on ahead.

'So, if the energy is a little off at lunch, it's because I'm trying not to rip his head off.'

'I will eat in silence, let you two murder each other with your eyes.'

'He'd better be accommodating,' Savi snapped, reeling her attitude in quickly before she risked taking it all out on Marco and ruining his tour of LA.

'I don't care if he is or not. I'm not here for him, really. I'm here for you, I don't need him to be nice to me. It's not going to impact our deal, Savannah. I can promise you that. You can pretend to date me until Jesse gets his shit together and people stop caring about those photos, okay? I'm not going anywhere and I'm not gonna jeopardise it.'

Savi's entire demeanour softened, and she looked up at him, the sudden urge to wrap him up in a hug taking over. So, she did it. A real hug, not one for show. There was nothing fake about it. 'Thanks, Monaco.'

'Let's go find Dolly and Cher, shall we?' He clutched her hand tightly and pulled her along.

'You're on a mission to find Cher?'

'Hell yeah. She's a legend,' he replied, bursting into an obnoxiously loud rendition of 'Do You Believe?', impersonating Cher's voice and all.

'I thought you'd have wanted to see Andrea Bocelli or someone, you know . . .'

'Italian?' he laughed. 'He's more up my mum's street.

Maybe even my grandma's. I actually grew up on drum 'n' bass, which a lot of people don't know. My brother and I discovered it when we were about ten, and it honestly kind of shaped my teen years. I've been to my share of raves; Europe is really the best place for it. I'm lucky to live there.'

'I can see you at a rave, now I think about it.' She squinted at him, studying him.

He had that effortlessly cool thing going on, and it wasn't just in the way he dressed. If she were to compare the Marco she knew now to the Marco who had first started out in racing, there was a huge difference. It was a transformation which had been documented in interviews and media footage. He'd found his feet, grown into himself. Even in the months that she'd known him, he'd changed. It explained how he'd gone from crying in fields over a girl who didn't want him back to flirting with her and parading a hoard of women around.

'You should come to one,' he suggested.

'No way.' Savi shook her head. 'Not my scene, at all.'

'I vowed to forever hate country but look at me last night. I had a blast.'

'Country music at least has words you can understand, not just a mash up of sounds. I could create that kind of music on my computer.'

'But when that bass drops . . . there's nothing like it.'

'I'll go to a rave when you enter a rodeo.'

'Enough said, moving on,' he laughed, stepping over Tom Cruise.

'Are there any racing drivers with a star?' Savi pondered. It was mostly movie and television stars and musicians that were honoured, but she knew a few drivers had dabbled in such industries.

'Savannah. What planet are you on?' Marco threw his head back and stared up the sky, exasperated. 'Have you not heard of the iconic Steve McQueen?'

'Oh, shit! I forgot about him!' She slapped a hand over her mouth. 'I think I need my contract to be dissolved immediately. I don't deserve to be in this sport.'

'I am genuinely appalled.' He laughed and steered her further down the line of pink and gold stars, most of them needing a clean. 'Look, here's the King of Cool. Take my photo with him?'

'Did you know his grandson was almost a vampire? And he was a firefighter.' She tried to redeem herself, spouting out knowledge of Steve McQueen's family tree like she was a walking Wiki page. 'Fictional, obviously. Two of my favourite shows.'

'Oh, good. Hopefully we can meet his grandson one day and I can tell him you're an embarrassment to the industry.' Marco crouched down for Savi to snap a photo of him on the ground. 'Next you'll be campaigning for McDreamy to have a star.'

'Patrick Dempsey was *the* dreamboat of the early two thousands, does loads of charity work and produces and directs. And he's a damn good driver, too.'

'Okay, now I think about it, I can't even argue with you. He's also a really great guy, he's been in the Revolution garage a few times. Just stopped by to say 'Hi' and wish us luck. I have a signed model of one of his race cars on my bookshelf, if you want it.'

'What?!' she gasped. 'Please! I hope he shows his face this season.'

'Doubt it, he's busy in his new championship with his new team.'

'Oh.' Savi jutted her bottom lip out, genuinely disappointed. She had grown up watching him on her TV screen every week, and when he'd begun racing, it was like two of her worlds had collided and she'd been in heaven.

'Don't worry, Cowgirl. We've still got plenty of eye candy in the paddock, myself included.'

'You're so egotistical, Monaco,' Savi tutted disapprovingly.

'Comes with the territory.'

'I beg to differ. I'm very modest.' She may have been a little big-headed when it came to her career, but when it came to her looks? That was a different story.

'And you're one of the most beautiful women to ever grace the pit lane. Seriously, Savannah. Modesty looks good on you, don't lose that.'

She barely paid attention to his arm around her shoulders as they narrowly avoided being harassed by a rather dodgy-looking Mickey Mouse near the Chinese Theatre, instead wondering where that compliment came from. That wasn't part of their deal. But then again, neither was this trip. Marco seemed to be doing a lot of things that he didn't need to be doing, and for some reason, Savi was in no rush to put a stop to it. She liked having someone on her side, someone rooting for her. She'd had a lonely four years.

'Before he gets to the table, I'd just like to say he looks like an idiot wearing that hat in here.' Marco mocked Jesse's choice in outfit as they watched him navigate a sea of over-dressed A- and B-listers, most of them recognisable. Savi's red cowboy boots were firmly tucked underneath the white tablecloth, but they had certainly earned her a few second glances when she'd walked in.

'It's part of his brand.' Savi kept her voice low and a smile on her face.

'Don't ever let him come to a race wearing an outfit like that. The team will roast him.'

'I think you and I both know my boyfriend is never coming to watch me race.'

The reality of her statement stung, and she wished she hadn't said anything because now Marco was looking at her with pity all over his face for about the gazillionth time since he first learned of Jesse's existence, and Jesse was looking at *him* with unwarranted distaste.

'Afternoon.' Jesse sat down across from them. 'Have fun this morning?'

'Have fun last night?' Savi shot back, immediately feeling guilty. This wasn't the time or place to have it out with him.

'Would've rather not had to work, but at least it was productive. Unlike this conversation.' He was staring her down in a silent war, completely unashamed of their current company bearing witness to their lover's tiff.

'So, the Walk of Fame was cool!' Marco interrupted.

'Yeah?' Jesse's attention diverted to him. 'Did you do the whole thing?'

'We speed-walked it, which has made me super hungry.'

'You should go for the beetroot burger, or the jackfruit

Bolognese. I had the jackfruit last month when I was in LA, highly recommend it.'

Savi had already decided to keep her mouth shut, but what was he talking about? She knew his whole schedule, where he was in the country at all times, and there was no reason for him to have been in LA last month. He hadn't mentioned it. Why would he have kept that from her? She watched him across the table, oblivious to his slip-up.

'How long have you got left on the tour?' Marco asked.

'Few more months, then I move on to the European leg.'

'So, you're not gonna be home for a while, then? Isn't that hard on you, physically and mentally?' Marco glanced at Savi, almost as if he were asking her. Jesse had never made career decisions with her in mind, and she didn't expect him to, but her feelings weren't exactly taken into consideration. Only seeing him here and there, on his terms, took a toll.

'No, but I don't mind. I like seeing the world and I like performing. Home will always be there, but the opportunities won't be,' Jesse shrugged.

She wanted to say that home wouldn't always be there. His parents were getting older, his siblings were moving on with their lives, his grandparents were already gone, and he hadn't even taken time out to attend their funerals. And as for Savi? Who knew how much longer she could stick around before it all became too much for her. She was always fitting in around him, never the other way around. It would be nice to have someone who had the time to come to her races, hell, she'd take a trophy husband if it meant she was happy.

'I suppose. I guess Savannah and I are lucky that we get longer breaks between races. The season is quite spaced out, gives us plenty of time to focus on what's important,' Marco said, his dig missed by Jesse. But Savi had to fight to conceal her smirk.

'What was it like growing up in Monaco?' Jesse took a sip of beer, an unusual choice in drink for a place so upscale but it was very him.

'Uh, luxurious, to say the least. My family are quite well-off, I won't pretend otherwise. My love for cars came from seeing people pull up to the valet of my family's hotel in Ferraris and Lambos. But our house has a tennis court, and I had a personal coach. That kind of luxurious.'

'I'm surprised you didn't go to boarding school,' Savi laughed.

'I did . . .' He grimaced. 'But I hated it, so I came home and had an army of personal tutors instead. Had to live my life to a strict schedule, though, with the racing added to the mix. Probably why I like to explore so much.'

'Yeah, Gabriel had me on a schedule, too. Well, he made sure my parents kept me on it and checked in when he could. He even scheduled in time for video calls to discuss my progress, twenty minutes every Friday.' Savi remembered the early years of her career fondly.

'I'm grateful Sav has been there, done that and is still living life by a schedule now. Helps me sleep easier at night knowing even though we're so far apart, she's keeping busy. She's always been independent, just like me.' Jesse shot her a smile, irritating her once again.

She wanted to tell Jesse every detail of her day, tell him

all the mundane things and talk back and forth all throughout the day. Instead, she was lucky if they exchanged one message in twenty-four hours. He'd blame it on their schedules, but a text didn't require them both to be available at the same time. That was the beauty of technology. But there was always a reason, always an excuse. It wasn't a case of being independent, it was just Savi being tolerant.

'Still, don't you wish things were different?' Marco quizzed, looking confused.

'Sure, sometimes,' he shrugged.

'Only sometimes? If I had a woman like Savannah in my life, I would never let her go. I'd want her with me every day, I'd want to eat dinner with her and wake up to her and travel the world with her. Experience life together.' Marco's jaw was clenched, and Savi was stunned to hear him speak about her like that so openly. She was equally surprised to find that she didn't care how Jesse reacted. Maybe someone needed to remind him of what was in front of him.

'You know why we don't have that dynamic, Marco. It's part of the reason you're here, why I let you into our lives. You know what those photos would do to her?'

'This has nothing to do with the photos, Montalvo, and you know it. You should have been loving her out loud from day one, not hiding her. You could have protected her regardless of whether people knew about your connection or not. Those photos were probably only obtained *because* you keep your dating life so private, people were looking for some gossip.'

Savi sat there dumbfounded at her teammate's fierce defence of her. No man had ever stood up for her like that, even the man whose character was in question. She knew Marco was right, and it made it even more difficult to look her real boyfriend in the eye as her fake one rose from the table before their first course had been delivered.

'Mars . . .' she spoke softly.

'No. I'm sorry, Savannah. I can't sit here and listen to his bullshit.' Marco pulled out some money from his wallet and slapped it down on the table. 'That includes the tip. Thanks for flying us out here, Jesse. You put on a damn good performance.'

Marco left the restaurant in an explosion of anger, which may have been a little over the top but it was still valid. Everything he'd said was right, but Savi wasn't ready to face it yet. To have a conversation with Jesse that could change everything. She'd got comfortable over the course of their relationship, and Marco had swooped in and uprooted everything she thought she knew about herself and what she wanted. Just with his observation.

'Superstar,' Jesse sighed, 'this isn't working.'

'What?' She frowned, hoping she'd heard him wrong. It was too soon for this. 'What isn't working?' Savi stayed rooted to the spot, quite literally on the edge of her seat as she had been gearing up to follow Marco.

'This. Us. Whatever the fuck we're doing here.' He laughed. 'I mean come on, Savannah. You really want to be with me when people like Marco exist? That man could give you the whole world on a silver platter, and we both know I can't.'

'But that's just the thing, Jess. You can but you're actively choosing not to. Because, what? You can't be bothered?

You don't love me anymore?' She watched him take another sip of beer, rolling her eyes inwardly at his lack of ability to survive any social interaction without a drink. 'What did these last four years actually mean to you?'

'I thought we were a team,' Jesse shrugged. 'And then I realised, you've got a team. You've found your people. You don't need me anymore.'

'No, don't put this on me,' Savi bit out, anger rising through her body. 'There's no reason you couldn't step up, treat me the way you so clearly think I should be treated by someone else. And it was never about needing you. The only person I will ever need is myself. Just admit that while I spent all this time choosing us, you were only choosing you.'

He shrugged again, adding to the unfamiliar bitterness she felt towards him. For someone who wasn't ready to have this conversation, she was sure as hell feeling empowered the longer it went on. 'Yeah, I guess,' he replied, the beer bottle now half empty.

She held his gaze, wondering if he was going to add any more insult to injury. But as the seconds ticked by and it became evident he wasn't particularly bothered, she came to the conclusion that in actual fact, this was the perfect time to have this conversation, and that actually, she was ready. It was just a crying shame that he had beaten her to it.

'I think we're better off as friends, Sav. I'm sorry. This feels like more of a friendship, anyway, these days. Maybe that's all we were ever supposed to be.'

'It feels like –' Savi scoffed. 'Who's fault is that, Jesse?! You backed off without communicating! You stopped planning our future two years ago, is that how long you've had these doubts? Would you have said anything if Marco hadn't exposed the cold, hard truth about the kind of man you're incapable of being?'

'I was waiting for that spark to come back,' he mumbled, pulling a face like he was trying to gain some pity. It wasn't going to work. She'd fallen for lie after lie, letting every excuse wash over her. And it had all been for nothing. Since when had the spark been missing? It was sure as hell there when the photos that got them into this mess in the first place were taken.

'Waiting while doing absolutely nothing to help matters. Waiting, and wasting my time. Everything I've given you, Jess, all the hours I travelled when I was exhausted from working, moving my schedule around to fit in a video call, making sure you knew you were a priority. You never did the same. You let me do all of that, knowing you didn't want this.' She gathered up her things, aware that they were causing a scene but not particularly caring.

'I'm sorry, Superstar.' She felt nauseous at the mention of her nickname; one he had lost the right to use.

'I don't give a damn if you think you're sorry or not. Do you know what the last few years have been? Bullshit. And I'll tell you one thing, I'm glad Marco gave us a helping hand, because I can't imagine wasting a single second more on you.'

She rose from her seat with every ounce of dignity she could muster, left her own share of the bill, refusing to let Jesse pay for her uneaten food, exited the restaurant and chased Marco down the street.

She spotted him way ahead of her, marching on ahead as she ran to catch him up. 'Monaco!'

'Savannah?' He whipped around. 'You didn't have to come after me, I'm a big boy.'

'We're a team, remember?' She placed her hands on her hips, trying to catch her breath. 'And I'm not going to lie, after the conversation I've just had with him in there, I need my teammate by my side.'

'Cowgirl?' He held his hands out to her as her façade crumbled.

Savi looked up into his big brown eyes and swallowed back tears. 'It's over.'

'Oh, Savannah . . .' He frowned, pulling her into his arms. 'Was it his decision, or yours?'

'Uh . . . His? I think? I didn't really try to stop him, though.'

She breathed a sigh of relief as he held her tight, letting her know she wasn't alone even though she was miles away from everything she knew. 'Are you okay?'

'Not right now. I'm confused, and angry, and hurt. Also a little bit frustrated that I didn't just have more time to process my own feelings after he abandoned me last night, because that might have been my own personal nail in the coffin. But no . . .' she choked back a sob, 'he called it first.'

They stood in the middle of the street, ignoring the frustration of everyone around them as they blocked the pavement. Marco threaded his fingers through her curls, playing with her hair and soothing her. 'Tell me what you need, Cowgirl. Whatever it is, I've got you.'

'I don't know, I just know I need to get out of here, go

somewhere I don't have to think about who I am or what I want. I was going to head back to Wyoming, but I don't know that home is where I need to be while I get my head straight. I never thought I'd say that, but I can't handle the smugness and the *I told you so*'s just yet.'

'Can Wyoming wait until after the race?'

'What did you have in mind?'

'Come back to Monaco with me?' he asked. 'I'd really like to show you how I do things when we're not travelling the world for races.'

She pondered the offer, juggling the pros and cons in her mind. She'd never been to Monaco, and it might be nice to see how the other half lived. What else was she going to do? Fly halfway across the world solo and sit in a hotel room? Go home and have Weston celebrate the downfall of his baby sister's shambles of a relationship? She could get on board with a private tennis court, where she could smash tennis balls and pretend they were Jesse's face until she had no anger left within her. 'Fuck it, let's go.'

16

Savannah needed solitude, and that was exactly what Marco's tiny home country could offer her. An escape from reality, some peace and quiet. And more importantly, someone to remind her just how special she was. He could do that for her, just until she figured out who she was in a world without Jesse.

Marco wasn't lying when he said he had grown up in luxury. While he had been open about his upbringing when Savannah had asked, bringing her here was a whole different ball game. Thankfully he knew his family were still in Switzerland visiting his brother, and the only people here were the housekeepers.

Her eyes would fall out of her skull if she saw the way his parents dressed just to sit around at home. Not a day went by when his father wasn't in a full suit or a shirt and trousers. He was ready to drop everything and run to a business meeting at any given moment, and he frequently held them at the family home. They would petrify Savannah, and he knew she'd be self-conscious of her own choice in clothing. If only she knew his mum had a pair of cowboy boots hiding in the back of her walk-in closet.

Despite the stupid amount of money they had accumulated in their joint bank account, his family were incredibly down to earth and he was proud of that fact, grateful for the way he had been raised. Everywhere they travelled, they volunteered with the local community, educated themselves and immersed themselves in the culture. They'd built schools, hospitals, hotels which only hired local people and paid above minimum wage. And the rest of the world didn't know about any of it. His parents didn't like to brag, and they kept their social circle small.

His brother had taken all the money out of his trust fund and donated it to a medical research programme the same week he turned eighteen, and then promptly moved to Switzerland to meet a girl he'd been talking to online and started from scratch.

But Marco knew this was intimidating. From the tennis court and the swimming pool to the marble floors and multiple garages filled with sports cars, mostly gifts from car manufacturers for just . . . being a racing driver. It was a lot. And he wasn't oblivious to the fact Savannah hadn't come from money and was probably afraid to touch anything in there.

'I never realised you still lived with your parents,' she murmured, hovering in the doorway to the kitchen. After a guided tour, during which she had been stunned into silence, that was all she had to say? He was wondering if he should've booked her into a hotel or rented an apartment for the sake of a week. She might feel more comfortable.

'I have an apartment, but there's only one bedroom. I didn't think it was appropriate, plus it's in a building full of racing drivers and you would have been hounded by them all. They're nosy. You have your pick of three rooms here, and my family won't be returning home until we're en route to Brazil for the race.'

'I bet your apartment doesn't have a tennis court,' she laughed nervously, finally choosing to join him at the kitchen island, while the family chef whipped them up some pancakes. Vegan and packed full of protein and chocolate chips, just how he liked it.

'No, but it has a pool. On the roof, not private. And a community gym, too, which I don't use because I crammed as much equipment as I could into the spare bedroom. The reason for me not having an extra bed.'

'You know what my gym is back home?' She watched the chef work. 'Running the hiking trails and horseback riding. Mocha and I go out for hours sometimes.'

'Is it not dangerous, running the trails? Isn't the bigfoot out there?'

'I stay close to the ranch. I've grown up there, I know what to look out for. And bigfoot isn't real, idiot.' She rolled her eyes, and he grinned at her. He liked it when she called him an idiot. It made him feel like they were getting closer, close enough that they could insult each other without consequence.

'So, Cowgirl. Is there anything specific you'd like to do while you're here?'

'Am I allowed to indulge in the life of Marco De Luca for a while? Go to the casino, play some tennis, swim . . .' She took a bite of the food that was put in front of her. 'Eat these incredible pancakes. Oh my god! Maybe I do need a chef.'

'If you want to live my life, you're gonna have to ditch

the cowboy boots for a few days. Those won't fly in a place like this,' he laughed. 'I'll have to drag you out on a sunrise run.'

'Sun*rise* or sun*set*?' Her eyes widened.

'Rise. Shouldn't you be an early bird, growing up on a ranch?' He took a forkful off her plate, too impatient to wait for his own to be ready.

'Getting up early was Weston's thing. I always stayed inside and helped get breakfast ready for when he and Dad and the ranch hands came back from their early morning jobs.'

'So, if you're not up by nine every morning to run or train, I'll have to set the fire alarms off to get you out of bed. Noted.'

'I am capable of waking up early, I just prefer not to. I have enough of that during race week. Please also note that I am in mourning following the end of my relationship, so go easy on me.' She scowled, but in all honesty, she didn't seem as devastated as he had worried she'd be. He had even got in touch with Esme in case he needed back up, since she was the only friend who had known about Jesse. Her reaction had been explosive, and Savannah's phone had immediately lit up with a flurry of messages from her best friend. But she hadn't shed a tear in front of him since first leaving the restaurant, and she had hardly mentioned it on the flight to Monaco. Wasn't that a sign that it had been the right thing for her, whether the choice had been hers or not?

'I will take it into consideration. Eat up, I've got something really cool to show you.'

'How can it possibly get cooler than everything I've seen so far?'

'Trust me.' Marco gratefully accepted his pancakes from the chef. 'Give me two minutes and we'll head upstairs. You'll like it, it's right up your street.'

He scoffed his food down, thankful that he'd taught himself this recipe so he could have them any time the chef was off, or if he was in another country.

His mum could cook, but as the family hotel business grew and grandkids came into the picture, she had hired someone to take care of things. Most days, the house was empty, so their personal chef had shifts at their Monaco hotel, too, and helped curate the menu.

'How on earth did you eat those so fast?' Savannah watched him, her expression a combination of awe and disgust. 'That's not human, Mars.'

'I was hungry,' he shrugged, getting up from his seat and putting both plates in the dishwasher. He had never been one to leave things lying around for the housekeepers.

'There's hungry and then there's whatever that was. You're like a vacuum.'

'I like pancakes. Those you guys ordered for me from room service in Spa were right up there with some of the best I've had.' He used to hate mentioning that debacle, but now he could laugh at his misfortune. Yes, he'd embarrassed himself. But he wouldn't make the same mistake again. Well, aside from falling for someone he couldn't have. He was right in the middle of making that mistake now, stood in his kitchen. But he wasn't going to cry about it in front of anyone or declare his feelings in a garage full of people.

'This surprise better be good.' Savannah followed him up the staircase, constantly stopping to admire photos on the gallery wall. It was pretty much all Marco and his brother in black and white candid shots, from their teen years to now. 'Your brother looks like you.'

'Don't tell him that. He got papped once, back in the early days of my career, by someone who thought he was me. He's rejected every comparison since. But yeah, you can't tell us apart in some photos.' Marco pointed out one where they had matching football shirts.

'I'm adopted, so my brother looks nothing like me.' Savannah smiled fondly at the mention of her brother, a common theme. She obviously thought a lot of him.

'You're adopted?' He didn't know why that shocked him so much.

'Yeah. My parents were friends with my biological mum who died during childbirth. She had made arrangements so if anything were to ever happen to her, my parents would take me in and raise me like their own.'

'Savannah, I'm so sorry . . .' He didn't know if he should put his hand on her shoulder, hold her hand, or give her a hug, so he just stood looking at her, hoping he was doing a good job at hiding his adoration for her.

'It's fine. I don't know any different. I have an amazing family, I'm very lucky that they were there when I needed them. When my mum needed them.' She didn't look sad about it, she looked at peace. He wondered if her adoption was one of the reasons she fought so hard for her career, so she could give back to the people who had given her everything.

'The surprise is just at the top of the stairs here.' He pushed open the door to his safe haven: a room dedicated to his racing simulator.

Jasper had got him a new one at the start of the year with all the upgrades and extras he could ask for, and Marco had painted the room black and added neon lighting and huge wrap-around screens. When he sat down in the racing sim seat, it was like he was in the Revolution car. He even had temperature control in there so he could practise for the warmer races. The closet held his team merchandise and old racing suits, and one wall was lined with trophies and helmets. It was heaven for any driver, his own personal shrine.

'Wow, Monaco. This is next level.'

'Have you got your own racing sim set up yet?' he asked. Every driver was given one by the team when they signed their contract. Some of them even had two like Julien, who lived in two different countries. It helped keep their heads in the game during longer breaks.

'No, not yet. The ranch is a little chaotic, lots of stuff. I need to go home and clear it all out, fix the things that nobody else has time for. The stables are the next step, we're supposed to be getting new horses but there's no space for them.' She chewed on her bottom lip. 'Jesse was supposed to come home with me and help, but I guess I'll be doing it on my own.'

'Well, if you need a hand just give me a shout,' he offered, genuinely meaning it. Partly because he didn't want to leave her alone until he was sure she was truly okay, but also because he wanted to see what the Midwest was really like.

'Wyoming is a long way to go to help clean up someone else's mess.'

'Teammates, remember? Just consider it, I don't mind if you decide at the last possible second. I've got no plans after the race.'

'Thank you,' she whispered, coming across as very shy suddenly. 'So, which is your favourite helmet? I like this one.' She pointed to a pink and purple one with metallic paint.

'That's my favourite. It was one of my first IEC helmets, designed by one of my childhood best friends. She's done a few more for me since, but there's something special about this one.'

'It's beautiful,' Savannah agreed. 'Can I have a go on the sim?'

'Why do you think I brought you up here? It wasn't to show off,' Marco laughed. 'Take a seat, I'll adjust everything for you.'

He admired the light in Savannah's eyes as she lowered herself into the seat, pressing the button on the steering wheel and bringing the system to life. When Marco wasn't away, he was usually hiding out in here or at his small but equally luxurious apartment. He hated being at the hotel, where all the staff knew who he was. He woke up, went for a run, had breakfast and came home and raced until his next meal. Aside from last time he was home when he was on the yacht and clubbing with all those women . . . He was going to have to come out of hermit mode this week and show Savannah how people truly lived in Monaco. Show her the lifestyle of the rich and famous, since her waste of space of an ex had never shown her himself.

'This feels like the real thing!' she yelled above the noise of the engine. He'd forgotten to reduce the volume on the surround-sound speaker system, and his ears were paying for it.

'Because it's tens of thousands of euros worth of equipment, designed specifically for racing drivers!' he yelled back. 'Something tells me we're gonna be getting a flight back to Wyoming after Sao Paolo and getting your own sorted.'

'I think so!' she grinned.

He let her play around on it for the next half-hour, before deciding he should probably show her the room she'd be staying in. Their guest rooms were all immaculately set up, each of them decorated with all-white furniture and neutral beige accents. The whole house was the polar opposite to the De Luca family hotels, which featured bold colours, patterned wallpapers and luxurious velvet textures. The only colourful thing in this house was the neon lighting in the shrine to Marco's racing career.

'They sort of all look the same, but I thought you'd like this one.' He led her to one with a view of the ocean, his personal favourite and the room directly next to his. It was a big house, and he didn't like the idea of her being on the other side of it at night.

'It's beautiful. Did you have an interior designer?' She stepped further into the room, her suitcases already in there thanks to housekeeping. He had noticed she didn't usually unpack her things, but there was a walk-in wardrobe right there and something told him Savannah didn't often get the chance to utilise one of those.

'No, that was all my mum. She did the entire house. She's spent years curating every room, finding the perfect pieces that suit a specific style. Driving Dad insane in the process.' He laughed. 'She'd be glad to know it's appreciated, because we sure as hell don't care. The poor woman nearly had a fit when she walked into my all-black gaming room, filled to the brim with technology. She said it was like a dungeon.'

'Well, I can see where she's coming from. But I think I want my own set-up to look like yours. It helps draw you in to the simulation, shuts out all the noise.'

'Sooo . . . You do want my help?' He nudged her arm, hoping to score an invitation.

'Yes. Fine.' She rolled her eyes playfully, looking sort of pleased that he was coming with her. 'You can come to Wyoming. But you can't ride Mocha, and you'll have to help out around the ranch, and with dinner. Even guests have to get stuck in. It's the Hart family rule. Plus, cleaning out the stables and fixing up the stall means getting your hands dirty. Literally.'

'Any other rules I should know about?' His lip quirked with amusement.

'Laugh at my dad's jokes, no matter how bad they are.'

'Right. I can do that,' he nodded.

'Your family seem like a strict, rule-following type of family.'

'Well, yes and no. No embarrassing the family name in public, so my yacht drama wasn't well received, but as far as they're concerned, you and I have made up for that. We all spend time together as a family once every month to two months, even if it means everyone else must travel for my benefit. Uh, no women were ever allowed in this house growing up and I am still not allowed to bring them back here even as a grown adult.'

'Do they know I'm here?' Savannah shot up from her spot on the bed and smoothed out the sheets, looking around like someone was watching.

'Yes, they do,' he laughed, mocking her. 'You're not just a random woman, Savannah. They think you're my fully-fledged girlfriend, potential wife-to-be, and even if you weren't, you're my teammate and it's different.'

'Speaking of the contract . . .' she muttered.

'It still stands if you want it to, Cowgirl.' He shrugged, not minding in the slightest if they kept up the charade. It benefitted him in the sense that he could keep her close, but it also helped her out. 'You shouldn't have to deal with the media onslaught of a fake break-up in public as well as going through a real one behind closed doors. Besides, we don't really want to be labelled as a short-lived, whirlwind romance, do we? It only adds fuel to the fire for those who bashed you for dating your teammate in your rookie season.'

'That's a valid point. Do you mind?' She looked up at him through big brown eyes, silently pleading and tugging on his heartstrings. 'I know you're probably itching to get yourself back out into the dating world.'

'Not at all. You've got me for as long as you need me.' He offered her a small smile, grateful he was allowed to keep playing one of his favourite roles.

'Thanks Mars,' she sighed softly. 'But still, I hope your parents don't come home early.'

'They won't. I know their schedule like the back of my hand, we have a family calendar, and we all check it every morning for updates. It's how we all stay in the loop when we don't have time to talk. Like I know Rafael isn't working today because he's taking his oldest to a hospital appointment for his asthma. And Mum and Dad are taking his other kids out for a picnic.'

'And they know you're in their house with a *girl*,' she teased.

'It's my house, too. I pay my way even though I have my own place.'

'Well, I would hope so with the millions you earn.'

'I may earn millions, but I don't *have* millions. I donate most of it, as do my parents. We have everything we need and more, no need for the money to just sit there.' He never talked about money with anyone, nor did he boast about giving it all away. But he wanted Savannah to know the real him and respect the way he handled his finances, not wrongfully judge him. Frankly, the amount of money he earned made him feel nauseous.

'I like that. I wish my parents would take mine. They think I should keep it all, but despite seeing my contract with their own eyes and knowing the salary I was offered, I don't think they can quite comprehend how big the number is. I don't like to see them struggle, but they're so stubborn. They think it's wrong to take money from their kid, but if I can't take care of people, what's the point in having it at all?'

'How is it that we can be from two opposite worlds and yet we're almost the same person?'

'I'm just you but in cowboy boots,' she grinned at him.

'Hey, I'll have my own pair in a couple of weeks!' He was genuinely excited for it, to live the stereotypical cowboy life for a week or two. It was worlds away from what he was used to, and more importantly, it was Savannah's world.

'I guess I should incorporate that into your grand tour of Sheridan, Wyoming.'

'Oh, *grand* tour?' He raised an eyebrow.

'That was pure sarcasm, but if you want to be excited then I will try my best not to crush your dreams. Just . . . don't expect much. The ranch is old, it needs work, and my family are under a lot of pressure. They won't like us helping, but I need you to help me fight them on it. They're very proud people, and they'll be embarrassed.'

'Got it. I'll throw myself in at the deep end, force my love on them.'

'Like you did with Esme?' she sniggered. 'Sorry, that was really mean.'

He pretended to gasp and clutched his chest. 'You're cruel, Cowgirl.'

'She confessed it wasn't one-sided,' Savannah reassured. 'You just weren't the one.'

'Never am,' he sighed.

'Likewise, apparently.' She gave a sad smile. 'We've just got to have some patience.'

As Savannah started unpacking her suitcase and hanging clothes in the walk-in closet, Marco let his mind race with thoughts of her living under his roof, wearing his shirts and sharing his pancakes every morning. Being *his*. But she was in no position to entertain his fantasies right now, which meant that she just couldn't be right for him either. So, while he would be patient in his journey to finding his soulmate, he would never quite understand why the universe kept sending him women who were perfect for him but would never feel the same way.

17

Monaco was beautiful. Savi had complained about waking up at the crack of dawn to exercise on her first morning there, and then never again. By the end of her visit, she had been the one waking Marco up even earlier, begging to run further each day.

Their feet pounded the pavement day after day for an hour plus, all the hurt over Jesse fading with every step. Then they'd come home and have their protein pancakes and take it in turns on the racing sim for a few hours. Post-lunch was time for tennis which, it turned out, Savi was great at. Better than Marco, who'd had thousands spent on a coach. Dinner was always at a fancy restaurant, Marco's treat despite Savi's insistence, and they spent every evening in the casino or at a bar. They'd seen botanical gardens, museums, cathedrals, and soaked in every ounce of history Monaco had to offer.

Savi had fallen in love. With the country, the house, the port, the boats. All of it. It was so different from what she knew, and she'd never give up the ranch life forever, but she was incredibly grateful to have had a taste of the high life. Of course, with her position on a team like Revolution Racing, she could have this all the time if she wanted it. But home was home, and it was where her heart belonged.

She especially wished she was at home now, not in the

middle of a pre-quali autograph session with thousands of fans, most of them solely focused on her and Marco and demanding every detail. People were always invasive during these sessions, but security were edging closer and closer with every interaction. The team had insisted Savi and Marco sit on the end of each table, so they were next to each other, but it was pulling attention away from their teammates and Savi felt weird about it. This was their moment too.

The camera crew were acting like they weren't there, but at least Bea was getting shots of the others, too. In fact, the head photographer for the IEC and a close friend of the team had made it her personal mission to draw the focus *away* from the new couple, for the sake of their sanity. Still, Miko and Kodie were clearly irritated that the media were blatantly ignoring them. Savi could feel the fury radiating from her teammates, and she knew there was not a damn thing she could do to make it up to them. She didn't ask for this. She would just have to do damage control, take every opportunity she could to bring the attention back to them.

'People are so rude,' Kodie muttered. 'Like, hello, we're sat right here.'

'I'm sorry, Kodie. I don't like this either.' Savi spared a quick glance at her teammate, noticing her clenched jaw and harsh scowl and trying not to take it personally. She knew her friends were annoyed at the situation, not necessarily at her.

They may have thought Savi was a winner; she was bound to get sponsorship deals and brand deals because of the fanfare surrounding her relationship with a fellow driver, it was the dream scenario for a rookie, but she wished she could switch it off and on. She hadn't been thinking about any of that when she agreed to this, she'd just been thinking about the photos and what they could do to her reputation.

They signed a seemingly endless collection of autograph cards, model cars, flags, t-shirts and caps, so many fans wearing Revolution Racing's signature red, black and white zebra print merchandise. It filled Savi's heart with joy and was one of her favourite things about the job. To know that these people were here for the same reason as her; motorsport was everything to them. Life in Sheridan was quiet, mundane. This was nothing like that.

She was a key part of something important for the first time in her life, and she couldn't wait to go on Faith, Lucie, Bea and Esme's podcast later in the year and share her journey with millions of young girls. *Girls Off Track* had blown up and its success had played a pivotal role in Jasper hiring an all-female team. She might not have made it this far had they not done the work. Sure, there were smaller manufacturers with all-female teams in other race championships, but they were the only team at the top level. That was why this was so significant. They were setting the standard, showing up the multitude of teams who didn't give female drivers a second thought.

Signing the last red baseball cap with a black marker pen, Savi popped the lid back on and waved goodbye to the dwindling number of fans who hadn't quite made it to the autograph table. They had an hour set aside on qualifying day and another hour on race day for this, but there were always some left at the back of the queue who they just didn't have time to see. Revolution ran on a tight schedule with very little wiggle room but that was how Savi liked it. She liked to be busy, it helped kick her into gear and put her in the zone. Forget about the millions of questions directed at her love life.

'On to the media building next please, everyone. The room is jam-packed with journalists and we're on a tight schedule!' Jasper rallied behind them, herding the team out of the garage and across the paddock.

'You okay?' Marco threw an arm around her.

'Stressed,' she sighed, traipsing behind the team.

'Anxious?' He pushed for more.

'No, it's not that kind of stress. I just know they're going to bombard us in here, too.'

'It's just part of it, unfortunately. The press liaison will direct the questions the best they can, try to keep it to a minimum. But there will be a few.'

'Kodie and Miko aren't happy.'

'I know. They'll get their time to shine in there, don't worry. Not every journalist will want details of our relationship, only some. And it is their job to ask about that, too, so try not to get too upset about it when they do. If your teammates kick off in the aftermath, Jasper will tell them the same thing,' he reassured her.

'Thanks, Monaco,' she smiled.

'No worries. Sit on the opposite side to me, okay? It will make a statement to the media that we're not here to talk about us.'

They walked into a buzz of excitement and the flashes

of cameras, more than seventy journalists all watching them take their seats, their chairs lined up in row after row. The higher-ups from the IEC and Revolution Racing stood at the back as usual, monitoring their employees.

Savi knew of press conferences that had gone awry in the past: drivers swearing, making inappropriate comments, arguing with one another and landing themselves and their teams in trouble. Abandoning all their media training because the pressure got to them. Revolution's drivers consistently oozed professionalism, and Savi could only hope the girls would follow suit.

'First question, please,' a voice called out.

Journalist number one stood from their seat and took the microphone, giving the drivers a little wave. Most of them responded, aside from Julien who leaned back in his seat looking moody as ever. That had always been his thing. 'I have a question for Kodie. There has been talk of your father starting a NASCAR team. Would you ever cross over to a different championship?'

Kodie laughed sarcastically, but with a genuine smile on her face so she didn't come across as harsh. 'Not a chance. I know I haven't been in the IEC for long, but I can't imagine ever going anywhere else now. My father can do what he likes, but I'd rather have him involved with the team who gave his daughter a chance. So, who knows, maybe we can convince him to join Revolution Racing in the future.'

'Julien,' another journalist took the mic. 'Will your oldest daughter be going into motorsport? She's shown a lot of interest in the sport, coming to plenty of races over the past few seasons to support her dad. Maybe it's a potential career path for her?'

Julien shook his head. 'Jasmine is very set on medical school in the US. Soon she won't have time to come and see me race, but even if she wanted to go into it, I don't think I want my baby girl in a car that drives that fast.'

'You stick to the speed limits at home?' the journalist grinned.

'Always. Even on the empty roads around the island of Oahu, speed limits are there for a reason. I'd never drive fast with my family in the car, no matter how good I am. The safety precautions just aren't there on the open road.'

'Well said, sir.' The journalist nodded gratefully, handing the microphone back. Jasper looked pleased as punch in the audience. Road safety had been a big thing for the team last season, with Julien participating in an ad campaign in support of stricter speed limits in rural areas after he'd had a minor accident near his home in Malmedy while racing Marco.

'Marco, what made you decide to settle down so suddenly with a fellow teammate and a rookie, no less? You were seen with several women in the weeks leading up to you and Savi going public, how do we know this is real?' a female journalist asked, angering Savi.

Shouldn't a woman know better than to make a comment like that? So what if Savi was a rookie? What difference did it make to how he felt about her? She was getting mad like their relationship was real, but she couldn't stop herself. It was the principle.

'I'm not sure what Savannah being new to the

championship has to do with anything,' Marco frowned. 'It took us a little while to figure it out, but when we did, we agreed we might as well go all in. We just decided to stop messing around and face our feelings.'

Savi couldn't wipe the smug smile off her face. He may be lying to the entire room, but she still felt proud to be associated with someone who was willing to stand up for her. She and the girls had hit the jackpot having such supportive teammates and bosses, and any threats of sexism were quickly shut down. It helped being so closely associated with a company like *Girls Off Track* which was focused on advocating for women in motorsport.

'Savi, do you worry about what people will think of you for dating your teammate during your first season?' The journalist went straight in for the kill.

Savi may be feeling shaky on the inside, but she wasn't going to let it show. 'No, I don't worry about the close-minded opinions of others. I'm here to do my job and to bring the championship title home for my team. Who I date is totally irrelevant and doesn't change anything. Marco and I are both professionals and racing comes first.'

'Hell yes,' Jasper exclaimed enthusiastically from the far wall, quickly reverting to team principal mode when heads turned to look at him, his head ducking down in embarrassment. 'Sorry, continue.'

'But won't there be a time when your relationship has to come first? Like when you get married or have children?' That one stung. What was this woman's problem? Had a racing driver personally rejected her or something?

'Faith and Julien worked together, as do Brett and Lucie.

Both couples are going strong and the only impact their relationships have had on their work has been positive. I'm not sure that our fans are going to take too kindly to what you might be implying here, and I'm also not sure that the choices I may or may not make in the future need to be addressed publicly. I respect that you are here to do your job, but I would very much like it if the questions could be focused on my job, and the job of my teammates rather than gossip surrounding our relationships. If you do want to focus on relationships, why not discuss the team as a whole and how the mutual respect we all have for one another has allowed us to create some fantastic content and win races?' Savi crossed her arms when she was done, pleased that she'd shut her up but dreading the reaction from her bosses. Until she looked over at them and saw every single person lining that back wall had smirks or smiles on their faces. *Especially* Jasper.

'Nicely said, Savi,' Brett piped up. 'We're basically all married to each other, at this point. It's a bit cultish, but we wouldn't have it any other way, would we, guys?'

'No,' Miko smiled. 'We're all incredibly proud to be a team.'

The journalist sat down silently, looking mighty ashamed of herself. As she should.

Savi stared at her hands for the rest of the session, answering any questions aimed her way with as few words as possible. She knew she was going to walk out of this room to tension that she didn't want. Kodie and Miko had already let her know they weren't happy about having the spotlight taken off them in their rookie season, but now this? She knew it wasn't her fault, but it didn't stop the guilt clawing at her. Spiking her anxiety and threatening to cause a scene.

With Brett answering the final question, they traipsed out of the conference room. There was an air of defeat lingering behind them and as Savi watched Kodie and Miko enter the trailer, she stopped in her tracks. 'Woah, Cowgirl!' Marco knocked into her. 'Don't just stop walking like that! Are you okay?' He kept a tight grip on her to keep her upright.

'Fine. Just don't want to go in there.' She gestured to where the door was slamming shut behind them. 'But I need to get my things.'

'Walk in there, head held high, get your team colours on and come back out here ready to put in one hell of a stint. You shine in quali, Savannah. They know it, I know it and Jasper knows it. Hell, the whole motorsport industry knows it by now.'

'Okay.' She let out a shaky breath.

'They can be bitter all they want, but their attitude doesn't diminish your talent.'

'Thanks, Mars.' She had noticed she only used the nickname everyone else used for him when he was being particularly sweet. 'I'll see you in the garage.'

'Not a chance.' He followed her right up to the trailer door, leaning against the side of the structure with his arms crossed. 'I'll wait outside. And if you would feel more comfortable moving into our trailer for the rest of the race weekend, then I'll make that happen.'

She smiled appreciatively, reluctantly climbing the stairs

and opening the door to reveal Miko making a coffee and Kodie sitting on the sofa with headphones on. 'Hi, girls.'

'Hey, Sav,' Miko smiled back at her. 'Coffee?'

'No thanks, Meeks.' She set about gathering her things together: sunglasses, headphones, gloves. All the while, Kodie remained silent. Music blasting from her headphones, competing with the noise of the coffee machine. Savi wanted out.

'You know,' Kodie ripped her headphones off, 'you could have waited. You didn't have to make it public so soon, Savi. You didn't have to kiss in front of the cameras, let the whole world know about it.'

'Ko—'

'I'm not finished,' she interrupted, standing from the sofa and throwing her headphones into the nest of cushions. 'I know you didn't ask for the attention you're getting, but you knew you were gonna get it. And now the only thing anyone cares about is you and Marco and your perfect little love story. I'm happy for you, I am, but I just wish you'd waited until the end of our first season as a team. You made a choice, and you didn't take Miko and me into consideration.'

'I'm sorry, Kodie. I'm sorry to both of you, I really am.'

'I know you are and I'm proud to call you my teammate and to be on this journey with you, but I'm still angry and I still feel let down. It's unfair that you get so much attention just because you're dating De Luca, and it's unfair that you didn't at least have a conversation with us about it. You didn't warn us.'

'I should have talked to you about it, let you know we

were planning to go public. Asked how you felt about it. But truthfully, we didn't really plan it. We never talked about the implications, we just got caught up in the moment and suddenly stopped hiding it.' Savi felt sick to her stomach for lying, but it wasn't like she could tell them the truth so she might as well try to salvage her friendship with Kodie.

'Yeah, you should've.' She grabbed her headphones and stormed out of the trailer, leaving her racing suit still hanging in the closet.

Miko focused on her latte, smirking to herself. 'You two are as fiery as each other, but I really respect the way you owned up to your misplaced judgement just now.'

'My relationship with you two as my teammates is just as important as the one I share with Marco, and I hate to think that this is all having a negative impact on your careers. You're both equally as talented as I am, both deserving of your places on this team. I don't want to overshadow you, and I wish I could make it all stop.'

'I know, Savi. And Kodie knows it, too. She's just been having a hard time adjusting to the pressure of this championship and this is adding to her stress, but she shouldn't have taken it out on you. It is what it is, and the press will do as the press does. Just live your life, enjoy Marco.' She raised an eyebrow suggestively and Savi blushed. 'But, if you want to keep sticking up for us like you did in there then I'm sure it would go a long way towards making Kodie feel better about the whole thing.'

'She isn't the only one pissed off about it. I am, too. It's okay in small doses, more so when it's fans making a fuss, but bombarding us during media sessions is too far.'

'But you can get all hot and heavy with a super sexy Italian racing driver, so it's not all bad really, is it?' Miko grinned. 'I'll leave you to get dressed. See you in quali.'

Savi hurried to step into her suit and get her shoes on, making a mental note of everything she'd left in her cubby in the garage. Her helmet was still in there. She had to admit she was feeling a lot better about the whole thing, but now she was worrying that Jesse might have seen the livestream and noticed how defensive Marco was of her. Of them. He spoke as though this was real and she was his. Once again, treating her in a manner Jesse never had.

'You ready, Cowgirl?' Marco tapped on the window.

'I'm coming!' she called out.

'About time. You realise we have to be in the garage, like, now.' He was already walking before she jumped off the bottom step.

'Well, then. It's just as well we are literally feet away from it.' Savi ran ahead, racing him inside. 'Get a move on, Monaco, we've got grid positions to claim!'

18

Something felt wrong. The car wasn't reacting the way it should, and Savi was burning up as her anxiety increased. It was race day. Qualifying had been and gone and both Revolution teams had smashed it, earning first and third starting positions. But today, everything seemed to be going wrong, and they were less than an hour into the six-hour race. Savi was up first, and she'd locked up twice already, both times with her engineer on the other end of the radio, demanding to know what was going on.

She was convinced it wasn't her doing. It had to be the car. Savi could admit she was a little distracted thanks to a stream of angry, possessive texts from Jesse before the race, but she always left her personal life back in the garage. Always. It was one thing she was immensely proud of: her innate ability to shut the rest of the world out the second she shut the door.

'Jasper, it doesn't feel right. I know this car, and it's not behaving like it did yesterday.'

'Savi,' her boss came over the radio, 'I need you to be specific. What's happening?'

'It's the steering. You saw me lock up, right? I feel like I'm fighting the car.'

'Just keep going.' Her engineer's voice joined the conversation once again, this time a little less accusatory. Maybe he'd realised it really wasn't the driver at fault. 'We'll bring you into the pits and give it a once-over.'

'No, I'm telling you guys,' she shouted. 'Something's wrong. It doesn't feel safe.'

'Savi, it's fine. I can see the problem on my screen, it's an easy fix. You've got half a lap to go and then we can take a look.'

'No, come on!' She didn't *want* to stop the car and let the team down, drop out of the race. Not after her conversation with Kodie. But this wasn't normal.

'Savi, we believe it's safe to keep driving.' Jasper's voice was stern, snapping her out of her defiance. If they weren't going to let her stop, then she was desperate to just make it back.

She kept pushing, multiple cars up ahead of her and the race win slipping further from her grasp with every turn of the track. But she didn't slow down, the pit lane so painfully close. And then, in the blink of an eye, the race was over. Savi spun out on a corner, tyres screeching mere centimetres away from her opponents, and her car hit the tyre wall.

It ricocheted, and the marshals jumped out of the way as debris flew up in the air, their orange hi-vis jackets the only thing providing comfort as that moment of fear overpowered everything else. The front wing was gone, her front left tyre was rolling away from her into the gravel, and her ears were ringing as her brain processed what the hell had just happened. But as Savi grounded herself, taking a moment to adjust to reality, she realised she was fine. A concussion was likely, and she might not be one hundred per cent okay mentally after such a shunt, but the car? It was destroyed. The race was done.

She could hear it now, the uproar from the commentators as they debated what was wrong and analysed her every move on the replays. They could be so brutal at times, she wished she could have a flashing neon sign above the car that read 'Not my fault!'. Why did the blame so often fall on the one operating the car, and never on the car itself? Every vehicle was full of technology, but race cars were on a whole other level. Everyone knew technology failed.

The team were going to be mad, too, but not as mad as her. Her engineer should have listened to her intuition, as should Jasper. Most drivers wouldn't stand up for themselves against their bosses, but Savi wasn't most drivers. She knew she put her life at risk every time she got in that car, but she would also do whatever it took to win. Except risk the lives of every other driver around her, and that was what she had just been asked to do.

She wasn't having it. And if Jasper wanted to argue with her and berate her for calling him out, she would leave. It was her dealbreaker. A lack of concern for safety had almost killed her brother, and now he was in a wheelchair for the rest of his life. She would not reach the same fate, not if she could help it.

The marshals leapt into action, and she put her thumb up, indicating she was okay. Stepping out of the car, all she could offer the crowd was a wave. It was followed by a round of cheers and applause; fans always feared the worst. How could they not when a car crashed right in front of them at two hundred miles per hour? Most seasoned race-attendees had witnessed far worse than this and she genuinely wondered how they could keep showing up race after race, season after season, knowing a driver could lose their life right in front of them. It was probably the same reason the drivers were in the car in the first place: passion.

Savi trudged her way over to the medical car, letting them check her over. Her wrist was sore, but it was nothing she couldn't handle. She had spent years falling off horses on the ranch while she was trying to wrangle the rescues. Of course, she wasn't allowed to do that now she'd signed with Revolution Racing. She only saddled up Mocha, Java and maybe Cappuccino if he was having a good day. It wasn't worth the risk of injury.

'You're all set. You can go back to your team.' The medic sent her on her way.

Sitting in the back of the medical car, waiting to be taken back to the paddock, she watched her beloved race car get strapped up and lifted on to the back of the recovery truck. It was one of the worst feelings in the world, knowing she had been behind the wheel when the fate of the race was decided. At least Brett was still in it and there were no signs of anything being wrong with the guys' car. Not yet, anyway.

What she wanted to do was hide out in the trailer and lock the door behind her, but that wasn't what they did. Revolution Racing was one big team, consisting of both cars, and that meant until Marco or Julien took the second car across the finish, she would stay in that garage and offer her support. No matter how downtrodden she was, or how anxious she felt about her teammates' feelings towards her.

The medical car drove through the paddock at a painfully slow pace, passing lingering fans who were exploring the fan zones and all-access areas instead of sitting in the grandstands. They all stared, trying to get a glimpse through the tinted back windows. 'Can you park by the team trailers, please? I'd like to get into the garage without being spotted.'

'Of course,' the medic answered, swerving the car round the guys' trailer and getting her as close to the garage entrance as possible. 'Take care, Miss Hart.'

'Thanks for rescuing me.' Savi always liked being nice to the circuit staff and treating them as equals, especially the medics and track marshals.

She had been watching motorsport on television her whole childhood, and she hated seeing the way some drivers acted when they got out of the car. It was widely known in the motorsport world that drivers should be given space when they crashed, because they were so in the zone that they could act out. She'd witnessed a few punches. Yes, it was devastating. Yes, for some there were higher stakes than others. But the throwing of helmets and blatant disrespect towards people who were just there to help had never sat right with her, and she had vowed to never be that person.

'What the fuck happened out there?' Kodie pounced on her as soon as she walked into the garage, refusing to give her any personal space. 'You didn't even make it an hour!'

'Excuse me?' Savi snapped. 'Weren't you listening to the team radio? I very clearly said there was something wrong with the steering.'

'You could have driven more carefully, Savi.' She rolled her eyes.

'Kodie,' Miko followed along behind them with a disappointed frown, 'Savi is a fantastic driver, she was obviously being careful but if there was something wrong with the car then there was always going to be potential that something like this could happen. Just admit this is personal and you're being unfair.'

'Thanks, Meeks. I'm sorry, Kodie, but you're acting like I *wanted* us to lose out on the race. Why would I want that when it directly impacts me, too? We're a team, and I know you're upset with me as it is, but I would never be selfish when I'm behind the wheel of our car.'

'Ladies!' Jasper appeared, looking as stressed as Savi felt. 'Can I ask that you take this disagreement into your trailer or simply let it be.'

'Oh, I'm done here.' Kodie didn't quite have the audacity to snap at their boss, but she wasn't exactly friendly. 'I will be back at the hotel if anyone needs me.'

'Savi, can we have a quick chat?' Jasper pulled her into a room at the back of the garage, the roar of engines drowning them out and providing them with a privacy that was hard to find in this environment. 'Are you okay?'

'Bit bruised, but it's not a big deal,' she shrugged.

'It is.' Jasper's brow creased. 'I would like to hold my hands up and apologise to you. We should have asked you to stop the car as soon as you realised there might be a problem. I'm sorry that we put your safety at risk like that, I can assure you it will not happen again.'

She accepted the brisk hug he offered, and they walked

out together, all eyes on them. The entire team would know by now that they had collectively made the wrong call. The thing was, Jasper couldn't possibly promise something like that wouldn't happen again. It was the nature of the sport; even those with as much knowledge and experience as Jasper and the engineers were not immune to human error and misguided decisions.

She was waiting for Brett's pit stop for fuel when an arm slunk around her waist. 'Good to see you alive, Cowgirl,' Marco whispered into her hair.

'Is there a reason you're touching me, right now?' She sighed, but leaned back into him, nonetheless. 'You are providing some comfort, however. So don't go.'

'I saw the camera crew making their way down the pits and I would be a very bad fake boyfriend if I didn't come and check on you after your crash. That being said, I was also worried as a friend, and this is making me feel better.'

Just like he'd said, the cameraman walked in and immediately aimed the lens their way. For the first time, this interaction wasn't entirely fake. Not like their fake kisses and hand holds. She had a feeling Marco would still be standing behind her like this even if the cameras weren't hanging around, but he was using them as an excuse. She didn't mind. After surrendering the race finish and being yelled at by Kodie, she'd take all the comfort she could get.

'Jasper insisted I keep driving.' She crossed her arms over her chest, still angry and ignoring Marco's hands splayed across her waist and abdomen. 'I'm pissed.'

'I heard it on the team radio. We all did, and we all agree it was the wrong call.' He placed a gentle kiss on her head and then the cameras left them alone, but Marco made no effort to move. She had to admit the crash had rattled her, so she wasn't in a rush to send him on his way.

'He also personally apologised within seconds of seeing me get out of the medical car. So I won't be pissed for long. He was wrong and he knows it and I forgive him; I just need time to get over it. Move past my disappointment.'

'Understandable. I heard Kodie going off at you.'

'Yeah, well. Kodie needs to get over herself. I understand why she's upset, but I have explained my side of things. If she wants to hold it against me, that's on her.'

'Every team goes through teething issues, Savannah. The guys and I don't always get along, despite being friends and teammates for most of our careers. There will be disagreements and arguments, and you'll make mistakes, but that's just part of it. You're still learning about each other. You guys gel really well, and you were all chosen to join the Revolution Racing family partly because of your individual abilities to operate as a team player. Kodie will get over her personal vendetta, once she gets a big brand deal or hits a milestone on social media. You and I both know you deserve all the fanfare you're getting, with or without me being attached to it.'

'You give good advice, Monaco. Anyone ever told you that?' She uncrossed her arms, resting her hands on his. It felt a little strange, like the lines were blurring between real and fake.

'Quite often, actually. You on the other hand, do not,' he chuckled.

'Are you ever going to stop roasting me for that?' She

rolled her eyes but stayed put. 'I didn't know my advice was going to manifest into you embarrassing yourself.'

'At least I can laugh about it now that my world does not revolve around Esme Keelan.'

'Were you in love with her?' Savi asked.

'No,' he breathed out a laugh. 'I just thought I could be.'

'Well as much as I love Esme, I believe there's someone else out there who is a better fit for you.'

'But, Cowgirl,' he murmured, his presence still invading her senses despite the camera being long gone, 'sometimes we settle because we don't have the courage to explore what else the world might have in store for us.'

19

Savi had stayed glued to the screens for the last hour of the race, watching Marco do his thing. He was trying to climb back up to a podium position after they'd had a rain shower and he'd spun out during the fifth hour of the race. He'd fought the team when they'd tried to switch him out with Brett, claiming it was only fair that they give him a chance to redeem himself and undo the error that threatened to wipe the progress his teammates had made during their stints.

It had paid off. Big time. He had overtaken Talos Sport, followed by Eden Racing, then the second Talos car, and claimed the top spot. He'd crossed the finish to a roar of cheers, everyone in the grandstands on their feet, flags waving. Half the time in this championship, it didn't matter who won or came second and third in each class; even finishing the race was a huge feat. And the response of the crowds always reflected that. They supported every team even if they had their favourites and they queued up for autographs in front of nearly every garage.

The team were discussing celebrating their win with dinner and a few drinks, but Savi was considering bailing in favour of room service and a bottle of wine by herself. Her body was sore all over, Kodie was still being standoffish, and she was tired. Socialising with a large group of people seemed like too much to ask of her tonight, even if Brett had been trying his utmost to cheer her up since he'd found her sat at the back of the garage alone during Marco's stint.

Marco pulled her to one side. 'You don't want to go to dinner tonight, do you?' he asked, his voice low. He must have noticed how quiet she was, even if she'd tried to put on an act.

'Honestly? No. I can't think of anything worse. I'm going to head back to the hotel, leave you guys to enjoy your evening. I don't want to bring the mood down.'

'I'm coming with you. We'll make a night of it, order everything off the room service menu we fancy, have some drinks, watch a film and play cards. I don't want you being alone and miserable, but I understand why you don't want to hang out with everybody.'

'You should be with your team, Mars.' She gave him a look.

'You're part of my team. Besides, if you're feeling battered and bruised now you're only going to feel worse over the next few hours. What if you can't move around? I can be your slave for the night.'

'Okay, thank you,' she smiled, sort of looking forward to his company. They'd spent a fair amount of time together outside of work now, and there was never a dull moment.

'But first, we've got to get the podium out of the way. We've got about twenty minutes while they do the scrutinising, then it's go-time.'

'Why is Jasper making us all go up? We didn't finish the race.'

'Because we, as a team, just won our one hundredth race. That's monumental, we all need to be on that podium. We're getting our own, Savannah. After the teams in second and third have celebrated.'

'Okay, I will admit, that's pretty cool.'

'Exactly,' he grinned.

Then she saw her, walking through the paddock with guilt etched across her features, and Savi's world shattered. 'Marco,' she whispered shakily.

'What?' he asked, then his eyes followed her gaze. 'Why is she here?'

Savi watched Sapphire get closer, flanked by one of the team's security guards. She knew this was bad. If it was enough to make Sapphire fly halfway across the world, it had to be something Savi didn't want to hear.

'Savi . . .' Sapphire muttered as she reached her. 'Is there somewhere we can talk?'

She looked around the paddock, full to the brim with drivers, caterers and team personnel. Nowhere was private, nowhere was safe. 'Um, I don't –'

'My trailer,' Marco interrupted. 'Come on, the guys have cleared out already.'

They let the security guard go, leading Sapphire up the steps of the motorhome. Savi felt like she was going to throw up, and barely a word had left the woman's mouth.

Marco gestured for her to sit down and fetched her a glass of water, setting it down on the coffee table. He was being so polite, so civil, but Savi's gut was telling her he was going to regret it any moment. Sapphire had guilt etched all over her face.

'What's going on, Sapph?'

'I'm sorry, Savi. I'm so sorry . . .' Sapphire burst into tears. Her face was blotchy, her breathing harsh and her forehead drenched with sweat. 'The baby. It's his.'

Savi felt like the world was closing in on her, and she could've sworn she could see stars. What did she mean, the baby was his? How could her baby be his? She was months away from giving birth, which would mean . . . No way. It couldn't be. He couldn't have. *She* couldn't have.

'Jesse is going to be a dad?' she choked out; for some reason that hurt more than the fact he had cheated. He was going to have the future she had wanted with him, with someone else. No wonder he hadn't wanted to build anything with her.

'Jesse cheated on Savannah?' Marco added, his tone dripping with sheer disgust.

'With me, yes. But he lied to me too, he told me you were over. Then next thing I know, you're showing up at his gig and he's telling me that you're back together. It's only now that I've put the pieces together that I realise you were never on a break in the first place.'

'No, we were together right up until I left Los Angeles a few weeks ago.'

'Yeah, about that . . . Savi, it's not just me that he cheated with. And with me it was just the once, but I have watched him with so many women since me. I dread to think how many he was with before then. And every time he would tell me you had left him, but then I would hear him on the phone with you, or you would come out to Tennessee, and I just knew every word out of his mouth was a lie. It had been since the start. I don't know how far back this goes, Savi...'

'But it could be four years...' Savi choked out, Marco's hand finding her knee.

'It could be. I've scoured my text messages and emails, tried to work it out. But I don't have all the details, so I can't be sure. I just needed to tell you in person, so you could throw all the questions you have at me. Yell at me, scream at me.'

'I'm not going to do any of that,' Savi sighed, burying her head in her hands. This hurt more than the break-up itself. 'Is he taking care of you?'

She didn't mean emotionally; she wanted to know if he had put things in place financially that meant Sapphire didn't have to worry about how she was going to afford to raise her baby. He had all the money in the world, and this was his child. It was the least he could do.

'No,' she sobbed. 'Savi, he doesn't want anything to do with us. I understand not wanting to be with me, I mean, I don't want to be with him either. No offence, but he's a real asshole. I don't know how you put up with him for so long. But for him to wipe his hands of his own child, refuse to be involved?'

Savi scoffed. 'Can't you demand a DNA test?'

'What's the point?' Sapphire laughed. 'It won't change anything. My baby is going to grow up without a dad, and he won't do a test anyway because it gives me too much power. I could go to the press and ruin his career.'

'He's pathetic. It's no wonder he didn't give a fuck if I was all over his girlfriend or not. He was too busy getting into bed with anyone who threw themselves at him,' Marco said, finally making a worthwhile contribution to the conversation.

'Does he know you planned on telling me? *Did* you always plan on telling me?' Savi asked her, reaching out to hold her hand. Maybe Sapphire's morals had been a little off for sleeping with him in the first place, but at least she hadn't knowingly betrayed someone. And now she was scared and alone and Savi couldn't help but want to protect her.

She was beginning to realise just how manipulative Jesse really was, and everything he had over her. He could take her down just as easily as she could ruin him, too. The difference was, he deserved it and all the hell that would rain down on him.

'I text him this morning. But he knows you won't do anything.' Now she knew why he hadn't contacted her all day; the guilt was probably eating him alive. That was if he was even capable of holding remorse.

'Well . . . what if I did? I could go to the press. I could tell the world what he's done, my voice is credible. What reason would I have to lie?'

'Savannah,' Marco growled, 'the photos.'

'What if he's done this before, Mars? What if your baby,' she gestured to Sapphire, 'isn't the only innocent child he's neglecting? How many other lives has he ruined, who else has he lied to? Who else *will* he lie to? I can't sit back and let him get away with it, thinking he can keep doing whatever he wants without facing some sort of consequence.'

'Okay, but you can't just expose Sapphire's personal situation to the world.'

'Oh, she can,' Sapphire nodded enthusiastically. 'You have my permission. It will be better coming from you and not me; if it comes directly from me, people will just assume I want his money. And I'll be honest, I don't want a cent from him. I just want a happy, healthy baby.'

'I can't believe who he's turned out to be,' Savi laughed in disbelief. 'How can someone be so self-absorbed that they're willing to lead a double life and hold no remorse? Was he ever going to tell me?'

'Probably not. People like him live for themselves and they have no regard for who they hurt in the process. You're both better off without him, and so is that baby,' Marco said.

'I'm sorry again, Savi. If I had known, I would have come to you immediately. He's just so good at manipulating, he's mastered it.'

'Even more reason to expose him for who he truly is.'

'Maybe it's partially my fault for being so naïve.'

'Not in a million years,' Savi shook her head. 'Are you going to be okay, Sapph? Is there anything I can do to help you?'

'To help *me*?' she asked. 'You don't need to help me, Sav. I should be helping you.'

'I just want to know that when you walk out of here, you're going to be okay. That you can raise your baby with everything you'll both need, and you have a support system.'

'I'll be fine,' Sapphire smiled sadly. 'Thank you so much.'

'If you need anything, I am a text or a call away. If you're ever struggling with this, I want you to tell me. I want to help you so please, utilise me. I'm sorry he's done this to you. To us. We both deserve better.'

'Sav, I don't mean to interrupt . . .' Marco placed his hand on her shoulder.

'I know,' she murmured. 'Sapph, we really need to go. We've got a big team achievement to celebrate and do press for up on the podium.'

'Oh!' She jumped up. 'Of course. My timing couldn't possibly have been worse. My sister is waiting at our hotel, so I'll head off. Thank you again, Savi. For not ripping my head off, too. But for the record, if you ever speak to Jesse again, I hope you tell him what a piece of shit he is.'

And then Savi was hugging Sapphire goodbye, wishing her luck with the birth of her ex-boyfriend's baby and sinking back down on to the sofa, staring straight ahead. It felt like her entire world had just crumbled around her; all the positive affirmations she had been repeating to herself for the last few weeks a total waste of her energy.

'Savannah?' Marco crouched down next to her, resting a hand on her knee, just like he had when Jesse had walked out on her. 'What do you need?'

'I don't know, Mars . . .' She covered her mouth with her hand like she could hold it all in, stop the tears from flowing. 'All I do know is that I'm not okay.'

20

Savi was locked in the bathroom of the trailer, sobbing her heart out, letting herself feel every emotion under the sun. She was going through the five stages of grief in the space of five minutes, and all the while Marco was banging on the door. She couldn't face him. She couldn't face anyone, including her own reflection.

After telling him she wasn't okay, he had tried to comfort her the best way he knew how, holding her in his arms like every time before, but she had brushed him off, barrelling into the tiny bathroom to cry it out in peace.

'Savannah!' He smacked his fist into the door again, causing it to rattle. 'Open the damn door. You don't have to do this alone.'

'I don't want you to see me like this,' she murmured, just loud enough for him to hear her, the mirror in pieces on the floor. How was she supposed to explain this to Jasper? At this point, she might as well tell him. Her dignity was in tatters, what difference did it make?

'I've seen you in a state before, Cowgirl. It doesn't faze me. Please, let me help.'

She reached up and unlocked the door, but she didn't make an effort to open it. He would have heard the click. The door swung open like it was some sort of big emergency, and Marco rushed into the room in a panic. 'Hi,' she smiled weakly.

He smiled back and set down a glass of water next to the basin. 'I hate to go all tough love on you, but you have got to get it together. Like, *now*. We need to be on that podium in five minutes, no matter what. Both of us, Savannah. No exceptions, no excuses. That's the rule.'

'I can't, Mars,' she sobbed.

'You can, Cowgirl.' He knelt next to her, narrowly avoiding his knee landing on the glass and brushing her hair out of the way while she took deep breaths to calm herself down. 'Because you have to. Savannah, if you're not out there with us . . . it's not going to go down well. This is a huge moment for our team, don't let him ruin this.'

'I know, Marco. I know. But this is just . . . I've never known betrayal like it. How can I have missed all the signs? I was living in fucking La La Land, so adamant we were happy and in love and it turns out not only was I not even happy for the last year or two, but he hadn't been happy from day fucking one. The entire relationship was a lie. But hey, I know all about relationships built on a lie, right? That's what you and I are.' She laughed, the sarcasm bitter on her tongue as she said it. She knew that wasn't what this was, and she felt the guilt creeping up her spine the second the words left her mouth.

'Savannah, no. You and I? It's different and you know it. I know you don't trust yourself right now, you don't know what's true and what isn't, but I'm not Jesse. And you are not fragile. You're not going to break just because the man you loved lied to you, because you're not going to give him the power to destroy everything you've built. You're not going to let him win. Think about everything you've got going for you: the career of your dreams, a supportive family, a close-knit group of friends. But most important of all, you've got yourself. And as long as you're focused on rebuilding and healing and loving yourself, you're always going to come out on top.'

'Am I really that unlovable? What did I do wrong?' she sobbed.

'No sweetheart,' Marco shook his head, looking equally heartbroken. 'You're not unlovable. You're *made* from love, it's who you are and everything you stand for, and not everyone is going to know what to do with that. It's part of life, and sometimes the lessons life wants us to learn are dealt to us in the most unfair ways.'

'I don't understand why I wasn't good enough for him. I tried, I really tried. To support him, to lift him up. I rarely complained when he neglected me, I didn't hound him when he didn't talk to me for days. I took a back seat so he could chase his own dreams while I chased mine. I flew thousands of miles just to be with him and he didn't give me the same effort even once. What did all those women have that I didn't?'

'It's not that you weren't good enough for him, it's that you were too good. What he did to you says everything about the kind of person he is and has no reflection on you. Don't let him crush your spirit, please. Don't change who you are at your core. Because there are people who love you exactly as you are.'

Savi stared at Marco's shoes, tracing the scuffs with her eyes. 'I can't go out there looking like this.' She choked back the lump in her throat, no more tears falling down her cheeks. She was all cried out for the time being. 'It's being broadcast to millions of people across the globe, and they're going to zoom in on me and I'll be a laughing stock. I can feel the mascara running down my face, how puffy my lips are . . .'

'You've got no choice, Cowgirl. It's got to be done.' Marco rose to his feet and reached for a cloth, running it under cold water. Seconds later, he was back down at her level, holding the damp washcloth to her forehead, then her neck.

'You don't have to do that.'

'Yeah, I do. I'm not getting yelled at when we both miss the podium celebrations, and I also don't want you to do something you'll regret. But as much as I wish I could tell you to take your time and calm down . . .'

'Okay.' She drank the water in record time and checked her watch. 'Time to go.'

'Oh, thank *god*. I honestly thought I was going to have to leave you in here while I went and made excuses on your behalf.'

'Work comes first. Always.' She took a deep breath, shook herself out and threw open the trailer door. Marco was right, she couldn't let Jesse have all the power here.

'Well,' he chased after her, 'right now, yes. Work. Otherwise, Jasper will rip your head off. I know he seems nice, but that's because you haven't pissed him off yet. I strongly recommend avoiding doing so.'

The world was moving in one big blur as they headed to the podium, and despite her marching out of the trailer on a mission, her bravery soon subsided. By the time they navigated through the paddocks, Marco was all but dragging her by the hand and she was running to keep up with him.

'Mars . . .' She hesitated when their team came into view, alongside the other teams who had made the podium in different classes. They were all looking at them, evidently panicked by their late arrival. 'Marco, I –'

'You can do this, Savannah. I'm right here with you.'

She swallowed nervously, noticing her teammates looking at her strangely. Could they tell she'd been crying just minutes before? 'Feeling a bit emotional there, Savi?' Julien grinned. 'It's a lot to take in, isn't it?'

'You could say that.' And then she realised just how big this was. Revolution Racing had made history, and every single person who was part of it was celebrating today, whether they were here or at HQ. Savi was part of something incredible, and she couldn't take it for granted.

Screw Jesse and his selfish, narcissistic ego. He was never going to change, never going to grow. But Savi could. She could keep pushing herself in her career, continue to build her legacy. Alone. Except she wasn't alone, because she had her family, her team. She had Marco. So that was the other thing she would do: remain open to the idea that good men existed. Marco had proved that time and time again and she wasn't going to let Jesse taint her view.

21

Marco felt like a little kid at Christmastime. They were in business class, about an hour away from landing, and he'd been asking Savi questions since the minute they'd boarded the plane. He wanted to know what her mum was likely to cook for dinner, how many ranch hands they had, what a typical day on the ranch looked like, if she hung out with her friends when she was home, and most of all, how she was feeling following the bombshell Sapphire had dropped.

'My dad will probably have some embarrassing sign, so please ignore what it says.' Savi had her eyes closed, head leaning back against her seat. 'He always does it, thinks it's hilarious.'

'Is he a hugger? I hugged him at Spa without giving it much thought, but I don't know if that's his thing.' Marco was a hugger. His own dad was a scary guy to everyone else, but to him, he was a softie. Always had been. Mars had got his soft side and his work ethic and not a lot else. Both brothers were a clone of their mum looks-wise.

'Oh, definitely. Didn't you notice he is basically Gabriel but with less of the CEO energy? It's no wonder they became fast friends. My entire career stemmed from Gabriel and my dad chatting about hot dogs at the karting track, and Gabriel asking him which kid was his.'

'That's adorable,' he teased. 'So . . . everyone in Sheridan genuinely believes that you and I are together, don't they?' He raised an eyebrow at her. 'Does this mean we're going to get swarmed at the bars?'

'We will be swarmed every time we head downtown. We won't be able to pick up groceries without someone I know coming to introduce themselves.'

'Great,' he muttered, his tone laced with sarcasm. 'Just what we need.'

'It's different at home. They're a bit invasive, but they mean well. They just want the best for everyone there, so no, we won't be left alone but it's comforting. They're excited to see Savi from Sheridan, not racing driver Savi. They're good people.'

'Is your dad a bar kind of guy?'

'Definitely not, so it will just be the two of us heading out on Friday night.'

'What about your brother? I'm looking forward to meeting him most, I think. We can bully you together.' He nudged her arm teasingly, but stopped when he saw a strange expression decorate her features. She looked uncomfortable. He didn't want to pry, but there was obviously something she wasn't telling him.

She snapped out of it and shrugged. 'He likes to stay home.'

They spent the rest of their flight in silence, only speaking again when they were at baggage claim and figuring out where to go. Marco almost hoped his luggage was lost so he had an excuse to buy the most extravagant outfits he could find. He wanted to wear flannel and denim and anything stereotypical, but instead he only had a selection of t-shirts and shorts. He'd been warned it was hot in Wyoming at the moment, and it was likely going to be hot at Le Mans in two weeks. He always tried to pack for all weather so he could just get up and go anywhere the wind took him. Once again, it had paid off.

It didn't mean he wouldn't treat himself to some cowboy gear and cram it all into his suitcase, though. On second thoughts . . . Savi *always* had two bags. He was sure she could find some extra room for his things, too.

'Savannah, I found your parents.' They'd made it through baggage claim smoothly and had barely got through the automatic doors before Marco spotted the older couple waving manically, holding a sign that read 'Welcome home from prison'.

Calvin, her dad, looked far more comfortable and at home than he had at Spa. He was a tall, broad man and wore a battered brown cowboy hat, beaten-up work boots and dirt-covered jeans with a red flannel shirt. He was standing proudly next to a shorter lady in jeans, riding boots and what looked like one of Savannah's oversized band tees. They looked so excited, *he* wanted to drop his things and run to them, but instead he watched as Savannah did. One of her cases rolled away and he grabbed it, using his foot to kick her second one towards them. 'Oi, Cowgirl, I know you're excited but a little help here!'

'Let me get that while the girls fuss over each other,' Calvin chuckled and rushed to Marco's rescue, trying to give him a hug whilst simultaneously helping steer the cases out of the way of the streams of people trying to get out.

'So good to see you again, Marco. Welcome to Wyoming, sort of. We'll be there in no time.'

'Hi, Calvin,' Marco squeezed him back. 'Thank you for having me.' They had flown into Montana and were a short drive from Savannah's hometown. Short if you were American, at least, where everything was miles apart. You could get from the south-west of England to Malmedy, Belgium in under twelve hours. Europe was much more appealing to him.

'Come and meet the wife.' He led him to where Savannah and her mum were still squealing at each other, and it was only then Marco realised their t-shirts were matching.

'Hi, Marco!' Her mum rose up on her tiptoes to embrace him. 'I'm Bonnie.'

'Nice to meet you, ma'am.' He grinned at Savi over her shoulder. 'Your daughter has told me great things about your cooking.'

'Now, I understand you're vegan. I've found some recipes I think you might like; would you mind going through them with me before tomorrow? We're going to have a barbecue tonight but without the meat. I hear you want to try corn the traditional American way.'

'I do', he beamed, loving the fact Savannah had remembered something so small. 'And I'd love to look through the recipes. I really appreciate it.'

'How's Wes today?' Savi asked her parents.

'Very eager to meet Marco. Hasn't shut up about it.' Calvin wheeled both of his daughter's cases out to the pick-up zone, leaving Marco to lug his behind him. 'I think the horses know you're coming, too. Mocha was whining all night. I got out of bed three times to see if she was okay, and she just looked at me like I was the world's biggest idiot.'

'Have we got many kids' riding lessons this week? I want to give Marco a chance to ride Java, teach him how to be a cowboy.' Savannah patted Marco on the shoulder.

They stopped by a huge blue Ford pick-up truck, not dissimilar to one of many cars Julien had sat in the barns at his Malmedy farmhouse. 'Sav, come on honey. Let the poor guy ride Cappuccino. Let's not embarrass him with a tiny horse,' Calvin scoffed.

'He's never ridden before!' Savannah defended, jumping into the truck and slamming the door. The whole thing rattled. It wasn't an ancient vehicle, but it certainly wasn't new and shiny, and Marco wondered if Savannah had tried and failed to get them a replacement yet. They didn't seem like the type to want anything flashy.

'Cappuccino is in the middle of the two and she's come such a long way. She's not scared of every little thing, anymore, and she doesn't boot people off. We let some of the older riders take her out now. I'm sure she can handle Marco and vice versa,' Bonnie assured.

'Oh, I am more than okay riding the smaller horse. Whatever the professionals think.'

They drove the two hours from Billings, Montana and across state lines to Wyoming, blasting country music the whole way. Calvin notably skipped any of Jesse's music which apparently was a thing he did often, and he was taking great pride in doing so now he had broken his little girl's heart. He swore enthusiastically at the radio every time, and the more he did it, the more Savi laughed about it.

He felt at ease in their company immediately, much like he had with their daughter, and they were already getting him involved in their inside jokes. It made him miss his own family, who were basically a wealthy version of the Harts with European accents. At their core, both sets of parents were the same in terms of values and morals. They would get on like a house on fire.

'Marco, how do you feel about Sav overtaking you all the time?' Calvin asked.

'I think she's made it clear I need to up my game,' Marco laughed. 'She's certainly not afraid of a challenge, your daughter.'

'Her and Weston get that from Cal,' Bonnie smiled in the rear-view mirror, bursting with pride. Marco wondered if Weston was anything like his sister. If he was, this trip was going to be up there with one of the best of his life, and Marco had been to a lot of places with a lot of different people.

'Is this where you live?!' His jaw dropped as they drove under a battered wooden signpost that read 'Mustang Ridge', nothing ahead of them except a long, winding dirt road and a picturesque view of mountains and trees and everything Marco could have dreamed of. It was serene. He wanted Calvin to stop the car right this very second so he could hop out and stand there and soak it all in, but instead they were hitting every bump and pothole, the truck jolting.

'It is,' Savannah smiled. 'Beautiful, right?'

'Savannah, you could build yourself a race track out

here.' There was so much open space, and he imagined the Hart family owned most, if not all of it. It was a working ranch, not just a farmhouse on a bit of land. She could build a karting track and give local kids the same opportunity she had growing up, invest in the careers of junior drivers. He'd go into business on something like that in a heartbeat; he already sponsored a young driver from Glastonbury in the south-west of England.

'Don't give her any ideas! She isn't here enough to oversee it,' Calvin shook his head.

'Wouldn't Weston help out?' Marco asked, causing everyone in the car to go silent.

What was he missing here? Whatever it was, he was pretty sure he was about to find out. Calvin pulled up in front of a beautiful farmhouse, in the early stages of renovations. It looked new on the outside, white wooden siding, a new black roof and black window frames with planter boxes of fresh flowers under every window. But the porch had seen better days, and the landscaping needed some work. It looked like a proper home, though. One that was full of character and, more importantly, full of love.

'Wes!' Savannah yelled out as soon as she hopped out of the truck. 'Your favourite family member has returned, come say hi!'

Then the front door opened, and everything made sense. Weston wheeled himself onto the porch, beaming with pride, and held his arms out. Savannah ran into them for a hug, and he planted a kiss on her head of curls, looking over her shoulder to grin at Marco. 'Welcome home, Sav. Missed your face.'

'Missed yours, too.' She pulled back and whizzed around to face Marco, who was still standing there a little dumbfounded. He was trying so hard not to stare that he was coming across as more awkward than ever. But nobody else seemed to notice his moment of shyness except him. 'Monaco, meet Weston.'

'How's it going, man?' Weston offered a wave, snapping Marco out of it. He headed over and shook his hand, noticing he was the spitting image of Bonnie.

'Good! Nice to meet you, Wes.'

'Calling me by my nickname already? I like it.'

'Savannah does it all the time when she talks about you, so it kind of stuck,' Marco shrugged, shoving his hands in his pockets.

'Savannah?' Weston smirked.

'Don't start,' Savannah pointed a finger at him.

'Nobody gets away with calling her that, not even us.' Bonnie appeared at his side having left Calvin to get all the luggage out of the truck on his own.

'Mars kind of decided on it when we were having a disagreement and there's been no going back since. I think he's called me Savi a grand total of three times since we met.'

'What kind of disagreement would lead to you letting someone call you by your government name? You wouldn't even let them read it out at your high school graduation,' Bonnie frowned.

'It involved an Oscar-worthy speech, a garage full of people and some god-awful advice from your daughter,' Marco said. 'And that's all you need to know until I'm six beers deep and telling you my deepest, darkest secrets.'

'Oh, cool. We'll get the beers flowing and the campfire burning tonight, then,' Weston laughed. 'You can tell us how much of a handful Sav is when she's got nobody to rein her in.'

'You think he doesn't try to take on that role himself?' Savannah raised an eyebrow. 'Marco can give as good as he gets, you know.'

'Thank god you've got someone else to wind up,' Calvin joined them, bags in tow.

Marco reached for them, hauling them up the steps. He noticed a ramp on the left side of the porch, which must be how Weston moved around. 'Sorry, Calvin. Let me help.'

'Get your hands off, De Luca,' Calvin tutted. 'You're a guest.'

'But Savannah said . . .' Marco trailed off, watching his teammate try to hide her amusement.

'Let me guess, she told you everyone chips in around here, huh?'

'Yes.' Marco nodded.

'She's full of shit. We have paid ranch hands for a reason; guests are treated like VIPs at our home. That means you're fed and watered and your days are yours to do with what you wish.'

'Oh, okay, thank you but only if you're sure,' he frowned.

'He said he wanted to be a cowboy, Dad.'

'That doesn't mean he has to shovel horse crap, Sav,' Calvin laughed and clapped Marco on the shoulder, rather aggressively. Their builds could not be more different, Calvin's broad frame dwarfing Marco. 'Give the guy a break!'

'Yeah, Cowgirl, let me relax. Being chased around a racetrack by your determined little self is tiring, you know. Plus, I have to keep you in check off-track, too. Being a fake boyfriend is serious business, it's not for the faint of heart.'

'We both know the only one who's doing the chasing is you,' Savannah shot back, looking mighty proud of herself as she walked through the front door. 'Welcome to our humble abode.'

'We've sorted the guest bedroom out for you.' Bonnie rushed to reorganise the flowers on the coffee table. He knew there must be clutter hiding somewhere in this house, because Savannah had told him in order to set up her racing sim they would need to do a big clear out. But the open-plan living area which included a large kitchen and dining space looked pristine, which suggested they'd gone to an extra effort for his arrival.

'Which one is he in, Ma?' Savannah took hold of his case and started dragging it towards a long hallway. This house seemed go on forever, but it was simple and homely, and he loved it. No sign of marble floors, no sense that if you were to touch something it would shatter. He wished he'd grown up in a place like this; scenery included.

'The mountain room.' Bonnie left them to it, tossing Weston an orange from the fruit bowl while Calvin continued bringing the rest of the bags in and leaving them by the entrance to the hallway, allowing them some privacy.

Marco trailed after Savannah who seemed to be very keen to get him into his room, and when she opened the door he understood why. There was a huge mural on the back wall of some mountains, all dark and moody, accented with gold. It was stunning. The rest of the walls were black, and the furniture was all dark wood with a huge beige rug covering the wooden flooring. Although the décor was beautiful, it was the view from the window that was the real focal point. A perfect view of the mountains the house was surrounded by. 'Savannah . . .'

'This room is my pride and joy. I wanted a project to distract me from the stress of contract signings, so they let me loose in here. I didn't even have to beg them to let me spend my own money, this was mine to play with. Gave me a focus.'

'You've done a stellar job. This is magnificent. Did you paint the mural yourself?'

'No, a friend of Weston's helped out. She's an artist. She wants to design a helmet for me.'

'You should let her. You have good taste.'

'You would think they'd see my vision for the rest of the house and accept my help,' she sighed. 'But their pride gets in the way. In here, they can shut the door on it and go about their lives like their daughter isn't constantly battling to take care of them and give them what they couldn't give her.'

'Just do it without permission,' Marco shrugged.

'I have sent so many construction workers to the house when I'm not here, because they would shut me down in a heartbeat, but they won't send a stranger away. I got Weston's bathroom refurbished and turned into a wet room two years ago, last year I had a lift fitted to the basement so he could go down to his man cave and play on his games console with his friends like the old days, before his accident.' She looked like she was going to cry. 'I don't think they can grasp how much money is sitting in my bank account.'

'Hey,' Marco wrapped his arms around her and pulled her in close, 'it's a parent thing. Mine do the same thing even though my bank statements almost match theirs these days. We'll start clearing out the stables first thing in the morning, we won't tell them. Just pretend we woke up with this big idea, and then we'll go out and buy everything we need and bring it back here. They're not going to argue with you while I'm here, right?'

'I don't want to hurt their feelings,' she sniffed. 'Or maybe I just need to put my foot down. Force them to let me help them. I could give them so much if they let me, the house of their dreams. One that isn't falling apart. But it's Weston, too. He hates when I do things that benefit him, like when I pay off one of his many medical bills or get him new equipment that improves his quality of life.'

'They've worked hard their whole lives and it's hard to accept that they don't need to exhaust themselves just to get by anymore. They're traditional and they have strong morals, that much is clear. Your dad should be getting ready to retire, but he doesn't strike me as the kind of man who will ever stop and take a well-deserved break.'

'He won't,' Savi laughed softly. 'Weston would be out there with him if he could be.'

Marco ran his hands up and down her back in an attempt to comfort her. He didn't usually use that amount of physical touch to calm her down, but as they grew closer and therefore more comfortable with one another, he wasn't so afraid to test the waters. 'I'm really looking forward to getting to know your brother.'

Savannah pulled back from his embrace, glancing up at him. 'Thank you for not freaking out when you met him. I know I probably should've told you about him being in a wheelchair, but I don't like to talk about it. There's quite a story behind it, but I'll let him tell you. I have a feeling he'll open up to you about things that he usually keeps hidden from the rest of the world.'

'I hope so.' Marco turned and faced the room again, hands on his hips. 'Unpacking can wait, I want a tour of this place. Cows and all.'

'It's still early, don't you want to go and get your cowboy boots and a hat?'

'How is that even a question? Get moving!' He darted out of the room ahead of her, nearly careening into Weston on his way. 'Sorry, man!'

Weston brought his chair to a halt. 'No worries. Where are you rushing off to? Decided the ranch life isn't for you already?'

'Quite the opposite. Savannah is taking me to get some cowboy gear.'

'He's been going on about it since we met.' Savannah rolled her eyes.

'Cool, can I come?'

'*Really?*' Savannah's eyes looked like they were about to fall out of her head as she stared at her brother in shock. 'But you don't —'

'We'll take my car. Hasn't been used in ages so it could

do with being driven for an hour or two. Give it some oomph down the quieter roads, too. Get it going again.'

'Wes, are you sure about this?' Savannah seemed concerned and Marco stood there like a spare part, watching them have a conversation without words. 'You haven't been out and about in a while, and everyone will have missed you. You might get hounded by the locals.'

'I'm in a weird mood which appears to be diminishing any fucks I had left to give, so yeah Sav, I'm sure. You need cheering up, and that's my job. Plus, if you're worried about people papping us all, we both know they'll keep our secrets safe. They always have. So, let's go show Mr Monaco how we do things in Wyoming.'

22

'This might be the cutest town I've ever seen. I bet it's like something out of a film when it snows.' Marco hadn't stopped chattering since they'd left the confines of the ranch, and he was starting to drive Savi insane.

Her head was elsewhere; primarily on her brother who was sat in the back in his wheelchair, chatting back just as much. This was weird. Weston didn't go anywhere and yet here he was coming to watch their guest do a fashion show for them. Marco hadn't even been on the ranch half an hour before he'd successfully done the one thing Savi had failed to do every time she'd been home in the last few years.

'I haven't been downtown in so long,' Weston muttered, gazing out of the window as they passed the local bakery. A lot of the stores, cafés and restaurants in the area needed work doing to them, and most were in the process of having said work done. She would deny it if anyone asked, but she'd made a donation or two to help speed the town's development along.

'You don't get out much, Wes?' Marco questioned, causing Savi to inhale sharply and wait for an uncomfortable silence to follow but it never came.

'Not really. I don't like all the fuss when I leave the ranch. It's like the local outcast has finally left his hiding place and everyone crowds around me.'

'Wouldn't people fuss less if they saw you more often?'

'You don't know the residents of Sheridan,' Weston laughed.

Savi had endured this argument with him countless times, tried to encourage him to go out and give their friends his time. They'd rallied around him and sent gift baskets and cards when he was in hospital, then they'd delivered home-cooked meals when he first came home. She knew lots of them had reached out to him, too, invited him to dinners and drinks and backyard barbecues. He had just had such a hard time adjusting to his new way of life that he retreated into himself. But Marco was here now, and she was starting to see that maybe all he'd needed was an outsider to invade his personal space and force him to embrace his reality.

Pulling into a parking space in front of the only store Marco needed to fulfil his dreams, Savi stopped the car. 'We're here.'

'Don't forget to let me out!' Weston called out.

She opened the trunk and hit a button which allowed Wes to be lowered to the ground, and he immediately shot off. He got plenty of fresh air being out in the country, but this was different. He seemed excited. 'Race you to the store, De Luca,' he yelled, but he was already gone. Savi laughed as she watched two grown men chasing each other down the sidewalk, Marco purposefully lagging so he didn't overtake him.

'Hurry up, Cowgirl!' Marco yelled, grabbing the attention of a few passersby. One was a gentleman who had done some work at the ranch the previous summer for her dad. He looked pleased as punch to see Weston out of the house, but he kept it to himself, tipping his hat at Savi when she noticed and smiling away. If everyone could behave like that, Wes might do this more often.

She locked the car, another gift from her to her family, and followed them inside. Marco was almost doubled over looking at the sheer number of boots in here; they lined the walls, all different colours. There were browns, pinks, blues, greys. Any colour you could think of, this store had them. 'People come from all over the place to visit this one particular store.' She grabbed a pair of pink ones in her size, admiring the embroidery.

'I can see why,' Marco responded, eyes tracing every pair. Thankfully the selection of hats was much smaller, because she imagined they would be here for hours just for the boots. 'So, which colour do you think I should go for?'

'The obvious answer is Revolution Racing red, but I think tan or black would suit you better,' Savi answered, deciding to try the pink pair on. They would work great with her collection of white sundresses.

'But if a specific pair speaks to you, then you've gotta try them,' Weston added. 'Sav has about thirty pairs, each of them different in some way but they all have a story tied to them.'

'I have black ones with sunflowers on. Wore those the day we got Mocha and she nibbled on them – think she thought the flowers were real.'

'And you've got the white ones with red hearts which you wore for graduation,' Weston laughed. 'They stole the spotlight when you walked onto the stage.'

'I'm feeling like I need an entire outfit, guys . . .' Marco called out from the end of the aisle, where he'd found the back of the store which was filled with shirts and jeans.

'If that's what you want, we'll have you in the dressing room ASAP.' Savi picked up a pair of black boots with dark brown embroidery and held them out to him. 'How about these?'

'Love them. I'll get a just-for-fun pair, too.' He waited for Weston to wheel himself back up the aisle out of the way of the brown pair he'd been eyeing. The main part of the boots was a dark brown while the leg consisted of burnt orange flames with blue stitching, very apt for a racing driver. 'Or maybe two, because you're right, I need Revolution red. We can rock up to the next race with our matching boots and the fans will be screaming couple goals.'

'They already are screaming that and all you've done on camera is kiss a couple of times, which by the way, gross.' Weston scrunched his nose up in disgust.

'Wes, shut up. For once in your life.' Marco let out a loud laugh at their bickering. 'Don't laugh, Monaco, it will encourage him.'

'Yes, ma'am,' he saluted.

Savi clutched her new pink boots tightly and walloped him on the arm with them. 'Don't call me ma'am. Ever. I draw the line at Cowgirl.'

'Someone's feeling feisty today,' Weston commented, which only set Marco off more.

Savi pointed a finger at her brother. 'Don't think I won't hit you too, Weston Jameson Hart. Your wheelchair doesn't make you immune. Come on, Monaco. Let's get you a nice denim shirt.'

The two of them followed behind her still laughing but keeping any comments to themselves, and then suddenly Marco was lost in a maze of denim, leather, flannel and suede with his upper torso and head sticking out above the rails of clothing. 'How am I meant to choose? There are so many options, and they all look great.'

'We'll choose for you,' she suggested, picking out a few denim options. 'You know . . . you could go all out and get this.' Savi held out a denim shirt with the USA flag printed across the front and the shoulders.

'I'm sold. Pass it here.' He took it from her excitedly, adding it to his growing collection. 'You choose another one that's a little more subtle, and I'll go grab a hat. Wes, come with me.'

They came back ten minutes later to find Savi leaning against a rail, having chosen a second shirt within seconds. She was a thrifter by nature, so this came easily to her. She also had a fake boyfriend who dressed very well, and a willing model who had the perfect athletic figure. Marco would do well at the rodeo if he ever gave up racing.

'How much have you got?!' She gawked at the mountain of items on Weston's lap and in Marco's arms. They might as well have bought the entire store.

'I might be borrowing some of your suitcase space for Le Mans. Please pack light,' he shrugged. 'Right, dressing room. Wait here, guys. I'll be needing your advice.'

They waited for an age as Marco battled with zips, belts and buttons behind the curtain, giving Savi a spare moment to breathe. She had surprised herself with how level-headed she had been since the initial shock had worn off, and she was trying her best to focus on being home and being present. It just wasn't as simple as she kept letting herself believe. She wasn't sure if she was ever going to speak to Jesse again, and that sort of scared her.

'Are you done yet?' Weston shouted.

Marco's head popped out from the red curtain, his curls dishevelled. 'I don't think you're ready for how fucking cool I look.' And with that, he stepped out of the dressing room.

The belt he'd chosen had a huge gold and silver buckle with the brand logo on it, the denim shirt with the USA flag fit perfectly, highlighting his broad shoulders, and the dark blue jeans hugged his ass in all the right ways. Not that she was looking too closely. Then there were the red boots and black hat, both of which suited him in a way Savi couldn't quite explain. Marco was not the kind of guy who looked like he could pull this look off, until he put it all together. She was stunned. 'Wow.'

'I have never felt sexier in my entire life,' he stated.

'Damn,' Weston let out a low whistle, 'get this man on a catwalk.'

'Savannah, you trying anything on?' Marco looked at her own pile of clothes which she had slowly gathered since stepping foot in the store.

'I suppose I should try this dress on.'

'Don't forget the zebra boots you found a second ago!' Weston reached down by the side of his chair, picking them up and holding them out to her.

'Where did you find those?!' Marco's jaw dropped. 'Savannah, you have to get these. They match the livery of our cars, it's fate.'

'We'll see. They're in the thousands, and I've never spent that much on a pair of boots before. It just feels too extravagant.' She scurried into the dressing room next to Marco's, climbing out of her workout gear, a travel essential, and into the dress she'd found.

It was black, sleeveless, with a floaty skirt and a built-in corset. It was the kind of thing she would wear if she was going out somewhere fancy but still wanted to feel like herself. A dress she would wear if Jesse had ever taken her on a real date.

'How long does it take to put a dress on?' Marco muttered, his voice filling the silent store.

'I heard that!' Savi replied. 'And the answer is a while when it's got a corset!'

'Do you need help, Savannah?' She could hear the amusement in his tone, and she wanted to say no out of spite for him mocking her, but she was mature enough to admit she would be here forever if she didn't accept his assistance.

'Please,' she sighed and within moments, Marco was in the dressing room with her. He drew the curtain behind them to give her some privacy, even though it was only her brother and the store owner out there. 'It's a lace-up and I can't get it tight enough.'

'Right, brace yourself . . .' He waited for Savi to grip the walls and take a deep breath in before he set about pulling the strings as tight as they would go. He tied them up in a bow and stood back, admiring his handiwork. 'Done.'

Savi looked at herself in the mirror, studying the way it clung to her body in all the right places. She hadn't felt this elegant in a long time; her bare shoulders looked strong thanks to all the weight training she did, but her frame was still dainty. That was just genetics. Marco watched her reflection, his eyes catching on her chest. That looked great, too.

'My boots.' She pointed down at the black and white boots with the faux zebra fur detailing, realising she couldn't put them on herself. Trying to bend in a corset just wasn't going to work.

'Hold onto my shoulders.' Marco crouched down and lifted her leg up, the palm of his hand soft against her bare skin. He took his time sliding her boots on, one at a time.

'Thanks,' she whispered, watching him with a strange sense of appreciation. Her skin felt like it was on fire under his touch, and she didn't know if it was because they were in a tiny box mere inches apart, but she did know this was the first time she'd felt anything like this for someone who wasn't Jesse. And what made it stranger was, she was allowed to feel it now.

'What's going on in there?!' Weston's voice broke her out of her spell.

'Your sister is getting new boots.' Marco threw the curtain open. 'Look at them! What an outfit, Cowgirl. You have to get them.'

'But they're so expensive,' she pouted. 'They're six grand.'

'Sav, you deserve to be able to buy yourself nice things. Not just keep buying everything for everyone else.' Weston gave her a guilt-ridden smile, and she wished he didn't have to feel like that. He always acted like he was a burden, and she hated it.

'I'm buying them for you if you won't treat yourself,' Marco stated. 'Consider it a thank you for bringing me here and for being a wonderful teammate.'

'Mars, I can't let you do that.' She had tears in her eyes as she looked at him.

'You can. We have talked about my financial situation; you've seen where I live. Besides, every time you wear them I want you to remember the time you brought your idiot Italian-Monegasque teammate to Wyoming and let him go full Yeehaw.'

'You heard the man,' Weston grinned.

But all Savi could do in response was throw herself into Marco's arms and give him a suffocating hug, their bodies moulded together. Whatever this friendship was, she cherished it, and she never wanted it to end. Not when either of them parted ways from Revolution Racing, not ever.

23

'Thank you for fetching dessert.' Bonnie waved the box of pastries as she took it from Marco, who had clutched them on his lap the whole drive home.

'Did you find everything you were looking for, Marco?' Calvin was hauling coal out into the back yard where he had his barbecuing gear set up. Savi's dad loved hosting, and he'd spent the afternoon building a campfire while they were out.

'Three pairs of boots, two denim shirts, a flannel, a denim jacket, a suede jacket, a pair of jeans and a very fancy belt. Also, my hat, which as you can see is already a staple.' He pointed to his head. He'd only knocked it against the roof of the car once while getting in.

'You'll be requesting that the team's private jet lands in a field on the ranch just to get your new purchases to France,' Calvin chuckled.

The next race was Le Mans and Marco was determined that he and Savi were going to be matching with boots, hats and jeans. She had pointed out Le Mans was set to be too warm for jeans, and they would spend most of the week in full racing gear due to the amount of work they had to do in the garage and all the practice sessions out on track, but he'd fired back with the excuse of team dinners and their initial arrival in the paddock.

'Do you need any help with dinner?' he asked, looking like he was desperate to help in some way. He was sat at the kitchen counter, watching Savi and her ma peel and chop vegetables for the kebabs they were making.

'Wanna chop the sweet potato up?' Savi wondered if he knew how. He'd grown up with a chef and still had one to this day, and while she knew he could make chocolate chip pancakes, that didn't mean he had been taught the basics.

'I'm on it.' He took a knife from the drawer Savi pointed to and got to work. 'So, Wes is pretty great,' Marco commented quietly. Weston was downstairs on his games console, but sound travelled.

'I'm glad you guys are getting on. I think he's really missed having male company other than Dad, and he ignores his friends for the most part. He's really isolated himself and pushed them all away, so they've been sentenced to a friendship based on online gaming.'

'I just can't believe he asked if he could come with you today,' Bonnie said, welling up.

'Bonnie, don't cry.' Marco put the knife down and gave her a quick cuddle. 'I'll do my best to bring him out of hibernation for you, and hopefully when I'm gone he'll stay out.'

'You've been here less than a day and I already want you to stay forever,' she laughed softly, gratefully squeezing his hand. 'Savi is very lucky to have you as a teammate. I mean, what kind of man steps up in the way you did?'

Savi knew what her ma was referring to. First it had been the photos, then swooping in to take care of her when her world was falling apart. And she was right; not many people would do what Marco had done. But their connection went far beyond all that. 'Ma, Marco said he'll help me fix up the extra stall in the stables, so you can get another horse for the kids' riding lessons.' She spat it out while everyone was feeling vulnerable and emotional, hoping her mum would be more receptive.

'Oh,' Bonnie frowned. 'Savi, we shouldn't be asking that of him. He's a guest.'

'And you've got him chopping sweet potatoes,' Savi shrugged.

'It would be my pleasure to help, Bonnie. I wasn't lying when I said I wanted to go full cowboy, I really meant it.' Marco presented them with the result of his chopping skills. 'Plus, you and Calvin have plenty to do around here, so let us take a project off your hands.'

'I suppose it would get it done a lot faster, and we could finally take some names off the waiting list for lessons. We've had some kids on there six months plus.'

'Thanks, Ma.' Savi kissed her on the cheek.

'We won't spend a fortune or do anything crazy, promise. Just make it liveable.'

'Who wants to come and watch me barbecue?' Calvin called through the back door.

'Is he serious?' Marco glanced at Savi for confirmation. 'He wants us to watch?'

'It's his thing. He's very proud of his barbecuing skills, does all sorts of tricks with the utensils and drinks whiskey the entire time. We're basically watching him get progressively more drunk and risk setting fire to his apron with every sip, but it's good fun.' Savi had fond memories of helping when she was little, but for the most part it was his and Weston's time to bond while she and Bonnie sat back with their feet up.

'I'll just call Wes up.' Bonnie rolled her eyes good naturedly and headed to the basement.

'Woah, Cal. You didn't tell me you had this beast.' Marco took in the size of the grill.

'It was a birthday gift from Sav,' he beamed. 'She knows me well.'

'I also get him magnets and bottle openers from as many places as I can. The magnets go on the mini fridge, and he's got a tin full of the bottle openers. We've got a collection of beer mats which is a new thing. God forbid we get a mark on the table.' Savi showed him some of her favourites. 'If you ever find something with Monaco on, he'd love you forever.'

'I can get you a beer mat from my parents' hotel, but I think that might be the best I can do.'

'I'll take it. Appreciate it, bud. So, this hotel of theirs, is it really posh? I guess it probably is, being in Monaco.'

'Yes, but when there's racing on and the streets turn into a racetrack, we always provide huge discounts. It means we get fans from all over the world flocking to us, and they get the full Monaco experience without spending an absolute fortune.'

'I'd love to go to Monaco.' Calvin looked wistful as he grilled some halloumi.

'Really, Dad?' Savi frowned.

'Yes, but your mother doesn't want to go and we can't

really leave Wes on his own anyway, even if she did want to.' He shrugged it off.

'You're welcome to stay in our hotel for free, Calvin. Always. Or even in my family's home, with us. As long as the Monaco Grand Prix isn't on when Savannah and I are racing elsewhere, I'll come with you. I'm sure Savannah would, too.'

'You'd do that?' Calvin looked like he might cry, whether it be with excitement or gratitude or both. Savi felt like she might do the same.

'Of course. You've welcomed me here with open arms, it's the least I could do.'

Calvin pulled him in for a hug. 'You are the best fake son-in-law a man could ask for.'

'Dad,' Savi laughed. 'That's such a weird thing to say.'

'Your actual boyfriend never even offered to let us attend a local show, with or without you in attendance. He does realise nobody knows who we are, doesn't he? Your ma and I weren't going to blow your cover if we were in the crowd amongst thousands of people.'

'You don't even like his music that much,' Savi tutted.

'That's beside the point.'

Savi sat down with her cocktail, homemade with a little too much alcohol as per usual. She was never able to get it quite right, even when she followed a recipe. She spent her summers as a teenager making punch bowls for her friends' house parties, playing beer pong in basements and drinking in the fields and the mountains, not having much else to do when she wasn't riding the horses, doing schoolwork or karting. But cocktails were an art, and she had given up trying to perfect her attempt at a tequila sunrise.

She watched her dad in his element, happily grilling away. Marco was allowed a couple of goes before he somehow set fire to a mushroom and was sent to join her, Bonnie and Wes in shame. He told them stories of his own childhood and summer evenings with his family. Despite the clear divide in wealth, his stories weren't all that different to hers. They played board games, charades and did karaoke, all things that her family did. Maybe he was right; maybe their families would get on.

'This food looks incredible.' Marco took the piece of corn Savi passed down the table to him. They'd laid out all the food like a buffet in the middle of the table, all the mains and sides and condiments they could want. Not once did Savi or her family complain about the lack of meat available tonight. They weren't hunters like a lot of people around here.

'How's the corn?' Weston asked, right as Marco was mid-bite.

'Amazing,' Marco mumbled through his mouthful.

'So, your next race is Le Mans?' Calvin asked them.

'Indeed. Savannah's first time racing in such a prestigious event.' Marco had butter dribbling down his chin, and Savi couldn't resist getting a napkin and dabbing at it. 'She's in for a hell of a ride, but it'll be the best race of her life. That I can assure you.'

'If I even make it to the finish line this time,' she muttered, staring down at her plate.

'Will you stop beating yourself up about that? The car had issues, and the team made the wrong call. None of that was on you, Cowgirl. And hey, us guys won in the other car so we still got a podium *and* won the hundredth race.'

'I just know Kodie and Miko won't forgive me if there's a repeat. I'm already skating on thin ice within the team for launching what they think is a very real relationship to the public so early in the season and taking the spotlight off them.'

'The three of you just need to get in that car and give it your all. So much happens at Le Mans, it's a miracle if *anyone* crosses the finish line. Mistakes are made, things go wrong, but as long as you have done the best you can, that is truly all that matters.'

'Fuck me, it's like Ghandi is here with us,' Weston said, munching his way through the beetroot salad. He'd taken the whole bowl and gone in with a fork, rather than putting some on his plate.

'Mars is pretty wise, actually. He's not just been there for me with the Jesse drama, but he's helped with my anxiety on a couple of occasions.'

'You're still struggling with that?' Bonnie asked, concern etched across her face. 'Sav, if you need to go back on your medication . . .'

'No, Ma. It's not that bad. I can handle it, but you know, the start of the season has taken some adjustment. We're a few races deep now and I've got more of a handle on everything, even with what's been happening the last few weeks. Being home with you guys helps, reminds me I'm just some girl from Wyoming at heart. I've always got an escape route.'

'You'll never be just some girl, Savannah.' Marco was watching her with a look on his face that she couldn't quite read, and it was making her cheeks heat up. The sky was streaked with pink and orange as the sun went down, but nothing would hide how rosy they were under his gaze. 'Anyway, Weston. Been meaning to ask, what's your story?'

'My story?' Weston quirked a brow. 'Well, I was born in Sheridan. In Dad's old truck on the highway, actually. I was just so excited to see the world, I couldn't wait for the hospital.'

'Wes, you idiot.' Calvin threw a balled-up napkin at him and Weston dodged it. 'You know that isn't what he means.'

'I know, I know. Sorry.' Weston rolled his eyes. 'I was in a rodeo accident. Fell off a bull and it trampled me. Was in a coma, woke up paralysed. That's really all there is to it.'

'Shit, man. That's intense.'

'Wes was a rodeo star,' Bonnie chimed in. 'He was right up there in the rankings; had all the sponsorships he could dream of. That wasn't the first accident he had, but he had problems with his back after the previous ones and was warned against competing again.'

'Yeah, but us Harts don't do things by halves. I had to go out with a bang.' Weston took a swig of his bourbon. 'Rodeo was my thing, you know? It was what I was good at, what I wanted to do until I couldn't anymore. And here I am. Never expected it to end quite like this, but I'm still glad I had all those years of competition in me. I've got a collection of trophies in storage to rival yours, I imagine.'

'He's serious,' Savi smiled. 'I don't advertise that we're related because Wes disappeared off the face of the earth after the accident. He doesn't want all that attention again. He gets to live his life in peace, and now it's my turn.'

'Mind if I search you up?' Marco waved his phone in the air.

'Go for it, bud, but try *Wes Jameson*. I used my middle name as a stage name, probably half the reason Sav's fans haven't connected the dots yet.' Weston beamed, and Savi and her parents exchanged quick glances paired with subtle smiles. He didn't talk about his past with anyone, even them. It was hard to talk to him about anything personal these days, he would always change the topic.

'Wow . . .' Marco muttered, and Savi peered over at his phone, watching him scroll through countless articles about Weston's short-lived but extremely successful career. He was undoubtedly a star in his industry and was easily the rodeo equivalent of his younger sister.

'Entered my first comp when I was seventeen and competed right up until my accident when I was twenty-three. I'd already had one surgery before, and yeah, I was stupid for carrying on, but rodeo was part of me. It was all I knew. You get that, don't you?'

'I do,' Marco nodded. 'I can't imagine not racing. I'll do it for as long as I possibly can, and if there comes a time I'm forced to stop, whether it's my choice or someone else's, I'll find a way to stay in the industry somehow.'

'You kids,' Calvin laughed. 'So many people lack direction in life, and yet you guys had it all figured out before you even started high school. Dreams bigger than your fears.'

'I'm just glad that all three of you have seen so much of the world and experienced so much of what life has to offer.' Bonnie wiped her eyes, the wine obviously getting to her.

'Well . . . not so much recently.' Weston chewed on his bottom lip. 'Sav, how hard would it be to get me out to a race? To come and see you?'

'What?' Savi sat up straight. 'Is that something you want?'

'I've wanted that since day one. I almost came to your first race with Dad, but I wasn't ready, and I've regretted it every day since. I think . . .' he swallowed roughly, 'it might be time to bite the bullet and come support my baby sister from the sidelines.'

'If all of you come, I'll pay for it. Put you up in a hotel, get you VIP passes. The full works. And if you need a security team, I'll get that sorted for you.'

'Let me call Jasper tonight, see about bringing you to Le Mans with us when we leave here?' Marco suggested. 'It's the biggest race in history, Savannah should have her family with her.'

'Is it not short notice with hotels and everything?' Bonnie looked nervous.

'Ma, they're rich and their bosses are super important people.' Weston rolled his eyes. 'Let them take care of us. I'll have some champagne waiting on the jet, please. And oysters.'

'I mean, you can have those things, but we will judge you harshly . . . The jet is usually full of sweets and all the crap we shouldn't eat. Plus, water. A lot of water. Gotta keep hydrated.' Marco laughed. 'I'll shoot Jasper a quick text, put the feelers out. I can't imagine he'll say no to helping us out, and if he does, we'll just turn to Gabriel.'

'Oh, of course! A Gal reunion!' Calvin clapped his hands. 'Haven't seen my buddy in what feels like forever.'

'Gal reunion?' Marco frowned.

'Gabriel and Cal. Gal.' Calvin shrugged like it was obvious and Savi buried her head in her hands in embarrassment. The pair of them were a nightmare when they were together, and she had fond memories of them when she was younger, waving foam fingers at her from the grandstands of the karting track and making fools of themselves and her.

Marco leaned closer to Savi and whispered, 'Cowgirl, I think Gabriel has a clone . . .'

They spent the rest of the evening sat around the fire, Marco impressing them with his guitar-playing skills and singing, while her dad did some sort of interpretive dance to the music. She hadn't laughed so hard in so long, and watching her family do the same thing provided her with a comfort she'd been missing. Savi should be an ugly, crying mess, but she just wasn't. She was starting to grow very accustomed to the bubble that was formed to protect her against the reality of the outside world every time Marco was around.

24

'Please tell me this was for Halloween or something?' Marco held up a photo from behind a mountain of plastic boxes, a grin plastered across his features.

Savi climbed over the boxes to get a closer look, immediately snatching it from his hands and hiding it behind her back. 'I can't believe you found that.'

They were in the basement, sorting through the Harts' family photos purely to embarrass Savi as per her teammates' request. So far, he'd taken photos on his phone of at least fifteen of them, and she just knew he would bring them out at the next team bonding event. He'd even sent some into the group chat already.

'The green isn't even the right shade!' Marco cackled. 'And the costume is so big on you.'

'Because I was six! *Monsters, Inc.* was my favourite film, and it was last-minute, so we just used the only green paint we had in our crafting supplies.' She smiled fondly at the memory. 'There's a photo somewhere of Weston dressed as Sully; we stuck bits of purple and blue fabric to a t-shirt, hat and gloves with a glue gun. Well, I say "we", Ma did it.'

'I would pay good money to see his Sully costume.'

'Didn't you ever have a fancy dress fail?'

'I was and still am amazing at fancy dress. Just last year I went to a Halloween party at Julien and Faith's house in

Hawaii dressed up as Michael Myers. Remind me later and I'll find the photos. His kids were terrified, Emmy smacked me across the face when I picked her up with my mask on.'

'I'm not surprised! They're still babies!'

'Didn't help that every adult there was dressed as something equally creepy. Jasmine was a horrifying version of Moana with fake blood and contacts. Scared even me.' He fake-shuddered.

'You like being an uncle, don't you?' Savi slipped the photo into an old photo album which still had space left over. None of their family photos were in order, they were a semi-organised chaos with two plastic boxes dedicated to them.

'It's one of most important roles I'll ever have. I probably see Julien's kids more than I see my brother's, but I love them all the same. I love their little imaginations, how they just say what's on their mind and cause havoc.'

'I hope I get to be an aunt one day. If Wes ever gets his shit together and starts dating again.'

'He might surprise you.' Marco put the lid back on the box he'd been rifling through.

They'd mucked out the stalls already, beating the ranch hands to it for the day, and were only inside for a breather and some refreshments. Marco had complained the entire time, but what he hadn't realised was that he was a damn good worker and got his side done twice as fast as Savi. They just needed to fix the gate and put some hay in there, and the extra stall would be good to go.

'Did Jasper reply yet?' she asked. The flights wouldn't be a problem; the jet was already coming to collect Marco and

Savi, and Kodie was already in France so that was one less stop. The hotel was tricky; they'd need an accessible room for Weston and if the hotels were already booked up by the IEC teams, there might not be anything left.

'Let me check.' Marco pulled his phone from the back pocket of his new jeans. 'He said their hotel rooms are booked as of this morning.'

'Oh my god.' Savi clapped a hand over her mouth, trying not to burst into tears. 'Ma and Wes get to see me race for, like, the first time ever. And at *Le Mans*.'

'Hell yeah.' Marco high-fived her. 'We'll have to take them out for lunch on the first day. I know a good Italian place; I'll reserve us a table.'

'This is all I've wanted for years.' She breathed out. 'Even in my junior championship, they never got to come to a race. The timing was off; as soon as I made it out of karting and into the big leagues, Wes had his accident. He needed them more than me.'

'Yeah, and now you need *him*. And it looks like he might be realising that.'

Another hour passed, all of the boxes were put away and they'd had a pitcher of homemade lemonade between them. 'Ready to do some retail therapy?' Marco came out of his room wearing his cowboy hat.

'Yep. I think I might donate Mocha's riding gear to this new horse and buy my baby something new, so maybe we'll grab that while we're out.'

'What are you going for? New saddle and reins?'

'I think so. She should have something bold, stand out against the crowd.'

'Sounds like a girl I know.' His voice was right behind her, sending shivers down her spine, and she realised he must have intentionally moved in closer to her.

'Boundaries,' Savi muttered under her breath, marching on ahead. She grabbed the keys to her dad's truck, having already got permission to use it this morning.

'What was that?' She whipped around to see him smirking.

'Boundaries.' She said it louder this time. 'You're blurring them.'

'Only if you let me.'

He was right and it only set her more on edge; something was there under the surface, and she couldn't decide if she should ignore it and hope it would go away or tackle it head on, letting him know it wasn't the right time. There might not ever *be* a right time. Maybe he didn't feel it at all, perhaps he wasn't flirting, and he was just comfortable enough around her to not have to filter himself.

Savi blasted the radio on the way to the first store on their list for the day, filling the truck with the sound of Jesse's country twang and hoping it acted as a warning sign to Marco that she was nowhere near ready. It had been less than a month since she had broken up with the man singing love songs about her through the speakers, and less than three days since she had discovered just how far he was from the man she'd believed him to be. Having said that, she was more okay than she had expected to be and it didn't make sense to her.

'Wanna grab something to eat first?' Savi lowered the volume on the radio as they neared the next town over, where the best hardware stores were.

'Sure, but will there be places that do vegan stuff? I notice everyone's quite big on meat around here, there are deer heads on the wall in the store and in your basement.'

'Shit! Dad was supposed to take Henry down.'

'Henry?' Marco quizzed.

'He's not real. My family don't hunt, and we don't like taxidermy, either.'

'Oh. Now I feel stupid.' He laughed as Savi found the perfect parking spot, metres away from one of her favourite restaurants. She knew they had a decent vegan menu which was rare to find around here, but they were famous in the area for it.

'Don't. We were still going to take him down because he's pretty realistic and we didn't want to freak you out. If you were to go down there in the dark to grab ice cream from the freezer, you'd jump out of your skin. He just sort of looms over you.'

'Okay, note to self, wake someone up to hold my hand if I want ice cream.'

'Someone, or me?' she asked, her cheeks flushing. 'Well, you're hardly gonna take Wes down in the lift, are you? That's a lot of effort just for some mint choc chip. His lift takes forever.'

'I'd take your dad,' Marco shot back and hurried ahead to hold the door.

She followed him with a grin and walked in to a chorus of 'hellos' and 'long time no sees' all courtesy of the usual patrons who took up residence in the old red leather booth seats surrounding the edges of the restaurant. She loved it in here. It was cosy, you knew what you were going to get and there were no airs and graces from the staff. It didn't try to be anything fancy; it just served good food, cooked from scratch by the chefs who always made themselves visible to customers.

'This the boyfriend?' Delores greeted them at the door, ready to take them to a table. 'Also, why didn't you tell me you were coming home? I'd have made you an apple pie as a welcome present. You know that's my thing.' The elderly woman who had worked here for years frowned at her.

'This is Marco, yes. Mars, this is Delores. And I didn't tell you I was coming because I tell you every time I'm the only one who eats apple pie at home, and I can't eat the whole thing on my own. It's too much, and I'm on an athlete's diet.'

'Excuses, girl. You've got this one to share it with now, I'll see about bringing one by Mustang Ridge in the week before you leave.' Savi rolled her eyes. Della had always tried to take care of the Hart kids, providing them with somewhere to do their homework for years and a place for them and their friends to come and grab milkshakes on weekends.

'Nice to meet you, Delores.' Marco reached out to shake her hand and she turned her nose up, staring at his open palm like he was diseased.

'Call me Della, and don't shake my hand. I do hugs.' She held her arms out for Marco to step into, winking at Savi when he looked to her for confirmation. 'Come on, boyfriend. I ain't got all day, got all these old biddies to cater to.'

Marco quickly jumped into action, giving Delores a hug

that turned into an almighty squeeze, which would be cute had she not whispered loudly in his ear about not daring to hurt Savi otherwise she would cut off a certain body part. He nodded in agreement and followed her to the table, one in the back corner. 'Gotta give the VIPs some privacy from prying eyes. Don't get too handsy, though. Bobby over there might have a heart attack, don't think he can handle the excitement.' She pointed to a man who was around the same age as her, hunched over a newspaper at the counter but peering over it, in their direction.

'Thanks, Della,' Marco smiled, taking the menu but not looking at it until she left.

As she went, Savi heard her mutter, 'Polite, I like him.'

'Savannah, they do vegan pancakes!' Marco gasped.

'How are you the size that you are?' She scanned the menu, choosing to try something vegan herself but instead settling on an all-day full English breakfast. She'd tried one in London the previous year and grown obsessed, choosing to have it for breakfast in every hotel that had it on the menu. It was because of her that the diner had started serving it.

'I swear I do eat vegetables, but these sound so good. I can't resist.' He looked as though his mouth was about to water. 'So, spoken to Kodie the last couple of days?'

'Yep. She touched base, said she's sorry for overreacting and she's going to miss me for the next two weeks. Asked if we could go for a drink in Le Mans. Just one, obviously. Got to be in top shape for a race like that.'

'I'm so excited for you girls to experience it. No driver ever quite understands the magic of Le Mans until they get to race it themselves. There's nothing else like it: all the history, the unpredictability. The whole pit lane is just electric for the entire week, and in those twenty-four hours it's like you're in another world,' he said, the excitement shining in his eyes.

Savi loved hearing other people talking about the industry. It was the way Gabriel spoke about the IEC with so much passion that had made her want to excel at karting, so he saw her value and helped her get there. She had worked hard so that she could feel that love for the industry for herself, and it still didn't feel real that she was here. She'd made it.

'Mars, we need to talk about this fake-dating thing. Enough time has passed that we needn't worry about the photos, but . . . the only other reason for doing it was to keep Jesse and I's relationship free of any suspicion. Isn't it about time we stopped?'

'Are you ready?' he frowned. 'To face the publicity that will come with our fake break-up whilst you're still healing from a real one in private?'

She sighed and shrugged, because that was just it. She didn't know if she was. 'Probably not, but it's not fair to keep you tied to me. You have your own life to live, Monaco.'

'Savannah, are you serious?' He rolled his eyes. 'This is my life right now, and I am very okay with what it looks like. I'm not tied to you. I'm choosing you. So if you need to keep up the pretending for a little while longer, I'm game.'

'Really?' she asked, her heart melting a little at how sure he looked. 'You don't have to do this, Marco. I can handle it, if you change your mind or if there's a girl you've got your eye on or something . . .'

'My mind has been somewhat occupied.' He smiled. 'How does keeping me on as your fake boyfriend until the end of the season sound?'

Savi reached out for a handshake. 'You've got yourself a deal.'

She let Marco take control of the conversation all the way through lunch, listening to him tell her all about his, Brett's and Julien's antics before she and the others came along. It sounded like even Faith and Lucie's influence hadn't completely tamed them. There were stories of mechanical bulls, bouncy castles, stolen golf karts and trips to Paris where they'd rented bikes and caused havoc across the city.

Marco spoke like she would soon be part of it, and while she would be somewhat involved because she was part of the Revolution Racing team, it sounded like they did a lot of things as couples and Marco tagged along as an extra. She wasn't sure she would always be welcomed like she was truly one of them.

By the time they got back to the ranch, the truck was loaded up with not just equipment for Mocha, Java and Cappuccino, but for all the other rescue horses they had at the ranch and up to three more. Saddles, reins, bridles, coats. Everything they could possibly need. She had spent a fortune, but she'd been able to buy all the things she had dreamed of having as a little girl.

'What in the world?' Bonnie's eyes went wide at the number of items in the back of the truck. 'I thought you were just fixing the gate!'

'We really went for it,' Marco grinned. 'The final reveal will be on Friday, please do not enter the stables until then.'

'Okay,' Bonnie blinked. 'Let Cal know if you need any more tools.'

25

Four hours later, they'd successfully fixed the gate and fences, sorted through all the equestrian gear, reconfigured the loft space where the ranch hands slept if they had to stay overnight, and given each horse's stall a quick lick of paint on the exterior.

There had only been one incident: Marco hitting his hand with a hammer. Savi had stepped in while Weston sat in the doorway making fun of them. He'd snapped multiple photos, and Marco had flipped him off in almost all of them.

'Dude, you're covered in paint. I'm shocked any even made it onto the wall.' Weston inspected Marco's t-shirt – an old one which he'd borrowed from Wes when he realised he didn't have anything that could be ruined.

'Like you could've done better.' Marco rolled his eyes but the Cheshire Cat grin made it clear he was just messing with him. The pair of them had been bickering back and forth all day, and Marco had even gone as far as wheeling him out of the stables and shutting the doors on him when Wes had insulted his driving skills during the first race where Savi had overtaken him.

'You two joining us for dinner tonight?' Weston asked.

'Actually, no,' Marco answered before Savi could. 'I've got a surprise for your sister.'

Savi frowned. 'A surprise?'

'Be right back!' He darted off towards the house, leaving her stood there dumbfounded while Weston narrowed his eyes at them both.

'How are you doing?' Wes asked.

'I'm fine, and you?'

'Not what I meant.'

Savi tidied the tools away, refusing to look her brother in the eye. 'But I meant what I said.'

'Are you really, truly fine? With everything that has gone on? Because I will get myself on a plane and go and deck that loser in the face if you need me to. Just say the word.'

'Don't get me wrong, Wes, I have my moments. When I'm alone and my mind replays something he said or did in the past that I should have paid attention to. All the signs were there, and I feel like the world's biggest idiot, but I have too much going for me to let one person tear it all down. Sapphire has it far worse than I do, it's her I feel sorry for. Not myself. I just feel angry for myself, *at* myself.'

'How is it that you're so much younger than me and yet so much wiser? The way you look at life . . . I wish that was me. That I had your resilience.'

She walked over to squeeze his shoulder. 'You do, Wes. You're a hell of a lot stronger than you might think you are.'

'Mmm. Well, for the record, ignoring the red flags from Jesse Montalvo isn't what makes you the world's biggest idiot. Ignoring the green ones from Marco is.'

'Oh, I see them,' she laughed. 'I'm just not so sure he's interested in me that way. We're just friends. Besides, I think he's still hung up on my best friend.'

'He lov—' And then Marco was back and Wes was backing out of the barn, jaw on the floor at the sight of what their guest was holding.

A wicker picnic basket, two wine glasses and a tatty old tartan blanket from the basement. Her surprise. She dropped the screwdriver she was still holding and wrapped her arms around him, standing on her tiptoes and squeezing him as tightly as she could.

'What's that for?' he laughed. 'For all you know, this is for the horses, not for you.'

Java whinnied behind them and she grinned. 'He doesn't like wine, better give his share to me. But seriously, Monaco. Thank you.'

'I haven't even got started yet. I've just this second walked in with the goods.'

She waited patiently as he climbed into the loft space, reaching down as she lifted the basket up to him. He laid the blanket out, sending the loose hay flying as he waved it in the air, and then set about emptying the basket. 'Am I allowed to come and help?'

His head peered over the safety railing. 'No, stay down there with the horses until I give you the green light. And no peeking. I hear a single step on that ladder and I will push you off.'

'Violent,' she tutted, but secretly, she was enjoying every second of this. She was all about the little things, so she wasn't sure why she had spent so long wrapped up in someone who had no interest in gestures, big or small.

Marco started to make his way back down the ladder. 'Okay, all done.'

'So why are you coming back down?'

'So I can make sure you get up there safely.' He said it so matter of factly, like it was the most obvious answer in the world. 'Head on up, I'll watch from down here.'

'I'm glad I'm not wearing a dress,' Savi muttered, eyes nearly falling out of her skull when she saw his handiwork. Candles, cushions stolen from the bed up there, and an array of homemade food with two glasses of wine sitting at the side of the blanket, one with her name on it. 'Oh, wow . . .'

'Move over, I'm coming up.' He appeared behind her, gesturing for her to make room. It was a tight squeeze up there, but it was cosy and intimate. It was starting to occur to her that might have been the vibe he was going for, and while she tried really hard to mind, she couldn't help but gaze up at him with admiration.

'What have we got here, then?' She looked around them as they sat sprawled across the blanket, limbs tangled together like this meant nothing. But it did mean something, and she wasn't sure what yet, but she could no longer pretend the sparks weren't threatening to spill over from their fake relationship to their real one.

'All your favourites, made by your mum. I set her a mission while we were busy out here and she came through. So I can't take much credit, here.'

'You absolutely can. It was your idea, right?'

He nodded. 'It was.'

'Thank you.'

'You don't have to thank me, Savannah.'

'God, Monaco, do you not see it?' She shook her head in

disbelief. 'I would have been lost without you this season. We're not even halfway through, and my entire world has been flipped upside down. You are the only person on the entire team who knows my story. All of it. And you haven't shied away from it, or from me, or the storm I have created in your life.'

'I like storms,' he whispered. 'Besides, it's what teammates are for . . .'

'No, Mars,' she smiled, her soft tone matching his own. 'You've gone above and beyond. You're so much more than just a teammate and you know it. There is something here, something I've been pushing aside so I could do right by Jesse. And now, I want to do right by you and not drag you further into my mess, but . . .'

'I'm already in it, Cowgirl,' he murmured, reaching out to pluck a bit of hay from her curls. His voice was low and velvety, the kind of sound that made Savi's heart flutter. His fingers lingered, gently brushing against her cheek, and she caught his wrist, holding it there for a moment longer than necessary. 'I know this might not be the right time for a confession with everything you're going through, but being here in Wyoming has made me certain that you're special. Whatever it is that I feel for you, it goes far beyond anything I've felt for anyone else. And I'm sorry if that feels like too much, but I can't keep my feelings in any longer . . .'

The barn seemed to grow quieter, as if the world outside had paused. The horses stopped whinnying, tractor engines stopped running and the only sound was the hitch in Marco's breath when Savi edged closer.

She kissed him slowly, the kind of kiss that starts soft but deepens and invites the abandonment of responsibility. Maybe she shouldn't be encouraging him like this when she wasn't sure if her heart was entirely ready to let him in all the way, but how could she not? Savi had spent too long chasing lows and this . . . Marco was her high. Pulling her closer until she felt the solid strength of his body against hers. The scent of him – sweet, with a hint of cinnamon – made her head spin. Her hands found their way to his chest, gripping the fabric of his shirt to steady herself.

Marco guided her backwards, the material of the red and white plaid picnic blanket soft against her bare shoulders, the straps of her vest top slipping off her shoulders like she had been trying to tease him all day when in actual fact, he had been doing just that with his biceps each time he slammed the hammer into the wooden gate.

His lips left a trail down her neck, warm and unhurried, as if he had all the time in the world to memorise the taste of her skin. Savi's hands slid up to his shoulders before winding their way through the curls at the nape of his neck, her breaths coming faster now.

'Mars,' she whispered, his name barely more than a sigh. He pulled back just enough to look at her, his eyes dark with desire but searching hers, waiting for her permission to go further. She nodded, her head fighting her heart with her hopeless romantic nature winning the battle. She had to explore this, in whatever capacity felt right for them both.

'Are you sure this is what you want?' he asked, squeezing her hip. 'Say the word and we'll stop, Cowgirl. This is your decision. I won't take offence if you –'

'Monaco,' she interrupted, reaching up to kiss him again, 'I'm sure.'

They undressed each other slowly, the quiet punctuated by soft laughter when fingers fumbled with buttons or caught on stubborn fabric. With her clothes tossed aside and her boots kicked off, Savi let Marco take a moment to soak her in while she did the same thing, admiring the physique he had worked so hard to maintain.

Instead of coming back to meet her at eye level, he placed tiny, delicate kisses from her breasts to her waist, then down to her thighs. 'I'm gonna ask one more time, Savannah.'

'Yes.' She breathed out a laugh. 'Please, just . . . yes.'

His tongue danced with her core, teasing her and bringing her closer to the edge while her hands gripped his hair, her body rocking underneath his touch. Just as she was about to let herself feel that sweet, satisfying release, he stopped, pulling a condom from his wallet. Thank goodness someone was prepared. A smirk adorned his features as he looked up at her from between her legs, that one stray curl falling over his eyes again. 'Are you ready for me, Cowgirl?'

She pulled him up to her and with one swift movement, their bodies met in a way that felt as natural as breathing. The world fell away, leaving only the two of them and the rhythm they created together. His touch was firm but gentle, his kisses deep and lingering, as if he wanted to memorise every inch of her. But Savi worried he may have to live with just a memory for a long while yet, because this was earth-shattering. Everything she could have dreamed of, and as he moaned into her ear, his breath hot on her neck while they came together, the stars and planets aligned. It just wasn't enough. Not yet.

They lay tangled in a nest of fabric and hay, their bodies glowing with the warmth of shared intimacy. Savi traced patterns on Marco's chest, her head resting in the crook of his shoulder. He held her close, his fingers idly stroking her back as they listened to the distant sound of crickets and the occasional soft whinny of her beloved horses below.

'I think,' Savi said softly, her voice shaky, 'that might have changed everything.'

Marco laughed, pressing a kiss to her temple. 'Yeah, but I think that might be a conversation for another time, Savannah.'

He was right. For now, she needed to let herself enjoy it for what it was. Forget her fears and all the reasons this was a bad idea, and just pay attention to the way her heart felt like it had found its home.

26

'Savannah, no way. That horse is a fucking giant. I can't get on that!' Marco backed away from Cappuccino, eyes wide with fear.

'You can, trust me. I know what I'm doing, Mars, and I won't let go of the reins until you're comfortable.' Savi ran her hand along Cappuccino's muzzle, keeping her calm and still. She was a nervous horse, and perhaps wasn't the best match for a nervous rider, but she trusted her dad's advice. She just had to get Marco to do the same.

'If I fall off, you can call Jasper and tell him your family tried to kill me out here in the Wild West.' Marco crossed his arms and Savi grabbed one of them, forcing it away from his body so he could stroke the horse.

'Just give her some love.' Savi rolled her eyes. 'And get a grip, you're a grown man who drives fast cars for a living. You can handle a horse that twelve-year-old girls ride.'

'I'm really not an animal person, Savannah. Lucie and Brett have goats in Malmedy, and they rammed me and knocked me over last year. The only animal I like is Faith and Julien's dog.'

'Marco De Luca, you are getting on this horse. You wanted the full cowboy experience, didn't you? I'd be doing you a disservice if I sent you home to Europe without having experienced the wind through your hair as you gallop through the mountains.'

'I already kissed a cowgirl, isn't that enough authenticity?'

'Monaco,' she scowled, blushing slightly. They hadn't addressed last night, but it wasn't awkward. It just . . . was whatever it was and she had no desire to label it.

'Okay, what the hell do I do?'

'Put your foot in the stirrup, grab this,' she pointed at the pommel, 'and haul yourself over. Then just sit there until I give the next instruction.'

She tried her best not to laugh at his misfortune as it took him several clumsy attempts to mount the horse, cursing each time before he finally made it. Cappuccino just stood there blinking, probably wondering who let this guy anywhere near her. Once he was up, Marco grinned proudly down at her.

Savi spent the next twenty minutes guiding him around in circles, teaching him how to control the horse's movements. With each step, he gained more confidence and eventually, she was able to let go. She mounted Mocha and joined Marco, waiting for one of the ranch hands to let them out of the gate. They were taking the easiest trail; one she could remember like the back of her hand. It led to a little brook so they could have a picnic on the rocks and let the horses cool off.

'You know, this is kind of like driving. You have to feel every movement, learn the horse and move together as one. I think I like it.'

'Yeah, your horse is an extension of you.'

'But they still have a mind of their own, and I swear to god if she runs off and I go hurtling through the mountains, I am never going to forgive you.'

'You'll be fine, Monaco. If Gabriel can handle it, so can you. Right, we're about to enter the trail and it's quite narrow. Not so narrow that you're going to fall to your death, but we can't walk side by side. Stay as close as you can, I'll keep checking on you.'

She led him through the trees, remembering just how lucky she was to have this on her doorstep. Hikers would sometimes come all the way through from one side to the other and end up lost on the ranch, but for the most part, they and a few neighbours were the only ones who ever used these trails. It was peaceful; the perfect place to escape and forget about the real world.

They stopped by the brook and she unpacked, waiting until they were sat down on the picnic blanket with a beer in hand to bring it up. 'So, um . . . How was last night for you?'

Marco swirled his beer around, staring through the mouth of the bottle, deep in thought. He was quiet for a moment, the only sound the running water and Mocha and Cappuccino's whinnying.

'Savannah, you're not ready for the real thing, are you?' He still wasn't looking at her when he spoke, which gave her time to do a double take.

'I don't think I am . . .' Her voice was barely a whisper, nausea rising in her throat.

'Cowgirl, it's okay. You don't have to pretend. If I was your rebound, just say so.'

'You're not my rebound.' Savi pulled her knees up to her chest, watching Mocha drink from the brook. 'I just . . .'

'Look, some people are just destined to disappoint us. It doesn't mean they're bad people, or that they intended to, it just means they're not ours to keep,' Marco stated. 'Look at Esme. I thought there was something real there, but she wasn't meant for me. In the end, she was just part of my journey. My feelings for her taught me patience while I wait for what's mine.'

'But what if this journey just looks different to how you think it should and it's worth waiting things out just that little bit longer?' She chewed her bottom lip.

'How much longer is a "little bit"? I know you're scared, but I can promise you that if we were ever to explore this further, it wouldn't be like it was with Jesse. I've told you before that if you were mine, I would be shouting it from the rooftops, showing you off to the world. Regardless of the risks. I am an all-in kind of guy, in everything I do.'

'He didn't let me choose.' She let out a sarcastic laugh, getting angry again. Mostly at herself for putting up with Jesse for so long when she knew it wasn't what she truly wanted.

'What, to go public or not?'

'Yeah,' she nodded. 'He insisted for four years that I couldn't handle the level of fame that comes with dating someone like him. That they'd rip me apart in the press. It's why he was so paranoid about the photos being linked to me. He thought he was doing me a favour by keeping everything under wraps.'

'But in reality, he kept you locked in a cage.'

'My career could handle the blow if people realised it was me. I know Jasper would have my back, so would Gabriel. I'll admit that I was scared when they first got released in the press, but I could handle the humiliation;

these kinds of scandals happen to people in the public eye all the time and it's soon forgotten about when the next big thing hits the headlines. But instead, Jesse used the situation as an excuse to keep me as his dirty little secret.'

'And it also isn't your fault that the paparazzi are so vile, so invasive. They took advantage of you both in the privacy of your own home, bypassed a whole security team for a decent pay day. That's not on you, and fans and sponsors would take that into account.' Marco pointed out.

'I know you're nothing like him. I just need to be sure that his actions haven't fucked me up enough that I take you down with me.' Savi took her boots and socks off, tossing them to the edge of the picnic blanket and standing up. She needed to feel the earth beneath her feet, and this brook was one of her favourite places near the ranch. It was serene. It made her feel like herself again.

Marco joined her at the water's edge, his jeans rolled up to his knees. He looked ridiculous, but he looked peaceful the second his skin met the cool, clear liquid. 'You're too good for this world, Cowgirl.'

'Tell me about it.' She started wobbling her way over the pebbles lining the bottom of the brook, heading to the large rock that sat right in the middle. Once she made it over there, she felt like she was a million miles away from the outside world. She glanced at Marco who was cautiously eyeing the path she had taken. 'Come sit over here, live out your mermaid fantasies.'

'I don't have mermaid fantasies, Savannah. I've seen footage of them before, you know when people claim they've spotted one? They're terrifying.'

'They're edited.' She rolled her eyes as he worked up the courage and got closer to her, finally settling on the rock and gripping onto her thigh for dear life as his feet lifted from the ground. 'You *really* liked Esme, didn't you?'

'I did.' Marco nodded.

'How did you get over her?'

'I got under a number of other people,' he laughed.

Savi blinked at him. 'Is that seriously it?'

'No.' He shook his head. 'I'm not sure if that helped or hindered things. I'm just the kind of guy who thinks that what's for you won't pass you. That especially goes for soulmates. If you're supposed to be with someone, it'll happen. Sometimes the journey to get there is complicated and hard and it takes a while, but for the most part, I think it's supposed to feel easy. And it wasn't easy with Esme. It was all over the place.'

'It feels easy with you. Almost too good to be true.'

'Because you're used to chaos and pain. It's what you know, what you're good at. My parents really set the standard,' he said. 'The way they love each other . . . half the time I think they're on a different planet to the rest of us and their love is the only thing in the entire world that matters. The respect they have for one another, the way they support each other through absolutely everything no matter how big or small. It's all I want in life. God, it's more important than my career. To love and to be loved; it's what I was put on this earth for.'

'I grew up around that exact kind of love. My parents would die for each other, and it's beautiful. It influenced the way I see the world. So why did I settle for less than that?'

'Because you got the fairytale once. You got the racing career, then you got the contract of your dreams. You've found your home away from home with our team, given your family the ability to provide for Weston and keep a roof over their heads. You love hard. It's who you are. And you loved Jesse, but as a result it means you've suffered. You've got to love yourself more. *Let* yourself have all the things you desire. If that includes me, then I'll take it. But regardless of your choice in the end, I'll respect it.'

'I don't think anyone's ever been able to read me the way you do.' Savi rested her head on his shoulder, wanting to be close to him physically but unsure of how to go about it without crossing those lines once again.

'I'm just too good.' Marco took her hand in his, giving it a squeeze.

'Yeah, you are.'

27

Marco watched Savannah ride ahead of him, the midday sun casting a golden glow on her bronzed skin. She was ethereal and it broke his heart in two. Even now she had cut ties with Jesse, she still wasn't going to be his. Not yet, at least. Maybe not ever. Everything he had said to her about her character rang true for him, too; he always suffered in the name of love.

It wasn't a conscious choice he made time and time again; in fact, he had avoided women for years because he couldn't be bothered with the heartache. But the first time he let himself get close to someone, he'd got hurt, and then the second, he'd somehow wound up being given permission to hold her in public but had to live with knowing that she belonged to someone else in private.

Except now he seemed to have convinced Savannah to believe that the only person she belonged to was herself and he risked forever being labelled the rebound, no matter how much she insisted he wasn't. Marco was sick of being a rebound. He wanted the kind of love he and Savi had just talked about and while he was trying hard not to let himself get in too deep with his teammate, the harder he tried, the more he failed.

She was effortlessly beautiful, and watching her on the ranch, in her element, had only made him fall ten times harder. Then there was last night. Pure bliss, the most intimate experience he'd shared with a woman. It might not have meant much to her, but it meant the world to him.

This wasn't like it was with Esme. It felt easy even though it wasn't supposed to be. This was not a straightforward love story, and it may forever remain an unrequited one. The only thing Marco was certain of was that he had to stick by her through thick and thin. They were a team far beyond the racetrack and that bond was unique; nobody knew what it was like unless they'd been in the same position. He had seen the real Savannah now, the one nobody else got to see. He cherished that, and he would learn to appreciate their connection in whatever form the universe wanted it to be.

'You're being too slow, Monaco!' she called out from in front.

'You're an IEC rookie, you should understand I'm a rookie when it comes to all things cowboy! My hat doesn't make me an expert, Savannah!'

'Really?' She pulled Mocha to a halt and Cappuccino panicked when Marco reacted too slowly, almost knocking the horses into each other. 'I thought you were the next Buffalo Bill.'

'Who?' he frowned, calming Cappuccino down. She might be scary and unpredictable, but he was developing a soft spot for this horse.

'Never mind,' Savannah laughed. 'Come on, we're almost back at Mustang Ridge. How do you feel about a race?'

'Oh, Savannah . . .' he sighed. 'You know I can't say no to a race.'

'I know,' she grinned.

'What if I fall off?'

'You won't. Remember what I taught you?'

'It's ingrained in my memory forever.'

'You'll be fine. I'm there to catch you.'

He watched her gallop on ahead, knowing he would never catch her up. He laughed at the reality of the situation; Savannah Hart may never be the one to love him, but he would always be there to pick up the pieces when her life got turned upside down.

Savi sat round the campfire with her family, listening to Marco and Wes sing Italian nursery rhymes. She should be enjoying her evening, spending time with her family. But instead, she felt nothing except dread for the phone call she was going to have to return when she got back to her room. Jesse had been blowing her phone up for an hour on his work number, which she had stupidly forgotten to block.

'I think I'm gonna get an early night.' She stood up from her chair. 'Feeling tired from all the riding and I've got a headache coming on. Thanks for dinner, Ma. Are we riding again tomorrow, Mars?'

'You've got it.' He gave her a smile, but it was one full of sadness. He had seen her check her phone multiple times, which meant he knew what she was going to do.

Taking a deep breath, Savi sat down on the edge of her bed. This room was full of her childhood self: her teddy bear and photos of her and her friends, the floral bedding she'd picked out when she was sixteen and obsessed with lavender. She should feel safe from Jesse's influence in here, but she was terrified to make this call.

'Savi?' His face filled the screen at the same time his voice echoed around the room, and she regretted selecting the video option. Jesse scowled at her, looking angry — more than just a little disgruntled. 'Why didn't you pick up?'

'I was with my family. Why did you call so many times?'

'I wanted to talk things through. See if we could salvage this.'

'There is nothing to talk through, Jesse. You fucked up, you ruined us. I just want to know all the reasons you didn't want to take our relationship to the next level. Why you pursued other women, when I was right here, willing to give you everything you said you wanted.'

'Sav.' He rolled his eyes. 'We've been through this countless times. Don't you listen?'

'We should have been buying a house, getting married. All the big life things. But we got stuck at square one, Jesse. You said you wanted those things.'

'We had the cabin! I don't know what more you wanted from me. I was too busy to give you everything else, Savi!' he cried out.

'*Your* cabin. My lingerie might be in the drawer, but no part of that cabin was ever mine. You told me you wanted to build a life with me, Jess, but you refused to actually make any moves that would allow us to have the happily ever after we used to talk about.'

'Life isn't a fucking fairytale, Savi. I don't know what else to tell you.'

'Actually, I think it can be. If you let it be, life can

be pretty magical sometimes. And I have had plenty of moments where I've thought magic might be playing a part, some of those were shared with you back when we first met, but those moments have mostly happened alone, or with my team. Where were you for that? You haven't come to a single race.'

'You know I couldn't come to any races. I had no reason to be there, so everyone would know about us. A quick internet search tells you we grew up twenty-five minutes apart, it wouldn't take long to connect the dots.'

'You could've asked to come to Spa, Monza or Sao Paolo with any number of other celebrities who come to watch the race and soak up the atmosphere. Even Weston is pushing past his reservations and coming to watch me compete. He's opening himself up to all these questions from the media about his condition by being there, but he's doing it because he loves me. He wants to support me. He's putting me first.'

'Your brother finally got the balls to leave Mustang Ridge?' Jesse laughed.

Savi felt the colour drain from her face. 'Excuse me?'

'That might have been too far.' He had the decency to look guilty, but then the emotion disappeared from his features, and he reverted to being cold and uncaring. 'But what I'm getting at is, life doesn't always work out the way you want it to. Shit goes wrong, you get thrown curveballs. My life has become utter chaos since Sapphire told me she was pregnant.'

Savi laughed. 'No shit. And who's fault is that, Jess?' She waited for him to say more, but the words never came. 'I've tried. I've really tried, and I've pushed for more and you haven't been receptive to a single attempt. I loved you; I wanted you. Forever and always. But I guess I should've known the day you signed your record deal that things were going to change.'

'What are you saying?' He swallowed roughly, his hands on his hips.

'I'm cutting all ties, Jesse. For good,' she said, her eyes welling up with years' worth of tears for her past, present and future self. For the little girl who had just wanted what her parents had, who believed in the magic of fairytales and true love. 'Not once have you taken accountability for the other women, or for your baby. I don't recognise you anymore. Hell, I barely recognise myself.'

'Maybe we really are better off staying out of each other's lives, then,' he sighed, acting like this was all his idea, trying to twist the narrative until it seemed like he was doing her a favour by not fighting for her.

'Don't contact me again, Jesse. At least have enough respect to let me move on in peace.'

And then he was gone, and Savi was sinking to the floor at the foot of her bed. She let the tears fall, feeling like the last four years of her life had just crumbled to pieces in front of her. How could she have been so naïve? She'd known for months, if not years. Jesse didn't know how to love anyone except himself; he barely knew how to communicate. There had been hundreds of instances where he'd forgotten to tell her he was home safe, or he'd not bothered letting her know which state he was in or which country he was flying to next. Sapphire had kept her more informed than he had half the time. She was angry at herself, at him, at the universe for bringing him to her at that stupid county fair.

'Savi?' Marco's head of curls in the doorway was all she could see through her tears. 'What happened?' He rushed towards her, crouching down in front of her and holding onto her knees, trying to pull her hands away from her face.

'He couldn't even apologise,' she sobbed.

'I know, Cowgirl.' He tucked a stray curl behind her ear. 'Men like him can do no wrong.'

'You were right,' she choked out. 'I was right. He was never mine to keep.'

'Oh, Sav . . . Come on, get up off the floor.'

She caught a glimpse of herself in her mirror. 'I look hideous.'

'Don't worry about that. The crying is giving you a nice rosy glow.' He held her hands to his lips and gently kissed her knuckles. 'Get yourself dressed into your comfiest PJs, I'm going to get you a tea and then we're going to sit here and watch crappy reality TV and gossip about all the biggest paddock scandals we can think of.'

'Thanks, Mars.' She took the tea gratefully, scooting over to give him room and handing him the controls. 'You can choose. Although I like the sound of that new one that got released this week. Esme said it's nothing but drama and plot twists.'

'Sounds like the perfect medicine,' he agreed. 'Can I get under the sheets? It's kind of cold in here. I've been sat by a heat source for three hours.'

'Sure.' She held the sheets open and waited for him to climb in, still wiping her eyes as tears threatened to take hold again.

'He's an asshole,' Marco stated, pressing play on the TV. 'I know I've said it before, but you weren't ready to hear it then. I will say it every hour of every day until you're over him if I have to. You know your own worth, Cowgirl. Don't you forget it.'

'I really appreciate you, Marco.' She looked over at him, a slight smile creeping onto her face. 'I'm sorry if it feels like I'm playing with your emotions, I'm really not trying to.'

'I know you're not, and hey, I know I'm not Esme or even Miko or Kodie, and I've never had a guy break my heart, but I've broken my own heart too many times. So I'll be here for you every step of the way until loving yourself is enough.'

And with that, she was off again. But this time, as the tears rolled down her cheeks and her neck and she soaked her pyjama shirt, she laughed. At what, she wasn't quite sure. Maybe it was at her own stupidity, or her misfortune, or maybe it was the fact Marco De Luca was sat in her bed with a cup of tea, watching a dating show and nursing her back to her old self.

'Sorry, I can't stop crying,' she sniffled.

'You don't need to apologise.' Marco checked his watch. 'It has, after all, only been four weeks since it ended. Takes longer than that to get over a break-up.'

'Whatever, I'm a big girl and big girls *do* cry despite what Fergie says.'

They sat in silence while they watched the first episode,

other than the odd commentary on someone's behaviour or rating the couples. So far, Marco had been very opinionated and cut-throat each time he opened his mouth, and although Savi was giggling through it, she couldn't help the odd outburst of crying. She was going to have a sore head in the morning.

'Would you like a cuddle? No strings, no expectations.' He looked nervous but he held her gaze nonetheless while she sat there and contemplated it. What harm could it do? She shuffled into his arms, immediately feeling soothed by the warmth of his embrace combined with the warmth of the mug in her hands. She'd missed being held. And this may not mean anything in this exact moment, but it made her feel something. It made her feel like she mattered to someone.

So she lay there long after the credits of episode six rolled, and her half-drunk tea had gone cold and been put on the bedside table. She stayed in Marco's arms, crying and laughing in turn until eventually she fell asleep on his chest, safe in the knowledge that just because Jesse couldn't support her the way she needed him to, it didn't mean her friends, family and teammates couldn't step in and fill the gap.

28

'Are we allowed to drink the champagne?' Calvin whispered out of earshot of the flight crew, lifting it out of the ice bucket and reading the label.

They had driven back to the airport in Montana, where the Revolution Racing private jet was waiting for them. Jasper had ensured it was fully decked out with everything they could want: champagne, sushi, a multitude of snacks, *decent* plane meals which were part of a custom menu, soft drinks and waters. The Harts were in heaven, and they weren't shy about letting Savi and Marco know about it.

'Yes, Dad,' Savi laughed and found him a glass. 'Let Marco pop the cork, he's good at it.'

'It's all the underage parties I snuck out to as a teenager,' Marco grinned. 'They trained me for the life I lead today. Including how to deal with hangovers quickly and quietly.'

Weston scowled, wheeling up and down the aisle, exploring every nook and cranny of the plane's interior. 'Can someone hurry up and help me get into an actual seat so we can get this show on the road? Or in the sky, whatever.'

'You happy for me to do it?' Marco asked, standing to give Weston a hand.

They'd grown close over the last couple of weeks, with Marco often assisting Weston with various daily tasks, taking some of the pressure off Bonnie and Calvin. It was lovely to see Weston letting someone into his bubble, and Marco had even persuaded him to invite a girl over for dinner when he returned from France. All the things Weston had shied away from doing since his accident, he was doing with a gentle shove from a total stranger.

Savi seemed to be the only one worrying what it might do to Weston if his presence at Le Mans caused a stir, which it may or may not. A lot of the world didn't know who he was, but all it took was for someone on the rodeo circuit to see him on their TV screen and he would no longer be living a private life behind the rickety wooden fences of Mustang Ridge.

Wes had deleted his social media apps weeks after he woke up from his coma and not touched them again since, even for personal use. He gamed and read books, and occasionally wrote in his journal. A habit picked up in therapy sessions he'd been forced to go to by their parents. That was all he did day in, day out when Savi wasn't home for him to wind up. Oh, and he watched livestreams of her races which, notably, was more than Jesse had ever done.

He seemed to be taking a lot of monumental steps in a very short period of time, and although she loved seeing snippets of the old Wes, she was too used to the version of her brother who just wanted to shut everything and everyone out. If the media attention got too much, he could shut down again and then there would be no hope of getting him back.

With Weston sitting at one of the tables with his spare gaming laptop in his bag, waiting for take-off so he could safely get it out, Marco settled in opposite him and opened a newspaper.

'I'm very impressed, Marco,' Bonnie nodded at the paper. 'Most people of your generation use their phones to access the news.'

'I'm not going to lie, I found it in the seat pocket, and I forgot to bring a book, so I figured it'll do until we're in the air and I can get my portable gaming console out. It's probably Julien's.'

'Is this also Julien's?' Savi pulled a fruit wind-up out of her own seat pocket.

'That either belongs to one of his kids or it's Brett's.' Marco squinted. 'Strawberry? Belongs to Brett. He's obsessed with those.'

'So, what should we expect when we get to Le Mans?' Bonnie sat down next to Calvin and opposite Savi, who had decided to let the guys do their own thing across the aisle. She wasn't part of the gaming squad, nor did she want to be.

'We'll get a private transfer to the hotel and check in, unpack and freshen up, then Savannah and I are going to take you all for lunch at my favourite restaurant in the city. Show you the architecture, do a bit of shopping. It's not really a tourist town, but it's pretty.'

'Do you think I'll find a magnet or a bottle opener?' Calvin's ears perked up.

'Probably,' Marco laughed. 'We'll likely have an early night as we'll be the first ones there, but first thing in the morning we're going to head straight to the track for a practice session. You guys can get breakfast in the team HQ building; we've got caterers so you can take your pick. We'll also introduce you to the team, reunite you with Gabriel, show you where to get merchandise if you want any.'

'Oh, I want *all* the merchandise,' Weston interjected. 'We need lots of t-shirts to replace the Jesse Montalvo tour tees. We're coming back on the jet, right?'

'You are. Savannah and I will be joining the rest of the team in the UK for Silverstone, and then I think Savannah has a workshop with *Girls Off Track* in London, right?' He looked to her for confirmation, and she nodded. 'I'll probably tag along with her.'

That was news to Savi. Not that she was complaining, she just hadn't given it much thought. In fact, she wasn't sure what the rest of the season had in store for her when it came to travelling; they had yet to race in Shanghai, Fuji, Qatar and Sebring. All she knew for certain was that she would be back home in Wyoming when Sebring was over since it was in the United States.

She had weeks to fill in between, where usually she would be catching up with Jesse, and now she had to choose between going back to her family or carving out new adventures for herself with her team. She wouldn't say no to a trip to Hawaii, for example. Or returning to Monaco and meeting Marco's parents, maybe even flying out to Switzerland to ski and hang out with Marco's brother. Except their relationship dynamic was even trickier than it had been on her last visit, and if she was going to meet his family, she wanted things between them to be clear.

The flight dragged on forever, in part thanks to Weston's constant complaining that planes were boring. The rodeo had taken him around the US in a specific order which meant he'd never had to travel too far, and most trips were done on the road. The jet had televisions and board games, but they spent a long time sat on the ground during their layover while the jet was refuelled. Thankfully everyone was asleep for the last few hours except for Savi and Marco, who were sharing headphones and watching more of that reality show they'd started, Savi having shuffled over to his side of the plane.

'Welcome to Paris.' Their flight attendant poked her head round and smiled at their sleepy faces. 'You're welcome to exit the plane now. Your car is waiting for you.'

They waited for Marco and Calvin to get Weston back in his wheelchair, not an easy task when he was itching to get off and enjoy some fresh air. That was another thing he'd complained about; not being able to open a window. He was too used to being in the open air back on the ranch, being able to wheel out onto the front porch whenever he felt like it. Thirteen hours on a plane was hard work.

'I wish we could see Paris,' Bonnie sighed wistfully, looking around like she'd see the Eiffel Tower from here. They'd flown into Charles de Gaulle Airport and were driving the rest of the way. Another two and a half hours, much to Weston's annoyance.

'You'll have to come next year,' Marco suggested, holding the car door open for Savi's mum.

'I might not be racing next year, you don't know,' Savi said.

Marco looked at her, his expression flat. 'Cowgirl, I beg you, shut up.'

'Yeah, what he said,' Calvin added.

'What?!' she laughed. 'Shit happens!'

'There's a stronger chance of Julien retiring to raise another set of twins than there is of you being kicked off the team, and you know it.' Marco huffed and sat in the back of the SUV, next to Weston. 'No more negative comments, please! We're only allowed to have fun from now on.'

Savi hoped this was the first trip of many, and that Weston wouldn't be put off attending future races. He'd supported her in her karting days and having him there felt right.

She'd attended several of his rodeo competitions, too, even sitting in the crowd on the day he'd had his accident. She could remember it like it was yesterday; the way he'd cried out in pain as the arena fell into silence, a cloud of uncertainty hanging in the air as they waited to see if he would get up from the ground. He never did. He was carried off on a stretcher, and Savi had left her spot in the audience to get to him, following him in the ambulance and calling their parents on the way.

She'd missed three races while he was in his coma and when he woke up, the first thing he'd made her promise was that she wouldn't give up on her dreams just to stay home and help him recover. She had wanted to. She'd felt guilty putting her own life at risk after they'd nearly lost him, but a promise was a promise, and her brother wanted to watch her shine. Why should she suffer just because he was?

*

The drive into the city of Le Mans was pure magic; the history-filled streets rolled by and as they drove under the bridge, multicoloured flags hanging from wire the whole way through, Savi was reminded of just how special this was. So many drivers from other championships dreamed of being able to compete in this twenty-four-hour race, some celebrities even seeking out opportunities to get behind the wheel of a race car with this weekend as their end goal.

It had been going for over one hundred years and had just celebrated its centenary with an exhibition of more than sixty cars which had previously won or marked the history of the race, a drivers' parade through the city where fans gathered and cheered the drivers on, wishing them luck for the weekend. They even had drone shows and live entertainment at the circuit. Savi wished she could have been there for that, but she'd missed out by one season.

'Do you think we could stop for food first?' Weston asked, holding off on making another complaint when Savi turned to glare at him. 'I could do with some local cuisine.'

'We're going to an Italian,' Savi deadpanned.

'Close enough. Italy is only one country away.'

Marco asked the driver to stop, agreeing that their bags would be taken to the hotel and dropped to their rooms by the staff. Another perk of being a VIP that Savi didn't think she would ever get used to; people trying to do everything for her. She'd walked into her hotel room for the second race of the season and someone had unpacked on her behalf, freaking her out when she realised the staff must have seen and handled her underwear. It was weird.

'This is beautiful,' Calvin commented, standing on the pavement and looking up, not at the restaurant building, but at the cathedral opposite. 'Can we go in?'

'The three of you can come back into the city in the week, I'll have someone from the team drop you in,' Marco suggested. 'We have plenty of assistants and interns who can ferry you around. The circuit isn't far from the city centre, so it won't take much time out of their day.'

It was relatively quiet in the area immediately surrounding the restaurant, and they were shown to a table as soon as they entered. It was nothing like Savi expected, and not the kind of place she thought Marco would choose to dine in. The tables were all dark wood, the walls red and there was some questionable décor, like the side table which seemed to have no real purpose except for displaying a single dying plant, with marble elephants acting as a table leg. Nonetheless, it was homely and seemed authentic, and she loved it.

They'd pored over the menu, settling on a range of pastas and pizzas and calzones, ordering all the side dishes they could manage between them, then they'd said hello to a couple of drivers from Camino Endurance Team and let Weston and Calvin take photos with them, both of them looking pleased as punch to be speaking so intimately with people they'd admired for years.

They were waiting for dessert when a group of fans approached them: a group of five or six girls who were decked out in Revolution Racing merch. They'd spent the duration of their meal glancing over at Savi and Marco and whispering, until Marco had waved them over and given them the green light to interrupt.

'Hi, girls,' Marco smiled. 'Thanks for waiting for us to finish eating.'

'It's no problem,' one of them smiled back, acting as their spokesperson while the rest of them seemed too nervous to speak. 'We were wondering if we could get photos and autographs? We know we'll see you at the parade, but you'll have so many people to see then.'

'Sure,' Savi agreed, taking a black marker pen from one of them and signing a collection of hats for them all. They each had a *Girls Off Track* hat which she signed, too. Her signature sat amongst around ten others, black ink standing out against the pastel pink fabric.

'We're trying to get autographs from as many females in motorsport as possible, but you were our top priority this season,' the quietest girl of all spoke up. 'We've been following your career since you were first announced as a driver in your last championship and went on the *Girls Off Track* podcast, and when you signed your contract with Revolution Racing we just knew we had to meet you.'

'Yeah, Revolution having an all-female team for their second car really changed the game. We even collectively signed up to a *Girls Off Track* workshop, we met Faith and Lucie!' another chimed in. 'We're all studying degrees in college which should help us get into the industry.'

'That's amazing. Keep doing as many of those workshops as you can!' Savi said. 'I think they're doing an internship programme next year where they'll invite select people to work the race season under them, so if any of you get accepted for that you could well be working with us.'

'What?!' their spokesperson gasped. 'As soon as they announce it on socials we'll get on that. Do you think you'll ever join forces with them?'

'Maybe, as their company expands. I think I need a couple of race seasons to settle in with the team before I try to branch out to other projects,' Savi said, smiling over at Marco, knowing he was a silent partner in his friends' business.

'Hey, girls . . .' Marco smiled. 'What are your names and social media usernames? I'm gonna get you some VIP paddock passes for this week. My family can't make it so I've got some spare. You can watch Savi and the girls in action, and you'll get to meet Lucie, Faith, Esme, Bea . . .' He pulled his phone out to take their information down.

Savi couldn't stop grinning while they all took turns taking photos, her dad stepping in to help with the group shots. They were crowding the aisle of the restaurant, blocking the waiters, but nobody seemed bothered. The staff were probably used to drivers dining with them and fans catching wind of their locations. She loved that she had the power to make fans' dreams come true, like she was some sort of motorsport fairy godmother. Although it was Marco who was doing the wish granting this time, she had done plenty herself.

'Thank you both so much. We'll see you at the track!' The girls gathered their merchandise and phones and scarpered off, back to their table, leaving Savi and her family to enjoy their dessert in peace.

'Ma?' Weston poked Bonnie in the ribs, laughing. 'Are you crying?'

'Bonnie, are you okay?' Marco tried to catch her eye but she was hiding her face.

'Sorry, I'm just so proud of you, Sav. I know it's not been an easy few years, but I think being here it's all just hitting me. You defied the odds and actually fucking made it.'

Savi gasped. 'Oh my goodness me, Ma's swearing. But seriously, thank you. You guys have had my back from the very beginning, and I know even without Gabriel's financial input, you would have made it happen. Somehow, some way. I couldn't have done it without you.'

While she joined Bonnie in tearing up, she felt Marco's hand drop to her thigh under the table. He didn't give it a squeeze, or even move at all, but he held his hand out with his palm facing upward. A silent invitation to take hold of it and use him as an anchor. She did exactly that, managing to hold back her emotion so as not to cause a scene in a restaurant full of people who recognised them. The last thing they needed was close-up shots of Savi's ugly crying face hitting the internet; her teammates would never let her live that down.

'I'm going to make it my mission to come to one race a season, even if I have to take a commercial flight on my own,' Weston said.

'Not a chance, I'm coming with you. I'm not missing my little girl on that podium if I don't have to,' Calvin stated, seemingly forgetting that he had a ranch to run. It was a miracle that he'd left to watch her race at the start of the season, let alone that he was here for this too.

'Please do come to as many races as you can,' Marco said, 'because I'm really going to miss you all. I feel like part of the family.'

'Well, duh. You are.' Weston rolled his eyes. 'We'll be wearing our Revolution Racing shirts for you, too, De Luca. You can't escape us now; once a Hart, always a Hart.'

Savi was sitting on the edge of the claw-foot bathtub in her hotel room, dressed in her pyjamas and moments away from falling into bed. Except she was actually moments away from walking down to Marco's room and giving him a hug.

He had wheeled Weston all around Le Mans, playing tour guide to her family and not once complaining about how much strength it took to push a six-foot-something ex-athlete over cobbled pathways. Weston's expensive new wheelchair was no match for those cobbles. They'd made it to the cathedral after all and found Calvin a magnet. Both experiences that everyone had soaked up every moment of until Weston started to say that his medication was making him sleepy. He'd been on anti-depressants for two years, something Savi had briefly tried to keep her anxiety under control; she had just concluded she would rather keep any kind of medication out of her system.

Deciding that her need to thank him overruled the voice in her head telling her they needed some space between them after spending so much time together recently, she made her way down the corridor and pressed the button to buzz the elevator up to his floor. The rooms next to hers were empty; waiting for Kodie and Miko to fill them when they showed up tomorrow.

She tapped on the door lightly, sort of hoping he wouldn't hear it so she could run back to bed. It was one a.m., and they were supposed to have had an early night, but she hadn't been able to sleep. One second, her mind was on Jesse, angry at herself for sticking by him for so long when she knew there hadn't been a future there. Then the next, it was on Marco and all the times she'd thought she felt something and squashed it down in favour of being loyal to the man who wasn't treating her like a partner. She had only known Marco was awake because the group chat was alive thanks to him and Brett bickering back and forth about mundane crap.

'You're still up?' he said, looking surprised but not confused to see her standing at his door at this time of night. He beckoned her in, closing the door softly behind her.

'Couldn't sleep,' she shrugged. 'And I realised I haven't thanked you for today. For taking my family under your wing and showing them round. In fact, I haven't thanked you for coming back to Wyoming with me, either, and helping me decorate and picking up the pieces when Jesse left. You've really gone above and beyond for us all, and you've opened Weston's world up again and –'

'Savannah,' he interrupted, 'you don't have anything to thank me for. I've had the best couple of weeks getting to know you on a deeper level, living out my cowboy fantasies.'

'But still, you didn't have to do any of it,' she mumbled.

'I wanted to. It's as simple as that.'

'Thank you.' She said it again, one last time, but this time he clamped his hand over her mouth, and she let out a muffled laugh. 'Thank you, thank you, thank –'

'Shut up, Cowgirl. Do you want to stay and watch

something? We have a few episodes of that show left. I know we have to be up early, but –'

'Yep,' she nodded. 'Which side of the bed is yours?'

'Left.'

She leapt up onto his king-sized mattress in her leopard print PJs and fluffy slippers, brought halfway across the world with her for the first time ever, and settled into his sheets, the pillows nearly swallowing her whole. 'You coming?'

He raised an eyebrow at her, eyes raking her body in that way he'd done so often and she had ignored. 'How does such a small person take up so much space?'

'It's my big heart,' she grinned. 'I require the extra room.'

'Yeah, well, hope you don't mind some physical contact because I'm not watching TV from the far-left hand side of such a humongous mattress.'

Savi raised her eyebrows, feigning a threatened look because in truth, that small dose of physical contact with someone who knew her and respected her may well have been what she'd come looking for tonight. So, she really, really didn't mind.

29

Marco watched as Savannah's eyes lit up with every merch tent they passed, every food truck or display of historic cars. They'd walked the twenty-five minutes from their hotel to the circuit so they could take in everything at their own pace, appreciating the walk despite it being the crack of dawn and their eyes barely being open.

One episode last night had turned into two, then three, and before they knew it they'd had three hours' sleep, nose to nose. They had somehow managed to wake up before their alarms went off, and then Savannah had high-tailed it back to her room to change.

They were expected to wear official team clothing all week because Le Mans was so high profile; the media were constantly on the prowl for drivers to interview, and the cameras were always rolling to get B-roll footage ready for the international television broadcast over the weekend. Marco's dream of matching cowboy gear would have to wait. He wore his usual red tee and black jeans, and Savi had borrowed his spare black tee after deciding that her own red one didn't hang off her body the way she wanted it to. She wanted oversized for fashion purposes, and the team had only supplied her with fitted.

Marco felt somewhat smug that she was wearing his shirt, he just couldn't help but wish it were in an entirely different context. Still, they walked into the paddock hand in hand, having not quite worked out how and when or even if to tell people they were no longer a couple and never really had been. As far as Marco was concerned, the threat of those indecent photos being linked to Savannah was still looming over her, and therefore he didn't intend to go anywhere.

'De Luca, my boy.' Brett clapped him on the back in a bone-crushing embrace, 'Savi, my lady. How was your little Western getaway?'

'Do not ever call me "My Lady", this isn't the eighteen-hundreds,' she tutted. 'But it was *really* good. Please excuse me while I go and find Kodie and Meeks, catch up later!'

They watched her in silence as she headed into the garage, and then the second she was out of earshot, Brett pounced with all the questions he'd been dying to ask.

'So how was it, meeting the parents?' he smirked.

'It must have gone well because they're here with us.'

'No way, man! That's amazing. What are they like?'

'Everything I expected them to be and more. Being with them felt like I was at home away from home, and honestly? I'm sad that we had to leave.'

'I get that, I feel the same every time Lucie and I visit her parents in Tuscany. I think a lot of racing drivers feel like they have family in all four corners of the world, and it's just such a good feeling, right?' Brett gushed, reminding Marco of how much he missed his friends when they weren't exploring the world together.

'Anderson, I've *really* fallen for her.' He emphasised by widening his eyes as he said it. 'She's in a league of her own, seriously.'

'Is this more intense than Esme, then?' his teammate questioned. 'Because you were pretty into her judging by the way you buried yourself in chocolate chip pancakes... and those women.'

'Absolutely. It's not even a question. Savannah is just... magic. I don't know how else to put it. She lights up every room she's in, she's sassy and the perfect mix of serious and fun, and most importantly, she makes me feel seen. I know I'm going to have to separate from her at some point when we have to go to our individual homes, but man, I can't bear the thought of it.'

Marco wasn't just saying these things to try and sell their relationship anymore; he was so far past that. He meant every word, and call him crazy, but he was starting to think Savannah might be starting to question her own feelings towards him. There had been something in her eyes when she showed up at his hotel room last night. He didn't know what it was, but when they'd woken up that morning, they'd spent a long time lying there just looking at each other as they let the world come into focus. Something was different. It was as if the end of her relationship with Jesse had planted a seed in her mind.

'Don't go home,' Brett shrugged. 'She's said a couple of things about wanting adventures, hasn't she? So, take her on some. See the world with her, show her things from your point of view. That's one of the best things about being part of this team; not having to do shit alone. Hell, come visit the rest of us in Malmedy, if you want. Let her in on our little clique.'

'We are not a clique,' Marco frowned. 'Everyone's welcome.'

'Yeah, but we don't really know Miko and Kodie very well yet, outside of the buddy scheme, although we would like to soon because they seem great. It's just that Savi is basically an extension of you. We want to see what the fuss is about, you know? You can't hog her forever.'

'She'd probably love that,' Marco nodded. 'I just know she loves to help out at the ranch when she can, and we just set up her racing sim in the guest bedroom . . .'

'End of the season is coming up fast. No reason you can't travel for a month and still have plenty of time to see family. Speaking of, where are they? Are they at the track yet?'

'They're still asleep. We ended up doing a tour of the city immediately after getting off the plane, so I imagine they're shattered. It is only seven a.m. after all, and they're probably pretty jetlagged too.' Marco rubbed his temple, trying to rid himself of the headache that was threatening to form.

'Don't tell me your head hurts from lack of sleep,' Brett scowled. 'You're new at this I guess, sharing a room with your girlfriend in race week. You'll soon learn that having sex past ten p.m. is out of bounds if you want a full night's sleep. What did you squeeze in, two rounds? Three? If it was more than that then I have no sympathy at all.'

'If you must know, we watched a dating show and fell asleep. She also isn't officially in my room, yet. She's got her own, but she couldn't sleep so she came to mine.' He wished he could tell Brett the truth about their situation and get his friend's advice. After all, he'd been friends with Lucie for years before they got their happily ever after. He understood the pain.

'That's adorable.' Brett wrinkled his nose, 'But still, you tell her she's banned. And for the love of all that is holy, do not have sex *during* the twenty-four hours of Le Mans. You won't survive it; you might think the adrenaline will help but you'll be exhausted.'

'Brett, you don't need to tell me these things. I have had sexual relationships before, you know. During race week, too.'

'Have you?!' Brett gasped. 'We all thought you were a bit of a monk.'

Marco left him standing outside the trailer, confused, while he headed into the garage after Savannah. He left her to it when he noticed her standing to one side, chatting animatedly with her teammates and laughing away, all tension from the last race dissipated. He didn't want to intrude, so he busied himself with the stat screens and catching up with his engineer, trying not to glance over at her too often. She was admittedly a bit of a distraction.

'De Luca,' Jasper joined him, 'how you feeling about giving us our first test lap of the week?' He folded his arms, doing his classic authoritative team principal pose.

'Yeah, I'm keen. Let me just change into my suit and grab my helmet.'

He disappeared into the trailer for less than five minutes, having perfected the art of getting race-ready in record time. When he came back out, Savannah was at Jasper's side, deep in conversation. Alarm bells were ringing in Marco's mind; she seemed anxious, and their boss looked concerned, but he didn't want to intrude so he went over to the car and greeted the mechanics, climbing into the seat.

He drove down the pit lane, bypassing multiple garages busy with teams rushing to fix issues with their cars or doing interviews with the press. They were all focused on the biggest race of the season, but Marco? He was focused on his cowgirl and how he wanted to give her the entire world on a silver platter, all the things she'd wished for. But still, even after she'd left the man who had wasted four years of her life and no longer owed anyone her loyalty, it wasn't Marco's place to do so.

Marco didn't know if what he was feeling was even real. After Esme, and believing that could be something, his radar for the spectrum of human emotion was wildly off kilter. This thing with Savannah could just be a friendship, a unique bond that came about because they were teammates, and he felt a duty to protect her and care for her.

But then he thought about Lucie, Faith and Bea who were also part of his team, his inner circle, and while he would forever be willing to go into battle for them, he didn't get butterflies in his stomach when he looked at them.

He didn't have to constantly resist the urge to brush his hand across their cheek, move their hair out of their face or place his hand on the small of their back. He didn't lie awake hoping they'd knock on his door or look forward to their spontaneous evenings of binge watching the latest TV shows cuddled up under bed sheets, wondering if they would move away if he moved a couple of inches closer. Savannah was different. She was special, one of a kind, and every second that he spent with her only further solidified their connection.

That night they'd spent together in the barn had been

incredible, but maybe that was all it was ever going to be. Just one night.

He tried to pay attention to the car, searching within himself for the fire that he found each time she was out on the track with him, challenging him. Today was just a practice session, it didn't mean anything. It just let the mechanics and engineers know how the car was handling, so they could ensure everything was running smoothly and finalise their race strategy. But the further he got and the more he got to grips with it, the more that fire started to burn. He'd found the spark.

He was angry at Jesse. Angry at him for not recognising what was right in front of him this whole time and for stringing Savannah along. What was the point? Was he just using her for what she could offer him? For sex and intimacy and admiration? Was he comfortable? Savannah might have stayed with him because *she* was comfortable, but that was fine. She hadn't done it knowing she was never going to give him the future they'd talked about. She had stayed because she loved him and was the kind of person who fought for the people she loved.

'De Luca, how's the car feeling?' Julien's voice came over the radio.

'Good, man. Hey, Moretz, what's the lap record here?'

'Uhm . . .' Julien hesitated, asking the people around him to look it up, 'Why are you asking?'

'Just got some stress to unleash.'

'Mars,' Brett intercepted their conversation, 'this isn't the actual race. You know that, right? Speed doesn't matter in this scenario; we're just getting a feel for the car.'

'I need to let it all out and the only way I know how to do that is on the tarmac.'

'Sex also works,' Julien suggested. 'When I've got a lot going on, Faith can just sense it. Came back to the hotel room at the last race and she was –'

'First of all, don't want to hear it. Second, not really a viable option while I'm sat behind the wheel. And in case you haven't noticed, while you've been trying to talk me out of it, I've only been getting faster. Wish me luck, lads.'

He didn't hit the mute button, but his conviction was enough to silence them and leave him to go about his mission in peace. He pushed his foot on the accelerator, letting his frustration at the world fuel him as he kept up the pace. There were so few other cars out on track right now, he could get away with taking risks. Like going over the white line in places where he typically wouldn't, going against everything that felt natural. Every racing driver pushed themselves sometimes, but they were still careful. Still semi-cautious.

Right now, Marco was being the opposite of that. He was driving with reckless abandon, and even his engineer couldn't slow him down as he came onto the airwaves.

'De Luca, slow the fuck down.'

'But why? It's just me and the car out here.'

'There's no need to be driving that fast in a practice session.'

'That's not a viable reason. If I can do it, why not let me? I'm getting the car warmed up, seeing how hard it can go. That's what we need to see, isn't it?'

'It's your head, not mine, man,' his engineer sighed.

'Just tell me how close I am to hitting that lap record.'

'You Revolution boys are a fucking nightmare . . .' he said through gritted teeth. 'But yeah, you're close. I'm gonna shut up now and let you crack on. But if you do this again, if you push too hard unnecessarily, I will report you to Jasper.'

Marco just smirked behind his visor, because he knew he was going to do it. It may not be as significant because it wasn't mid-race, but he would still make the history books. He kept driving like the world was going to end, no longer being cheered on by his fury but instead by pure passion for this job. And then it was time to go back into the pits, to be celebrated or disciplined, he wasn't sure. But he didn't care; he could feel in his bones that he had broken the record.

'I saw all of that.' Jasper approached him as soon as he was out of the car, arms crossed and eyes narrowed. 'Do we need to talk?'

'No. That was a one-off.' Marco swallowed roughly. Despite what that little show of arrogance might suggest, he was scared of his boss. Sometimes. Only when he got behind the wheel; because he knew that every decision the drivers made on track was closely analysed and scrutinised by the entire team.

'If you're going to smash lap records every time,' Jasper raised an eyebrow, 'don't let it be a one-off. Listen to your engineer, but damn, De Luca. That was an excellent performance.'

After his team principal clapped him on the back, he left him alone and Marco was given a split second to process his achievement before his teammates were at his side, congratulating him. That was going to hit headlines later. And he was bound to be interviewed, too. He was just glad that team radios weren't accessed by the media team during practice sessions, because his refusal to obey his engineer wouldn't go down too well. Marco never wanted to be labelled as a difficult driver, and that wasn't what he was. He'd got carried away, used his job as therapy.

'Bro . . .' Brett beamed at him, knocking on his helmet. 'You did a classic Jules Moretz, there. Big fan of the diva attitude, it weirdly kind of suits you.'

'I don't pull moves like that anymore, I'm past all that.' Julien rolled his eyes. 'Don't go all *Fast and Furious* during qualifying tomorrow, or the race, but yeah, that was impressive.'

Marco removed his helmet and balaclava, offering his teammates his signature cheeky grin and accepting the hug Julien offered. 'Thanks, Dad.'

'Go find your girlfriend, she was on the edge of her seat watching you.' Julien sent him to the other side of the garage, where Savannah shot up at the sight of him.

'What was that?!' She smacked him on the arm.

'That was me realising I might need therapy, or anger management or something.' He shrugged. 'Aren't you going to say "well done"?'

'Well done, you big idiot. That was dangerous, Monaco.' She scowled at him, looking more cute than angry. 'What were you so mad about?'

'You getting your heart broken by global superstar and biggest asshole in country music, Jesse Montalvo. It pissed me off, Cowgirl.'

Savannah's face softened as she looked up at him, her big brown eyes full of appreciation. It made him melt. 'You don't need to be angry on my behalf, Mars. He may have caused some damage, but he certainly didn't break my heart. I won't allow him to have that much power over me.' She reached her arms out for an embrace, and he took the opportunity to pull her close into him, glancing down at her. 'Do you know what would break my heart? You getting hurt because of me.'

'I knew what I was doing, but I promise not to do anything that stupid again. You have my word. And for the record, I will always be angry at anyone who doesn't realise how lucky they are to have my Cowgirl's heart.'

30

Savi had sent her family for a tour of the circuit with Gabriel, needing some time to herself. Her head was bursting with what ifs and reasons not to do what she was about to do. At some point over the course of the week, she had decided she was going to reveal all to her team principal, cover all her bases in case everything with Jesse came out. She didn't trust him or his team to protect her anymore.

'Savi, come on in.' Jasper welcomed her into his office. He had a much more professional and luxurious set up for Le Mans, because absolutely everything about this race was kicked up a notch. The exotic plant on his desk was her favourite new addition. 'How are your family finding everything? Your brother looks like he's having a whale of a time. Caught him and your dad racing Gabriel in a golf kart earlier today.'

'They're loving it. Thank you so much for sorting everything out for them; I never thought they'd make it here, but you've made it so easy for us all. The access to the plane, the accessible room, the transfers and the personal assistant. We really appreciate it.'

'It was the team's pleasure. We'll do the same for any race they want to come to, so please don't be afraid to ask.' He smiled. 'So, what brings you to my office?'

'I might be about to become Revolution Racing's problem driver . . .' She chewed her bottom lip, taking a seat when Jasper gestured to the plush leather chair in front of his desk.

'I find that hard to believe,' Jasper frowned. 'Before we begin, I will keep this as confidential as I can, depending on what the issue is. If you need the team's protection . . .'

'You've done this before, haven't you?' She laughed awkwardly, not wanting him to think she was making light of anything. This was big, and he might choose to wipe his hands of her.

'With Brett and his mental health problems, and prior to that, Julien and his daughter. Every driver has personal matters that are required to stay private sometimes. Having said that, damage control is a fine art and I have mastered it.' Jasper sat down himself, linking his fingers together.

'Okay. That makes me feel better. Um, I will offer context but I suppose I should just dive right in for now. There are some indecent photos circulating in the media linked with Jesse Montalvo. They're a couple of months old, and the attention has died down, but . . .'

'You're in them, too.' He nodded slowly, letting it sink in. 'Are you okay?'

'What?' She blinked, not understanding why he was asking.

'You had your privacy violated in a horrific way, Savi. I'm asking if you're alright.'

'Oh.' She sat in silence for a moment, stunned. 'Yes, I'm fine. Nobody knows it was me, but I fear it may only be a matter of time. I have a horseshoe tattoo which is visible in the photos, and my hair is quite distinctive . . . There's just no reason for me to be publicly linked with someone like Jesse so I can only imagine that's why it hasn't got out.'

'Were the two of you . . . involved?' He frowned.

'Yes, for four years. But we no longer are.'

'I don't mean to pry, I'm just a little confused.'

'Marco and I aren't really together.' She sighed. 'It was Jesse's grand idea to throw everyone off the scent and Marco was happy to go along with it to protect me. And I know we should have come to you when all of this went down, but I was embarrassed. I thought I could handle it, and I'm just scared that now Jesse and I are over, he's going to do something stupid and the whole world is going to know it's me in those photos.' She could feel her heart beating in her chest, the stress of the entire situation building.

'Okay. So, who else knows you and Marco aren't together? And about the photos?' He pulled out a notepad and pen, ready to take names down.

'Esme Keelan, my parents and brother, Jesse's PR team and his ex-manager. That's it.'

'Ex-manager?' Jasper questioned, looking concerned.

'Sapphire Maravel,' Savi confirmed. 'She quit a few weeks ago, but I don't think she'd say anything. Might want to keep her on our radar. I'm so sorry, Jasper.'

'You don't need to apologise for those vultures taking advantage of you, Savi. It's my job to look after you as one of my drivers, and I'm just glad you feel comfortable to come to me now.' He reached out and passed her a tissue, smiling sadly. 'I'm going to get in touch with our PR team but I'm going to keep the amount of people involved to an absolute minimum. If these photos come out, I will not let it ruin you. I promise. And your position on this team is secure regardless of anything that happens.'

'Thank you,' she nodded. 'I promise I don't make a habit of lying.'

'When you signed the contract to be part of this team, at no point did it state you had to disclose every detail of your personal life, Savi. I don't expect that from you, nor do I expect you to be one hundred per cent honest all the time unless it's involving something that directly impacts the race, or team dynamics. Although I do have to ask, how are you and De Luca planning to let the team know none of it was real?'

'Um . . . I guess we'll just tell them it fizzled out naturally. There's no need to make a scene, and we don't want them to think we've been keeping them in the dark for months because we didn't trust them. I just can't explain it to them. I can't sit there and tell them the details; it's too humiliating and I don't want anyone to think badly of me for roping Marco into my mess.'

'From where I'm standing, it appears as though he's very happy to be dragged into your chaos. He lights up around you, Savi. I say that with nothing but good intentions. I've known Marco a long time and I thought he might be spiralling, but getting close to you seems to be balancing him out again. He's back to the old De Luca we all know and love.' Jasper smiled, looking pleased as punch to have the opportunity to play matchmaker. Savi wondered if he'd done this before.

'He did also get to pretend to be John Wayne for two weeks in the Wyoming mountains, and I think that perked him up a bit,' she laughed.

'Do yourself a favour and keep him close, Miss Hart.

He's a wonderful friend and confidant for us all and I have no doubt that the journey you two have embarked on is only just the start of a lifelong bond. Now that he is in your corner, he will fight to the death to protect you.'

Savi smiled, looking past Jasper's head at the photos on his office wall. Black and white shots of him and the guys, a couple of her, Kodie and Miko. The way he talked about his team told a story; Revolution Racing was his family. It made Savi feel better about all of this. She felt safe in the knowledge that she didn't just have Marco on her side but her team principal too.

'If you have any questions, please ask.' Savi stood up, throwing her tear-soaked tissue in the waste basket. 'I'm going to find my team, see how they're feeling in the lead-up to qualifying.'

'Okay,' Jasper nodded. 'Before you go, Savi ... You're doing an outstanding job. You should be proud of yourself, because I am and Gabriel is, too. You've found your feet.'

She left his office with her head held high and hurried to the trailer, hoping to find her teammates waiting for her. Miko always liked to play chess before a race and she sometimes managed to persuade Kodie to be her opponent, no matter how little she knew about the game.

So, it was no surprise when Savi found them staring each other down over Miko's Koa wood chess board, a 'welcome to the team' gift from Julien, who had got it custom made for her in Hawaii. Kodie's gift had been a signed wheel arch from a Formula One driver's championship winning car, and Savi's was a vintage leather jacket that looked and felt like it was made for her.

'Am I interrupting anything important?' She perched on the edge of the sofa.

'Yeah, I'm about to fuck up Meeks' reputation of being the best chess player in the paddock. She's probably going to cry or throw something. You should stick around.'

'She won the last game and is about to win this one so now she thinks she's all that,' Miko added. 'Needless to say, I'm still the expert.'

Savi watched them as they did nothing. They sat in silence, Miko's brain working overtime to salvage the game while Kodie sat there looking smug. She finally no longer felt awkward around her own teammates, instead realising that it was still early days. They could iron out their disagreements, learn to love each other the way siblings did, because that's what this was: a family. And families fought, and they got angry and frustrated, but they were still tied to one another in a way that made it near impossible not to still love them.

'Girls, could we do something soon?' Savi sighed. 'Go somewhere new, see the world away from a racetrack. I miss you both, and I know we've had a few hiccups. I just want time with my teammates without the stresses of work getting in the way.'

'I'm down,' Kodie shrugged. 'Meeks?'

'Yeah, sounds good to me. New Year's trip to Japan?' she suggested. 'My family can put you up in one of our Tokyo hotels and we can immerse ourselves in some culture. It's worlds away from what the two of you are used to, and when we go to Fuji we won't get to experience much because it's such a tight schedule with the race. I know New Year is months away but planning the itinerary is half the fun.'

Savi nodded enthusiastically, knowing that Miko would do everything in her power to make the trip as authentic as possible. She'd heard all about her favourite restaurants and the Tokyo nightlife that Miko had experienced at university, and she was keen to see it for herself. Ramen from the packet while she did her high school homework in the basement was the closest Savi had got to Japanese culture.

'Get booking, Meeks,' Kodie agreed. 'And give up on this game, I've won.'

Miko threw herself against the back of the sofa and sighed dramatically, giving in to the fact she was losing her title. 'Fine. Hate you.'

'You love me,' Kodie grinned.

Standing up again, Savi excused herself while they argued back and forth about all the wrong moves Miko had made throughout the game. She needed to find Esme and fill her in on all the drama she'd kept to herself the past couple of weeks. This thing with Jesse was still weighing on her mind, and she hadn't spoken to Esme since. They had the kind of friendship where they weren't in constant contact, but one text or phone call and either of them would drop everything to be there for the other. Savi was counting on that right now, because as much as she appreciated Marco's presence in her life, there were some things she couldn't discuss with him.

She found Esme in the Eden Racing garage, catching her eye and pulling her away from the editing she was doing. She always felt strange being in another team's garage so she would hover at the back, feeling like an intruder trying to learn all their secrets. This championship wasn't like that; the grid was an extended family beyond each individual team or manufacturer. Everyone supported everyone else, stopped for chats and welcomed each other into their garages, hospitality buildings and HQs, but Savi was new here. She hadn't earned anyone's respect.

'Sav, my girl!' Esme gave her a hug, trying not to knock her over the head with the vlog camera she was holding. 'How's life treating you?'

'Ha!' Savi let out a fake laugh. 'Fantastic.'

'We're long overdue a proper catch-up. We can use my team's trailer,' she suggested, leading her out to it, 'The guys are figuring out their race strategy in the office, so they'll be a while.'

She followed Esme up the steps, immediately noticing how stark this trailer was in comparison to either of the ones that belonged to Revolution Racing. It was bright white; the lights were blinding and there was no sign of life except for everyone's racing gear and a single pair of sunglasses on the coffee table belonging to one of the drivers.

It was horrible. She liked that her own team's trailers were messy and chaotic and warm because they felt like home, and they all had photos stuck to the walls wherever they could, reminding them of what was waiting for them after race week. The girls had a faux fur rug under their coffee table with personalised mugs next to the coffee machine and the guys had a stack of computer games and Julien's CD collection next to their television so they could unwind during their downtime, both trailers providing a safe haven away from the garage and press conferences.

'Ew, I hate it in here.' Savi wrinkled her nose, trying to make herself comfortable on the sofa and failing. There weren't even any cushions. 'Eden Racing need to step it up.'

'It's a brand-new trailer for this season, and nobody's bothered to decorate,' Esme shrugged. 'I agree with you, though. It's awful. Anyway, enough deflecting, are you okay?'

'I don't know?' Her voice went up at the end, like she was asking herself the same question.

'I'm so sorry I wasn't there for you in person, Sav. I should have flown out to you as soon as Marco got in touch. I just thought since you had Mars . . .'

'It's okay. If I had needed you, I would have called and begged you to get on a plane. But you're right, I did have Marco. And he helped more than I ever thought he could. Picked up the pieces, refused to let me wallow in self-pity for long. He distracted me in the daytime and held me while I let it all out at night, talking things through with me.'

'I'm glad you had him. And how do you feel now? Honestly. Don't put on a front with me,' Esme pushed, smiling softly.

'Part of me feels like a weight has been lifted, as strange as that sounds.'

'It doesn't sound strange, Sav. I get it, and things weren't right between you for a while. I think part of me is relieved, too. And it's been hard even for me to lie to everyone.'

'I'm sorry I ever asked you to lie for me, especially when it turns out Jesse wasn't even worth the hassle,' Savi scoffed.

Esme reached for her hand. 'But *you* were worth the hassle. I'd do it all over again.'

'Now that I'm out of the relationship and looking back on it, I'm starting to wonder if maybe I started to fall out of love with him when he started pushing me away,' Savi frowned. She'd barely given herself a chance to think about it that deeply; she had just accepted the situation for what it was and focused on moving on. But now she was analysing, and it was making it easier in the sense that she knew there were bigger and better things in her future, but harder because she was angry at herself for sticking it out as long as she did.

'Which goes back two years, if not more.'

'Exactly. But there's more to it, Ez . . . Towards the end of it all, I started making comparisons between him and Marco. Comparing the way Marco made me feel safe to the way Jesse made me feel, and I realised Marco was doing everything Jesse should've and didn't. It was like there was part of me that had feelings for Mars but my brain hadn't quite caught up to the idea.'

'*Do* you have feelings for him?'

'That's the thing. I don't know if I do now, but I think that I could. There's a connection, that's obvious, but is it romantic? What if I'm just trying to look for what I was missing with Jesse, and I've made it all up?'

'If you're questioning it, doesn't that tell you it's not just a friendship? Look at Lucie and Brett, they had a connection from day one and it took them ten years to figure it out, but it was inevitable. They could never just be friends. You took him home, Sav. You let him in, showed him your world. You don't do that with anyone, but you did it with Mars. Why?'

'I can't have romantic feelings for Marco.' Savi buried her face in her hands, groaning with frustration. This was why she'd needed Esme's input, but now she was facing the reality of the situation, it was overwhelming.

'According to who? Society? So what, you broke up with Jesse over a month ago. But you began the process of moving on from him the first time he fucked up and shoved the idea of a future with you to one side in favour of his career.'

Savi just sat there staring at her, trying to make sense of it all. Esme was probably right, but moving on so fast didn't feel right. Until she thought about the fact that they were going to have to slowly reduce the amount of time they spent together and stop touching each other in public so that everyone thought their relationship was coming to a natural end, and she realised she didn't want that. She would miss it, miss him. 'Fuck,' she whispered.

'Coming from someone who has had that kind of affection from Marco in the past, I'm telling you now, Savi, he's down bad. I can see it every time I pass you two in the paddock, or when I watch interviews and social media content. It's staring you right in the face, but you and I both know he's been hurt before, and you've been hurt too. So, I beg you, if you're going to consider turning this fake relationship into the real thing, make sure you're certain you're ready. Be sure that what you feel for Mars is real, and there's no chance you'd let Jesse back into the picture if he asked. I don't think he can take another heartbreak.'

31

The grid was alive in a way Savi had never seen it. It was full to the brim with journalists, TV crews, drivers, mechanics, engineers, team principals, social media teams, influencers and VIP guests, and it was near-impossible to move around freely. The Revolution Racing team had formed a huddle and were watching Savi's brother do an on-camera interview, looking mighty pleased with himself as he talked at length about their relationship and how it had evolved as they'd grown up and grown into themselves.

'Weston is so proud of you,' Marco murmured into her ear. 'He's practically bursting at the seams. Look at him, can't stop smiling.'

'Don't start, Monaco. I'll be an ugly, crying mess.'

'Told you before that's impossible, but you do look like you're about to physically melt. Are you feeling alright, Cowgirl?' He scrutinised her, and it only made her cheeks more red.

While most of the sweat plastering her hair to her forehead was a result of her usual pre-race anxiety combined with the fact they were all in full racing gear bar helmets and the sun was beating down on them, Marco's hand constantly hovering above her waist or hip was also a contribution.

'I feel really hot,' she breathed out, wishing she could

shove the sleeves of her racing suit up her arms to allow some relief from the sticky heat.

'Faith?' Marco flagged their social media manager down as she whizzed past on her way to shoot yet more content of the car. 'Sorry, are you able to hunt down a portable fan for us?'

'Sure! Jules doesn't look like he's using his.' She poked him, 'Oi, Husband. Give Mars your fan, will you? Savi looks about ready to collapse. We've been out here so long, it's ridiculous.'

'Take Brett's, too. He's an Aussie, used to the heat.' Julien handed them both over. 'I don't know why they made us come out here so early, the band haven't even made it out yet.'

Right on cue, the drummers started pouring onto the grid and getting in position, all of them dressed in red, white and blue. Savi had seen this on television over the years; the drummers performed, then someone sang the French national anthem, the French Air Force aerobatic demonstration team performed a flypast over the pit straight and they finished with someone parachuting from a French Army helicopter to deliver the national flag to the official race starter, who was usually a celebrity or ex-racing driver. This year, they had an NBA player who was a huge endurance racing fan and sponsored an IEC team.

Savi didn't want her anxiety to ruin this weekend for her, but she was feeling claustrophobic, and she couldn't leave. This was part of her contract, and she was starting the race. She needed to get it under control before she totally lost it.

'You're okay, Savannah . . .' Marco turned the fan on

and held it up to her face while Kodie placed a reassuring hand on her shoulder. She was so glad she'd confided in people about this so she didn't have to do it alone, but she wished her body had done this back in the trailer instead of waiting until she was on the grid in front of tens of thousands of people and cameras which were broadcasting live to millions and pointing right at her. She didn't want to show weakness moments before the biggest race of her life began. 'I've got you.'

'Is it anything specific worrying you, darling?' Her mum moved in close, speaking just loud enough for her to hear over the noise of engines, drums and screaming fans.

'Everything,' Savi laughed. 'Having a bit of a delayed reaction today, I think. I felt okay when I woke up this morning, and the autograph session didn't phase me. But then the second we walked out here, the anxiety kicked in. There are just mountains of pressure on us this weekend, you know? I don't want to screw it up.'

'You're not going to screw anything up, Sav,' her dad added, coming back over with Weston now they were done with interviews. 'You're here for a reason, don't forget it.'

Their words weren't helping her feel any less overwhelmed, in fact her dad telling her she was here for a reason only added to her stress. That was half the issue; she was here for a reason. To help get her team to the finish line, to score points, to give the fans and sponsors and her bosses what they wanted. That was a lot to put on someone.

She looked at Marco, who was still holding a fan to her face, like her very own personal assistant, and silently pleaded with him to help her. She didn't know how, but she knew Marco would think of something. He always did.

'Let's escape for a moment,' he suggested. 'We can hide out in the trailer just to give you some relief from the chaos, say you needed a bathroom break or something. If we're quick, nobody will even notice.'

'Run, we won't tell anyone.' Miko shooed them away and Marco hastily grabbed Savi's hand, moving her through the crowd with confidence but not in such a rush that people paid them any attention.

'Mars,' she cried out from behind him, forcing him to stop as soon as they made it to the back of the garage. 'Wait, I can't . . .'

'You want to stay here?' he asked. 'Sit down quick, nobody can see.'

They were hidden from view behind a temporary wall, near the drivers' bedrooms, and Savi sank to the floor, doing her best to fight the full-blown anxiety attack. Marco lowered himself to the ground next to her and didn't say anything, instead taking her hand in his and raising it to his lips. She breathed in and out with a purpose, desperately attempting to pay attention to anything except how she was feeling. Marco's thigh pressed against hers, his lips on her skin, his shoulder brushing her own. He was grounding her without even realising. Savi let her head rest against the wall behind her and closed her eyes, staying put for a few minutes. It worked. She felt human again, and when she opened her eyes, Marco was looking at her, his brow etched with a mixture of concern and something else she couldn't quite place.

'I'm ready,' she smiled.

'Are you sure?' He placed one final kiss across her knuckles and waited patiently for her go-ahead. Savi nodded, standing up and holding her hands out to him. He took them and joined her, grabbing her for a quick hug before they made their way back out to the grid. They bypassed questioning glances from other drivers and reunited with their team, where Jasper shot them a quick thumbs up. Savi returned it, glad to have his support.

'Hey, Savi.' Lucie joined them, her camera pointing down at the ground, but they could tell she was itching to raise it and aim it at them. 'Are you up to some quick-fire questions? Both of you, ideally. It's just a fun little segment we're doing for the channel.'

'Go for it,' she smiled, pulling Marco to one side so they could film somewhere a little quieter, which was hard given the environment they were in. Their new backdrop was the wire fencing next to the track, that faced the grandstands and the thousands of fans who were watching the grid activity from their orange and white plastic seats.

'Okay. Before we start, it's a "who's most likely to" so I'm going to ask you a question, and then I want you to tell me which of the two of you is most likely to do the thing I'm talking about. It won't all be motorsport related, either. This is a fun one.' Lucie waited for them to agree. 'Cool, first up, who is more likely to regret a tattoo?'

'Savannah.' Marco blurted out with zero hesitation, earning himself a whack on the arm. 'What?! I know you have one and you hate it!'

'Who is most likely to miss a flight?'

'Marco!' Savi yelled out. 'He's hopeless, honestly. He dillydallies too much, or he stops for food and forgets he's still got to get to the gate.'

Lucie snorted with laughter because she knew Savi was right, then she continued, 'Who is most likely to oversleep during race week?'

'Savannah again. Not just during race week, either. That girl can be out like a light for a month straight, given half the chance.'

'Shut up, I was up early for a run every day in Monaco,' Savi scowled. 'You were the one making a fuss about it, Mr "I go for a run every morning", didn't see you run once in Wyoming except for when you were running away from the cows.'

Marco feigned shock at her unapologetic exposure of his secret fear of the massive creatures her family kept on the ranch. 'They were making weird noises, I didn't trust them.'

'Speaking of big scary animals, who is most likely to survive in the wild?' Lucie smiled at them, and Savi knew she and Mars were in the middle of creating some stellar content for the Revolution Racing social platforms.

'Me,' Savi cut in before Marco could even say her name. 'I think that has been established. Mars got himself all the cowboy attire while he was in Wyoming with me and hiked and rode a horse, but he wouldn't last an hour in the actual wilderness.'

'She's not wrong,' Marco huffed. 'Next one, and try to make it a question that works in my favour, yeah Luce? She's brutal.'

'Most likely to –' Lucie stopped to laugh. 'Marco, I'm

sorry and I love you, but most likely get the drunkest at a post-race celebration?'

'Lucie, why would you put that in there?!' Marco cried out. 'I hate this game.'

'Easy, the answer is Marco,' Savi grinned. 'Witnessed it first-hand. In fact, that was the first time we hung out properly, at Faith and Julien's house in Belgium.'

'Yeah and now look at us, you're bullying me live on camera.' He rolled his eyes. 'Wow, I'm a lucky fella. It's just as well I like you, Cowgirl.'

'That brings me to the final question actually . . . Who is the most likely to give the other person a nickname?' Lucie smiled warmly at them, going all gooey-eyed as she glanced between them and waited for an answer.

Savi couldn't stop smiling as she looked up at Marco, who was already grinning down at her with adoration. 'That would be both of us. He calls me Cowgirl or Savannah, never Savi.'

'And Savannah calls me Monaco, or she uses Mars like my friends do. Sometimes De Luca, just depends on our moods.'

'Perfect, thanks guys. I doubt that video will take much editing, but I'll get it out on socials at some point during the race.' Lucie flounced off to find Faith, leaving Marco and Savi in their own little bubble, away from the rest of the team.

'I think Monaco might be my favourite nickname anyone's ever given me.'

'Really? I like Mars, it's cute. Suits you.'

'I'm not cute, Savannah. Trust me, and you know that. You've seen what I can do in the bedroom.'

She felt herself burning up again, but this time she wasn't fussed about trying to make it stop. He hadn't flirted with her like this for ages; could he sense that her boundaries were shifting? Was he pushing them knowing that she was becoming more open to it? 'We should go back to the others . . .'

'Agreed,' Marco said, but his eyes flashed with desire. She wasn't making this up; this was not just a friendship. Savi wanted this, in some capacity. She wanted to see that side of him.

'Look what they gave me!' Brett yelled as they got closer, and they saw him holding a t-shirt cannon and aiming it at the grandstands opposite the pits. They watched him shoot rolled up navy IEC shirts at the fans as the crowds erupted in screams of joy, and waited for Gabriel to announce over the speakers that it was time to get in their cars.

'Savi, Julien . . .' Jasper joined them. 'Ready to get us started?'

'Yep, aren't we, Sav?'

'We are,' she nodded. The anxiety had dissipated, and now the excitement and adrenaline were building as the entire grid came to a standstill. The planes flew over, unleashing red, white and blue smoke over the pit straight. She felt euphoric, and this was just the beginning. She had twenty-four hours of this ahead of her.

'Right, we all need to clear off. The army guy is about to deliver the flag, and then the official countdown will start,' Faith explained to Savi more than anyone else, then she kissed Julien goodbye. 'Good luck, everyone.'

Savi's family crowded around her, wishing her luck and

telling her how proud they were of her. It didn't matter how often she heard them say it, she would never tire of it. Everyone was starting to leave the grid in preparation, Savi and Julien heading over to their cars which sat side by side, ruby red paintwork glistening in the sun.

Climbing into the cockpit, Savi took one final deep breath and gripped the steering wheel, mentally preparing herself for the next three hours before she switched out with Kodie. It was a long twenty-four hours, she knew that from watching it and talking at length with the team. But she was ready: to enjoy it, to fight and to do her teammates proud.

'I'm going to be in your garage while you're in the car, not mine,' Marco crouched down by the car, 'I want to be with your family, so I can explain stats and things to them. I'll be third in our car, so I'll be there when you get out, but I'll leave you be when you join them.'

'You don't have to leave me be, Monaco. Ever. I want you there, in fact, I'd prefer it if you were. If you can be, obviously. If you hadn't pulled me off the grid when you did and sat with me in that garage, I might not have made it back out here. You've been a huge support for me so far this season, and I know we're only just halfway through, but I've grown so much as a driver and a person. You've played such a big part in that. So please, don't leave me be.' She held his eye, hoping he understood what she was fighting so hard not to say aloud.

'Okay,' he nodded, pausing when Gabriel's voice interrupted them, letting the drivers know it was time to get in position. Marco kept looking at her, waiting for who knew what.

'What's wrong?' she frowned, her helmet stopping him from seeing anything except her eyes. 'You've got seconds, Monaco.'

'I know,' he sighed. 'I just . . . I'm so fucking proud of you, Cowgirl.' He reached for her glove-covered hand, removed it from the steering wheel and peeled her glove back just enough that he could place a gentle kiss on the inside of her wrist. 'See you on the flip side.'

32

Savi's stint was one of her best performances yet. She had successfully held off Talos Sport and Kahan Racing for ten laps and then overtaken Brett towards the end, leaving Kodie with a solid lead going into the final six hours. She was currently curled up on a camping chair in the back of the garage, watching Miko and Marco's progress like a hawk.

He'd spun out at one point and her heart leapt out of her chest, but he'd got it together and kept driving with minimal damage. A quick trip to the pits to replace part of the rear wing and he was good to go.

Her parents were fast asleep in the trailer, but Weston was still wide awake in the garage next to her, wrapped in a blanket and watching Savi watching Marco. 'What's the deal with De Luca, Sav?' he quizzed, squinting at her suspiciously.

'Hmm?' she mumbled, still focused on the television screen which was tracking Marco's fight with Ricardo De La Rosa, Bea's partner.

'You and Marco. Something you wanna tell me?' She turned around to see his eyes were still narrowed, and his arms were folded.

'Nope,' she shrugged. 'Nothing at all.'

'Okay, but there's something I wanna tell you,' he retaliated. 'You're blind, Savi.'

'Am I? Well then, looks like you're not the only one in the family with a disability.'

That made her brother laugh, but she could sense he wasn't going to shut up about this and she was going to end up confessing her deepest, darkest secret to him. She seemed to have had a few of those recently. At least if he started giving her advice and insisting she take it, she could do the same to him about that girl back home who kept trying to insert herself into his life.

'You two have so much chemistry, it makes me want to tear my hair out. It's like watching a romcom coming to life in front of my very eyes. I saw it from the moment you rocked up on our doorstep with him, and I watched it blossom into way more than friends while he was on the ranch with us. Now, I don't know for sure that something went down in the barn, but whatever it is between you was building long before the truth came out about Jesse.'

'I wasn't disloyal to Jesse.' She frowned, hating that it could look that way.

'I didn't say you were, Savi. That's not who you are. I'm just saying that the universe brought De Luca to you for a reason, and I don't think the timing was a coincidence. You knew in your heart it was time to go, and Marco was your vessel for moving on. You haven't told me to shut up yet, which means I'm on to something.'

'Fine . . . You are indeed on to something. And yes, something did happen in the barn and it changed everything. Even if I told him I wasn't ready,' she confirmed, wincing when he whacked her on the arm. 'Ow, Wes! I hate it when you're right.'

'Are you serious, Sav?! What are you waiting for?' Weston asked, looking like he'd just been told Santa Claus was real.

'Call me crazy, but I think jumping into something new mere weeks after finding out my ex-boyfriend of four years is fathering another woman's child and cheated on me more times than anyone can count might not be the best idea. But I've been hoping he might stick around, you know? Wait for me to figure out what I want next.'

'What I'm hearing is the feeling is mutual.'

'Maybe,' she shrugged, trying to pretend she hadn't been overthinking it.

'I'd like to have him as a brother-in-law.'

'Jesus, Weston. I'm not marrying him. I'm just contemplating whether we might be more than friends, if I want to try taking that leap.'

'Savi, I would give anything to get my time back, relive those years I spent on the rodeo circuit but make the most out of other areas in my life, too. Go on more dates, let love in. I'm definitely gonna call her, you know? Monica, that old high-school friend who keeps fighting to stay in my life. Sure, I might fuck it up, she might get scared of being with someone with my issues and trauma, but life's too short not to try. It's why I encouraged you to chase this IEC dream of yours, why I finally got a grip and left Mustang Ridge to come here.'

'So basically, I need to get a grip.' She raised an eyebrow.

'Yes,' he laughed.

'Thanks for the input, I will take your opinion into consideration.'

She snuggled down in her camping chair, taking a corner

of Weston's blanket and throwing it over her knees. She needed to sleep; she'd only squeezed in an hour here and there when she wasn't in the car. But they were so close to the end of the race, and she wanted to watch Marco and Miko take both cars over the finish.

It was in the final hour that things started to go wrong for the team. Miko was complaining over the radio that she felt unwell, and she didn't think she was going to make it. When you were in such a confined space, your senses were heightened, and you could start to feel overwhelmed very quickly. Savi headed over to Jasper's side, listening intently to the radio conversation between her teammate and her boss.

Jasper took his headphones off and turned to her, 'Savi, do you think you've got a few more laps in you? She needs to get out of that car, but we can't surrender the race in the final moments.'

'Yep,' Savi nodded with zero hesitation, 'bring her in.'

She rushed to collect her balaclava and helmet, ignoring the cameras being shoved in her face as she moved around the garage. The only thing that mattered was getting that car across the finish line. 'She's coming, Sav!' Kodie yelled out, and then the car was in the pits and Savi was all but yanking Miko out of the car so she could switch out in record time. Drinking tube connected, seatbelts on.

This was what drove her to victory time and time again. High stakes, adrenaline coursing through her veins. She checked her mirrors for cars coming out of the pits behind her and pushed on ahead, her grit and determination spilling out onto the track along with the car.

Marco was right there in front of her, a reminder of what this meant. She was getting to finish arguably the most iconic race in motorsport history with her teammate by her side, her family watching from the garage. It wasn't just special, it was magical. A feeling nobody could possibly understand unless they were in this industry and succeeded in such an incredible feat.

'How are you feeling, Savi?' Her engineer's voice filled the car.

'Stressed, but getting into the groove.'

'Just relax, you've only got three laps to go. Marco is there with you, keep close to him. We want you over the line together, it'll look good for the cameras and give us some fantastic photographs for the history books.'

'Who goes first?' She grinned behind her helmet, knowing Marco would never willingly let her overtake even by mere millimetres.

Her engineer laughed, 'That's up to you to decide. Just don't do anything stupid.'

Savi breathed out deeply, gripping the steering wheel with more determination than ever before. Crossing the finish line with Mars by her side was a dream she didn't know she had until it was here. It was happening. To be able to do the thing she loved most in the world with one of the people she . . . well, she might not quite be ready to admit that out loud but in her head? Marco De Luca was easily levelling with her love for racing.

She did as her engineer instructed, keeping Marco within touching distance. They shot past grandstands full of fans from all over the world, streaks of evergreen trees and cars who were more than fifteen laps behind them but still winners in their own classes.

But then, just as they were about to cross the finish, one of those drivers, who was in a car that was nowhere near as high-tech as Revolution's and had half the experience of most drivers on the grid, locked up at the worst possible moment in the race. The *last* second.

The car jerked to the right, careening into Savi, who in turn went sailing towards Marco. Debris went flying, right there on the pit straight. She spun three hundred and sixty degrees, feeling like she was suspended in time. *Marco*.

His car was crushed up against the pit wall, the whole team on the other side unable to do a damn thing about it. 'Marco!' she yelled, no sound coming out. Her car had come to a stop in the gravel but she couldn't see him, couldn't see much of anything except black dots in her vision. But she wasn't injured, she wasn't in pain. Her inability to see straight was the shock, the fear that Marco hadn't been so lucky. She needed him to be safe, needed to be able to hold him in her arms while she let herself feel everything she'd been shoving down. She needed *him*.

There was a knock on her window, and she looked to her left to see a white-gloved hand. It was him. Out of the car, standing on his own two feet, trying to yank her door open while she sat there too stunned to move.

'Cowgirl, are you okay?!' he shouted through the door. 'Can you open the door?'

But she could barely muster up the energy to reach for the handle, instead bursting into tears at the sight of him. Crashing was one thing, but bringing your teammate into it was a whole other level of stress and guilt. The other driver was already out, slamming his fist down on the roof of his car in frustration while Marco continued screaming at Savi.

She threw the door open, knocking him back in the process. 'I'm sorry, I'm –'

'Hi, Cowgirl.' He helped her out of the car and gripped her tightly, arms wrapped around her waist like he was just as afraid to let go as she was. 'Don't fucking scare me like that.'

He lifted her helmet off, then her balaclava, running his fingers through her hair and holding her face in his hands, wiping away her tears. She just looked at him, taking in every detail of his face. His chiselled jaw, that one curl that never stayed in place and fell onto his forehead, the way his brows creased so intensely when he was focused. He caught her eye for just long enough to snap her out of it.

She didn't shy away, didn't avert her gaze. What would she have done if Marco hadn't made it? If *she* hadn't made it. Weston was right, life was too short, and it was fragile. She didn't want to waste any more time, letting Jesse's actions keep her from what was meant for her.

'Monaco . . .' she murmured, reaching up to run her hand along his jaw. His gaze shifted to her lips, and she smiled at him, 'Hear me out, trust that this isn't just the shock talking and I would never say this without meaning every word . . . Mars, I think you might be my person.'

'Really?' He breathed out a laugh, 'I'm your right guy?'
'I think so,' she nodded.
'About time.'

And then his lips were on hers, thousands of fans screaming at what they thought was an act of relief between two lovers, who had come close to losing one another. Which it was, but it was so much more than that. It was the beginning of a beautiful chapter they had yet to explore, one in which Savi was free to be herself, express her fears and hopes and dreams and know that she would be met halfway. This kiss felt different to the one they had shared in the barn, because she didn't have to worry what it meant. She *knew* what it meant. She was his, and he was hers.

He parted her lips with his tongue and she let him, not a care in the world at how far the camera zoomed in on them. Let them see. Let people see what a real relationship looked like. His hand travelled down her body until he reached the back of her thighs, silently encouraging her to jump so that her legs were wrapped around his waist. Revelling in each other for a few moments, they broke the kiss, instead clinging to one another like their whole lives depended on it. She didn't want to let go, but there was a bigger issue at hand.

'Monaco.' She pulled back. 'The race. What about the team?'

'Cowgirl, look around. Look where we are.' He gestured to the finish line with his head, and she gasped. It was metres behind them, which meant . . .

'We did it?!'

'Fuck yeah, we did.'

Then she noticed the red flag waving, which meant the race was done, and everyone had been given the positions they were in when the race finished whether they had crossed the line or not. This couldn't be taken away from them because of the crash. Revolution Racing had won, and as the race marshal's voice came over the track speakers and confirmed the winners, everyone in the grandstand opposite got to their feet, flags waving and arms flying up in the air to offer their applause. It was the best moment of every race, when thousands of people came together to celebrate the incredible feat of every team who had participated, and the team's hard work paid off. But this? Finishing a twenty-four-hour race in such a way? Nothing would ever compare.

They'd done it. They'd scraped through by the skin of their teeth, and they'd not only completed it, but they'd *won*. She'd never felt pride like it.

Once they had been checked over by the medical team and made it back into the garage, their teammates swarmed around them. The atmosphere in there was strange; like they were torn between celebrating and being respectful of the fact two of their drivers had just collided and the aftermath could have been so much worse.

'Thanks for covering me, Sav,' Miko smiled weakly. 'If I had known that would be the way it ended . . . Well, I'm just glad you're okay.' She hugged her, pulling Kodie in with them.

'Could have happened to any of us, Meeks. But we're safe, and we won!'

'Savannah Hart, don't you be so blasé about what happened out there.' Her mum marched over, and her teammates scattered so she could scoop her up in a crushing embrace. 'Of all the races to crash at, you had to do it at the one where your dad, brother and I were watching from behind the scenes,' she tutted.

Calvin chuckled, 'But we are very glad you're okay.'

'And proud of you,' Weston added. 'For completing the race, and also for facing your fears with De Luca. Glad to see my advice got through that thick skull of yours.'

'Yes, what was *that* about? Real or fake?' Bonnie's eyes went wide.

Marco joined them, wrapping an arm around her waist. 'Real.'

'Clear out, team!' Jasper shouted above the noise, 'Podium time!'

The IEC podium had become like her second home over the first half of the season. She and her teammates had placed first, second or third in every race so far. That was standard for Revolution Racing, but it was beyond incredible for a team full of rookies. Sponsorship deals had been pouring in ready for next season, and she knew her success was going to skyrocket overnight when her rookie season was over and done with.

She, Miko and Kodie stood on the platform for second position, next to but slightly lower than Brett, Julien and Marco. Jasper and Gabriel were amongst the crowd below them with her brother, who was manically waving the USA flag, and her parents. All of them looked close to tears. The team's mechanics and engineers were quiet, with subtle smirks and stunned expressions across their features, in disbelief at just how much they had achieved in the past twenty-four hours.

They'd fought sleep the entire time, changed the race

strategy halfway through, battled extreme heat and rain and storms, replaced broken rear wings and panels, kept their drivers in high spirits. Revolution would have been lost without them, and Savi wished they could all come up on the podium with them. They belonged up here.

'This is magical,' Miko commented. 'Look how many people have gathered.'

Fans were running across the circuit towards parc fermé where the cars sat stationary in a grid formation, behind large signs that read 'first', 'second' and 'third' in bold letters. The IEC had four classes and Revolution Racing were in the top class, which meant the other classes had already had their celebrations while Savi and Marco had been getting checked over. She looked down at her feet and saw a few stray pieces of champagne-soaked red confetti on the floor.

'I think that's my favourite part. How they all cling to the fences, no security to stop them. It's a free-for-all in the best way; they haven't had to pay thousands of euros to gain VIP access. All they'd have to do is leg it from the grandstands and here they are. Celebrating alongside us.'

'I was them once. There's nothing like it,' Kodie added.

Savi focused on the fans, on her family and on her team, glancing over at Marco and earning herself a small smile. She had spent all that time angry and hurt that Jesse had never bothered to show up for her, but now? She was relieved. This was one thing that was hers and only hers. He'd never been willing to share it with her, never made any effort to try. And that meant he couldn't take the joy out of this for her. He wasn't part of this. But Marco was, and she'd chosen him to be her teammate in every phase of life.

'Have you seen the trophies?' Brett whisper-yelled over to them. 'They're fucking *crystal*.'

'Oh, wonderful. The kids will break that in no time,' Julien muttered.

As each winner was announced, the crowd roared, and Savi felt alive. And when it was her turn to take hold of her trophy and lift it in the air, she looked directly at her parents. Her very first teammates in life who had listened to every dream of hers and Weston's and not once told them there was a chance they might not make it. This win may be hers, but it was shared with Miko, Kodie, her team, her family and every single person who stood in that crowd and beyond wearing Revolution red.

Champagne rained over them, soaking Savi's curls and trickling down her neck. She looked up to see Marco grinning down at her and laughing as Julien did to him what he had just done to her. 'Couldn't help myself. It's tradition.'

'Mars . . .' she whispered, choking back a sob.

'Savannah?' He immediately pulled her up to his level, his arms wrapped around her tightly. She knew the cameras were on them at this precise moment; how could they not be? The world saw a connection between them and right now it was at its strongest.

The dam burst. She didn't know why she was crying this time. It was a combination of everything: anger at Jesse, hurt over what he'd done to her, joy over earning a Le Mans podium and her family being here to witness it. But it was the final thing on her list that provided the most tears; she had fallen for her best friend. He had come at exactly the right time, despite what they may have said on that ride back in Wyoming. The universe knew what it was doing, it had just been up to Savi to let him love her in the midst of her heartbreak.

33

Healing looked different for everyone. For some, it involved journaling, meditating and breath work, reducing the size of your social circle, throwing yourself into an intense gym routine and therapy. Not for Savi. She had already integrated most of those things into her daily routine in high school. The therapy had started after Weston's accident, a necessary route to deal with her own trauma from almost losing him, spending months watching him lying in a hospital bed and then watching him navigate his new way of living in a cloud of fury.

She needed to do more. *See* more. They were at the very end of the race season with one more to go, and she had spent the last six weeks travelling with Marco, Kodie and Miko in between work trips to Shanghai, Fuji and Qatar. They'd taken that girls' trip to Tokyo, too, got a taste not only of Japanese culture but the life of Japanese billionaires. Miko's family were loaded, and Savi had been so blown away by every little thing that she hadn't thought of Jesse once that whole time. Then she'd got on the plane to go to the next destination and been left with too many hours in solitude to reflect and been back at square one.

Social media made healing look easy sometimes, like a straight line. But it wasn't. Her emotions could switch up in seconds, and she often found herself zoning out and staring into space, thinking about nothing in particular. She liked those moments; the world felt still, more manageable, and she was numb to her pain.

Marco had taken a step back, allowing her the space to do what she needed to do and make sense of her emotions. She hated that she required space from him of all people, but it was the nights she spent cuddled up with her teammates that allowed her to know with absolute certainty that Marco was not and never would be a rebound, because it was always Marco she wished she was waking up to the following morning.

And now here she was, doing exactly that, in the suite he'd booked for them in a Swedish spa, miles away from anyone. And at night, she felt miles away from her problems and her past and the only thing in the world that mattered was them.

'You heard from Sapphire today?' He sat down next to her, lowering his legs into the pool, the warm water rippling with the movement. They'd been here for days, pretending today wasn't happening. Then this morning, it felt like someone had thrown a cold bucket of ice over them.

'She's got lawyers on standby, just in case Jesse tries to pull something. Not sure what exactly, but he's going to feel like he's being attacked from all sides so he'll look for any defence he can. My own lawyers are prepared, too.'

'Let's hope he just owns what he's done and never does it to anyone else.' Marco sighed, rubbing his temple. 'Want a drink before it all comes out?' He offered her his bottle of beer.

'Why are you drinking at this time of the morning?' She raised an eyebrow.

'Because I know hell is coming your way, and I don't like it one bit.'

'I'll be fine, Mars. Worse things have happened.'

'The news articles and social media comments are going to be brutal, Savannah.'

She tried not to laugh out loud, because he was right. They would be. Savi was about to confess to the entire world that it was her in those photos from the cabin, in an article posted by a third-party organisation. She was opening herself up to an onslaught of hate, sexist and misogynistic comments, all because her privacy being violated in the first place was wrong and staying silent didn't sit right with her. 'I know, but I'm ready for whatever they throw at me.'

'Are you going to let me read it now?' He nudged her arm, staring at the phone she had been clutching all morning. It could blow up with notifications any second; the article was late going live. Something to do with last-minute checks by the lawyers.

'Sure. Let me show you the proofs.' She scrolled through her emails, finding the correct version. It had been thoroughly edited to ensure she didn't say anything that could get her in trouble. Aside from the defamation case she suspected might be landing in her lap soon.

Peering over his shoulder, Savi started to read the article and tried to put herself in the shoes of the millions of other women this had happened to. Mothers, daughter, wives, sisters, friends. But photos being leaked wasn't the only thing she had mentioned.

She'd also taken it as an opportunity to expose Jesse for

who he really was, a liar and a cheat. Because she might not be the only one, and Sapphire might not be the only woman raising his child alone. She would be damned if he was going to be allowed to lie to anyone else.

'The Woman with the Horseshoe Tattoo: An Exposé by Savi Hart.' Marco read aloud, and then he sat quietly, soaking in every word she'd written.

I was recently the victim of a sex scandal and after months of hiding in the shadows, I'm ready to reveal my identity in the hopes that I can help anyone who has ever been in my position. Earlier this year, I was staying in a cabin in Tennessee, with someone I had been in a relationship with for four years. It was protected by a security team, but an individual got past them and decided that our privacy and dignity were less important than a decent pay day. If I had known he were that desperate for money, I'd have written him a cheque myself. You expect to be able to enjoy intimate moments with your partner in your own home without the risk of someone photographing you without your knowledge and selling those photos to the press. I was embarrassed and ashamed, but recently I realised I have no need to be. I didn't do anything wrong. It was everyone else. I was participating in a consensual, intimate act with someone I had loved deeply for four years, and it was the media who took advantage of that.

Not only was my dignity stripped away by that photographer and the media and everyone who was trying to find the woman in the photos, but I was also manipulated by country music megastar, Jesse Montalvo. The man I loved and trusted. Little did I know, he had spent most of our relationship entertaining countless other women, not only betraying my trust but putting me at risk of sexually transmitted diseases and not once disclosing any of this to me. Either I'm lucky or he was careful, but whichever it was, he is not the man I thought I loved. A man who has fathered a child with another woman, and refuses to acknowledge his part in creating a life.

Jesse even persuaded me to enter into a fake relationship with my teammate, assuring me it would keep the press off the scent of my relationship with him and keep my identity under wraps. He suggested we keep it up for a whole race season, long enough for the media circus surrounding the photos to die down. If only I had realised he was trying to keep me off the scent of his own betrayals. As a result of his actions coming to light, I have found a fire within me. I'm ready to fight the consequences of the media's actions with my family, friends and my team behind me, and I'm ready to reveal that the relationship with my teammate is now very much real.

I wasn't sure if I should write this article, but I can no longer let those photographs dictate the way I live. I also need other victims to know that someone else making an active choice to tear you down is no reflection on you. I have chosen to no longer live in fear of being exposed as the woman in those photos. I am the woman with the horseshoe tattoo, and I am taking my power back.

'Thoughts?' Savi frowned at his expression; he gave nothing away.

'I think I want to kill everyone who ever shared those photos around, whether it was on news platforms or social media or groupchats...' Marco's jaw tensed and he gripped her phone, his knuckles turning white. 'How can anyone do that to someone? I was angry before, but reading it all in your own words like that makes me furious.'

'I'm with you.' She pried her phone out of his hand. 'Do you think Jesse is gonna be mad?'

'Who gives a shit?' He threw his hands up.

'My lawyers.'

'Valid point.'

'I think Jasper is ready to unleash the Revolution Racing lawyers on him or anyone else who decides to take offence to this. Gabriel, too. They're angry, defensive. Protective of me, because the IEC is a family. They want to throw all the power they've got at the situation, and don't get me started on the *Girls Off Track* team. They want me to do a podcast episode, and then lead a workshop about how to tackle sexual harassment in the workplace.'

'Has that ever happened to you in the workplace?'

'Yeah, but not to the extreme that it had serious implications on my mental health. I've seen that happen before. A mechanic from my last team would consistently touch me inappropriately when I was getting in and out of the car. He was caught and fired, but that's not the point. He had normalised it in his own mind, and it was all kept hidden from the press to save face for the team. I've witnessed worse, heard stories. It's a very real issue that isn't talked about unless it involves someone high up.'

'What can we do, as male drivers?' he frowned. 'I'm not sure I've ever witnessed anything serious happen, but I guess it's in the little things. Subtle moments that we as men wouldn't take notice of. I remember in Faith's first season, there was an issue with a driver at one of Julien's parties. He got too close to Faith when she was drunk, we made him back off.'

'That. That is what you can do as men. Call it out when you see it, listen to us when we tell our stories. That's really all we can ask. Being a woman in this industry is hard, even on the good days. But also, the way female fans can treat male drivers sometimes is equally as abhorrent and we've all come to accept it as part of the culture.'

'I fucking hate the world.' He lay down, his back flat against the wooden deck.

'Me too.' She patted his chest, 'But come on, I want to turn my phone off and go for a spa treatment. Hide away from the real world again for an hour.' She knew she would return to thousands of notifications, and she had already decided she wouldn't be addressing any of them. What needed to be said had been published, and although she would use her voice when needed or when asked, she would like to move forward.

'Savannah . . .' He sat up again, looking into her eyes with an intense gaze. It was like he was trying to hear everything she wasn't saying. 'I need you to tell me you're okay.'

'I can't tell you that.' She bit her lip, and he immediately pulled his legs out of the water, swivelling to face her. It was the first time she'd felt truly vulnerable around him.

'I'm so sorry, Cowgirl.' Marco's eyes welled up with tears, and the vulnerability she had felt morphed into admiration for the man he was. It was no wonder she had always felt so safe around him, so at ease. So free to be herself. He made her feel seen.

'It's fine,' she shrugged. 'Well, it's not fine. But *I* will be fine.'

Marco reached up to tenderly brush his fingers along her jawline, smiling softly as his brown eyes melded with her own. 'You should be so proud of yourself. You're not just a superstar, Cowgirl. You're a fucking supernova.'

34

'Thank you so much for doing this, Savi.' Lucie led her across the carpeted floors of the *Girls Off Track* headquarters, her long dark hair swishing as she walked. That woman was always in a rush, and Savi hurried to keep up with her.

'It's my pleasure. Thank you for thinking of me. I know you didn't exactly have a gap in the schedule for this, but the fact you made space . . .' She offered a shy smile which Lucie couldn't see, because she was still too far ahead. 'It means a great deal to me.'

'Are you for real?' Lucie stopped and turned. 'Sav, there was no way we weren't having you on ASAP. That exposé you did raised so many important issues, and there must be so much you wanted to say but didn't have the word count for.'

'Some things I legally probably shouldn't say in this podcast, either.' She grimaced. There had been zero backlash from Jesse in the few weeks since the article went live, in fact there had been radio silence. Sapphire hadn't heard a thing, either. He hadn't even been spotted in public. He must be hiding in the cabin, so Savi didn't want to rock the boat.

The internet trolls had come out in full force to attack her, but she tried to focus on those who defended her and shared their well wishes. It helped that her teammates,

Marco included, had helped her through the worst of it. Marco had taken charge of Savi's social media for a couple of days so he could block accounts and delete comments.

'We'll try to keep this focused on the motorsports industry, make it more an informal discussion between friends and coworkers about some of the things we have seen and experienced as women,' Lucie said, gesturing for Savi to enter the recording studio.

Savi would never get used to how special it felt to be standing in the *Girls Off Track* studio. The neon pink sign filled the wall behind the sofas, with pink-on-pink chequerboard wallpaper and plush velvet sofas. Bea's influence was written all over it, and she looked mighty proud as she waved her over.

'Hey, Sav!' she smiled. 'Come sit down! Faith is just grabbing drinks for us all. Talking non-stop for two hours is thirsty work.'

'Two hours?' Savi blinked.

'They'll cut it down,' Lucie laughed.

Savi made herself comfortable and let Bea, one of the original podcasters for *Across The Line* before it became *Girls Off Track*, mic her up. She'd dressed comfortably for this, as suggested by the girls. A pair of yoga pants and one of Marco's hoodies that was the perfect amount of oversized on her. 'So . . . are you all doing this episode? Is Esme joining us, too?'

'Oh!' Bea exclaimed. 'Sorry! No, it's just Faith and I. Lucie is disappearing in a second. We thought that, you know, given my previous reputation as a bit of a paddock groupie, I might have some valuable insight. I have been on the receiving end of inappropriate conduct a few too many times, and . . . you know what? We'll save that for the podcast!'

And that was exactly what she did. Faith had long since sat down next to her co-host, and they were already over an hour in. They'd started out with an intro to who Savi was and how she'd started out, refamiliarising the podcast fans with Revolution Racing's new addition. Now, Bea was on a rant, and Savi was disgusted at what she was hearing.

'I have no shame in my sexual activities, only in the way I treated these men before and after. I was a gold-digger, I will admit that,' Bea shrugged nonchalantly. 'But what I will never be okay with is the way some drivers and engineers I did *not* wish to entertain made it sickeningly obvious that they were ready and willing, I mean, the comments I got when I walked down the pit lane . . . the wolf whistles, the cat calls. The way I was cornered in garages and hospitality tents. That's not acceptable. They were taking the freedom to choose away from me.'

'Oh, it was awful up until a year or so ago,' Faith added. 'Savi, you really came in at the right time. I don't know if they've all had an attitude change, or if they're just scared now there are more women coming into the industry. And I love that we're loud about it. We'll call them out, and I think your exposé made that abundantly clear. We're not going to sit by and let men get away with sexual harassment disguised as light-hearted humour.'

'They love to say they didn't mean offence, or they didn't realise something would be taken the wrong way,' Savi scoffed.

'Then they tell you to lighten up!' Faith yelled out, exasperated.

The three of them had spent most of this podcast session gossiping about the antics of the people they worked with, and finding themselves in constant states of disbelief at the stories they heard. If you asked Savi, none of it should be cut.

'So, Savi, how have you found it being a female racing driver?' Bea asked. 'It can't have been an easy journey to embark on. I know that all of us here at the podcast and the academy have struggled in our fields, but getting behind the wheel opens you up to a lot more scrutiny.'

Savi sat back in her chair again, relaxing into it. 'It's been a nightmare in some respects. The constant onslaught of sexist comments on social media, in my inbox. Especially after my exposé. Are we really still slating female drivers in this day and age? I honed my skill just the same as any male racing driver, and I've trained hard. Worked hard. I haven't just fallen into it without showcasing my talent and proving my capabilities. Why is my biology still a discussion?'

'Exactly! That's why these conversations are so important,' Faith nodded. 'And precisely why we wanted you on with us today.'

'Yes, thank you again, Savi,' Bea added. 'Our platform wouldn't be what it is without women like you sharing their stories with our listeners. You're the future of our industry, and it was our honour to provide another platform for your voice to reach people.'

She breathed a sigh of relief as the recording stopped, and both girls squealed with excitement. 'Savi Hart, you're a star! That was by far one of our best episodes yet. Esme is going to love editing it, too. So much content, so many important topics covered.' Bea stood up and hugged her.

Faith did the same, leading her back out. They had back-to-back meetings all day, which meant they really had fought to get this in. 'Is Mars meeting you here or are you heading back to the hotel solo?'

'He's waiting downstairs. Didn't want to come up and detract from my big moment.'

'Oh, bless his heart,' Faith laughed. 'Are you okay to head down without me? I need to make a quick call before our next client shows up.'

'Sure.' Savi nodded, calling out as she headed to the elevators. 'Can't wait to listen to the ep! And I will see you ladies in a few weeks at the next race!'

She buzzed herself down, and was greeted by a nervous-looking Marco. He'd been so worried about her doing this, but she knew herself, and she also knew she was in good hands. It was the safest way to continue taking control of the conversation.

'How was it?' he asked, taking her hand in his.

She sighed as they headed out into the street. 'It was good . . .'

'But?' He squeezed her hand.

'It was behind closed doors. How am I supposed to walk down the paddock like nothing ever happened, Mars?' she questioned. He pulled her to a stop in front of a coffee shop, neither of them caring that they were in the way. Marco was great at working out the exact moments Savi needed a pep talk and some words of encouragement.

'You don't. You own it. But if you need him to, Jasper can temporarily take you off press duties. Just say the word and he'll do it in a heartbeat. You haven't got to do anything you're not ready for.'

'Except show up.'

'Yes, but that's the first step.'

'It's a pretty big fucking step, Monaco. It's a mountain.' She let out a sarcastic laugh, and he silenced her with a quick kiss. She loved it when he did that.

'Then climb the mountain, Cowgirl. Think of it like the ones you grew up around. You were born and raised to climb them, so don't for one second think you're not capable of conquering this. This is your paddock. Your home. Revolution Racing and all the teams on the grid are your family, and if you want me to hold your hand physically and figuratively then that's what I'll do.'

'Please,' she nodded, and then stepped closer to whisper in his ear. 'But before I go climbing any mountains, take me back to our hotel so I can climb *you*.'

'You keeping those on?' Savi grinned at Marco's cowboy boots as he lifted his leg.

'Don't you like them?' He laughed, shuffling closer to her across the king-sized mattress.

'Mars, you're wearing booty shorts and a plaid shirt. It's criminal.'

He leaned in closer, capturing her lips in his. He rolled on top of her, their bodies morphing together. She smiled through the kiss, always unable to hide how happy she was with him. He had well and truly flipped her life upside down once more, but in all the best ways. She had never imagined she would feel so secure, so at home with another person.

His lips traced her skin from her neck to her collarbone, before he ventured to her breasts and then the inside of her thighs. Her entire body felt like it was on fire, and he'd barely got started; she just knew she was in for a treat.

In the short time they'd been together, they had rarely had rough, desperate sex. It was always slow, passionate. He took his time with her, made sure to check in with her every step of the way and prioritise her needs above his own. It was no different now, as he peeled her underwear down her thighs. 'Okay?'

'No, but only because you're still wearing booty shorts,' she laughed. 'I can't get lost in the moment with you dressed like a Ken doll, it's highly off-putting.'

'You're literally wearing granny underwear, Savannah,' he scowled playfully. Marco didn't care about things like that; never expected her to dress a certain way to impress him. He was lucky if she even got out of her pyjamas on days they had nowhere to be.

'There is nothing wrong with my underwear! It's comfortable. But the difference is, it's already round my ankles and your ass is still clad in vintage wash denim.'

He stood up and unbuttoned his shorts, a joke gift from his brother who thought it was hilarious that Marco was embracing the cowboy way, kicking them across the room. He whipped his shirt off, leaving him standing over her in nothing but his boxers. 'There. Are you attracted to me again?'

'Breathtakingly so.' She grinned back at him as he grabbed her hips and pulled her to the edge of the bed, her knees on his shoulders.

'Can I?' Marco asked, looking up at her with a devilish smirk. This was his favourite time of day, every day, and he made sure to see to her needs morning and night if she was in the mood, which she often was. How could she not be? He was Italian, he was built for this.

'You can.' She grabbed a fistful of his hair as he buried his head between her legs, already anticipating what was coming her way. His very first touch made her feel electric, his tongue going straight for the clit.

This was exactly how she liked it. Straight to the point, because to her, the best part was getting to have him. All of him. Oral never lasted long for either of them; they'd spent a lot of time learning each other's bodies over the last few weeks in Europe, at the track and at the hotel, and as a result, they both knew how to hit that sweet spot in record time.

Marco had been treading carefully initially, not wanting to push Savi too far. But once Savi had all but pounced on him when he'd walked through their hotel room door one night, they hadn't stopped.

There was rarely a day when one of them wasn't in the mood, and despite their friends telling them they were just in the honeymoon phase and this would pass, it was Savi and Marco's deep understanding of one another on an emotional level that made this feel so special.

And it was Marco's incredible talent for understanding Savi's needs that had her lifting herself from the bed as she climaxed, her entire body trembling while he kept a firm grip on her, letting her ride out her high.

He lifted his head, smiling up at her before gently placing a kiss on her inner thigh.

'Get up here,' she laughed, 'I want the rest of the Marco De Luca deluxe package, please.'

'It would be my pleasure, but uh, I'm diving right in . . .'

'What do you mean?' She frowned at him as he made himself comfortable, one arm either side of her. He peppered kisses along her jawline.

'I mean, if you touch me, Cowgirl, I'm not going to survive . . .'

'Oh! Did someone get a little bit too excited?' she giggled.

'My self-control appears to have been left on the Calais to Dover ferry.'

'Well, I'm ready when you are.' She shifted her hips up towards him, signalling for him to proceed. She didn't need time in between orgasms to get herself worked up again, all it took was one kiss and she was a goner. Every time. It made it very easy for their nights of passion to be exactly that, long nights with very little sleep.

She revelled in the taste of herself on his tongue, getting lost in her senses as he entered her slowly, moaning into her mouth in the progress. That was up there with one of her favourite sounds in the world, equalled only by his laugh and the sound of her race car's engine.

'Is this okay?' he asked. 'Are you comfortable?'

'I'm all good, Mars.'

He took it as his cue to speed up, thrusting into her a

little bit quicker with every moan that escaped her lips. She could feel every inch of him as he gave her every ounce of his attention, his big brown eyes gazing into her own with every movement. It wasn't until his fluttered closed that she felt the rest of her body tighten, clenching around his length while her hands gripped his shoulders like he was her lifeline. 'Savannah . . .' His jaw tensed, brow furrowed, and he opened his eyes again just in time to watch her climax along with him. In unison, just like everything else they did. Like they were two halves of the same person.

'Happy?' he asked, trying and failing not to collapse on top of her. She secretly liked it when he did, even if she pretended he was heavy.

'Always,' she smiled. 'I'd rank that performance an eight out of ten.'

'Shut up,' he laughed, 'I'll have you on your knees first thing tomorrow morning, don't you worry. I won't deprive you for long.'

'And that's why you're my favourite.' She kissed the side of his head, which was currently buried in her neck once again, only this time he was out of breath.

'I love you, Cowgirl,' he sighed. 'So, so much.'

She smiled up at the ceiling, thanking her lucky stars that the universe had delivered him when it did, and given her the courage to pursue what felt right and good and the one thing that gave her peace when her entire world was in chaos. 'I love you, too, Monaco.'

Epilogue

Marco wandered in from the balcony of their Monegasque apartment, the sun setting behind him as Savannah watched him from the sofa. 'Do you think you'll ever want to move back to the ranch permanently?'

'We literally just bought this place,' she laughed. 'But in answer to your question, yes. When we retire and we've seen enough of the world. Right now, I'm happy with our two-week-long vacations. Wyoming feels less like home the more time I spend here.'

'I was hoping you'd say that.' He sat down next to her, running his fingers over the script font that decorated her thigh, just above her knee. A tattoo for their first anniversary, influenced by wine but still one of her favourite memories. The word 'Monaco', forever inked on her skin to match Marco's fine-line lasso on the inside of his arm. Subtle, but a true representation of each other and their story. 'Because I'd like to bend you over this balcony at least once a week.'

'Marco!' she gasped, laughing when she caught the smirk on his face. 'Just as well we live in such a private complex, then.'

'The paparazzi would only see us if they were in boats, and the waters are monitored for that exact reason. Can't say the same for our neighbours, but we've got some young drivers around here. I'm sure they've got up to all sorts in their downtime.'

'Did you have all of this in mind when we were looking for a place?'

He glanced at her, the smirk still giving him away. 'Maybe . . .' He was no liar. A big selling factor for their permanent move to Monaco was the level of privacy they were blessed with. He wasn't going to risk a repeat of the Tennessee cabin photos when she had worked so hard to distance herself from that situation.

They had spent the last two years travelling the world together and making frequent stops in Belgium, Hawaii and Wyoming in between racing. It was bliss. They had watched Savi's brother get married, finally moving off the ranch and into a place downtown with his new wife. Calvin had retired at long last, and Savannah had invested in *Girls Off Track*, offering regular summer workshops in multiple states across North America with the help of Kodie and Miko.

Savannah had also become close with Marco's parents, who as far as they were concerned now had a daughter of their own. They encouraged her to play more tennis, wined and dined her, and she revelled in nights at the casinos. It was a different life here, and it was easy to get lost in it, but Marco wouldn't let her. He liked the cowgirl within her, the way she walked around the streets of Monaco in her boots without a care in the world. That was the Savannah Hart he'd fallen in love with, and no city was going to take that away.

Any time she started to miss Wyoming, either they

would get on a plane, or her parents would. Bonnie and Cal had embraced flying thousands of miles every few months, safe in the knowledge that Weston didn't need them anymore.

Everyone was making moves and Marco was just . . . well, enjoying loving on his girl. He wouldn't change a thing. Except he was on a bit of a mission to fast-track their happiness, wanting to max out the fairytale.

'You given any more thought to some little you and I's?' Marco asked. 'I could retire soon, you know. Be a stay-at-home dad. Have four or five little scamps running around. We could get them karting, let them follow in our footsteps and raise the next generation of championship-winning IEC drivers.'

Her eyes widened, 'Four or five?!'

'I was pushing my luck there, I'll admit,' he shrugged. 'One or two would be fine.'

'Okay, let's keep it in mind,' she agreed.

'Wait, really?!' He sat up, hovering over her.

'Really, but we're not starting any kind of *trying* until this season is over. And you know, you might want to make an honest woman out of me while you're at it. I'm an old fashioned kinda gal.' She lifted her head and pecked him on the lips, snapping him out of his surprise. She had just given him the green light to propose after months of saying she wasn't ready.

'You want to get married?' he murmured, and he could see her eyes lighting up.

'Not right now, if that's how you're gonna ask me.'

'You'll know when I'm really asking.'

Savi grinned. 'Why, because you'll be a blubbering mess?'

'Precisely,' he grinned back. 'Because, Cowgirl, who wouldn't want you to be their teammate forever?'

'I do have one question though. Before you start planning a proposal.' She smiled, leaning in close. 'Do I get to wear cowboy boots with my dress?'

'Savannah, I wouldn't want you any other way.'

'Right answer, Monaco.'

On a station platform, with nothing to read,
and a four-hour train journey stretching ahead of him...

That's where the story began for Penguin founder Allen Lane.
With only 'shabby reprints of shoddy novels' on offer,
he resolved to make better books for readers everywhere.

By the time his train pulled into London, the idea was formed.
He would bring the best writing, in stylish and affordable
formats, to everyone. His books would be sold in bookstores,
stationers and tobacconists, for no more than the price
of a ten-pack of cigarettes.

And on every book would be a Penguin, a bird with a certain
'dignified flippancy', and a friendly invitation to anyone who
wished to spend their time reading.

In 1935, the first ten Penguin paperbacks were published.
Just a year later, three million Penguins had made their
way onto our shelves.

Reading was changed forever.

—

A lot has changed since 1935, including Penguin, but in the
most important ways we're still the same. We still believe that
books and reading are for everyone. And we still believe that
whether you're seeking an afternoon's escape, a vigorous debate
or a soothing bedtime story, all possibilities open with a book.

Whoever you are, whatever you're looking for,
you can find it with Penguin.